THE
DAUGHTERS
OF
TEMPERANCE
HOBBS

THE
DAUGHTERS
OF
TEMPERANCE
HOBBS

A NOVEL

KATHERINE HOWE

A Holt Paperback
Henry Holt and Company   New York

Holt Paperbacks
Henry Holt and Company
Publishers since 1866
120 Broadway
New York, New York 10271
www.henryholt.com

A Holt Paperback® and ® are registered trademarks of
Macmillan Publishing Group, LLC.

The Library of Congress has cata loged the hardcover edition as follows:

Names: Howe, Katherine, author.
Title: The daughters of temperance hobbs : a novel / Katherine Howe.
Description: First edition. | New York : Henry Holt and Company, [2019]
Identifiers: LCCN 2018035472 | ISBN 9781250304865 (hardcover)
  ISBN 9781250231444 (international)
Classification: LCC PS3608.O947 D38 2019 | DDC 813/.6— dc23
LC record available at https://lccn.loc.gov/2018035472

ISBN 9781250774439

Our books may be purchased in bulk for promotional, educational, or business use.
Please contact your local bookseller or the Macmillan Corporate and Premium Sales Department
at (800) 221-7945, extension 5442, or by e-mail at MacmillanSpecialMarkets@macmillan.com.

Originally published in hardcover in 2019 by Henry Holt and Company

First Holt Paperbacks Edition 2020

Designed by Kelly S. Too

P1

For Louis

THE
DAUGHTERS
OF
TEMPERANCE
HOBBS

PART I

AETITE

And Ruth said, Intreat me not to leave thee, or to return from following after thee: for whither thou goest, I will go; and where thou lodgest, I will lodge: thy people shall be my people, and thy God my God.

Ruth 1:16

King James Bible

The Devil has made us like a *Troubled Sea*; and the *Mire* and *Mud*, begins now also to heave up apace.

Cotton Mather,

The Wonders of the Invisible World, 1693

Prologue

The first clod hit Livvy Hasseltine's face—a starburst of cold mud exploding hard on her jaw. Livvy spat dirt, dropped her basket, and turned to run. The taste of dirt and sheep soil in her mouth.

"Get out of here!" one of the boys screamed. The others bayed like hounds. Another clod sailed by her ear. Livvy hunched her shoulders, trying to make herself small. Cloak flapping behind her like sparrow wings.

Split-wood fences and stacked stone paddocks walled both sides of the road. Cold late winter mist lay so thick that Livvy couldn't see much farther into the fields behind the fences than a rod or two, but she could hear the soft lowing of shaggy-backed cows, their jaws working the cud as she fled by. One of the fields had the bull in it. She didn't know which one.

Livvy grasped up her skirts around her knees, her boot heels landing hard in puddles touched with ice. Veering left, she slithered through a gap in the fence, hoping she had guessed right, dashing past a knot of sheep settled together in a wooly row against the chill, soft ears flapping. She slid down a rolling hillock of damp turf and her coif flew off, a pale dove lifted away by fingers of fog. Brown fringe of hair falling into her eyes. She glanced behind her, through the cloud rolling heavy between the cottages of Easthorpe, this mean little village where they never used to live. How many boys? Three, their shadows moving after her down the lane. She could hear their breath. Their syncopated feet.

"You! Satan spawn! Longtooth demon beast! Best you run!"

"Which way she go?"

"This way!"

"I got her."

Another clod came sailing through the fog and fell with a splat six feet behind her. Livvy picked up speed. Woolen stockings bagging at her knees.

Livvy's breath came high and tight in her chest, her cheeks flushing scarlet. She wasn't a runner. She didn't like to go outside the cottage, most days. She preferred it near the hearth, teasing the flames with a poker, helping their landlady by sweeping up ashes or shelling peas. It was a mistake, to go out. To be seen. Livvy was a watery girl, prone to fevers. Her skin clammy and hot. Livvy craved quiet, and warm things, and she loved her straw pallet in the attic and holding the turnspit dog to her chest, feeling him warm asleep and his heart beating under her hand. Livvy wished she'd stayed in their rented corner of the cottage loft. Invisible. Unknown.

The mud clinging to her eyelashes made her eye start to water. Sure, the water was from mud. Not from crying.

"We're coming for you, little girl!" Laughter, shouts. Sheep bleating in alarm.

Sweat soaked through her shift and darkened the wool of her dress, painting circles under her arms and a vee down her back. Sweat plastered her ragged fringe to her forehead. Through the mist Livvy could only see rolling green-brown turf dotted with sheep, some goats, round-bellied and rubbing their horns together.

The mists parted before her as she ran, and knitted behind her, as though she were running in a dream, her feet not touching the ground, wet clods falling farther behind. Mist thickening. Gasping, Livvy spied half a dozen sheep trotting apart like the ripples in a pond full of stones. The boys were still coming.

Ahead, a shape—another cottage maybe, behind a line of trees. Livvy dug into the mist with her elbows, breath exploding out of her chest, pushing herself faster. The trees were thick and old, she didn't know what kind, her mother would scold her for not knowing. No, she knew this one—an ash. Good. Livvy skidded behind the ash's trunk, old with gnarled elbows, some branches hanging low. She flattened herself against the trunk. Hidden. Chest heaving. Hearing herself breathing, trying to force herself quiet, she swallowed her breath away, nostrils flaring.

"Where'd she get off to?"

"Footprint here."

How close? Livvy's pulse throbbed at her throat. The ash bark wet and crumbling under her fingers.

"She be running thataway."

Murmuring behind hands, shuffling feet. They talked about her with oaths in their mouths.

Sounds of sleeves wiping noses and grumbling and the three boys— she didn't know their names—jogged down the slope, leaping first one, then the next and the next, over the shallow, rocky creek that wound its way across the bottom of the field. Livvy held still.

The three voices called out for her, after her, they thought, stopping to pick up clods of mud and rock and hurl them into the mist where they thought she had fled. They drew away, down past the creek.

Livvy caught her skirts in her hands and dashed on the balls of her feet to the looming shape before her, stone walls, leaded windows, peaked slate roof. When she drew into its shadow she saw that it wasn't a cottager's house after all, but the church. A sedate little steeple at one end. Gothic points over narrow, dark windows.

St. Mary the Virgin.

Her mother warned her away from popishness.

"Naw, she didn't go this way," a distant male voice called.

"Let's go back," another suggested.

Livvy crept to the church door. Heavy, solid, oak, with iron latch and hinges. Livvy pushed on it with her shoulder and it creaked open, and she slipped inside and the door whumped closed behind and she was safe.

Dark. Damp. Cool. Almost cold. Livvy folded her arms across her narrow chest and peered into the dimness within. Rows of pews. A few candles on an iron stand in the chancel, flickering under an effigy of the Virgin with a naked baby standing on her lap. The cloying smell of melted wax and pine garlands left hanging since Christmas. The cold saints' eyes stared down at her. Following as she moved.

Idolatry. It was a very great sin.

Livvy edged around the stone walls, hunting for a place to conceal herself. Splinters of color moved over her face, cast from feeble sun through the stained-glass windows. Christ at the Resurrection.

She'd have to go back for the basket—they only had two. And the other had a ragged hole in the bottom, chewed by mice. She'd been carrying scrap greens, dandelions gleaned from the edge of a field. They'd be scattered and eaten by a goat by now. Livvy hated Easthorpe.

The alcove leading to the south door beckoned her, pointed roof and cool stone, shaded in darkness. Livvy crept around the corner, pressed her back to the stone wall, and slid to the floor. Outside, the boys called one to another. Close by. What would happen if they caught her? Perhaps they didn't know themselves.

Brick quoins framed the pointed door. The church was sturdy. Ancient. She didn't have a guess how old. She huddled on a rectangular stone slab fixed in the floor, the kind that hides a narrow stairwell leading down to tunnels stacked three deep with long-moldering corpses. The church walls draped with the clinging skeins of marriages and sacraments and deaths, centuries of private stories unspooling under the watchful eyes of the saints.

The voices outside faded. Livvy hugged her knees, staring into the late-afternoon darkness of the alcove. She watched the door. It was a boon being hidden away. Hiding in these few moments of quiet. In the cottage there was no hiding. She slept at her parents' feet, with their landlady—a distant cousin of her mother's—and her husband and her bevy of children snoring in the hall below. Eleven of them altogether. The attic air got heavy and wet from so much breathing.

Livvy's eye tripped over a carved human shape at the topmost point in the quoin over the south-facing door. Something out of sorts about that shape. Odd, and like it was watching her. Only not like the dead-eyed Virgin.

Livvy got to her feet, touching her fingertips to the wall, and pushed her fringe away from her eyes, straining for a better look.

The keystone over the doorway was a different color and texture from the other stones. The church was multicolored rock cobbles, a rainbow of grays, and smooth stone—granite?—framing the doorways and the stained-glass windows. The keystone was different. Wrong. Sticking out of the shadows like a stubbed toe.

It was black chalkstone. Oblong, oddly shaped. Livvy crept nearer.

The carved shapes on the keystone were rough, untutored, unchurch-like. The kind of work a family would do for a headstone when they couldn't afford to pay someone. Lines and curves, nonsense-shaped. Livvy stared harder, getting used to the darkness, and presently the scorings in the chalkstone resolved into the figure of a woman.

The woman was naked, save for a coif that covered her hair and ears. A tiny smile on her face, and round, staring eyes. Eyebrows drawn up, as though asking a question. Her ribs showed, breasts hanging, and she was squatting, the attitude of her hands insisting that the beholder stare upon her most secret parts. Her nakedness was bawdy. Unashamed. Carved alongside her, lightly, Livvy could just make out letters: *E L U I.*

Livvy smiled. She imagined that the chalk effigy smiled back.

"You there!" The voice shattered the peace of the alcove, and Livvy started.

"What do you think you're doing?"

Livvy turned to find the young and disapproving face of the vicar. Black robes and a tight collar. His hair was thinning, and he had no cap on. In his hands hung pine garlands, drying and brown. Taking them down for Candlemas.

"I was just—" The silence in the church rang heavy in her ears.

"Who are you?" The vicar stepped nearer, squinting down at her.

"I'm . . ." Livvy had a horror of talking to strangers. They'd only been in Easthorpe some weeks. Enough to arouse suspicion, but not enough to have made friends.

"You're one of Goody Redferne's boarders." He kept moving nearer. He had pox scars on his cheeks, making him look raw and burned.

"Aye," Livvy managed. She took a step backward without meaning to and hit her heel on the wall. Pain flared up the tendons in her foot.

"From Lancashire," he said, and when he said it his mouth twisted, and something changed in his eyes. "Just arrived."

Above the southern door, the crouching carved woman seemed to be giving birth to all manners of escape.

"Aye," Livvy said at length. "Pendle Hill."

The pine garlands sighed softly to the vicar's feet.

"And who be your mother, little girl from Pendle Hill?" He stepped nearer, his slipper crushing the desiccated needles. Livvy's nose twitched at the sharp scent of the pine oil.

"Anna be her Christian name. Anna Hasseltine."

"No," the vicar said slowly. "I asked you, *who be your mother?*"

Confused, Livvy crept with her toes nearer the door.

"She—She's—" Livvy stammered. "I'm—"

"What do you want here?" He was so close, only an arm's length away.

"I was only—"

"You were only what?"

Livvy's eyes traveled up to the squatting black chalk woman. Her hands on her knees. Her smile saying, *Yes. Look at me. I know you. I knew you before you knew yourself.*

"You be an abomination," the vicar said, softly and so friendly-like that at first Livvy thought she must have misheard him.

"What?" Livvy said.

"You best be getting on," the vicar said, dropping his voice to a sinister whisper. "Wee Cromwellian. Little spawn of the Pretender. I'm just back from London, you know." He stepped near enough that she could feel his wet breath on her cheek.

Livvy's wrists ached. In the pillory, back in Pendle, she'd been left so long the bones in her wrists grated together like dry pebbles.

"Oh, aye." The vicar's poxed eye gleamed. "I saw it all. Cromwell's body dragged through the streets on a sledge. Hanged for a day, then his head hacked off. Driven on a pike twenty foot high. Mounted above Westminster Hall. Can you conceive it? The Lord Protector himself, slack-jawed, pecked by crows?"

Livvy's feet inched her along the wall, away from the vicar, nearer the door. Three feet. Then two. Almost near enough to grasp the handle.

"Go on. Get out of here," the vicar snarled. "There's no call for the likes of you in God's house."

Her hand fell on the door. Pushed it open. The evening mist drifted in, carrying the smells of sheep and darkness.

"This were never God's house," Livvy said, too loudly, and stepped into the coming night.

Chapter One

Cambridge, Massachusetts

Early February

2000

"It would appear that we are nearly out of time," Janine Silva said, eying her vintage Spiro Agnew wristwatch, and Connie Goodwin's vision blurred with a surreal sense of déjà vu.

For six years, every major event of her graduate student life had taken place in this room. The new student welcome reception was held here—Connie had worn flip-flops, of course, which was appalling, but true. Her reading seminars were taught here. Her oral exams—the longest four hours of her life, so stressful that she had basically blocked them out the moment they were over. That was here too. Her practice job talk, before a panel of fellow doctoral candidates each wanting to ask a question more probing and picayune than the next, also here. And the dreadful, stultifying holiday parties, year after year, which she'd attended mainly so that she and her roommate Liz Dowers—Liz of the half-dimple smile and ability to actually lecture in medieval Latin—could make off with the cheese platter at the end. Years and years she had spent trapped in this room, like Theseus in the Labyrinth, an endless vista of sameness around this one conference table. And then, all at once, never again. Not since her final defense. In, what? 1995. Five years. A long time. And not a long time at all.

The room itself was essentially the same as she remembered. Pitted conference table, with a few fresh pairs of initials here and there, tattooed into the wood with ballpoint pen. The same stained blackboard, now hidden behind a freestanding whiteboard with an announcement for an undergrad study break next week—*free pizza!*—in blue dry-erase marker. The same white-whiskered portrait of an anonymous old man, gazing boringly out at his own receding importance. The same grimy window, with the same shutters, now pinned open to catch what remained of the thin winter light. Four in the afternoon, and already almost dark. February was the cruelest month in New England.

Janine Silva, chair of the newly renamed Committee on Degrees in Women's, Gender, and Sexuality Studies, folded her hands in front of her and smiled at the faces assembled around the table.

"I believe we have time for one more question," Professor Silva said. "Who would like to do the honors?"

Janine looked expectantly into each face in turn. To Janine's left, Marcus Hayden, specialist in African American history, newly lured from Dartmouth with tenure and, it was rumored, a house in Belmont for him and his wife and four (four!) children. Marcus was a superstar. He'd gotten the Bancroft history prize with his first book (first!), and he appeared regularly as a commentator on cable news networks. He was the kind of guy Connie found herself thinking about in parenthetical interjections (a Bancroft!). If he had any shortcoming at all, it was that Marcus knew he was a superstar. He'd barely acknowledged Connie when she came into the room. He was cordial to Janine, but in an aloof, superstarish way. He had no notes in front of him, and was also looking at his watch—an expensive one. Well-cut sport coat and no tie. Too handsome for a tie. He had already moved on from this otherwise unmemorable afternoon. No way would the last question come from him.

To Janine's right, Professor Harold Beaumont leaned back in his library chair, eyelids heavy, fingers knitted over his sweatered belly. Professor Beaumont had published a thousand-page Civil War monograph twenty-one years ago, with a university press that listed it for sale in hard-cover at a cost of eighty-nine dollars (all but guaranteeing it would never be adopted for any course), and then he'd settled into tenure with com-fortable indifference. Connie doubted he remembered having been on her own orals committee. Or if he did, he didn't much care. He passed his days teaching one seminar a year, generally consisting of no more than four students at a time (they all had to buy his book), writing a regular column for the *National Review*, and going on cable news shows, though not the same channels as Professor Hayden. He had notes between his hands, the selfsame typewritten ones that he took to every examination like this one, but Connie was reasonably certain that he was about to fall asleep.

On the opposite side of the table, eyes wide, buttoned into an ill-fitting navy blue blazer that had the look of being borrowed from a friend, radi-ating the vibrating crackles of panic that perhaps Connie alone around the table could remember having felt, sat the reason for this gathering—a young, curly-headed graduate student named Esperanza Molina. Zazi, to her friends. Enduring the longest four hours of her entire life up to this point. Five pounds skinnier from months of studying. Light-headed, desperate for escape. Hands tightly folded, thumbs crossed as if in prayer. Her eyes met Connie's and begged, *Please let this be over.*

"I'll do it," Connie said.

Janine beamed. "Professor Goodwin? By all means. Go ahead."

"Miss Molina." Connie leaned her elbows on the table and looked pointedly at the young woman—girl, really. Grad students looked younger to Connie every year. "Would you kindly provide the committee with a concise but complete history of witchcraft in North America?"

The second hand ticked on Connie's watch. And kept ticking. It ticked long enough that Connie noticed it ticking. Her question was meant to be a lob. An easy tossup that Zazi could smash into the corner of the court—Connie had never actually played tennis, but same difference—and go out of her oral qualifying exam with a bang. This was a gimme question. Zazi's eyes were open so wide that Connie could almost see the whites around her irises. What was happening in there? Was Zazi hunting through all her mental index cards—she probably didn't use index cards, none of the grad students did anymore—shuffling through drawer after drawer, looking for the answer and finding them empty? What would Connie do if Zazi couldn't answer? She would have to throw her a life preserver. Give her a hint or something.

Connie glanced at the other professors around the table, weighing how a life-preserver hint would go down, and what it might mean for Zazi passing the exam. Janine would probably let it slide. Maybe. Depending on how she felt about Zazi's writing. Harold? Oh, he wouldn't care, would he? Unless he felt like causing a problem just because he could. Connie wouldn't put it past him. Plenty of professors—more than she'd like to acknowledge—took more pleasure from exercising their power over their students than they did in seeing their students succeed. She glared at him as she thought this, but he didn't notice. And what about Marcus? His lips pressed together, flattening his mouth. Dammit. No way would he give Zazi a pass. No freaking way.

Zazi straightened in her chair, drawing her shoulders back and lifting her chin. She looked from one professor's face to another, settling at last on Connie.

"Northeast, South, or Southwest?" Zazi said.

The Harvard graduate student of American history, as Zazi was, and as Connie had been, must demonstrate mastery of a dizzying array of facts, details, arguments, and agencies of staggering obscurity before being advanced to candidacy for the doctorate. This demonstration took place before a panel of professors, each chosen by the graduate student to form a committee carefully balanced between the competing interests of mentorship, influence, power, and ego. From Connie's perspective, Zazi had chosen well. Two senior people, of differing politics and spheres of influence. A young superstar. And a young not-exactly superstar. Also of differing politics. And certainly different spheres of influence. Connie had never been invited on any cable news programs. Not a lot of call for commentary on early American colonial religious history on cable news. Thank God.

The questions Zazi had gotten that afternoon had been par for the course, and as wretched as any oral exam Connie had ever presided over. Discuss, if Zazi would, the major themes and publication details of some of the most widely disseminated escaped-slave narratives circulated in the eighteenth and nineteenth centuries. In what ways, would Zazi say, did the Antinomian Crisis find expression in the political and religious organization of the European colonies? Would Zazi please describe the first Wedgwood ceramic pattern put into mass production, and its importance in the history of American class signification and practices of consumption?

Awful. Just awful. Though Connie thought she was doing okay so far. Maybe not awesome, but totally fine. Connie glanced at Marcus again under her eyelashes.

Maybe not fine. Hmmm.

Zazi needed Connie, and not just for the lob. Zazi had come to Harvard straight out of the Plan II honors program at the University of Texas, and she intended to study American colonial history. She also had a secondary interest in syncretic and folk religions of the South and Southwest, specifically Hoodoo, Vodun, and Santería. Connie was doing her best to steer Zazi away from a dissertation on that, though. Hard to get a job with that topic. No university teaching positions listed "occult expertise a plus" after "Ph.D. required."

As Connie knew well.

Zazi had arrived in Cambridge owning zero sweaters, breezed through her coursework, had frozen her first winter, bought two sweaters, and had been all set to sit for her oral exams on time when her plans had collapsed into wreckage around her. Steven Hapsburg, assistant professor of early colonial American history and Zazi's advisor, had been denied tenure and would be leaving Harvard at the end of the semester. Rumor had it he was leaving academia altogether and moving to Puerto Rico to live on a boat. (Smart move.)

Hapsburg had come to Harvard in 1994, replacing Connie's own advisor, Manning Chilton, when Chilton suffered an abrupt, appalling, career-ending distemper. Hapsburg was young, and earnest, and straight out of the University of Delaware with a studious dissertation on Connecticut shield-back chairs. He loaded up with courses and advisees and tutorials and got involved in residential life and published three articles (one in *American Quarterly*, even. *American Quarterly!*), got his book under contract with a decent university press, and then— kablooey.

Hapsburg's ignominious departure should have come as a surprise to exactly nobody. Harvard's history department hadn't tenured a junior faculty member since the 1950s. They preferred to hire superstars from peer institutions, to be guaranteed they were getting the best. (Marcus Hayden, Exhibit A.) But no one had bothered to tell Zazi that.

One night the previous November Connie had been sitting her in office at Northeastern, a pile of one hundred and fifty blue-book mid-term exams on her desk, already two weeks past when she'd promised her United States Survey 1580–1860 undergrads she'd have the exams back, starting her fourth mug of coffee for the day and drumming on her head with a pencil, when her office phone rang.

It was Janine Silva.

"She's very upset," Janine said, in a mild tone that reminded Connie that Janine had stepped in when she, Connie, lost her own advisor to a devastating illness just as she was beginning dissertation research. In the background, a nose blew, and weeping continued audibly.

"He can't stay on to see her through the exam?" Connie said. Outside a breeze kicked up, rattling dry maple leaves against her office window like loosened teeth.

"He's moving onto a boat."

"There's no one else on faculty who can do it? What about someone in religious studies?" Connie's hand found her forehead and pinched an eyebrow.

"I'm not asking you to be her advisor," Janine pointed out. The radiator under Connie's office window rumbled to life. *Like I did for you*, Janine didn't say. "Third reader. Second, at most."

"Isn't Thomas a lecturer now? Can't he do it?"

Thomas Rutherford had been Connie's undergrad thesis student when Connie was in grad school. He was now a lanky postdoc, half a foot taller (who knew boys still grew in college?), and as pale and studious as ever. Connie still met him for lunch, on occasion.

"You know that won't do her any good when she goes on the job market," Janine said. "She'll need a professor. For her letters."

"But—" Connie picked up the pencil from her desk and pressed her thumbnail into it, digging a crescent into the wood.

What she couldn't say to Janine was that this was the year Connie was up for tenure herself. She had grad students of her own. She had nearly twice as much committee work as her colleague who came in the same year (a guy, of course). She had a book to finish. And, in theory, she had a life (ha ha). She couldn't take on some wayward grad student at another institution. It wouldn't help her tenure case at all. It would just eat up her time.

On the other end of the line, in the background, the nose blew louder, and Janine said "Here, dear," with her hand over the receiver. Probably passing over the box of tissues. One of the first lessons of being junior faculty: keep a big box of tissues. They'll be needed for the coming wave of dead grandmothers, career-ending B pluses, and dead-to-rights plagiarists feeling abrupt remorse.

Connie rested her forehead on her desk, staring into her plaid-skirted lap. There was a tiny moth hole over her knee.

"Okay," she said.

"Wonderful," Janine said. "I'll let her know. And that you'll be her respondent at the graduate student history conference in the spring."

Connie replaced the telephone receiver without lifting her head.

"I want to go live on a boat," she said to her empty office.

". . . was one of the reasons Catholicism was so adept at absorbing the rituals and folk practices of so many cultures," Zazi was saying.

Connie pinched herself on her arm to force herself to pay attention. It had been a long day. A long week, if she was honest. What was this, Friday? Friday already. At least she could take the whole weekend to write. Unless they had plans. Did they have plans?

"Can you give a concrete example to support your argument, Miss Molina, rather than sweeping generalizations?" Marcus sounded unimpressed.

Zazi's smile wavered. She looked at Connie. Her dark eyes were worried. Connie gave her a subtle head nod. Zazi folded her thumbs in the opposite way.

"Well," she said. "In Louisiana voodoo, for example, oftentimes the figures of worship or spiritual significance were mapped onto Catholic saints. Instead of seeing them in opposition to each other, as might be expected, practitioners held the saints to be embodiments of the same spiritual properties and ideas. The figure of Papa Legba, for instance, is a voodoo loa—a saint, basically—who stands at the crossroads. He intercedes on behalf of humanity, so he is prayed to, but he is also served. We can see how that role, the role of intercession, maps onto the figure of Saint Peter, one of the Apostles. Peter was the rock on which Christ said he would build his church. Peter stands at the crossroads between the divine—Jesus—and man. It's basically like all the same thing."

"And what does that tell us about witchcraft?" Connie prodded, in part so that Marcus wouldn't have time to press Zazi any further. Superstars can be impatient with garden-variety brilliant people.

"Well," Zazi said, "I guess I see witchcraft as kind of a catch-all term. That encompasses many different forms of folk spiritual practice. It's a way for people—often women and people of color—to claim power for themselves."

A mildly wicked thought entered Connie's head. Zazi's was a good answer. Connie was satisfied. Zazi was definitely going to pass. In a few moments she would be welcomed as a colleague, rather than an apprentice, and her work would begin in earnest. Connie knew it, the other professors around the table knew it, and she suspected Zazi knew it too. She knew Zazi well enough to tease her. Just a little.

"One last question," Connie said, walking her pen over her knuckles and smiling prettily at the grad student on the other side of the conference table. Zazi smiled back, but carefully. Connie could tell she was trying to keep it together. Only a few minutes more.

"Yes, Professor Goodwin?" Zazi asked. Polite. Happy. Almost over.

"Think any witches were real?" Connie asked, waiting for the thud of silence that had fallen when Manning Chilton asked her that exact question in this exact exam almost exactly a decade ago. Janine gasped aloud, Marcus muttered, "You've got to be kidding me," and Harold was asleep. Connie sat back, folding her arms over her chest, smiling out of one side of her mouth.

"Nope," Zazi replied without missing a beat. She was grinning.

"Well done," Connie said.

Janine was laughing behind one jeweled hand. "Okay then," she said, trying to swallow her laughter. "Marcus?" Professor Hayden nodded in the manner of a man ready to go home. "Harold?"

Professor Beaumont twitched and woke with a grunt. "Right, right, yes," he said.

"If you'll just give us a few minutes, Esperanza," Janine said.

Zazi stood up, her face shining in triumph. Had Connie looked that way when she was sent out of the room to await the committee's verdict? Maybe so. Regardless, Connie knew what she had to do. After quashing Marcus's objections—he would object because he felt obligated to keep the proceedings from being a rubber stamp, not because he didn't actually intend to pass her—Connie would take Zazi to Abner's Pub for a drink to celebrate. Just as Janine had done for her. A warm glow washed up Connie's cheeks. As much as she took pleasure in her own meager successes, she might be enjoying Zazi's triumph even more.

Quarter past five, her watch read. Later than she thought. She had promised to be home.

Just one drink. It wouldn't make her too late. She hoped.

Chapter Two

"Dammit," Connie muttered, bending over and feeling around on the stoop in the dark for where she had dropped her keys.

A chill wind kicked up and rolled down Massachusetts Avenue, stirring her plaid skirt and licking up her thighs. She reached a hand behind her to hold the skirt down so she wouldn't flash the homeless guy bedded down in the doorway of the yoga studio across the street. Where had those keys gone? Her fingers were going numb. If she couldn't find them she'd have to ring the bell.

Connie definitely didn't want to ring the bell.

A group of three undergrad girls tripped by, catching their stiletto heels in the bricks, naked legs pale with cold under short shimmery dresses and insufficient coats. On their way home from a final club probably. Drunk and chattering, excited, happy. One teetered over to the side and ended up in a snowdrift, her friends hooting with laughter as they scrambled her back to her feet. Connie eyed them with mild envy. Even when she was an undergrad, at Mount Holyoke, Connie had never been naked-legs confident like that.

Her fingertips stumbled over the keys, grasping the largest—an antique iron one, hollow, with a long shank, that she'd found years ago. Hidden in a Bible, of all things. It didn't go to anything. But she liked having it. A fob for the chain. Or a talisman, maybe. A reminder that secrets can sometimes be discovered when one looks closely at ordinary things.

She straightened and stirred the keys in her palm, stroking the antique one before picking out the one that fit the front door of the Green Monster.

The Green Monster was what Connie called the squat, peeling apartment building where she lived, just outside the busiest section of Harvard Square. The Monster had once been a grand Cantabridgian house of the Gilded Age, all dentil moldings and curving oak-railed staircases and marble fireplaces. When the Gilded Age curdled and yellowed into the twentieth century, whoever owned the house realized there was more to be gained from carving it into a warren of small apartments to rent to students and other wayfarers. Three or four apartments per floor, three floors, dusty stairs and the muffled mewling of cats across the hall. In the rear a punk girl lived on the largesse of her parents, occasionally modeling for tattoo magazines, but mainly smoking marijuana that Connie could smell in her kitchen. Upstairs a single father with a drinking problem lived in a studio on one side, and three MIT grad students who rarely made eye contact shared a one-bedroom on the other. What had once been a carriage house in the rear had been transformed by the 1920s into an auto repair shop. What had been a garden was now a parking lot. The house took its name from the particular shade of Fenway Park green that covered its peeling face, the same color as the line-drive-eating billboard of the same name.

Connie shared the parlor rooms on the first floor, lit by a bay window overlooking Massachusetts Avenue and one stubborn, determined, but nearly snuffed-out rosebush. Being on the parlor floor meant soaring ceilings and elegant mantels on the one hand, and street noise and mice on the other. Most mornings, Connie was awakened by the car mechanics talking under her cracked bedroom window. Or by the smell of coffee from the kitchen.

She fitted her key into the door to her apartment, trying to turn it silently so as not to awaken the sleeping occupants. The bolt slid, the door creaked open, and Connie slipped into the darkened living room, dropping her shoulder bag full of exam books at her feet and easing the door closed behind her. As it clicked shut two furry paws materialized at her ankles, and whiskers appeared snuffling her shins. That was one occupant she hadn't fooled.

"Hey, Arlo," she whispered. She bent down and collected the wiggling animal into her arms and hoisted him to her hip. Two terrier-like feet scrabbled at her throat, and a happy tongue tackled her cheek.

"Am I in trouble?" she asked the vaguely sized creature in her arms. His tail brushed her thigh.

"Uh-oh," Connie said.

She surveyed the dim outlines of the living room, lit in cool blues and oranges from the streetlights outside. A couple of beer bottles on the coffee table. An open laptop in sleep mode. A plaid shirt draped over the back of the couch. Signs of waiting, finally abandoned.

Connie tiptoed with Arlo under her arm down the hall of the apartment, past the door to the bedroom. It was cracked open. Dark inside. When Connie passed the door the ball of her foot pressed on a board that creaked in protest. She stopped.

Sounds of rustling sheets inside the bedroom—someone rolling over.

Then a soft snore drifted out from behind the bedroom door. Connie continued creeping to the galley kitchen at the rear of the apartment.

In the kitchen, Connie snapped on the light, set Arlo down, and went for the fridge. She and Zazi had shared nachos at Abner's—the kind made with "nacho cheese," which Zazi loudly derided, on the grounds that she was Texan and had things to say about nachos, but which they'd devoured anyway. Disgusting, yet oddly satisfying, and here, only a short time later—okay, maybe not a short time later—Connie was starving.

Her hand fell on the fridge door and her eye on the whiteboard mounted to the freezer. Below the running tally of household expenses kept to figure out who owed what to whom at the end of each month, Connie found a scrawled note. She pulled the end of her braid up under her nose in a kind of mustache as she read.

Grace called. Said call back ASAP. Late okay.

Below that, in block caps:

GRACE ALSO THINKS YOU SHOULD GET A CELL PHONE.

"Oh, man." Connie looked around for Arlo, but he had disappeared.

Inside the refrigerator Connie found bread and mayonnaise and sliced deli ham that was probably still good and some mustard. She hunted up a cleanish plate from the sink and started assembling a sandwich.

Connie doubted that her mother had called for any real emergency. Once Grace Goodwin had called her daughter six times in a row at her office, leaving voicemails of increasing stridency, until Connie, panicked, with fifteen minutes between classes, called her back to discover that Grace was upset because one of her tomato plants had died.

"*Mom*," Connie had said. "Oh, my God. It's a tomato plant."

"It was heirloom," Grace said, as if that alone could explain the emergency.

After raising Connie on her own in a shabby farmhouse in Concord, which Grace had run as an anarcho-syndicalist collective (Connie was never able to establish whether Grace actually knew the definition of anarcho-syndicalism, but whatever), Grace had followed her bliss all the way out to Santa Fe, New Mexico. While there she had cleansed auras and raised succulents and wondered aloud why Connie didn't know herself better. They'd passed several years this way, speaking haltingly on the phone—or rather, Connie spoke haltingly, and Grace spoke at length and on any number of arcane topics, most of which didn't interest her bookish, rationalist daughter. Then when Connie was halfway through grad school, after the wretched summer when Manning Chilton ripped a neat hole in the center of Connie's intellectual life, Grace had abruptly pulled up stakes to move back east. Grace now lived on the North Shore, in the house she had grown up in, about an hour away from Cambridge. Close, but far enough to pretend she wasn't close.

Connie sank her butter knife into the bread, slicing the sandwich in two neat halves. She probably owed Grace a visit.

The wall separating the kitchen from the bedroom was old horsehair plaster, browned and bubbling from generations of neglect. Behind that wall, the other occupant of the apartment slept the sleep of the disappointed.

Maybe she should go see Grace tomorrow.

She stuffed some sandwich into her mouth, chewed, felt a wave of revulsion at the taste of the meat, opened her mouth and let the chewed glob fall into the sink. She ran the water and put her mouth under the faucet and drank. The water felt good. Cold, from being held in cold winter pipes. Was Grace remembering to leave the water trickling in the antique house where she lived? A house older than electricity. Older than plumbing. A house that treated plumbing as a person might treat a new third arm—uninvited, perplexing, potentially useful, but also a rank intrusion. Sometimes it seemed as though the house was trying to grow the plumbing back out of it, like a splinter.

Yes. It would be good to go up and see Grace. She'd go. This weekend.

Connie slid the remnants of her sandwich into the garbage and slunk out of the kitchen.

In the darkened, silent bedroom she slipped out of her blouse, unhooked her plaid skirt, and dropped it to the floor. She'd pick it up tomorrow. She was exhausted. Head buzzing with the exam, with the writing she had planned for the weekend, with Grace's call.

"How'd it go?" a sleepy male voice asked as Connie slid under the covers.

"I thought you were asleep," she said softly.

Sam Hartley was a steeplejack who had dropped—literally, on a belay line from the rafters of a mid-restoration meeting house—into Connie's life halfway through her years in grad school. Connie's life fell into two halves: before Sam, and after. Sam made up silly nicknames for her and told bad dad jokes and hogged the covers. Sam spent a lot of his time waiting: for the library to close and spit her out preoccupied and tired, for the end of her midterm grading, for her book to be done. Connie liked finding him there, waiting, whenever she was ready to step out of the past and back into the world where she nominally lived. In a way, Sam was the world. A whole universe of memory and feeling, contained in the form of a tired ex-punk in his mid-thirties who was waiting on a small-business loan from Salem Five Cents Bank to buy another truck and hire some scaffolders.

Her universe yawned and stretched his arms over his head. "I was," he said. "Sort of. What time is it?"

"Late," she said, inching closer to him. She could just make out the profile of his nose—beautiful, straight, yet broken once, long ago. His hair cut short and sticking up in sleep. Sometimes she missed it long.

"She pass?" he said, voice tired.

"With flying colors." Connie found the swell of his lightly furred chest below his collarbone, the part that fit her cheek most perfectly, and rested her head there, sliding her arm around his waist. But when she did so, his chest was tight. His jaw too. A wave of tension vibrated along the length of his body.

"Sam?" she said softly. She couldn't see his face.

Somewhere inside the plaster wall, a mouse rustled.

"You could've called," he said at length.

Connie's stomach turned over from a sour combination of bad sandwich, nachos, and guilt.

"I didn't think it would—"

"You never do." Two beer bottles in the living room. That meant he would have been waiting for her, alone, for at least three hours.

Connie sat up. Sam eased himself up in the pillows, leaning on the headboard.

"It was work," she said, and while it was a good excuse when she spoke it inside her head, spoken aloud it sounded pathetic.

"I know." His hands rested lightly on the duvet. She wanted to touch him.

"It took longer than I thought it would," she said.

"It always does," he pointed out. Not angry. Matter-of-fact.

"I couldn't . . . There wasn't a good opportunity to call. I didn't go back to my office."

"If you had a cell phone, this wouldn't be a problem," he said, in the tone of someone rehashing an exhausted argument.

Connie didn't know what to say. Okay, sure, she could see why he might have worried. Three hours was a long time to wait. But her work had to come first. Why couldn't he understand that a lot of her work didn't look like "work"?

He waited. Looking at her. He'd taken his septum ring out a couple of years ago, and without it, with the shorter hair, he looked older. Steady, tired, with deepening smile lines around his hazel eyes. A man, instead of a boy. Even with the tribal tattoo around his upper arm.

A man disappointed in her.

"It's not like we had plans or anything." She knew as she said it that it was a feeble excuse.

"That's not the point," he countered. Head leaning on the headboard. Still not angry. Calm. Maddeningly calm.

"So what *is* the point?" Her voice rose more than she meant it to. "You know I can't just leave those things whenever I want to. I have to make nice with senior people. I have to do them favors when they ask me to. Janine and Harold could be called on for letters for my tenure file. Everything I do is under review, all the time!" Her hands twisted the bedsheet.

Sam closed his eyes.

"I know, Cornell," he said, voice ragged with exhaustion. It was his nickname for her. An old inside joke. He used it to tease her whenever she got too bookish and impossible. Which was most of the time these days. "I guess I just wish—"

From the floor came the sound of a creature stretching out short legs, readying for sleep.

"Wish what?" She was afraid of the answer.

He stared at her for what seemed like a very long time.

Then he pulled the covers up over his shoulder and settled in the bed on his side, facing away from her.

"Nothing," he muttered.

What was she supposed to do? His work was cut-and-dried—when you're up on the scaffolding scraping and re-gilding a steeple, you're at work. When you're at home, you're at home. Connie was never not at work. Never not thinking about her writing, about her teaching, about the deadlines looming on the horizon or the journal articles she had on submission or her book, that awful book dangling over her head, grazing her scalp like the sword of Damocles.

"Sam?" Connie tried to keep fear out of her voice.

"I have to get up in five hours," he said into his pillow.

She settled gingerly down next to him, fingers knitted over her belly, and stared up at the ceiling. Before long his breathing evened and slowed. Arlo, on the floor, breathed at a different rate. The darkness in the room deepened, then thinned, then grayed, unveiling the egg and dart molding along the ceiling one mesh at a time before Connie finally fell into a restless sleep, just before the dawn.

Chapter Three

The Volvo groaned in protest as Connie entered the rotary by the Nahant causeway. She downshifted, pumping the brakes, and eased the exhausted car onward through pure force of will. In the past several years the speckles of rust on the sedan's tired body had spread, rashlike, and the air-conditioning had died last summer. It was only a matter of time before she'd have to get the thing started by running with her feet through the floor, like Fred Flintstone. Connie knew it didn't make sense to keep it. It was in the shop more often than not, and Volvos weren't exactly cheap to fix. At least she could take it to the auto repair shop outside her bedroom window. A fortunate outgrowth of the car's constant need for repairs was that Connie rarely had to hunt for street parking in Harvard Square. The Volvo was usually on the lift in the shop.

A soft whimper emanated from the backseat, and Connie checked the rearview mirror to find Arlo, a thin droplet of drool hanging from his chin, looking green under his mottled fur.

"Only a little farther, sweet animal," Connie said. He smacked his lips stoically and lifted his nose to the cracked window, sniffing the ocean air.

The Volvo swung them through the rotary and along the shoreline drive. Off to the right, the steel-gray winter ocean rolled away under a heavy cloud cover, breathing onto shore like a hibernating animal. Connie cracked her window and lifted her own nose. The air tasted salty, sharp, and cold. The clouds hung low enough to suggest snow without promising it.

Connie had heard Sam get up with his alarm, at the impossible hour of five a.m., but she'd pulled the covers over her head and immediately drifted back to sleep. It was Saturday. No classes to teach.

When she woke up a couple of hours later, there was no coffee.

No note, either.

Her stomach knotted in on itself.

She eyed the scrawled note on the whiteboard from last night, telling her that her mother had called. And that she should get a cell phone.

"Why don't we just go?" she'd said to the creature on the floor.

She scrawled a hasty note announcing where she was going on the whiteboard, signed it with a little heart with an arrow through it, gathered up Arlo and her shoulder bag of exams to grade, and left.

She hadn't been up to see Grace since Christmas. A long time for her mother to be alone on the North Shore. Marblehead was an hour away on a good day, and most days in greater Boston weren't especially good. Saturday afternoon in the winter, though, was about as good as it got, trafficwise. Connie downshifted into Swampscott only forty-five minutes after she had fired up the Volvo's beleaguered engine and pulled away from Cambridge.

Why was Sam so unable, or unwilling, to understand the kind of pressure she was under? He'd understood when she was in grad school, up late at night finishing her dissertation, shattering her circadian rhythms so thoroughly that she once spent an entire week working 'til nine in the morning and sleeping 'til three in the afternoon. When she was in the job market the first time, he'd stood by her without flinching, even going with her to the American Historical Association annual conference, held that year in New York City (a town to which both Connie and Sam had a pronounced allergy), waiting in the bar of the Hilton while she went to her first-round interview for a job she didn't get, held—as most first-round interviews were—in a hotel room that required everyone, committee and applicants both, to sit on the side of a bed.

He'd talked seriously about relocating with her, should the only job in her field happen to be somewhere else—as most of them were. He hadn't even complained when Connie picked their apartment for its proximity to Widener, the Harvard University library—necessary for her, she thought, as she revised her dissertation into a book—even though it meant an hour's commute to most of his steeplejack clients on the North Shore.

Connie gripped the steering wheel more tightly as they rolled down a small hill, past a hillock of lobster pots stacked one on top of the other and overgrown with ivy, and over the town line into Marblehead.

Arlo put his paws up on the window and let out a bark.

They rolled through the sedate downtown, past Chinese takeout and video rental and the ice cream shop. The temperature on the bank clock read forty degrees. Cold enough to set the bones to chill, without the crispness of freezing. Wet cold. Almost colder, even, than ice and snow.

Sam was mad because she hadn't called. Okay. Sure. But that was a chimera, a stand-in for the real thing.

She knew what the real thing was. She just didn't want to admit it.

Connie put her blinker on and the Volvo oofed around a corner, rolling down a weedy alley named Milk Street, a graveled road closely lined with houses that had stood, barely changed, for almost four hundred years.

Milk Street snaked deeper into the heart of the peninsula, the houses growing sparse, until the road finally petered out, without ever properly ending, into a narrow path lined with old oyster shells that trailed into the woods. This time of year the woods were gray and sleeping, the forest floor matted with dead leaves and webbed with fallen tree branches.

The Volvo rolled to a stop outside what appeared, to the casual observer, to be an overgrown thicket at the mouth of the woods, framed by an alder, an ash, and—however improbably—an American elm. Connie rested her wrist on the steering wheel, her breath fogging the window glass, staring until she could see Granna's house. Only after a few minutes of careful gazing in just the right place could the outline of an iron gate be discerned, embedded in the overgrown hedge. And above, rising from a mesh of vines and leaves, all naked and brown with winter, Connie could almost make out the turret of a chimney that had been standing for a very long time.

"Come on," Connie said as she climbed out the driver's-side door, but Arlo had already vanished from the backseat, appearing an instant later at the gate, sniffing, tail helicoptering. Connie slammed the car door with a rusty creak, slung her bag over her shoulder, thrust her hands in the pockets of her jeans, and walked, head down, to Granna's.

Even though Grace had been in solitary residence for the past several years, Granna—Sophia was her name—had lived here until her death when Connie was small, and so Connie still thought of the Milk Street cottage as Granna's house. Grace had grown up in this house, but when Connie was a child they had rarely made the trip from the Concord commune to this New England outpost. Grace and Sophia must have had brambles of their own, just as Connie and Grace did. Connie hadn't even known they still owned the cottage until Grace asked her to ready it for sale that summer in grad school. The summer she met Sam, and her advisor had a breakdown, and her life split into everything before, and everything after.

The summer of weirdness, Connie thought of it now. It happened almost ten years ago. A fillip in her life. Hard to believe. Harder still to explain. When it was over, Connie had returned to what she thought of as her real life. Sam came with her, stepping into her real life—her work, Liz, Cambridge, Abner's Pub. In Sam's body, Sam's nearness, Sam's observing, amused hazel eyes, Connie had proof that the summer of 1991 had really happened. Without him, she could almost pretend that it had been a fever dream, brought on by too much stress and not enough air-conditioning.

Once Connie was safely back in Cambridge, in the fall of 1991, back in grad school where she belonged, her dissertation under way, her life restored to some semblance of normalcy, Grace had reconsidered her plans to sell Granna's house. She had packed up her herbs and Reiki books and crystals and moved from Santa Fe back into the family homestead, wiping grime from the windows, blooming the garden into even lusher life, and clearing the auras of any clogged-chakraed person who cared to go to the trouble to find the house at the end of Milk Street. There were more people like this than Connie had expected, actually.

Arlo wormed his way through a hole in the hedge. Connie heard the sound of him frolicking, and a woman's voice saying, "Well! Fancy meeting you here! Did you bring her with you?"

Connie's hand fell on the rusted gate latch. "Hi, Mom," she called.

Once inside the hedge, the garden, though sleeping for the winter, nevertheless seemed to glimmer with hidden life. A winding flagstone path made its leisurely way to the door of the house, lined on both sides with tufts of sage, thyme, rosemary, and lavender, grayed with cold. In place of grass, the earth on either side of the path was a riot of plants in varying stages of hibernation and decay. To this side, the dried stalks of full-grown asparagus rustled together. In the far corner, their roots sunk into the wood of the house, an array of nightshades—tomato plants, dried and brown, the gnarled tangles of henbane and moonshade lying in wait for spring. The webbed vines overhead cast the garden in long blue shadow, blurred at the corners, hard to make out, and yet strangely the air inside the garden was not as bitingly cold as it was in the outside world.

At the bottom of the garden, under the alder, a pair of reading glasses applied to her nose, her hands busy with a suet cake in a cage overhead, long gray hair hanging down her back, Grace Goodwin balanced on tiptoes in overlarge L.L. Bean winter boots and a woolen poncho.

"Hello, my darling," she said. She clicked closed the suet-cake holder, wiped her hands on her jeans, and moved among the plants to the flagstone path. "How was the drive? Was it awful?"

Connie picked through the sleeping garden until she reached Grace and folded her mother in an awkward hug.

"Not too bad," Connie said, breathing in her mother's smell. Baby powder and patchouli and lavender. But her mother stiffened under her embrace in a way Connie didn't expect, and embarrassed, Connie pulled away.

Grace peered into her face. Some quality of Grace's expression had changed. Connie couldn't quite say what it was. Was Grace annoyed she'd stayed away so long? Her mother knew how busy she was, didn't she? Well, she was here now, that was the important thing. Connie's answering smile became uncertain. Grace took Connie's hands in hers, stretched them out to the side, and scanned up and down Connie's body, as she used to do when evaluating whatever preppy castoffs Connie had decided to wear to school.

"What?" Connie asked, dubious.

Grace dropped Connie's hands and pressed her palms to Connie's cheeks and looked into her eyes. Grace's eyes were the same pale blue as Connie's, and seemed to grow paler in the winter months, as all things did. Dry and cool.

"I'm just so pleased you're here," Grace said, but some quality in her voice made Connie certain her mother wasn't telling the truth.

"Okaaaay." Connie never could get a straight answer out of her mother. Everything Grace said was wrapped up in hippitude.

"Come in," Grace said. "Let's get warm."

"She's going to offer us herb tea, you know that, right?" Connie said to Arlo, who trotted after them along the flagstones.

"None for him," Grace said.

The rusted shadow of a horseshoe hung over the front door, but the door itself had been painted within the last few months. A glossy black that highlighted the ancient ridges and the knobs of nailheads.

Inside, in the narrow entry hall before the ladderlike stair, Grace and Connie stomped their boots on the doormat out of habit, even though there was no snow to loosen, and pulled apart their bootlaces and stepped out into stocking feet. Grace's socks were striped and hand-knitted. Connie's were too—knitted by Grace.

"You sit." Grace waved a hand at the sitting room to the left of the front hall. The sitting room glowed from a gentle fire crackling in the fireplace, filling the house with the smell of charred apple wood.

"Let me help you." Connie started to follow her mother into the darkened dining room to the right of the front hall.

"Nope! Sit!" Grace disappeared into the kitchen in the back.

The sitting room was the same as it had been the summer Connie lived here, and probably the same as it had been fifty years before that. Granna's Chippendale desk pushed off to one side, where Connie had started work on her dissertation, now covered with ripped-open bill envelopes and miscellaneous lists. A couple of needlepoint armchairs, drawn near the fire, one with a basket of knitting sitting at its slipper feet. A sagging sofa, claimed by Arlo, who was curled into a mottled ball with his tail over his nose. In the window, a lush spider plant hanging in a crocheted planter, softly swaying in an invisible draft. Bookshelves groaning under the weight of successive generations of books. On the mantel, a tiny cornhusk doll, with a faded yarn bow around its neck and button eyes, leaned against a brass candlestick holder. Connie fingered the doll. That was another remnant of the summer of 1991. She'd found it one night, crushed and forgotten, hidden behind a book on the shelf. It was amazing, the secrets you could find in a house where the occupants never threw anything away.

"Mom?" Connie called.

Herb tea never took this long.

"Coming!" Muffled, from the other side of the house.

Connie peered back into the dining room, but seeing nothing except the dim, placid gaze of the woman in the portrait over the dining table, gave up and sank into one of the armchairs, stretching her stocking feet nearer the fire. She gazed idly around the room. The room gazed back at her. She snaked her hand into her jeans pocket and pulled out her keys to have something to fiddle with. She held the antique iron key between her two outstretched index fingers, staring at it in the light of the fire. She'd found it in this room too. Hidden in that Bible, the big one over there, on the bottom shelf.

"Just another minute!" Grace called.

The fire popped, scattering a shower of sparks on the hearth, sending a golden shimmer running along the shaft of the key. "You sure I can't help?" Connie's hands set to working the key away from the others, until it was free of the ring and lay alone in her palm.

"Nope!"

The key felt warm in Connie's hand. She rolled it over her knuckles, as she did with pens while she was writing or grading. Walking it from one knuckle to the next.

"What's she doing in there?" Connie asked Arlo after a time. But when she looked over at the sofa for commiseration, the animal was gone.

Presently Grace appeared in the doorway to the sitting room, carrying a small something in her cupped hand.

"The place looks good, Mom," Connie said, inanely, because she didn't know what else to say. She slid the key back into her jeans pocket.

"Oh, yes, I know," Grace said, waving the compliment away for what it was. She came over and sat on the sofa at Connie's elbow. "Let me see your hand a sec."

Connie eyed her mother. "What for?"

"A little tidbit I have for you," Grace said, in that fragile, artificially lighthearted tone that made Connie think she wasn't telling the truth.

"What kind of tidbit?" Connie asked.

Grace shushed between her teeth. "Come now. Left hand, please," she said.

Connie snaked her left arm out of the armchair, like a child reluctant to get a booster shot. With a *tsk*, Grace took Connie's hand in hers, gently massaging Connie's wrist with her thumbs. She moved her thumbs in little circles up along the back of Connie's hand, at the crispy bits between the bones. Connie's scalp began to tingle as the tension hidden between her bones started to dissolve.

"Sam's mad at me," Connie said softly.

"Hmmm." Grace drew her finger and thumb down each of Connie's fingers in turn, and then dug into the webbing between the fingers and thumb, discovering tiny planets of tension that Connie hadn't known were there. Connie leaned her head back in the armchair. Warm feet by the fire. Smell of old wood and dust. Home.

"I don't know why," Connie added, which wasn't true, and she knew her mother would be able to tell it wasn't true. She didn't know why she had said it. Maybe because she didn't want it to be her fault.

"Hmmm," Grace said again. She turned Connie's hand over in her lap. The fire popped. Grace's knowing fingers worked their way over Connie's palm.

Connie sighed. Her eyes closed. Her hand lay in Grace's blue-jeaned lap; then came a light tickling, and her mother's fingers knotting something quickly. Connie opened her eyes.

Grace had encircled her wrist with a simple length of braided twine, scratchy and knotted firmly. From the twine dangled a tiny gray stone, webbed in place by twine woven into a kind of basket shape. The stone was ugly and unassuming, like a pebble you'd find in a driveway.

"What the heck, Mom," Connie said, with the same venom she'd used in junior high the time Grace had hidden High John the Conqueror root in her book bag, making Connie's homework stink of rotting plant flesh for a solid month.

"It's an eagle stone." Grace bent and picked up her knitting from the basket at her feet.

"A what?"

"Eagle stone." Grace's needles clicked together, thumbs moving rapidly around yarn. The needles were making a small sock.

"Repeating yourself doesn't actually give me any more information, you realize," Connie pointed out, feeling at once like a frustrated teenager and a woman frustrated with herself for acting like a frustrated teenager.

"It's a kind of geode. Hollow. Shake it, see?" Grace reached over and tickled the pebble with a fingertip, and sure enough it made the tiniest rattling sound.

"And what have I done to earn such an elegant, glamorous item as this?" Connie put her hand in her lap and tugged on the twine with her right finger and thumb. The knots didn't budge.

Grace put her knitting aside and fussed out of the sitting room. "Tea's almost ready," she called from her way to the kitchen.

Connie examined the pebble in the firelight. It was plain, dusty, and ugly. And it rattled.

After a minute or two Grace came back in, this time with the expected two chipped mugs. She settled back on the sofa and offered one to Connie with an artificially prim smile.

"So," Grace said. "It's lovely to see you. What else has been going on?"

"Nice try." Connie sniffed the tea, which wasn't peppermint but different—green and tart. "What is this?"

Grace laughed once in surprise, and sipped her tea instead of answering.

"What is it? It's not peppermint," Connie said.

"Raspberry leaf. It's an excellent tonic. Drink."

It didn't smell bad by any means. Just strange. Connie took a tentative taste, and it was nice. Grassy and bright.

"I'm sorry to hear that you and Sam are in a fight." Grace was watching the fire.

"It's not a fight." Connie took another sip of tea so she wouldn't have to elaborate. She was sorry she'd brought it up.

"Ah," Grace said.

"I'm sure it'll blow over," Connie continued without really meaning to continue. "You know. It wasn't a big deal. Just a misunderstanding."

Grace sipped her tea. In the firelight her skin looked papery and soft, kissed with freckles that Connie didn't remember.

"It was," Connie insisted.

Grace's eye slid over to her daughter's face. Then down the front of Connie's plaid shirt. Then back up to her face. She smiled a tiny smile.

"*What?*" Connie said, frowning over her mug.

Grace set her mug on the end table and stretched her own feet nearer the fire. Her toes cracked.

"You know, darling," she said, in the thoughtful manner of one broaching a topic only with great reluctance, "it could be that the best thing is something different from what you expect."

"Something different?" The mug of tea felt hot in Connie's hands.

"Maybe the kindest thing you can do for Sam is to let him go." Grace's voice was soft, but she stared hard into the fire.

"Let him go?" Connie exclaimed. "What are you talking about? I thought you liked Sam. You always said you liked him." Everyone liked Sam. Liz Dowers, her half-dimpled former roommate, even used to joke that she kind of liked Sam more than she liked Connie now. Of course, Liz was only kidding. Probably.

"I do. I like Sam very much." Grace's eyes were pale. She reached again for her knitting.

Connie sipped her tea so that she wouldn't say something she would later regret. It was too hot, and it burned her tongue.

"Part of growing up—" Grace said.

"I'm thirty-four," Connie growled in a way she'd heard Arlo growl once, when she'd pulled a dirty root away from him.

"—is doing things you don't want to do. When it's in the best interest of someone you love."

"I know that," Connie said.

One of the logs in the fireplace sighed apart, dissolving into embers.

"It's possible," Grace said slowly, "that things could be about to change. For you." She continued knitting, thumbs looping yarn over long needles. Needles clacking together. "And it's possible those changes could be . . ." She paused. Her knitting fell into her lap. "I worry the changes could be bad for him. That's all."

"Mom!" Connie plunked her tea down on the floor. "Can you just give me a straight answer? Because the reason Sam's mad at me is he wants us to get married."

"He does?" Grace's voice sparkled around the edges.

"Yes. He does. I've told him I don't want to deal with any of that stuff until after tenure, because honestly I have about as much on my plate as I can deal with already. But his whole thing is that if I love him, there's no reason to wait. We had a huge fight about it a week ago and he's been weird and standoffish since then. So if you think I have a good reason for breaking up with him, whatever it is, I should probably hear it now." Blood throbbed in Connie's temples.

A week ago at the Chinese restaurant in Harvard Square, the one with cheap scallion pancakes on the first floor, a lounge on the second, and a pulsing nightclub on the third, Sam had led Connie up to the lounge, settled her on a banquette with a scorpion bowl bristling with straws and decorated with hula dancers and a fire in the middle like a little volcano, and he'd asked her to marry him.

She'd laughed. She'd said, "You've got to be kidding. Before tenure?"

It was awful.

"Oh, my darling," Grace said quietly. "What a lot of choices you have before you."

Connie leaned her head back in the armchair and stared at the ceiling. Oak beams, gnawed by powderpost beetles. Strong as rebar on the inside, even with the lattice of beetle holes on the outside. An illusion of weakness, masking phenomenal strength. Some day, after the fall of American civilization, after all the people were gone, and there were no more new roofs or sump pumps or spackle, these colonial New England houses would still be standing. Naked oak ribs exposed, waiting for whatever was going to come next.

Sam had told her that.

Connie fingered the little pebble that Grace had looped around her wrist. It rattled. That was going to get very annoying, very fast.

"You know," Grace continued quietly, "it was said that eagle stones could only be found in eagle nests. That they would fly all over the continent, searching for the stones, and carry them in their talons back to their nests, and hide them there. To keep their eggs safe."

"That sounds made up," Connie said, rubbing her thumb over a threadbare patch on the armrest of her chair.

Grace tied off the first tiny sock and began another.

"They're very powerful." The second sock was the same pale green as the first. Soft mohair the color of new clover.

"Uh-huh," Connie said.

Grace seemed on the point of saying something else, but stopped herself. The light was falling away from the windows that looked over the sleeping garden, drawing curtains of light away to reveal the night. Darkness collected in the corners of the sitting room and under the furniture, coloring in the scene slowly with navy blues and blacks. "I made up the guest room already," she said.

"Thanks, Mom." All at once Connie felt exhausted. Utterly, completely exhausted.

Grace gazed out the wavery glass of the window. "Imbolc," she said, almost to herself. "Did you see the snowdrops all in bloom when you arrived? At Imbolc, everything seems to be in stasis. Like the winter will never end. But it will."

Connie hadn't noticed any snowdrops, but if Grace was right, then they were early. Snowdrops and crocuses, nosing up through the snow earlier every year.

"Very soon"—Grace's eyes paled—"it will end."

Interlude

Easthorpe

Essex, England

Candlemas

1661

Livvy's breath was bursting, the torn basket banging against her knees. She sprinted bareheaded, cloak flapping, as the afternoon sky grew more leaden and heavy, threatening snow without delivering on its promise. She skidded around the stone fence, scrabbling for the gate latch, sending some chickens clucking, and then she was at the door.

At the threshold, she stopped. Inside the cottage, raised voices and a slam.

"Get you back down here and talk on this!" a man's voice shouted. Her father, Robert Hasseltine.

"Quiet down, you!" thundered Goody Redferne, the landlady. Her mother's cousin. Then came a crashing, as of crockery.

Livvy shrank from the door, gripping the basket.

Before she could decide what to do, the cottage door jerked open and she was met with the pinched face of her father. His nose and cheeks were ruddy from cold. His hair, thinning on top, some strands askew. It took a moment for him to register that she was on the stoop. And another moment for him to see the bruise blooming across her face. Livvy could feel it, swelling as big as a cabbage. Her father's nostrils flared.

"Get inside," he said.

"Yes, Papa." The door shut behind her and she found herself in the hall, the kitchen fire smoking from going untended. Goody Redferne had a greased iron skillet in her hand, one of her sons wrapped in her skirts, her brow gleaming with sweat.

"Livvy," she said. "Where you been, then?"

"Where's Mama?" Livvy said.

Her father stalked out the door. It whumped shut behind him.

"She's up the loft." Goody Redferne placed the skillet on the trestle worktable in the center of the room and straightened her head covering, wiping her sweating forehead with a wrist. She disengaged the child from her leg and shooed it away. Then she noticed Livvy's face.

"Look at me." She took Livvy's chin in her hand and turned Livvy's face this way and that in the firelight.

Goody Redferne's eyes were piggish and sharp. They missed nothing.

"Well?" she asked.

"I fell," Livvy said, hoping God would forgive a thoughtless lie. For all she knew, the boys who chased her were kin to the Redfernes. It wouldn't do, to be sowing discord.

"Huh," Goody Redferne said.

She hunted down a roll of tattered cheesecloth. Then she reached up and pulled a leafy stalk from the rafter where different herbs hung drying, stuffed it into the cheesecloth, wrapped it tight, wetted it, and handed the poultice to Livvy. Keeping her gaze averted, Livvy applied the poultice to her swelling face. Her skin felt hot under the cloth.

Livvy eased the basket to the wide-planked floor, hoping its ragged hole and emptiness would go unnoticed. Her cousin was the mistress of the house, and Livvy's job was to obey and make herself useful.

Goody Redferne turned her attention to the kitchen hearth, stoking one of the fires with a poker and easing a hanging pot over the center of the hottest of them. A stew was bubbling, smelling of turnips and greens and potato and chicken fat.

"Best you go on up," Goody Redferne said without looking round.

Livvy edged to the ladder, mounting it with one hand, awkwardly scrambling up with hands and elbows to keep hold of the poultice.

The attic was dim, lit only by what firelight from below glowed through the hatch and peeked through the chinks in the floorboards. Up under the thatch it was humid and warm, a relief from the cold bite of the day. Livvy heard cooking sounds from below, bustling and chinking, and Goody Redferne humming a hymn. Under those comforting homelike sounds, came soft weeping.

"Mama?" Livvy spoke softly.

As the darkness receded before Livvy's acclimating eyes, she discerned a vague, lumpish form on the straw pallet at the far side of the attic. Her mother, Anna. Lying on her side, hands between her knees. Livvy saw only the swell of her mother's hip, the hunching of her shoulders, and her softly gathered stocking feet.

Livvy crept forward, trying to make her feet fall softly, as on clover. She got down on her hands and knees and crawled into the pallet. The straw rustled under her slight weight. Mice skittered in the thatch overhead. She formed herself to her mother's back, twining her arm around her mother's soft waist. The wool of her mother's dress was scratchy, and smelled familiar—of her mother's hair, and of something else unique to Anna's skin—licorice, or anise. And nutmeg. A richness and bitterness of herbs that Livvy loved.

Anna closed her hand around Livvy's and brought it up under her chin.

"We're to be off tomorrow," she said.

After traveling for months through heavy winter, on roads rutted with frozen wagon tracks and splinters of ice, they'd been at Goody Redferne's mere weeks. Livvy's mother barely left the cottage; she barely left the attic. Goody Redferne had seemed of two minds having them. Not overly welcoming. But matter-of-factness often passed for welcome, these days.

Livvy combed the hair behind her mother's ear with her fingers. She wanted to know why they had to leave. But it would be impudent to ask.

"Where we going?" Livvy tried instead.

Her mother shifted about on the pallet and lay on her back. Livvy's mother was just past forty, pale, with careworn eyes. Her skin was soft and papery, her plain nose smattered with freckles. Livvy's nose, too, was plain and freckled. Like she'd been spattered with mud.

"Why, what happened, daughter?" Anna cupped a hand to Livvy's bruised cheek. Her eye was nearly swollen closed.

Livvy groped for the poultice and put it back on her face. "I slipped."

Anna pressed her thin lips into a line. "No you didn't." She reached up and took a floss of Livvy's hair between her finger and thumb, and rubbed them together. Her thumb traced gently over the swelling fold of Livvy's purpled eyelid.

"'Mine eye runneth down with rivers of water for the destruction of the daughter of my people,'" Anna said.

Lamentations. Livvy had heard it read in meeting, back in Pendle.

Since the King had been restored, and the Pretender's corpse dragged through the streets, those of a mind for purification, like the Hasseltines, had found less welcome in the countryside. They subsisted in pockets, here and there, resistant moral islands eschewing Popery and its vile licentiousness, suspect in the eyes of the Crown. But there was something else too. Livvy's whole life they'd lived under a shadow. A haze knitted of whispers. What had spurred their abrupt removal from Lancashire to Essex, to the bony elbow of a village that was Easthorpe? There had been talk, and harsh words, and those pilloried hours with her head and Anna's hanging in the stocks to the jeers of their neighbors, and then one night her father had bundled them into a cart atop a scant few rolls of linens and a trunk of cookware and scraps of clothes. They'd jounced away without a farewell to anyone. Stopping in market towns here and there, speaking little.

Now they were leaving again.

Livvy wouldn't be sorry to go. Had word come they could go home?

"Mama?" she asked. "Where we going tomorrow?"

"Ipswich," her mother said, but strangely. Ipswich was a port town not so far away. The cart would make it in a day or two, if the snow held off. The cold might keep the snow at bay.

They knew no one in Ipswich. They would be strangers.

"Ipswich?" Livvy repeated.

"Yes, Deliverance," said her mother. "And thence to a land of peace, to a place named for peace. God has made a haven for us, where we can seed a new Zion in the wilderness."

"Where's that?" Livvy sat up, her voice sounding small and far away in her ears.

Anna smoothed the floss of hair back behind Livvy's ear. The turnspit dog pawed into the pallet with them, warming their feet. "In the Massachusetts," Anna said serenely. "A village named Salaam."

Chapter Four

Cambridge, Massachusetts
The day after Imbolc
2000

Connie leaned on her elbows at the bar in Abner's Pub, staring into the amber depths of her old-fashioned. The ice had melted. The maraschino cherry lolled in the bottom.

"I make you something else?" Abner asked.

"Huh?" Connie said. A moist droplet trickled down the side of the tumbler, and Connie smeared it with her thumb.

"You don't like it." Abner gestured at the glass.

"No, no. It's fine," Connie said. "Could I maybe get some nachos, though?"

Something about those awful nachos. Connie actually salivated at the idea of them. Melty fake cheese, canned black olives, canned jalapeños. Zazi would laugh her head off if she knew.

"Sure, kid." Connie knew Abner called everyone "kid" so he didn't have to remember regulars' names, but she appreciated the pretense of familiarity all the same. She also appreciated that in Abner's eyes, if nowhere else, she still qualified as a kid.

She twisted the glass on its coaster. The stone around her wrist rattled whenever she moved. Like the bell on the collar of a cat, designed to give backyard songbirds a fighting chance. Connie would never be able to sneak up on anyone ever again. Not that she made a habit of sneaking up on people, but even so. It was the principle of the thing.

"Boo!" a young woman's voice said next to Connie's ear, so softly and suddenly that Connie gasped "Oh!" When she looked around to discover the speaker, she found the mischievous eyes and half dimple of her friend Liz Dowers.

"Oh my God. You scared the pants off me."

"It was just too good. I couldn't help myself," Liz said, settling on the stool next to Connie's and waving a finger at Abner to indicate she'd like an old-fashioned too. "You were so lost in thought, I considered stealing your laptop bag just to see if you'd notice."

Liz and Connie had roomed together for the first half of their respective doctoral programs, Connie's in American colonial history and Liz's in classics. But while Connie had gone the academic route when her degree was done, clawing her way into the professoriate with single-minded purpose (to the apparent detriment of her major life relationships), Liz had vaulted into the museum world, landing in the softly feathered nest of the Harvard University Art Museums medieval antiquities department. She was now associate curator. Her specialty was . . . Oh, man. Liz's specialty was so arcane and specific that Connie didn't entirely understand what it was. Something about illuminated manuscripts. And poetry? That sounded right.

Liz's cheeks were flushed from rushing through the cold to meet Connie. She wore a blouse and pencil skirt and knee-high boots, her water-pale hair in an elegant bun at the nape of her neck, only a few strands loosened by her jog across campus. She looked like a grown-up. It was weird.

"Sheesh. Give a girl a little warning next time, why don't you," Connie said. "And don't steal my laptop."

"I would, if the girl would get a cell phone," Liz said. "Besides, your laptop is better than mine. Mine is from, like, 1995. It weighs about eight pounds." Abner delivered Liz's cocktail, and she sipped it with the relief of a woman who has worked under fluorescent lights for a ten-hour day in a room without windows. "You been waiting long? We said five thirty, didn't we?"

"Yes," Connie said. And then, without any warning whatsoever, and for no reason that she could discern, something broke open inside her, and she started to cry.

"Oh, hey! Whoa!" Liz folded a concerned arm around Connie's shoulders. "What's the matter?"

Connie fumbled for a cocktail napkin, and, finding one, honked her nose in it. "I don't know!" She sniffed, wiping under her eyes.

"Did something happen?" Liz asked gently, rubbing Connie's arm.

"Sam and I had a fight, and Grace thinks—Grace thinks—" Connie sobbed. "Grace thinks I should break up with him, and she tied this stupid rock on my wrist and I can't get it off!"

Liz squeezed Connie tighter, but under her squeeze was gentle laughter. "Poor muffin," she soothed. "You want me to ask Abner for some scissors?"

Connie looked into Liz's warm, sympathetic face and started to laugh, tears still winding down her cheeks.

"Look at it! It's horrible!" Connie raised her imprisoned wrist for Liz's inspection.

Liz took the eagle stone between finger and thumb and twisted it critically in the dim light of the bar.

"Wow," she said. "That's the most Grace thing I've ever seen. Like, ever."

Connie laughed harder and blew her nose again. Abner slid the nachos between them and refilled Connie's water. Next to the plate he left a pile of cocktail napkins.

"I know, right?" Connie dandled it with her finger. It rattled obediently.

"It rattles? I bet *that* isn't driving you insane." Liz toyed with a nacho and wrinkled her nose in distaste. "Did you actually order this?"

"It is driving me insane." Connie peeled up a tortilla chip trailing a long tendril of fake cheese and piled it into her mouth. Salt and fat and oh, it was good.

"So what's it supposed to do?" Liz asked, subtly edging the plate of nachos closer to Connie and farther away from her.

"What?" Connie said through a full mouth. Tart jalapeño. Salty olive. Delicious. She peeled up another.

"The pebble that rattles. Grace wouldn't give you such an elegant item unless it had some divine purpose. Your chakras need balancing or something? Mercury going retrograde again?" Liz took a sip of her drink. "That would explain a lot about the date I went on last night, actually."

Connie chewed, looking at the eagle stone. "It's supposed to be protective. Folklore claimed that eagles used them. To safeguard their eggs."

Liz coughed, a mouthful of cocktail snarfing up her nose. "Wait, what?"

Connie shrugged.

"Their eggs?" Liz repeated.

"That's what she said."

Liz turned sideways on her barstool, grabbed Connie's hands, and held them out on either side of her body. She scanned Connie's sweater and her plaid skirt and her confused, pink-nosed face.

"Are you pregnant?" Liz asked with suspicion.

"What?" Connie said, her voice coming out much higher than usual.

"Eggs? Safeguarding? Come on. That's Grace talk for 'pregnant.'" She dropped her voice. "Is that what you and Samuel fought about?"

Liz always called Sam "Samuel." It was an ongoing joke among the three of them, all three of whom were known by official nicknames. Connie, Sam, and Liz. Constance, Samuel, and Elizabeth. Strangers who shadowed them everywhere. Elizabeth was the one wearing a pencil skirt. Not Liz.

Connie hadn't been home to see Sam. She'd stayed overnight with her mother in Marblehead, suffering a chilly and fitful sleep in one of the four-poster twin beds in the attic bedroom in Granna's house. She'd awoken to strange pale-gray light through the upstairs shutters, quilt over her head in a rainbow of cut-up squares. When she looked at her watch, she realized she had slept past ten in the morning—almost twelve hours. She never slept that late. When she got up the house was empty, save for Arlo resting on his side under the dining table, enjoying the watchful gaze of the woman whose portrait kept vigil over the dining room. She had a creature under her arm too.

"No?" Connie said.

"What do you mean, 'No, question mark'?" Liz leaned closer, blocking out three laughing undergrad guys in sport coats with a pitcher of beer between them.

Connie's thumb roamed along the surface of the bar. Initials carved into the wood and blackened with time. "I mean. I don't think so."

The truth was, Connie didn't pay much attention to her body. She trusted it to carry her around safely, to do what she needed it to do, and for not much else. Her body was the Cartesian vat in which her brain lived. Even when she was alone with Sam, in private, and quiet, and all she wanted to do was feel, the transition from her head into her body was a bumpy one. It seemed safer inside her skull. More under her control.

"You mean you don't keep track?" Liz was incredulous.

"Who keeps track?" Connie said, equally incredulous.

Liz arched a pale eyebrow at Connie, dragged a fat day planner bristling with receipts out of her shoulder bag, flipped it open to January, and pointed. Sure enough, in the corner of the squares for the week of January 20, little red ink dots. For four days.

"Oh," Connie said. She filled her mouth with another nacho so she wouldn't have to say anything else.

"How long's it been?" Liz stuffed the day planner back into her bag.

Connie shrugged. But now that Liz was asking, it was an interesting question. Connie cast her eyes up at the ceiling of the bar, thinking. Was it? No. Wait. Was it?

"Oh, for Pete's sake," Liz exclaimed. "This is madness. You cannot possibly be as clueless as you seem right now. Wait right here."

Liz put a cardboard coaster on top of her cocktail glass to show she was coming back, cast another disapproving look at the plate of nachos, pulled on her coat, and hustled out of the bar.

When Liz was gone, Connie said, "All right, then."

She turned her still-untouched old-fashioned one revolution on its coaster. Then another.

"Abner?" she called.

"Uh-huh?" He cleared away three pint glasses abandoned by the undergrad boys and wiped the rings off the bar with a cloth.

Connie pushed her glass away. "You think I could just get, like, a Coke or something?"

If the barman had overheard their conversation, he was good enough at his job not to show it.

"Sure," he said, whisking the tumbler away and setting a small fizzy cola into its place. With a lime wedge. Nice. The Coke smelled good. Sharp and sparkling. Connie didn't remember Coke ever having a smell.

"Thanks," she said. She squeezed in the lime and gobbled another handful of tortilla chips soaked in fake cheese.

There was no way Liz was right. Was there? Impossible. Her body would never do that to her. She had tenure coming up.

In the fragmentary reflection of the mirror behind the bar that read ABNER'S in a faux-historical font, Connie looked the same. Some freckles. Long, bark-colored braid snaking over her shoulder. Well-made nose. Eyes that Sam liked to call zombie eyes, they were so pale blue. Cheeks slightly hollowed from stress. Fair Isle sweater, the comfy one with the hole in the elbow that Grace had patched with suede. She looked the same as she always had. Maybe a little sallower. But, God, she was thirty-four.

Nope. That was totally not happening. There was no way she could deal with that before tenure. No way. Everything would just have to wait. That would wait. Marrying Sam would wait. After tenure, she'd deal with it.

On Sam's face, smile lines bracketed his eyes. Even while he slept. She liked to trace the little arcs softly with her fingertip, and see how long she could do it without waking him up. A baby! Would it look like him? Babies don't have smile lines. They don't even smile right away. They're basically like silkworms at the beginning. Wriggling blobs. No. She had to get her book done first. Anyway, there was no way. She was far too careful. She was . . .

"Okay, I'm back. Let's go," Liz said. She'd been gone barely ten minutes. She stood before Connie clutching a small plastic bag from CVS. "Ladies' room. Chop chop."

"What? Here?" Connie blanched.

"Come along, Constance," Liz said in a false schoolmarm tone. "No dilly-dallying."

Liz hustled her along the bar to the tiny ladies' room in back, a narrow affair with two stalls hardly big enough to turn around in.

"Here." Liz thrust the bag into Connie's hands and pushed her into a stall. She turned her back to wait. Connie could see the heels of Liz's boots under the door.

"You're just going to stand there?" Connie said.

"You can't wimp out," Liz said.

Connie grumbled and opened the box. Foil wrapper, an accordion of instructions in English and Spanish.

"God," she groused. "This is mortifying."

"I don't hear peeing," Liz singsonged. One of her booted feet tapped to make its point.

Connie got situated with the weird stick thing and got her plaid skirt bunched up around her hips and shimmied her underpants down.

"You know how to use those, right?" Liz said.

"I have a graduate degree!" Connie said, too loudly.

Liz laughed.

Then, silence. What an appalling situation. She peed next to Liz all the time, but usually they were talking or something. Connie tried to relax.

"Think babbling brooks!" Liz interrupted.

"Liz!" Connie cried. "Shut up!"

The inside of the stall door was covered in a decade's worth of graffiti.

Josh is a douchebag.

TH + SH, inside a heart drawn with permanent marker.

Hit me baby one more time.

A straggly marijuana leaf.

Connie sighed and loosened and then it came.

"Good girl," said Liz.

Connie put the cap back on the stick and wrapped it in toilet paper and got herself cleaned up and stepped out of the stall, holding the stick between finger and thumb like it might be radioactive.

"Now we wait," said Liz. "The trick is not to stare at it while you're waiting."

"Terrific," said Connie. She laid the stick carefully on the edge of the single sink and washed her hands.

"The waiting is the hardest part," Liz said.

Connie leaned against the bathroom mirror and wrapped her arms around herself. "You sound like you speak from experience."

"I had more fun in college than you did."

"Apparently."

"So." Liz rummaged in her handbag and produced a lip gloss, tracing its pale pink sheen around her mouth as she gazed at Connie in the mirror. "What are you gonna do?"

The door opened, bonking Connie on the hip as a middle-aged mom-type pushed into the ladies' room.

"Ow," Connie said between clenched teeth.

"Hi," Liz said to her with a prim wave.

The woman glared at them and went into the stall Connie had just vacated.

"I'm not," Connie said. "So it's moot."

"Okay," Liz said, leaning a hip on the sink. "But if you are?"

The sound of urinating came from inside the stall, and Connie could see the mom-type's sneakered feet. Connie didn't want to be a mom-type like that. Sort of withered and sexless. At what point did a woman stop being a woman and become a mom-type? Did it happen overnight? Or was it a gradual thing? She also didn't want to be a mom like Grace, though. Not that Grace was a bad mother by any means. But growing up on a commune in Concord with a shifting cast of drifters, kale and brown rice for dinner, and a gaping hole in the roof wasn't Connie's idea of an ideal childhood. She supposed she had overcorrected for the chaos of her upbringing with the regimented way she had built her own adult life. Feeding her need for control. Seizing it wherever she could find it. Grasping for it even in places where it couldn't be found.

"I'm just not." Connie crossed her arms over her chest.

The mom-type flushed and came out of the stall, and she and Liz had to edge around each other awkwardly in the tiny space for her to get to the sink. The plastic stick sat on a paper towel under the mirror, right in front of the woman. She saw the stick, recoiled, glared at them, shut off the water, and edged around Liz again to get to the door, with a last irritated look over her shoulder.

"Yeah, bye," Liz said after the door closed.

Connie rubbed the palms of her hands over her eyes and wished she were back at the bar. She just wanted a nice chill catch-up with Liz, not this. The nachos would be getting cold. Cold and congealed.

Liz looked at her watch. She picked up the stick and peered at it.

"Well," she said. "Glad to hear you've got it all figured out, then."

She held the plastic stick out for Connie to see.

"Shit," said Connie.

It was after dark when Connie got to her office in Meserve Hall on Huntington Avenue in Boston, across the river. A Sunday night in February, clotted snow blackened with dirt clinging to the curbs, hard and dark as blocks of granite. Campus was deserted, and the building echoed under her hurrying feet. When she reached her office door, Connie's hand shook as she tried to fit her key into the doorknob.

"Shit," she said to herself. She'd been saying it in a pretty steady stream from Abner's Pub all the way back to her Volvo, and while she gunned the engine loudly enough to wake Arlo from where he appeared dozing in the backseat. She said it as she drove from Cambridge across the Charles into Boston, away from her apartment and from Sam. He was expecting her home by dinnertime. But dinnertime was a broad and flexible temporal category, potentially encompassing many hours.

She would go to her office. She would work. Just for a couple of hours. She needed to work.

The lock finally gave, and Connie slipped gratefully into the narrow, single-windowed nook that, while lacking in any decorative distinction, at least contained almost enough shelves for her books. Her desk. Her computer. Her reading chair. Her desk lamp left over from grad school. The radiator rumbling under the window, often as not leaving the glass webbed with frost from meeting the cold outside.

Connie sank into her desk chair.

She turned on the lamp, casting a small yellow circle on the institutional desk, illuminating a stack of papers waiting for her to grade them. She booted up her computer, listening to it hum to life. She opened the file labeled *Completehistoryofmagicandwitchcraft.doc* and tried to read.

The words blurred together on the page. She rubbed her eyes, red from fatigue and her unexpected crying jag at Abner's. Where had *that* come from?

She dropped her hands and stared at the long, dense blocks of text. She was stuck on chapter five, on witchcraft's transition from being a crime, as it was in the 1600s, to being a matter for folk belief but not the legal system. She traced the change to around 1735, when the anti-witchcraft statute in England was revised. Instead of witchcraft being listed as a felony crime, punishable by death, after 1735 the crime became *pretense* to witchcraft. Witchcraft for profit, essentially. Taking advantage of people's belief in witchcraft for self-enrichment. Connie was arguing in her book—her book, which was two months overdue to the imprint at Cornell University Press to which she had promised it—that the wording of the revised law didn't actually suggest that witchcraft stopped being important in North American culture.

In fact, belief in witchcraft remained so widespread and deeply entrenched that the law sought to protect people from their own credulity.

However, one challenge Connie faced was that by the eighteenth century, she had fewer sources to rely on. Witch trials after 1735 would only be for cunning folk who village people believed were *fake*. Con artists, basically. Court cases wouldn't tell her anything about cunning folk who villagers widely believed were the real thing. Those crafty people in every village, herbs in the rafters, charms for sale, cats who might be spirit familiars stalking in the shadows.

It was Sam who had first pointed out to Connie that belief in witchcraft was real, insofar as it was a historical force of its own. Through his eyes Connie had started to see the secret signs of belief in charms everywhere she looked. Horseshoes over doors. A boundary marker, carved with a hex sign. Once she started seeing them, she could never unsee them. They stalked her, shreds of magic clinging to the real world everywhere she turned.

It started that summer. 1991. The summer she'd met Sam. Connie looked down at her hands hovering over the keyboard, made pallid by the blue-white light of the computer screen. A shadow of pain, as if her nerves had memories of their own, bloomed across her palms and down to her fingertips, and she flexed the fingers to get rid of the sensation, and the memory lying underneath it.

Connie turned to her email. One from her editor, gently asking how the manuscript was coming. Ugh—she'd reply later. One from her department chair, reminding her about a faculty meeting the following week. Delete. One from Janine, giving her details for the panel she was to moderate for the history graduate student conference at Harvard in a couple of weeks. No response needed. One from Thomas Rutherford, her old thesis student, asking if she was free for lunch sometime soon. He wanted to discuss his book project with her, and could they meet at the Harvard Faculty Club?

"Sure," she typed back, "just say when."

Another one from Zazi, asking for an appointment during office hours, and saying she knew how Connie felt about doing a syncretic religion project for her dissertation but she was really excited about it, and could they just talk about it one more time?

"All right, but let's discuss it first. I want to make sure you know what you're getting into," Connie typed.

Zazi's answering email arrived almost instantly. "Great! I'll see you Thursday! Thanks Prof. G!!!"

What was Zazi doing on her email on Sunday night? Shouldn't she be out? Or something? Not at work. Like Connie was.

Connie was at work.

Alone.

On a Sunday night.

In the dark.

"Shit," she said to the empty room.

She reached for the phone.

Grace picked up before the second ring. "You left!" she said without preamble. "I brought us back some nice Swiss chard from the market. I was going to make a frittata."

"How did you know?" Connie said.

A thin silence flowed down the lines and into the receiver in Connie's hand.

"Mom," Connie said in a warning tone.

"Well, it's obvious," Grace said mildly. She didn't elaborate. Grace was like that. She knew things. It drove Connie crazy. Grace also liked to insist that Connie knew things, if she would only pay attention. "The real question is, what are you going to do."

"You mean, am I going to keep it?" Connie said.

"You are," Grace said, and though Connie bristled under her mother's certainty, she knew the moment that Grace said it that she was right.

"What is there to do, besides bust ass on my book and hope tenure goes through before the committee finds out I'm going to have to go on leave for a whole semester and they yank tenure out from under me like a tablecloth under lots of expensive crystal and china and I have to leave academia completely and go live on a boat?"

"What?" Grace sounded confused. "No, my darling. About Sam."

"Sam?" Connie's first thought was that Sam would be beside himself. Forget putting him off about getting married—he'd just march her over to the courthouse in Central Square and see the clerk and then they'd meet Liz afterward for tea at the Ritz. Probably tomorrow. Maybe his parents could drive up from Rhine. And the guys Sam played bar trivia with, who he knew from grad school. They still met every month or so at the BU pub—one had his own timber framing business and one was at a historical society on the South Shore. They'd want to come. And Grace. She could drive down from Marblehead for the afternoon. Did they let people into the Ritz wearing caftans? Maybe she'd even ask Janine Silva. That sounded kind of nice, actually. No invitations. No muss. No hassle. No silly headwear. Connie hated silly hats. She would even wear a dress. Sure. Why not? Not a wedding dress, but like a regular dress. Liz probably had one she could borrow. When was the last time she had worn a dress?

"Yes, my darling," Grace was saying. "You have to let him go. You have to let him go right now."

"Wait, what? What do you mean, let him go? Why would I do that?"

The cursor on Connie's computer screen blinked once, twice, three times.

"Frankly, I'm surprised I have to explain it to you," Grace said.

Connie sat up straighter in her chair, her hand tightening around the telephone receiver.

During that first summer together, after weeks of dashing through backyard gardens in Marblehead and rooting through church archives and swimming in the moonlit harbor and realizing that this was real, this thing they were kindling together, Sam had fallen ill. He had been working on a church ceiling up in Beverly, and he had some kind of convulsion, and he fell and shattered his leg. But that wasn't the worst part. The worst was that even while he was in the hospital, the convulsions kept coming. They racked his body like an earthquake. None of the doctors knew how to stop them. His parents had come. It was horrible. Connie could barely stand to think about it.

And then, the convulsions had stopped. The doctors were at a loss to explain what had happened. But the darkest part—the part she had kept secret from Sam, and from Liz, and from everyone but Grace, who only knew because Grace somehow always knew secret things—was that Connie had discovered Sam's illness was part of a gruesome pattern.

Her father, Leonard, had gone missing in Southeast Asia, in the service, just before Connie was born. Nothing inherently unusual about that. Lots of young guys disappeared in Vietnam. Connie reached across her desk and fingered the only photograph she had of him, its colors whitened by sun and Kodachrome development. The photo showed a shaggy-haired young guy with muttonchop sideburns, grinning goofily into the camera, his arm tight around Grace, herself impossibly young, freshly dropped out of Radcliffe, her hair long and stick straight and parted in the middle.

Grace's father, Lemuel, had lived longer. Grace had actually known him, when she was a girl. But he'd died suddenly one winter afternoon when Grace was in high school, crushed under the woodpile at the back of Granna's house. An accident. Tragic.

Through the research Connie had been doing that strange and distant summer, she had learned about a whole other skein of distant Goodwin women (not Goodwins, clearly, as women's names always changed, but that was how she thought of them—as Goodwins like herself). Prudence Bartlett, a staid Revolutionary-era midwife. Connie couldn't remember what horror had befallen her husband. But something had gotten him, leaving Prudence to raise her daughter alone. Prudence's mother, Mercy Lamson, lost her husband in the middle part of the eighteenth century, crushed by a loose hogshead while offloading from a ship. Mercy's mother, Deliverance Dane, lost her husband, Nathaniel, to a broken wagon wheel. Though that horror had been the least of Deliverance's considerable misfortunes.

Deliverance Dane had been tried as a witch at Salem. And found guilty.

It was dangerous work, Connie had thought at the time, living in the past. But for the men who married into her family—the men who became fathers in her family, Connie realized with dawning horror—it was just as dangerous living in the present.

She had thought she had broken the pattern, that summer of 1991. Connie was so sure the pattern was broken that she had ceased thinking of it as a pattern. But now she saw that she was wrong. Horribly wrong.

"What you're saying is, I can't have both," Connie said with sickening finality.

Connie listened to Grace breathe on the other end of the line. Arlo's chin appeared on Connie's knee, his vaguely colored gaze staring up at her.

"I'm only saying," Grace said at length, "that no one ever has."

Chapter Five

Cambridge, Massachusetts

Mid-February

2000

"Connie?"

"Huh?"

Connie looked up from her plate, where she was stirring a beet and goat cheese salad around, the tines of her fork chinking against the china. Thomas Rutherford leaned over his steak tips and mashed potatoes, reached across the table, and touched the back of her hand.

"Are you okay?"

"Sure," Connie said. "Sorry. What were you saying?"

Her former thesis student, who in the past decade had sprouted from a nervous, earnest college boy into a rangy, mop-haired young man with wire spectacles and an intense gaze, stared curiously at her. She put down her fork.

"You sure?" Thomas said.

Connie smiled thinly. He was a postdoc now. He'd defended last year—"Dr. Rutherford, in the flesh!" she'd greeted him after his hooding ceremony, when they repaired to Abner's to celebrate—and though she thought of Thomas as a friend, she still held herself at a mentorish reserve. He didn't need to know what was making her preoccupied. Anyway, how would it sound? *Oh, sure, I'm great. You know, nothing much going on—just up for tenure, my book is late, I'm knocked up, and I'm afraid my boyfriend is going to be struck by lightning or possibly hit by a bus unless I break up with him, because it's quite possible I'm losing my mind.*

"Tenure packet goes in pretty soon. I'm stressing, is all," she said.

It was the truth. Partially.

Thomas pushed his glasses up on his nose with a finger. "Yeah," he said. "I stopped eating too, before my defense."

"You? Stop eating?" Connie said gently. Thomas was one of those drawn-out-chewing-gum-shaped guys who could eat his weight in food. He probably weighed less than she did. When they were younger, she used to tease him about having a tapeworm.

"Believe it," he said, spearing a cut of steak and forking it into his mouth.

Connie tried spearing a beet to see if that was going to work. She looked at it critically. It glistened in the soft, plush light of the Harvard Faculty Club, a purple globule of cold vegetable flesh shining on the end of her fork.

"So what do you think?" Thomas asked.

"About?" Connie swallowed thickly and put her fork down, beet still on it.

Thomas pressed his lips together, exasperated. "My book idea."

"Oh. Yeah. No, I think it sounds great," Connie said. What had he said his book idea was? His dissertation had been about Oliver Cromwell, the Interregnum, and politics in the Glorious Revolution.

"Do you really think it sounds great, or are you just saying that?" Thomas asked. Almost testy.

He wanted to write something about altered states in the early modern period. Religious ecstasy, psychoactive drugs. That was it.

"I'm serious," she said, reaching for a sip of iced tea. "There's a lot of exciting work happening in the history of science right now. I think it's a smart project. Especially for when you go on the job market in a year or two."

Thomas's left ear flushed pink. Just the left one. Weird. "Actually," he said slowly. "I was thinking of going on sooner than that."

"Oh?"

He still had two years on his teaching postdoc. Enough time to get his book together, give a few conference papers, strengthening his odds. Should she advise him to wait, or would he take that as her being meddlesome, or controlling? He had worked with Steven Hapsburg too, and been left mentorless when Hapsburg bailed for greener pastures. Or bluer shores, as the case might be. Thomas had basically been intellectually orphaned. Not as badly as Zazi had been, since he at least had had time to finish. But still.

"Thinking about it," Thomas said. Ear now crimson.

"Must be some job." She pushed the beet from one side of her plate to the other.

"It is," he said, voice low.

Thomas was sawing the remainder of his steak into itty-bitty pieces and smearing a precise dollop of mashed potato on each one. Why wasn't he telling her where the job was? What was it, professor of early American surfing at the University of Hawaii?

"You're not going to tell me where it is?" She dipped the tines of her fork in the salad dressing and slowly wiped them clean on the edge of her plate.

"I'm sworn to secrecy." The flush in his ear started to fade. He'd always been a twitchy kid.

"Well, if it were me," Connie said, "I'd finish out the postdoc, get your book under contract, and then go on the job market with a stronger curriculum vitae. But that's just me." Three hundred new PhDs in her field per year. Maybe four tenure-track jobs. Six in a good year. And she had gotten one of them. What did she know?

"You think it's a cool topic, though?" Thomas said. "I know most people's first books come out of their dissertations, but I don't know. I wanted to expand my field. And . . ." He toyed with the remnants of his steak tips.

Connie smiled at him. "And you're done?"

Thomas nodded with apparent relief that someone understood. "Yeah," he said. "I'm done."

Connie pulled her mohair scarf up over her nose and her knitted pom-pom hat down over her ears as she crossed Harvard Yard, her shoulder bag knocking on her flanks. It had been good to see Thomas. He reminded her of the real world, out here. Where ideas mattered.

A light dusting of snow had salted Massachusetts, and Connie's boots crunched softly, snowflakes as fine as ash under her feet. Sam was up in New Hampshire, consulting on a Congregational meetinghouse in Derry. He'd be back in time for the weekend. Should she tell him then?

Probably.

How would she do it? She could write it on a cake. No, too cheesy. Or, she could trick him into playing Trivial Pursuit, and somehow plant a card in the question deck. That would be funny. Hard to pull off, though. Hmmm.

Also ticking through Connie's mind was the question of whether New Hampshire was far enough away. Far enough away for him to be safe.

From her.

From them?

No. She wasn't ready to think of herself that way. She was still just herself. Herself with a new, unfamiliar medical condition that somehow made beets unappetizing and volcanic pimples bubble up under the skin of her chin.

She passed the library, moving under snowy elms, their naked branches reaching into the snow-pale sky like twisted fingers. Her first advisor, Manning Chilton, had told her that Harvard faculty had the right to graze their cattle in Harvard Yard. "Does that mean grad students have the right to graze a single sheep or something?" Connie had joked at the time. "It's worth making inquiries," he'd said around his pipe.

Chilton. She hadn't been to see him. There was a time when she thought she should visit. They had been close, once.

She wasn't even sure he was still alive. Though something told her he was. Some niggling instinct, persistent as a mouse gnawing a hole in a thatched roof.

She passed through Johnston Gate and waited to cross Brattle Street, stamping her feet to keep the blood moving, cars rolling by on snow-muffled tires. Connie shivered and looked over her shoulder. Why did she do that? No one was following her. No one knew where she was going. There was nothing special about an assistant professor of history spending a frigid February afternoon in a library at a different institution.

Behind Connie, the Yard was nearly abandoned, only a few shadowy figures scuttling through the cold, most likely undergrads on their way to class. They shuffled past the statue of John Harvard lording over the Yard like Abraham Lincoln, his knees spread, his brass toe rubbed golden by gullible tourists.

Connie crossed Brattle, her head down, her boots picking through snow crusts between the bricks of the sidewalk. She passed the leaning headstones of a long-sleeping cemetery. Then a plain Episcopal church with a Revolutionary musket ball embedded in its doorframe. All was as it should be on a winter afternoon in Cambridge. But Connie's unease continued.

She should have told Sam at the beginning. But when she'd tried to tell him some of the things that were happening then, he hadn't believed her. And why would he? She barely believed in them herself. The rare times Connie let herself think back to that summer, everything that had happened seemed impossible.

Connie looked down at her mittened hand and rubbed her thumb over the tips of her fingers. Her muscles remembered. Her nerves did too. The pain was real. The pain meant it had happened.

Her hand moved over her still-flat stomach, hidden under layers of coat and sweater and skirt and tights, and rested there. More pain to come. Would it feel the same? That sort of hot, blue, snapping feeling? Or would it be different? Connie made her way along Cambridge Common, up Garden Street to what had once been the Radcliffe Yard. Sometimes when she came here she thought of Grace. Wool knee socks and Peter Pan collars her freshman year. Then the sixties hit, and everything changed. A yard that had once been crowded with bookish "Cliffies" was now a quiet center for advanced academic research. Prize-winning authors. Electronic-music composers. Scholars from Europe. No more wooly-knee-socked girls.

The only constant was change.

Today, the yard was deserted, abandoned to the cold. Connie mounted the steps to the Schlesinger Library. Darkness was creeping across the quad already, even though it was barely three in the afternoon. Rock salt crunched under her boots.

Inside Schlesinger, Connie climbed out of her winter layers and stashed her shoulder bag in a locker, taking only a notebook and pencil with her. She hoped she remembered the call number.

In a nod to those long-vanished Cliffies, the Schlesinger Library at Radcliffe was known the world over for its collections on the history of women. The library held the papers of Susan B. Anthony, Betty Friedan, Amelia Earhart, and Harriet Beecher Stowe, to name only a few. It archived books that had once been owned by Ella Fitzgerald and Marilyn Monroe. It collected ephemera, like Riot Grrl zines from the 1990s. It shelved whole runs of magazines, like *Godey's Lady's Book* and *Good Housekeeping* and *Brides*.

And the library had cookbooks.

Lots and lots of cookbooks.

Connie reached for a call slip. Only a few other researchers were in Schlesinger—a couple of grad students from the looks of it (shabby jeans, circles under their eyes). At least one senior professor (textured Eileen Fisher wool wrap, reading glasses). Nobody she recognized.

With care, Connie wrote down a long call number, for a particular roll of microfilm. The microfilm held images of a book that had at one time been in the Radcliffe library special collections, but that had since been lost. The book had no author—or rather, it had many authors, most known only to Connie, but even she knew only a fraction of their names. She had no idea how many hands had gone into the making of this book.

Under "Title," she wrote "Untitled book of recipes—early American."

Connie tapped the pencil against her lips. Then grabbed a few more call slips, filling in other call numbers for other archived antique recipe books.

That way anyone looking at her call slips wouldn't be able to tell which manuscript she really wanted to see.

The librarian at the reference desk collected her slips, flipped through them briskly, and said, "Cool. It'll be a couple minutes. We'll deliver them to the microfilm reading room, downstairs."

"Awesome," Connie said, trying to keep her voice casual. "Thanks."

"I made a syllabub, once," the librarian remarked. She was cool-looking and young, with straight Bettie Page bangs and dark-framed ironic nerd glasses. Connie marveled at girls who could pull off nerd glasses. When she tried them on, she just looked like a nerd.

"Oh, yeah?" Connie said.

"With sherry and lemon juice. It was pretty good." The librarian peered at the top call slip.

"I'll have to try it," Connie said. She doubted that the book she wanted would have any recipes for syllabub.

Downstairs, in a windowless room lined with metal shelves that had once held magazines, which were slowly being digitally scanned for storage, Connie settled in front of her favorite microfilm machine. It was back in the far left corner, away from the door, and through some magic of institutional oversight this particular machine did not charge for printouts. She slid her copy card into the slot, feeling a slight twinge of guilt that was ameliorated by her recollection that she was down to three hundred dollars in her research budget at Northeastern. Some day, she pledged to herself, she'd send Schlesinger a nice fat donation to make up for her stolen microfilm printouts. Just not today.

The room was empty and silent, save for the occasional rumble in the heating ducts overhead. A thin film of dust coated the top of the microfilm reader, flecked with chips of paint from the ductwork. Connie pursed her lips and blew a puff of air at the dust, the paint flecks ticking softly onto the desk next to her. There was no silence like the silence of passing-away technology in the corner of a library.

After a few minutes the librarian with the cool nerd glasses appeared at her elbow, carrying a cardboard tray full of smaller cardboard boxes.

"Here we go." She set the tray on a rolling rack with a squeaky wheel next to the film reader. "You know how to work these, or you need me to show you?"

"Oh, I'm all set with microfilm. Thanks, though."

"No problem. Just bring them back up to the desk when you're done."

"Thanks." Connie's hand twitched, eager to grab up the box that she wanted from within its nest of decoys. She waited until the librarian was gone, then moved her finger down the spines of the small cardboard boxes, each holding a roll of film that contained on one long spool the photographic images of all the pages of very fragile, very old, very obscure books.

She found the one she wanted and lifted it with exaggerated delicacy. She didn't know why she was so anxious. The microfilm wasn't fragile. Perhaps it was because she knew how delicate, how fragile the original had been.

How easy it had been to destroy.

Connie slid the spool onto the spoke, threaded the leader film under the glass frame, and tucked it into the spool on the opposite side. She thought back to an afternoon in the stacks, years ago, when Manning Chilton, at the beginning of his splinter with reality, appeared and demanded this very source from her. Threatened her. Frightened her. She had been uneasy in deserted stacks ever since. Which made no sense—she knew where he was. There was nothing he could do to her. With a last look over her shoulder—the microfilm reading room was deserted, she was safe—she flipped on the machine.

First, black screen. Then white film leader. Then a frame with dates showing the reel had been photographed in March of 1990. Number of pages—265, unpaginated. Connie advanced the viewer one frame at a time. A blank frame. A blank frame. A blank frame.

Then, handwriting, faded and blurry. Connie adjusted the brightness level on the machine and the letters took shape. They were old, spider-like, sometimes shaky and poorly formed. A variation on English secretary hand, in which the letter C looks like the letter R, and the letter X looks like C. Reading old handwriting could feel like code breaking, sometimes.

The pages slid by one at a time, illuminating Connie's face with soft yellow light. The shadows of handwritten lines moved over her eyes as she scrolled. A familiar phrase rolled into view, out of focus. Connie manually adjusted the lens.

Method for the redress of fitts.

Connie reached over and hit "Print."

Chapter Six

Boston, Massachusetts
Mid-February
2000

"What's that?" Zazi asked, pointing to a thick sheaf of white printer paper, hole-punched and bound in an unlabeled three-ring binder. It was sitting on the edge of Connie's desk at Northeastern.

Connie fought through yet another wave of nausea, her hands flat on her desk, hoping Zazi didn't notice that her face had gone waxy. Each morning, she woke to the musical curses of the guys in the auto repair shop outside, and at first she wouldn't remember that anything was different. She would lie in bed, splayed like a starfish, luxuriating in her plans for the day—which lecture she was giving, what meetings were on the schedule, how much grading she had left. Then a small doglike tongue would lick the knuckles of whichever hand dangled over the side of the bed, and she would sit up and the nausea would come. It would wash over her like a wave, rising in her chest, coating her tongue. She'd spent the past week subsisting almost exclusively on a diet of seltzer water and toasted English muffins. Sam was starting to notice.

"It's—a primary—source," Connie started to say, but speaking wasn't going to be a good idea. Zazi had perfume on—something fresh and bright and young, orange zest maybe, and vetiver oil—and Connie could tell that the smell was technically pleasant, but all she wanted to do was barf.

"Is it for your book? Can I look?" Zazi asked, eyes shining with interest.

"Ah." Connie didn't want to show the manuscript to anyone. She'd planned to show the original to Sam, when she first found it. But there hadn't been time. Now she felt strangely possessive of it. It had taken her such a long time to find, and an even longer time to understand. It felt like something private.

Of course, it wasn't private. And it wasn't hers. It had been assembled by generations of invisible hands. It belonged to them. Or to everyone. Or to no one. Regardless, Connie discussed the manuscript at length in her book, the one that was overdue to Cornell University Press. Soon the entire world—and by "entire world," Connie meant maybe two dozen other historians, but whatever, some worlds are small—the entire world would know about this one very special, very strange, very difficult book.

Zazi probably wouldn't think there was anything all that unusual in an early modern physick book. She wouldn't necessarily know what made this one different. How could she?

"Sure," Connie said finally, getting unsteadily to her feet. "Go ahead. I need a sip of water anyway."

Zazi squeaked with excitement and pulled the binder into her lap as Connie stepped out of her office. She shut the door behind her and walked down the hall to the water fountain, trailing her fingers along the wall for balance. She held her braid back with a hand and bent to drink. It was cold, from being in winter pipes, and it tasted metallic. Connie rinsed her mouth and spat. She leaned over the water fountain, gripping it with her hands, and stared down at her warped reflection in the drain.

"Get it together, Goodwin," she whispered. Her distended reflected mouth moved, open and closed, when she spoke. God. She would not vomit in the water fountain. She would not.

She closed her eyes, waiting.

When she made it back into her office she found Zazi sitting cross-legged in the worn floral armchair that Connie used for reading, paging happily through the printout in the binder.

"I've totally seen this before!" Zazi cried, her finger holding a spot on a page about a quarter of the way through the manuscript.

"You have?" Connie said.

At that moment high, tinny disco music started playing. Zazi fished a small Nokia cell phone out of her shoulder bag.

"Sorry," she muttered before answering. "Mami? *Mira*, I told you not to call me when I'm with my professor. No, listen—" She switched into Spanish. She went on for a minute, castigating whoever was on the other end of the line, and then said, "Okay, love you, bye," turned off the phone, and stuffed it back into her bag.

"Everything okay?"

"Ugh! My mom calls me, like, all the time. It's so distracting." Zazi picked at a tuft of loose thread on the armrest of her chair.

Zazi sounded just like her, complaining about Grace. But Zazi was farther away from home than Connie had ever been. She wondered if Zazi's mother had, like Grace, an uncanny insight into the least convenient time to telephone her daughter.

"But look, though," Zazi continued, switching tacks almost instantly, bending her curls over the manuscript in her bluejeaned lap. She was always doing that—able to drop one topic and pivot instantly to the next. Connie wondered how many different tracks were running along at once in Zazi's mind. She suspected it was a lot. Probably more than Zazi let on.

"Show me." Connie came over and leaned on the back of the armchair she'd had since grad school, peering at the page marked by Zazi's finger.

"How old did you say this was?" Zazi asked.

"I didn't," Connie said. "But it's a tricky question. The manuscript doesn't have just one age. The newest entries are from the mid-eighteenth century. At least, that's my guess, from the handwriting."

"What's the earliest?" Zazi asked with interest.

Connie thought. "Don't know. Late medieval, maybe?"

Zazi rested her chin on her fist. "That's earlier than I'd have thought."

"Oh?"

"Yeah. This one? Like I said, I've seen this one before. In fact, I talk about it in my paper, for the conference."

Her finger was resting on the handwritten description of what the book called *The collinder and sheares*.

A chill traveled slowly up Connie's spine, wrapping around her ears, and tingling across her scalp. "You do?" Her voice sounded muffled by the blood in her ears.

"Yeah," Zazi said. "I forget now where I read about it. Maybe Zora Neale Hurston? Whatever, it's in my notes."

"You're kidding," Connie said. "Like, *Their Eyes Were Watching God* Zora Neale Hurston?"

"Oh yeah. She was an expert in this stuff. Did folklore studies all over the South. Talked to people, wrote a bunch of books about it. Got initiated into a voodoo cult, even. I've seen the pictures. I don't remember if her writing's where I saw this, but I've definitely seen it before. The exact same thing. You take a sieve and you balance it on an open pair of scissors, see?" Zazi mimed with her hands.

"And then what?" Connie asked, not letting on that perhaps she herself had had occasion to experiment with this technique.

"Then you, like, hold it out in front of you and you ask whatever question you want to know. And if the sieve tips over, it means one thing, and if it doesn't tip over, it means something else. Exactly like this, only this looks early modern, judging from the spelling."

"How old was the reference you saw?"

"That's just it," Zazi said, wrapping a corkscrew curl around one finger. "It was way later. Late nineteenth, early twentieth century. And it was in Alabama. And it was hoodoo."

"Hoodoo? Like voodoo?' Connie felt foolish. That was the problem with being an early Americanist. It could give you blinders. Like everything worth knowing suddenly stopped in 1800.

"Not exactly." Zazi paged deeper into the manuscript. "Kind of. But no. Voodoo is a syncretic religion from Haiti. There's a version of it in Louisiana, 'cause all these white people who got kicked out of Haiti after the revolution dragged their slaves with them. The part everyone's obsessed with, about voodoo, zombies? Like in the movies? Essentially, a zombie is a body being forced into mindless, soulless, backbreaking labor, without even death as a respite. Total analogue for slavery."

"I'd never thought about that before. You're right."

"Hoodoo's different. It's . . ." Zazi gazed up at the ceiling. Connie knew from personal experience that the right words weren't written on the ceiling. But she looked for them up there herself pretty frequently. "It's just . . ." Zazi tried again. Then she shrugged. "You know. Charms. Portents. Hexing and unhexing. Swamp doctor stuff."

"You mean cunning folk?" Connie said. Of course. It made total sense. The argument of Connie's book was that belief in witchcraft didn't go away after the 1700s. It merely changed. Went underground. Why wouldn't it have spread? Mixed with other traditions? Many streams, bubbling together, coursing together toward—what?

What happens to witches when they aren't called witches anymore?

Zazi paged deeper and laughed when she came across a recipe for a poultice for "piles of the fundament."

"Dang," she said. "How nasty was it living back then, huh?"

"Pretty nasty." Another wave of nausea gently rose into the back of Connie's throat. How long was this supposed to last, anyway? She should probably find out. Shouldn't she be taking vitamins? And avoiding fish? Or something? These were the kinds of things responsible adult women already knew. That she didn't know these things was ridiculous, and meant that she was probably not ready, and probably didn't deserve to have her job, or live on her own, and maybe it would be better for everyone if she just gave up and moved back home with her mother.

She should make an appointment with a doctor.

She should tell Sam.

Or she should break up with Sam.

"What is this, Latin?" Zazi was squinting at a page covered in strangely formed letters.

"No." Connie got to her knees by the chair so that she and Zazi could bend over the manuscript together. "I mean, I don't think so. I think it's cipher."

"You mean like a code?"

"Yeah."

"How can you tell?"

"Well." Connie had noticed the strange entry before, when she first found the book. Back then she'd spent an afternoon at the paw-footed desk in Granna's house staring at the cipher through a magnifying glass until the letters bent and moved across the paper. She'd intended to go back and spend more time on it, but then . . .

"Oh, look!" Zazi interrupted her train of thought. "There's kind of a pattern."

"Yeah," Connie said. "Some letter groupings repeat."

She reached over Zazi's lap and pointed to the letters *T U R*. They showed up grouped together several times.

"That's a cool bracelet," Zazi said, fingering the eagle stone. It rattled.

"Oh," Connie said, embarrassed. "Thanks."

"So what's it say?" Zazi wiggled in the armchair. They both leaned in, peering at the arcane script.

It looked like this:

TURTURJUSQUIAMUSANGUILLAVIRGAPASTORISAN GUI
LLAALNUSTURTURJUSQUIAMUSANGUILLAROSAVIR GA
PASTORISORIGANUMROSAMILVUSIRISSALVIATUR TURORIG
ANUMORIGANUMSALVIATURTURROSAORI GANUMURTICA
HIRCUSIRISALNUSHELIOTROPIUM JUSQUIAMUSIRISD
AFFODILUSIRISURTICAHIRCUSTURTURJUSQUIAMUSANGU
ILLAVIRGAPASTORISANGUIL LAALNUSTURTURJUSQUIAM
USANGUILLAROSAVIR GAPASTORISORIGANUMROSAMILVUS

Zazi and Connie mouthed the letters to themselves.

"You know what? I don't know," Connie finally admitted.

"You should totally try to figure it out!" Zazi cried. "How cool would that be, to have in your book? What if it's like some kind of crazy thing that nobody has ever seen before?"

"You know about my book?" Connie was confused.

"Well, duh. I read your dissertation. That's why I wanted to work with you." Zazi blinked. "Didn't Professor Silva tell you?"

It would seem there were several cunning women at work in this story. "You know," Connie said, "she didn't mention it."

"Oh yeah. I got it on interlibrary loan at UT. It was really good." Zazi turned another page in the binder in her lap. "Kind of wordy, but."

Connie was taken aback by Zazi's frankness. What was with these kids now? What would it feel like, to be that self-assured?

"Are you going to try to translate it?" Zazi pulled on the reading lamp over the armchair, spilling orange light over the binder in her lap. "I can help if you want."

What was Connie hoping to find, anyway? If Deliverance Dane, the first woman Connie knew to have owned this book, hadn't figured out a way to free herself from this—this *thing* Connie didn't even believe in, but feared, what made Connie think anyone else had? But she didn't know where else to start. She had been able to transcribe almost everything in the book, except for a few ciphers and some of the longer passages in Latin script which she would need Liz's help to understand anyway. What did she have to lose?

"Okay," Connie said, weakly, as Zazi squealed and clapped her hands together.

"Look, I can start already," Zazi said. "Doesn't that look kind of like 'daffodil'" to you?"

The letters all looked the same to Connie, as if designed to make their meaning opaque. Or else she needed reading glasses. She pinched the bridge of her nose and looked again. Daffodil?

Sure enough, near the center of the otherwise nonsensical, yet clearly patterned, block of text, she could make out the letters $A F F O D I L$.

"Holy cow," Connie said aloud. Zazi passed her the binder and they switched places, Connie sinking into her armchair. Zazi, meanwhile, climbed into her coat and scarf and pulled out her cell phone. "Zazi," Connie exclaimed. "You're amazing!"

"I know, right?" Zazi said, but her cheeks flushed with pleasure at the compliment.

Connie said, "Let me know when you've got a draft prospectus ready so we can go over it before the grad student conference. If you're sure you really want to do syncretic religions as a topic."

"I'm sure." Zazi wrapped a bright fuchsia scarf around her neck and tied her curls into a pouf on top of her head.

"I can't talk you out of it?"

"Nope." Zazi shook her head.

"You'll never get a job," Connie warned, arching her eyebrow.

"Yeah, yeah. So listen. Give me your cell number and I'll text you mine." Zazi held her phone with her thumb poised to tap in a long string of digits.

"I don't have a cell phone," Connie said.

"You what?" Zazi looked baffled.

"We'll talk soon," Connie said, her finger touching the page on top of "A F F O D I L."

Interlude

———

Around her, Livvy heard the groans and creaks of the hull's wooden plankings, and the wind screaming in the rigging. It sounded like a woman's screams, if a woman's screams could rise and fall without her taking a breath. Under the wooden groans, she heard soft weeping, and above her, on deck, the beating of feet and shouts of men. She drew her knees up to her chest and shivered. A trickle of water dripped between two boards overhead, drips plopping one after the other on her shoulder. The water was icy cold. It soaked into the wool of her sleeve and worked its way through her layers of linen until its frigid finger touched her skin.

Next to her, in the twilight half-light of the hold, a woman from Ipswich bent double and heaved into a felt hat held under her chin. The acrid stench of vomited salt beef drifted across Livvy's nostrils, and she swallowed the rising bubble of bile in the back of her throat. The cabin sole was slick with moisture, and vomit, and urine. They hadn't been able to go forward to the head in days, because of the northerly gale breathing down on them like Neptune with his cheeks blown blue and cold. Finally everyone gave up, huddling in corners, barely able to keep their footing with the rocking of the ship, its rising over the peaks of waves and crashing down in the valleys.

On Livvy's other side, her parents, Anna and Robert Hasseltine, leaned together, their square-toed shoes and the blackened hem of Anna's dress grimy with ordure. Anna held her hands folded and wedged under her chin, in prayer but also for warmth, with Robert's arm around her shoulders and his other hand gripping her upper arm. They swayed together with the creaking motion of the boat. Anna squeezed her eyes closed, her mouth moving over words Livvy didn't know, but Robert stared upward, his eyes tracking the movement of the sailors' feet on deck overhead.

"Steady! Heave!" shouted someone on deck, followed by the loud creaking of ropes under heavy strain. The ship groaned through its ribs. Livvy edged nearer her mother.

There were about forty passengers in all. Three or four fine ladies with their maids sequestered in the main cabin at the stern—Livvy had caught sight of them when they boarded at Ipswich, and had castigated herself for admiring the ribbons on their lavishly gathered sleeves—and the gentlemen of quality who went with them grouped merrily together in the roundhouse, where there was no shortage of strong beer and wine. The rest of them crowded together into the gun deck, men and women and children and babies jumbled together. They'd hit a gale the first week at sea. The gun deck transformed from plain, uncomfortable wooden quarters to a sordid sewer of sickness and despair, and continued so for near on a month. Two weeks earlier, someone's baby had died. A week after that a woman, younger than Livvy's mother, pinched-faced with terror and great with child, fell so ill that they had rigged up a hammock for her; she swayed with the motion of the ship, glassy-eyed, one hand dangling in space.

Livvy didn't know any of the others. A few families like theirs, worried-looking parents with smaller children who kept close. Some pairs of siblings, fifteen, seventeen, nineteen years old, indentured to service, their cheeks sunken with poverty, not meeting anyone's eyes. None had the haunted look of Anna and Robert, though. The look of people in flight.

The ship heeled sharply, causing the lanterns to swing, crazily bending shadows of the passengers and dancing them across the sole. A few screams rang out, faint under the omnipresent sound of the wind.

"All hands!" shouted a man's voice from above. The shout passed from man to man, down the companionway, along the gun deck. "All hands on deck!"

Robert tightened his grip on Anna's arm. "I ought to go."

Anna's pale eyes fluttered open, shaking her out of her prayerful reverie.

"Don't," she said.

Around them, pounding feet as the second watch hurried from the crew quarters forward, up the companionway stairs. Robert looked up, the muscle in his jaw tight. "I must," he said. "I can't stand by."

"What do you know of sailing?" Anna cried with unaccustomed venom. Livvy had never heard her mother castigate her father. He was the head of their household, as Christ was the head of the church.

Robert got unsteadily to his feet. "Nothing whatever. But go I must. I have two hands."

Anna grabbed her husband's arm, her fingers digging sharply into his muscle.

"Let me go," he said quietly.

Livvy got to her feet too. "Papa?" she said from behind her mother's back.

"I will not!" Anna shouted. A few of the other passengers watched from the corners of their eyes. A baby squalled and was shushed. "You've pledged to protect us. It's your duty."

Robert shook off her hand roughly. "I'll not stand idle and have us all perish in the belly of the whale!" he bellowed, and started making his unsteady way through the gun deck, head hunched low to be clear of the beams.

"You'd leave us alone in the Devil's wilderness?" Anna cried.

He didn't turn around. He took hold of the ladder in the companionway and climbed until he reached the hatch, pushed it open, and disappeared.

Anna collapsed to the floor of the gun deck, her face buried in her hands.

Livvy's fingers fumbled with the cloak ties at her throat, double-knotting them and pulling up her hood, and then she followed after her father.

The companionway ladder was slick with seawater and rain, and Livvy's boots scrambled for purchase as she pulled herself up. She reached the hatch and pressed her hand against it. It was heavy. She climbed higher and put her shoulders to the hatch, straining until it creaked open and a swirl of gale and rain reached its fingers underneath and ripped it away.

Livvy was out of the hatch and on her hands and knees on deck before she knew what had happened, skirts plastered to her legs as the deck canted away underneath her. Everywhere shouts and running feet. Someone swore at her but didn't stop. Livvy squinted against the needles of ice-cold rain, hunting through the hurrying forms for her father. A wave rolled underneath the boat, lifting it until its bow aimed straight into the heart of the gale, 'til it shot clear of the water and fell into a trough with a deafening crack. The deck rose up and smacked Livvy under her chin, rattling her teeth and breaking starbursts across the back of her eyelids.

"Papa!" she screamed, but her scream was too small over the screams of the rigging. Barefooted men, moving shadows in the rigging, the flapping of canvas as they tried to reduce sail. Shouts, formless in the void of the wind.

Livvy hunched her shoulders against the fury of the storm, her cloak flapping around her, and started to crawl for a coiled pile of hemp rope at the base of one of the masts. As the deck canted upward on a fresh swell, a torrent of icy seawater bubbled over her hands and around her knees, dragging on her skirts and filling her shoes. They went over the peak of the wave, airborne, hanging for a moment before crashing down again, the deck smacking her chest and face anew.

"What you doing? Get you below!" a man's voice boomed in her ear, but Livvy didn't heed him. She kept crawling, thinking she could hold fast to the ropes and not be rolled about the deck with each surge. A row of men, some passengers among them, heaved together on a line to turn one of the spars, but the wind was having none of it. Then the ship fell,

the deck falling away beneath her, and for an instant Livvy hung motionless in the air, borne aloft on the wind, before crashing back down on
the deck, the jolt jarring hard through her palms and knees. She couldn't
tell her father from the other men. They all looked the same, wet through,
wet hair clinging to their foreheads, wet beards, wet clothes, illuminated
momentarily by the crack of lightning zigzagging through the sky like
the wrath of God.

At last Livvy reached the mast. She struggled to wrap her arms around
it, but it tipped away from her, striking her in the shoulder as the ship
rose on yet another towering swell. Pain bloomed through her arm and
trunk, and she gasped with the force of it. Taking ropes in her hands,
Livvy inched herself closer, 'til she got her arms around the mast and
hugged herself to it. If she held tight enough, she and the mast moved
together, like a squirrel riding a tree branch as it blew in the breeze. The
ship leaned upward, borne aloft on a fresh swell as tall as a cottage, up
and up and up, the bowsprit aiming into the sky, into the black heart of
the storm, and that was when Livvy spied her father.

He had lost his hat, his thinning hair streaming out behind him, his
face locked in a grimace against the wind. He leaned with some other
men, their hands around a rope, their heels digging into the deck. His
coat was soaked through.

Livvy knew what she must do. But she didn't know how. The maelstrom made her small. The task was too great. She couldn't let go the mast
to use her hands.

She wrapped her legs around the mast, pressing her cheek to its sodden wood, and thrust her arms through some looped ropes. She lifted
her hands before her eyes. Wind whistled between her fingers, pulling
on her cheeks, peeling up her eyelids. She formed her fingers into a basket shape, fingertips not touching. Through the sphere of negative space
formed by her hands Livvy looked at the men on the rope. Her father
looked old and tired next to most of them. The sailors were short, and
wiry, and young, with taut muscles like strangling vines.

Her mother had taught her the words to say, but Livvy struggled to
remember. Most of the recipes were in English, but this one was in Latin.
It was very old, her mother said. No one knew how old. Anna had made

her memorize it. When Livvy had asked what the words meant, Anna hadn't known.

"It doesn't matter," she'd said.

Livvy had her doubts. She didn't like to use words she didn't understand.

She closed her eyes and pulled herself into her mind, tried to forget the wind, tried to close her ears to the screams. In her mind's eye, she made the image of her mother's recipe book. The book itself was wrapped in cambric and tied with twine in the bottom of their trunk, buried under rolls of linen and wool, wrapped up with their Bible and the letters for their passage. But she could use the version inside her head. She saw the oil-patterned endpapers, blood red, swirled with black and gold. Saw the heavy pages, etched by the pen scratches of many hands. Here, a bit of physick for piles, scribbled down by Anna's mother. There, a list of herbs for poultices for burns, written by Anna. Livvy paged deeper. Where was the weather work? Where?

There it was.

Livvy steeled herself.

It was going to hurt.

Chapter Seven

Cambridge, Massachusetts

Early March

2000

The binder was too big to fit in her shoulder bag, so Connie shuffled it from one arm to the other and wedged it under her chin as she rummaged for her keys. Her undergrad survey students had had their midterm exam that afternoon, and her office hours right afterward had been a steady stream of students already panicked that they'd gotten too many of the identifications wrong. Would she offer partial credit? Would there be a makeup exam? Would she consider letting them do an extra paper? When had undergrads become so fragile? Or maybe she was getting tougher. Hard to know.

She was an hour late, not too bad all things considered, and she'd called Sam from office hours to let him know there was a line out her door. So far so good. She was giving herself a solid B for today. Not top of her game, but better than passing.

As Connie dug through the mess of crumpled receipts and restaurant matchbooks and half-melted cherry ChapSticks and pens in the bottom of her bag, the door at the end of the hallway opened and an angry young female face popped out. The face had a be-ringed nose and heavy cat's-eye eyeliner.

"Do you have a screwdriver?" the face said.

Keys in hand, manuscript clutched to her chest, shoulder bag digging a red ribbon into her shoulder, Connie said, "Sorry, Sara. This isn't exactly a convenient time."

"Bitch," said Sara.

The door slammed shut.

"Nice to see you too," Connie said to the closed door.

Maybe today was a C.

She fitted her key into her apartment door and edged it open with relief. Inside, she slid her shoulder bag off and let it drop to the floor.

And she was met by an inexplicable riot of yellow.

Every surface—the coffee table in front of the futon in the middle of the living room, the breakfast table in the bay window to the right, the bookshelves on the far wall, the marble fireplace mantel on the left, the bookshelves on either side of her desk, the desk itself—all were crowded, covered, obscured by daffodils. Daffodils in vases, daffodils in beer steins, daffodils in toothpaste cups and mason jars and coffee mugs and water glasses. Delicate paperwhites, pale buttery yellows, rich egg-yolk oranges, their petals curling, breathing the soft, sugared breath of spring throughout the apartment. Connie laughed.

Where had the daffodils come from? There couldn't have been this many in all of Boston. Her back pressed to the door, Connie clutched the manuscript binder to her chest, marveling at the unreality of it all.

"Hey!" Sam appeared in the hall carrying a casserole dish. It smelled like chili, made from beans out of a can. But not in a bad way.

Sam put the casserole on top of an oven mitt on the table. The table was set in three places, paper towels sloppily folded under each fork. Two lit taper candles. A cereal bowl full of daffodil blossoms floating in water.

"Where did these all come from? How did you do this?" Connie exclaimed.

"Magic." Sam put his arms around Connie's waist and smiled down at her.

She'd stared into this face almost every day for the past—what, eight years? Nine. Lines around his eyes. Short cropped hair sticking up, never entirely clean. Nose broken once, and indifferently set. Rappelling gear in heaps all over the house. Thick books on architectural history stacked tall enough to serve as end tables. Chili made from beans out of a can.

Connie knew, with a certainty she had rarely felt in her life, that she could no more leave Sam than cut off her own leg. Not only that, but she would have to tell him. She saw with perfect clarity that everything was going to change, that it was going to happen in an instant, and there would be no going back to how it was.

And that was fine.

Blood rushed into Connie's head.

Sam saw it, saw something changing in her face, and leaned in closer and whispered "What?"

She clutched the manuscript binder to her chest. She could fix this. She must. But first, she had to tell him.

"Um," she said. And then she started giggling, a panicked sort of unreasoning giggling.

"Are you okay?" Sam said.

Her giggling worsened, spread to her chest and into her head and all down her arms and legs, and then Sam started giggling too, and it was almost as if she'd already told him, or he already knew. Or something. Could he tell?

Do you know? she asked him inside her mind.

He leaned down and pressed his lips to hers. Warm, and dry, a little chapped, and tasting of the bourbon he had been sipping while making beans-from-a-can-chili. Connie lost herself in the taste of him, in the thrilling nearness of him, his smell—Zest soap and sweat and a faint whiff of turpentine—and let herself kiss him back. Softening against him. And somewhere, inside the silent recesses of her mind, Connie thought she heard him softly whisper, *Yes.*

"Hello?" a woman's voice said behind them.

"Oh!" Connie gasped.

"You guys! Always canoodling." Liz Dowers waved a wine bottle wrapped in brown paper from where she stood in the open front door. "Am I early? Whoa. What's with the flowers?"

Sam's hands disappeared from Connie's waist. He planted a kiss on Connie's forehead.

"I brought wine," Liz said, smiling lamely at having interrupted them.

"That's great," Connie said.

"Two-buck Chuck?" Sam relieved Liz of the wine.

"Please," said Liz, climbing out of her coat. "We're adults. I spent upwards of five dollars on this."

Connie hunted for a good place to put the manuscript and settled on the armrest of the couch, the only flat surface not already bearing daffodils. Then she hugged Liz hello as Sam disappeared into the galley kitchen.

"Have you told him yet?" Liz said in a low voice.

"Shhh," Connie said.

"Connie."

"I know. I know."

"When," Liz said into Connie's ear.

Sam reappeared, carrying two glasses of red wine. He passed one to Liz and kept the other for himself. He waved his glass under his nose in an exaggerated way, and said "Hmmmm." He took a tiny sip, held the glass up to the light. "A bit flinty," he pronounced.

He knows, Connie thought.

After dinner, their bellies full of chili, Sam and Liz lolled on the couch, Liz's socked feet propped on the coffee table. Connie knelt by the hearth, fanning a small lip of orange flame curling over a twisted log of newspaper until it sparked the pine cones she had heaped on top. The fire popped, and Connie sat back on her heels, satisfied.

"We need to find you a boyfriend," Sam said to Liz.

"Ha," Liz said. "Good luck." Sam refilled her wineglass and she took a meditative sip. Arlo appeared from under the couch and strolled beneath Liz's propped legs.

"There's got to be someone." Sam stuffed the cork back into the wine bottle and smacked it down with a palm.

"Sure. Plenty. All married. Or gay. Or married and gay." She reached down and combed her fingers through Arlo's fur. "Why can't you be a human, little man?" she said. "Loyal. Furry. Doesn't play video games."

"You need a love philter?" Connie walked on her knees to the unassuming-looking manuscript on the armrest at Liz's elbow.

"Why not?" Liz said, staring moodily at the ceiling. "I mean, I've already plowed through everyone on SparkMatch, so."

Connie pulled the binder into her lap and riffled through its pages. "Here's one," she said. "Do you have a red candle in the shape of a phallus we can use?"

Sam laughed, and Liz said, "What are you talking about?"

Connie pointed at an entry in the book.

"Oh my God, you printed it out?" Liz sat up and put her wineglass down hard on the coffee table.

Sam said, "Wait. What?"

"I printed it out," Connie confirmed.

"Someday they're going to fix that microfilm reader, I swear to God," Liz said, and Sam said, "Are you serious? That's it?"

Connie passed the manuscript to her friends on the couch.

"Lemme see, lemme see!" Liz cried. Sam said, "You didn't tell me you had this!"

Liz brushed her fingertips over the pages as Sam supported the heavy spine with one hand, both of them peering at this strange source that had dominated Connie's research for almost a decade.

"I always wanted to see it." Liz flipped to a random page in the middle of the manuscript, and flipped again.

Connie fingered the little stone charm at her wrist.

"Deliverance Dane's honest-to-God physick book," Sam said into his wineglass, brushing it thoughtfully over his lower lip. "I'm surprised it's this legible, all things considered."

"Yeah, the imaging is pretty good," Connie said.

"I thought you were going to leave it hidden until your book came out," Liz said, turning one of the pages sideways and peering at the text.

"What changed?" Sam said. There was something behind his question, but Connie didn't know what it was.

If she told Sam, and he didn't believe her, it would ruin everything. Wouldn't it? But then, if he thought she was crazy, he might break up with her, and then he would be all right. She hoped. She had no idea if that would actually keep him safe or not. What was the mechanism of this . . . this. . . . *thing* she didn't believe?

"This is Latin," Liz said, eyes gleaming as her fingertips ran under lines of text.

"Some of it is," Connie said. "Some is cipher, though."

"Well," Liz said, "the spacing is off, and the words wrap around, but this is definitely Latin. See?"

Connie came over on her knees and put her elbows on the couch. The firelight danced over their three faces. The sugary scent of daffodils drifted through the air.

Liz's fingers were working carefully over the same block of text that Connie and Zazi had puzzled over earlier in the week.

"Hand me my reading glasses?" Liz waved a hand at her bag by the front door.

"Reading glasses?" Connie teased.

"Shut up?" Liz said pleasantly.

"I wear them too," Sam said behind a hand.

Connie hunted up the spectacles. Liz applied them to her nose and peered at the printout. She made letters with her mouth, silently, as she read. Connie watched her, fingertips tingling.

"Do you have some notepaper?" Liz asked.

Sam fished a small notebook held closed with an elastic band from inside a pocket of his jeans, and a nub of pencil from another. Liz took the notebook from him, flipped to an empty page, and started copying. Connie and Sam leaned nearer, watching. From underneath the couch came a soft, doglike sigh.

After a few minutes, Liz sat back and looked at her work.

"Weird," she said.

"What does it mean?" Connie asked.

Liz held the slip of notepaper up for them to stare at.

It read:

Turtur
Jusquiamus
Anguilla

> *Virga*
> *Pastoris*
> *Anguilla*
> *Alnus*
> *Turtur*
> *Jusquiamus*
> *Anguilla*
> *Rosa*

The text continued on like that, a long, repetitive list. Many of the same words—*turtur, aguilla, jusquiamus*—showed up over and over again. Others only appeared once. There didn't seem to be any pattern.

"It's a list," Liz guessed.

"Could be," Connie said. "What's it mean?"

"Well," Liz paused. "*Rosa* means rose, I can tell you that much."

"*Iris,*" said Sam. He pointed at one of the few recognizable words in the list.

Connie saw that *A F F O D I L* was part of *daffodilus*, wrapped around within the block of text. Daffodil. Obviously. Zazi was right.

"Are they all flowers?" Connie asked.

"*Heliotropium?*" Liz said. "Maybe. *Turtur* might be turtle, though. And *pastoris* means shepherd."

"*Anguilla,*" said Sam. "Isn't that a place?"

"An island." Some obscure tidbit of Caribbean history rose from deep within the filing cabinets of Connie's mind. "In the Lesser Antilles."

"It also means eel," said Liz.

Sam and Connie looked at her.

"What? It does," Liz said.

They all looked back at the list.

"*Virga,*" Liz murmured. "That could mean rod. Or staff. *Virga pastoris*—that could mean a shepherd's crook, if you put them together."

She drew a little bracket around the two words to show they should be grouped as one, and then drew a question mark next to the bracket. Though that didn't clarify anything, beyond opening the possibility that the words' meanings might change if they were put in relationship to one another.

"It doesn't look like a recipe," Connie finally said. "Unless the repetition is supposed to correspond to amounts. Like each mention is a unit of measure."

"Could be. Like in a cocktail recipe," Sam added. "Two parts lemon juice to one part sugar syrup, or whatever. Where the size of the part matters less than the proportions."

"Maybe," Liz said. "But why would they be listed out of order?"

"And why a turtle?" Sam said.

"And why an island name?" Connie asked.

The fire popped, and an unbalanced paperwhite fell out of its jelly jar on the mantel.

"Well," Liz said, setting the manuscript under the coffee table and the notebook on top of the manuscript and picking up her wineglass. "A mystery."

The fire licked up and settled down again, embers glowing with the downdraft of the last cool snap of early spring. Connie lifted a thumbnail to her mouth for a meditative chew. She'd managed to stop chewing her nails a few years ago, and when she caught the taste of thumb skin in her mouth she lowered her hand and stuffed it under her thigh on the floor.

"Poor Livvy Dane," Liz said, tracing a fingertip around the lip of her wineglass. "Do you think she had any idea what was in store for her?"

Liz was staring into the fire. Sam was staring at Connie.

"I doubt it," murmured Connie.

"You guys never told me what the deal was with all the daffodils," Liz added.

"Don't ask me," said Connie, her eyes on Sam.

"Daffodils," Sam said softly. "First sign of spring. It's how you know everything is about to change."

Chapter Eight

Cambridge, Massachusetts

Mid-March

2000

Connie reached over for another waffle fry, dragged it through the glistening globule of mayonnaise in the waxed-paper-lined plastic basket, stuffed it into her mouth, and chewed, enjoying the burst of salt and fat on her tongue. Oh, but it was good. She slurped some Cherry Coke to wash it down and reached for another fry. She should slow down. This was her second basket in an hour, and she still had forty midterms to go.

The exams were worse than she had expected. No wonder the kids were panicking in office hours. She didn't think a single person had gotten the correct identification for "cambric." Which was crazy, given that she'd talked about it in class. What the heck were they doing while she was up there yammering for forty-five minutes at a stretch? Ridiculous. So far the highest grade in the class was a 90. Which was pretty good, all things considered, but the mean was shaping up to be around a 72. She should probably think about curving the grades, or she'd have more tears and nervous breakdowns heading into the final than she or her TAs were ready to handle.

She picked up another waffle fry.

She had gained five pounds. That was what the nurse had said. Which explained why the waistband of her plaid skirt was feeling tight. Dang. She'd have to get different clothes. When? Would she really have to? Maybe she could make do with Sam's button-down shirts. And yoga pants. Not that she did yoga. Or owned yoga pants. For how long? For the whole time? Connie's mind tried to skip ahead, all the way to the end of the summer, but her reason rebelled. That seemed like a world away. Outside, wet fat snowflakes drifted from a leaden sky, collecting in sodden heaps in the gutters of Cambridge. She still had wool tights on under her skirt. August was a whole other school year.

Connie stuck the soda straw in her mouth, resting her elbows on the table, and slurped.

"You'll have to watch what you eat," Dr. Belanger had said. She looked too young to be a doctor. It was weird to think that people her own age were doctors. And lawyers. Samadhi Marcus, who'd grown up in the Concord commune with her, was working for the Bush campaign. Typical. He was always a closet Republican. When all the other kids in junior high were trying to figure out how to get weed, Samadhi was scheming to get steak.

"No sushi, no unpasteurized milk," Dr. Belanger had gone on. Grace would scoff at that. Grace believed in doing everything the natural way, even if it meant having milk that went off in a matter of days, and eggs with the occasional curled-up baby chick inside, bristling with pin-feathers.

"No alcohol, obviously," Dr. Belanger had continued. "And you should probably try to limit anything highly processed."

Connie lifted a waffle fry between finger and thumb and examined it in the half-light of Charlie's Kitchen, the dive bar where she did her grading. It was still a potato. Basically. She popped it into her mouth and chewed happily, turning a page in the blue book between her elbows and clicking open her red pen.

"Hey!" a young male voice called from over by the bar. Connie put a red X through a definition of "cambric" that read "An early American word for clutter, like bric-a-brac."

"Come on." Connie wrote in the margin, "Did you take notes?"

"Connie?" The young male voice was at her elbow. She looked up.

"Thomas?" She didn't think Charlie's was on Thomas's Harvard Square circuit. He wasn't the kind of guy to go places that had bar stools bolted to the floor. He pushed his eyeglasses up his nose with a finger and gave her a nervous smile.

"Hi!" he said. "Can I join you?"

Connie had promised to give the exams back next week, and this weekend she and Sam were due at Grace's house for dinner, so that was basically the whole weekend gone. She really had to finish. And she'd told Janine she'd serve as a respondent at the Harvard history grad student conference next Wednesday, which meant reading a panel's worth of student papers and being prepared to say something useful about them other than "Six pages of references to Foucault and Derrida don't actually add up to an argument."

Thomas smiled hopefully down at her, a beer in his hand. Well, she guessed she could spare a minute or two to hang out with Thomas.

"Sure," she said.

"Grading?" He settled in the booth across from her.

"Yep." She quickly put a red check mark next to a correct identification for "Wedgwood."

"How do they look?" he asked, following with a sip of his beer.

"Oh, you know," Connie sighed. "Terrible. They look pretty terrible."

Thomas laughed. "I sure don't miss grading for the survey. That sucked."

Connie glanced at him under her eyelashes. He looked more drawn than usual. Paler. She tallied up the number of points on the exam, wrote "82" and a few words of encouragement on the back cover, and placed it on the done pile. Thomas's Adam's apple moved up and down in his throat, and he shifted in his seat.

"How are you doing?" she asked, with an inflection of careful interest.

He smiled at her, fleetingly, and then looked away and took a sip of his beer. "Good," he said. His left ear was flushing pinkish. "I'm good. How are you? Get the tenure packet in?"

"I'm waiting on one more letter," she said.

He nodded, not really listening.

"What about you?" Connie asked. "How's your stuff going?"

Under the table, Thomas's knee was bouncing. "Oh," he said, smiling a tight smile. "Good! You know. I've got grading for my tutorial coming up. Otherwise, you know. Good."

"That's good." What was he doing at Charlie's? He hadn't come in with anyone.

Not meeting her gaze, Thomas asked—very casually—"So how's your book coming?"

"Actually," Connie started to say, but was interrupted by a squeal from over by the bar.

"Oh my God, you guys! It's my professor!"

Connie shrank down in her chair. Undergrads often seemed surprised whenever they caught their professors living regular lives: shopping for groceries, eating dinner. Once one of her students had turned up next to her in the line for the fitting room at Filene's Basement in Downtown Crossing, the old-school women's fitting room with no curtains or dividers. They were both carrying armloads of bathing suits. Connie nodded, said hi, hung the suits back on the rack, and left.

She reached for another midterm and opened the blue book. "Cambric—a lightly woven, cheap cotton fabric, commonly used in the eighteenth century for clothing and miscellaneous household uses."

"Close enough," Connie muttered, placing a red check mark next to it.

"Hey, Professor G!" someone said by her elbow.

Connie and Thomas both looked up and were met with the beaming face of Zazi, holding a pint of beer, her curls in a wild knot on top of her head. Eyeliner on. She looked like a girl out with her friends on a Friday night. When she saw Thomas her smile wavered, but only for an instant.

"Hey there! Do you guys know each other?" Connie said. Thomas and Zazi were only four or five years apart in the same program, and they'd worked with the same professor. Or had intended to, before Zazi was left high and dry without a mentor.

"Uh-huh," said Thomas without any warmth.

"Nice to see you again," said Zazi with uncharacteristic formality. She angled herself ever so slightly away from him and addressed herself to Connie. "How're the midterms? Are they the worst?"

"I think there's hope," said Connie. "You want to join us?"

"Oh," Thomas started to say, as Zazi said, "No, that's okay. I'm here with some people. I just wanted to say hi. And I was wondering if you ever got anywhere with that code? Cause if you didn't, I was going to see if you wanted to give me a copy and let me work on it for a while."

Connie had meant to talk to Zazi after Liz figured out the code was really a list, but the exams had taken over. "I did, actually," Connie said brightly. "I was going to email you, but then I didn't. Wanna see?"

"Heck yeah, I wanna see!" Zazi scooted into the booth with them as Connie dug through her shoulder bag for the small notebook in which Liz had copied the list of Latin words.

"What kind of code?" asked Thomas. Both his hands were wrapped around his beer glass, holding tight.

"Turns out," said Connie to Zazi, "you were right. It is Latin." She showed Zazi the list.

"It did say 'daffodil'! I'll be damned," Zazi said, running her fingertip down the page.

"What is that?" Thomas leaned forward, digging his way back into the conversation.

Connie popped another fry into her mouth and chewed. "Remember your senior year, when I was looking for my one perfect primary source for Professor Chilton?"

"Well, yeah," Thomas said.

Connie tapped the notebook in Zazi's hands. Across the bar, a cheer broke out when the Red Sox scored their first run of the night.

"Wait." Thomas reached across the table and grabbed the small notebook from Zazi's hand. She cried, "Hey!"

Thomas scanned the list of Latin words. "This is from that book Chilton wanted you to find for him?"

"Yeah," Connie reached over and plucked the notebook back out of his hands and returned it to Zazi.

"But you said you—" Thomas's voice was rising, not quite to a shout, but loud. His hands gripped the edge of the table, growing white between the knuckles.

Connie lowered her voice. "They'd microfilmed the cookbook collection, remember?"

Thomas's Adam's apple rose and fell in his throat. "Did you ever show it to Chilton?"

"Sort of," said Connie, voice darkening at the memory. "Turned out, he wanted to piggyback on my research for himself."

"I have to see it," Thomas said.

Zazi and Connie both looked up from the notebook.

"What for?" Zazi asked.

"Because. I have to see it, that's all," Thomas said. To Connie, he said, "What's the call number?"

The Sox scored again, whoops and pounding on the bar giving Connie time to digest what Thomas wanted.

Sharing research was a tricky prospect, in history circles. On the one hand, it was considered collegial to be open and accommodating, especially about new source bases. On the other hand, no one wanted to be scooped. Connie had heard of that happening to people. You work on a book for years, you get it under contract, sometimes your career is riding on it, and then someone else releases a book on the identical subject, or making a very similar argument, months before you. She could point to cases where junior faculty had been so utterly scooped by a senior person at another institution that the junior person's career never fully recovered.

Her book was almost done. She couldn't be scooped. Could she? Connie was unaccustomed to feeling protective of her sources. Especially with Thomas. But then, Thomas usually wasn't this insistent.

"I don't know if it would make that much difference to your new project," Connie said carefully. "But in any case. It's right there in Schlesinger. You can find it."

She bent and took another slurp of soda from her straw, a not-so-subtle way of saying, *I'm not going to do your research for you.*

Thomas's eyeglasses slipped.

"I don't see why you can't just tell me," he said, pushing them back into place.

"This one time, when I was at UT?" Zazi broke in. "I went to office hours 'cause I wanted to ask my professor to tell me about the history of this one mission settlement in central Texas? And she goes, 'Hmmm, let's see.' And she walks over to the bookshelf behind her desk, and pulls a book down, and hands it to me." Zazi looked between them, waiting for someone to laugh.

"That's pretty funny," Connie allowed.

"Fine," Thomas said tightly. "Good luck with your grading." He crumpled a paper napkin, tossed it on the table, and got up and left.

"See you Wednesday," Zazi said to his back.

He didn't even take his beer with him.

"Huh," Connie said, watching Thomas shoulder his way through the throng back toward the bar until she lost sight of him.

Zazi slid his beer over to her side of the table with one finger on the coaster. She lifted the beer glass and said, "To Latin."

"To Latin," Connie chinked her soda glass with Zazi's. And privately, in the secret recesses of her mind where she dwelled alone with her unreason, she added, *And to Deliverance Dane, whose book this is. Wherever she may be.*

Interlude

———

At sea, the north Atlantic

March

1661

"Papa!" Livvy screamed. She couldn't keep hold of the mast with just her legs and elbows. But she needed her hands. She'd never seen the work done without hands. She had no ingredients. She had nothing. Only the words. And she didn't understand them.

The rain needled harder into Livvy's cheeks, and when she looked at the deck she saw that the rain had turned to snow. Crusts of white weighed on every halyard and sheet, frosting over the glass panes of the skylights in the deck. The gale clouds still massed black and navy overhead, but now the ship lifted up over a swell of black water and thrust itself into a thin white mist of frozen air before shuddering down into the wave trough, raining sea spray over all the men on deck. Livvy's outstretched hands blued in an instant, and she flexed her fingers, trying to feel them in the dropping cold. The blood slowed in her body, and a shiver started deep within her trunk, moving in waves along the length of her arms and legs and ending with an uncontrollable tremor in her jaw. She tried to stop the terrible rattling, but she was powerless against it.

She basketed her hands before her eyes, flattening herself against the mast, and gazed at the men on deck through the frame of her outstretched fingers.

Deep inside her head, Livvy endeavored to still herself. To listen and hear only quiet. Only the sound of her breath. A white mist poured from her nose and mouth. The tempest pushed the temperature lower.

The sound of the storm fell slowly away. The screams of the rigging quieted, the creaks of the planking and groans of the water crushing against the ship's oaken ribs receded, a layer at a time behind the veils of her concentration. Livvy's pale blue eyes whitened, and then she was alone inside the silence, with no sound but the frigid air in her nostrils and the steady beating of her heart.

Her fingertips warmed. A ripping soreness alit on her fingertips and spread down the length of her fingers, across her palms.

Run, little saucebox! Devil's pack mule!

Livvy squinted against the recalled insult, the voices of boys back in Pendle.

Satan's spawn! Whorechild! I'll see you hanged, sure's I'm standing here!

"Leave me be!" Livvy screamed at the voices in her head, the trace recriminations of former neighbors and former friends. "Stop it and leave me be!"

You cannot do it, the voices laughed in a chorus. *Pathetic child. Weak as wormwood. Prideful to even try.*

"Stop it!" Livvy's shout vibrated with the chattering of her teeth in the seeping cold.

The voices laughed, their laughter rising, pouring over her with the sprays of ice-cold seawater, and Livvy steeled herself, closing her eyes and ears and shrinking deep within herself, retreating to some hidden attic in her mind where the voices didn't reach. She rooted within the pages of her mental book, digging until she found the list of words she needed. Slowly, with deliberation and care, Livvy formed each word in her mouth, dropping them one at a time, like pearls on a roll of velvet.

With each word, the heat in her hands quickened. A pinprick of lightning arced between her fingertips and thumbs, snapping and a curl of smoke. With each snap Livvy shuddered from the pain, but held her hands steady. A surging ocean wave, indifferent to the tiny girl-creature riding against the mast, rolled underneath the ship and began to lift it upon its heaving back.

Livvy was missing something important. Had nothing with her. Her mother also had nothing. She could not conjure it. But she could refer to it. Bring its energy and placelessness to heel.

Through the faint blue electric sharps bending and curling between her fingers, thickening into a hot bluish glow within her outstretched hands, Livvy saw the laboring shapes of the men on the deck, and among them, the bent and windblown form of her father.

Her eyes whitened around her pale irises, as though a veil of cambric had been drawn over her eyes. Within her hands the blue ball of light shocked and snapped and began, slowly, to rotate.

"As it grows, a plant beneath the sea," Livvy whispered, hardening herself against the deepening pain. "So shall it harden unto rock upon the air. Thus 'pon its liveliness decree, from here transport us safe to there."

As the final words fell from Livvy's lips, the wave hit its highest crest, and the ship, creaking under the pressure of the wind, sailed over the cliff-edge of water.

For an instant, time seemed to halt. The ship hung suspended in nothingness, water dripping from its barnacled hull. The men on the sheet froze mid-haul, their backs bent, teeth taut as ropes on a cleat. Snowflakes froze mid-drift, motionless and sparkling in the air. Inside the stillness, Livvy's feet lifted slowly, slowly, faintly, off the surface of the deck. Only an inch or two. Her skirts floated upward, her cloak and hair lifting, and Livvy's eyes widened, her ears roaring with the silence. The blue ball of woven electrical veins within her fingers coiled back on itself, spinning faster, and then with a roar of pain that shuddered throughout Livvy's entire small body the light tore free and arced across the deck of the ship.

A roar and a smack and Livvy was flat on the deck, cheek and chest and hands and knees smarting from the impact. Waves of snapping residual pain vibrated along her nerves, and she squirmed against the sensation, gasping for breath. She opened her eyes and lifted her head, daring to hope that her craft might have worked.

An aperture of blue had opened in the angry storm clouds overhead. As small as a basket. And as empty. The storm clouds closed black around the feeble shred of calm and blue, carrying with them a wind of renewed rage. The ship landed hard in the trough of a wave, its rudder spun, and the ship groaned over on its side, spars dipping into the rushing tide, roiling in white foam. Livvy opened her mouth to scream, but no sound came out. As the ship leaned farther, farther, broaching in the snowy black, a rogue wave as short and cruel as a fist raised its navy head along the rail of the ship, licking up the line of men hanging on the sheet. One after another they were knocked down like ninepins. And in among them, a fallen pin—Robert Hasseltine. Livvy's father.

She had failed. The weather work had failed. She was too weak. Too small. She couldn't maintain. She couldn't control. They were right about her, the harrying voices. She was a runt. Devil's spawn, gallows fodder, a trembling worm, naked and alone.

Chapter Nine

~∕

Connie didn't know him at all. But if she had to guess, she would say that Marcus Hayden was royally pissed off. He kept shaking his head and scribbling notes in the margin of the pre-circulated papers on the conference table in front of him, and when his pen ran out of ink, petering out to nothing in mid-note, the furious scribbling he did to get the ballpoint rolling again left thick, jagged zigzags of rage over the print.

The history grad students on the conference panel at the front of the room had no way of knowing that Marcus would, Connie guessed, sooner have set their papers on fire than comment on them. So much the better. Connie didn't think the papers had been all that bad. Not really. One kid, a blotchy second-year whose name Connie never could remember, had delivered a blah and unoriginal treatise on English legal precedents in colonial murder trials through 1790. Yawn. The second, an intense girl named Lisa Matthews with a ponytail so tight it pulled her eyebrows up her forehead and gave Connie a headache just to look at her, had delivered a paper so rife with jargon that it had essentially amounted to a long recitation of the same bibliography that all grad students recite when they first discover critical theory. Butler, Kristeva, Lacan, Derrida, Foucault . . .

"Everyone's read Foucault." Marcus had stopped her (stopped her!) with a raised hand. "You don't have to recapitulate his argument about the panopticon. All right?"

Ouch. Connie remembered that the girl with the tight ponytail had been admitted to her own program at Northeastern, and could easily have wound up being one of Connie's students. The girl had gone to Harvard instead, chasing prestige and funding, and maybe it was just as well. Connie didn't much care about Foucault anymore, either. No more than usual, anyway.

Thomas was the third on the panel to read, the last one being Zazi. As she waited for her turn to speak, Zazi fingered the papers on the table in front of her, petting the pages with her thumbs. She was wearing the same ill-fitting, borrowed blazer from her orals. Connie had looked over her paper—it was on syncretism and power in the American South, and its argument grew out of original archival research into a body of oral histories in Louisiana and Mississippi collected by an itinerant folklorist over the course of several decades, gathered together but never published. Zazi's paper was still in its nascent stages, but its perspective—that syncretic religion and folk magic practice represented an affirmation of subaltern power under a regime of white supremacy and economic marginalization—was thoroughly exciting. Okay, Zazi was looking at the nineteenth century, so edging out of her stated field of colonial history. But by the time it became her dissertation, Zazi could build in eighteenth-century sources. Connie found herself actually excited to hear Zazi give her paper. And that was saying something.

Marcus's rage, though on a low simmer for the first two presentations, hadn't fully boiled until partway through Thomas's paper. Connie was surprised to discover Thomas at this conference, which was, after all, meant to be a dry run for grad students so that they could get used to being eviscerated by professors they knew before they had to face intellectual disembowelment by a panel of strangers at the American Colonial History Association. Thomas was a postdoc now. Had been for a couple of years. He'd had six go-rounds of the grad student conference already. What was he doing here?

"I'm just going to stop you right there," Marcus interrupted.

Thomas looked up. His glasses slipped, and he pushed them back into place.

Marcus leaned forward on his elbows. "What would you say is at stake in this history?" he asked.

"What is—what?" Thomas's Adam's apple moved up and down in his throat.

"Why does this story need to be told?" Marcus clarified. "If you can't succinctly summarize that, then I think you're in the wrong field, don't you?"

Thomas's ear flushed crimson, and Connie's stomach soured. "Professor Hayden," she started to interject, wanting to protect her former mentee from this justifiable, yet painful, public dressing-down.

"Let him answer," Marcus stopped her.

The Harvard classroom where they were gathered—the panel of four grad students, an audience consisting primarily of their friends in the program and younger students who weren't ready to present their research yet, plus a few hard-eyed, driven undergraduates, and the responding panel of two professors, Marcus from Harvard and Connie, a guest from Northeastern, present only because Harvard found itself without a colonialist—was in one of the newer buildings on Harvard's campus, usually devoted to the study of science. Formica writing desks bolted to formed plastic seats, fluorescent lights buzzing overhead, beige carpeting. The room looked nothing like Connie's fantasy of Harvard, or her nostalgia for it. She had never thought she would be nostalgic for grad school. And yet, her disappointment in this drab and undistinguished room, which was like any classroom in any 1980s college-hijinks film, suggested that was, in fact, what had happened.

"I'm trying to argue," Thomas said, "that belief in magic invited altered states that filled a spiritual void left after the Reformation purged mysticism from the Catholic church. When the church no longer offered methods by which early modern people could exercise control over the uncertainties in their lives, or reach a transcendent state that helped them escape everyday suffering, they turned to magic unsanctioned by the church. It was a struggle for control, as well as escape."

"That's Keith Thomas," Connie interrupted. "The argument he makes in *Religion and the Decline of Magic*."

"Well, I know, but—" Thomas started to object.

Marcus flipped his copy of Thomas's paper facedown on the table in front of him. "You're referring to other authorities," he said. "Not to the archive."

Thomas's grip tightened on the papers in front of him. His ear darkened until it was almost crimson. "This is only a preliminary proposal," he said. "As Professor Goodwin knows, I'm taking my research in a different direction. This is merely the organizational prospectus."

Marcus looked at Connie.

"So what," he said.

"All Professor Hayden's saying"—Connie hurried to rescue Thomas—"is that even at the prospectus stage, conference respondents are going to want to see original work. Sources that haven't been plumbed yet. Zaz—Miss Molina's argument, for instance, is still coalescing. But her pre-circulated paper talks at length about the new archival sources that she will be using to build her argument."

Thomas glared at Zazi. She held her papers in her hands, careful not to look around at anyone. The vent in the ceiling overhead stirred the faint curls at her neck, but no other part of her moved.

"Look, you're wasting our time with this," Marcus Hayden said, flicking his fingertips at the pages facedown in front of him. "This is nothing more than a bibliography. It's no better than Miss Matthews's presentation." Miss Matthews, she of the tight ponytail, folded her hands on the table in front of her and failed to keep the twist of rage off her narrow face. Hayden continued, "Except her paper was a bibliography of all the most fashionable critical theory she's read since college, and yours is just a rehash of thirty-year-old secondary sources. You should be in dialogue with the arguments that precede you, not aping them."

Thomas turned his own paper facedown and said "Thank you, Professor Hayden. I clearly have more work to do before I can present this project."

His voice sounded tight in his throat. The words came out in a monotone. So much academic rhetoric was about domination and control. Thomas knew this and was ceding to Marcus. But he hated it. And his hatred showed.

Marcus said, "All right. Miss Molina, you're up."

Zazi rustled the papers in her hands, preparing to read. But Connie was looking at Thomas. And his ear burning bright, crimson red.

Chapter Ten

"Mom?" The rusted gate in the tall hedge that hid the Milk Street house was locked. This gate was so rusted that it was barely still a gate. Connie hadn't ever realized it had a lock.

"Maybe she's inside?" Sam suggested. He shifted a sack of groceries from the Cambridge Trader Joe's from one arm to the other.

"Why would she lock it?" Connie dug in the oyster shells of the road-bed with a toe. "She knew we were coming."

"Dunno," Sam said. He put a hand on the hedge and tried to peer through its leaves to the garden inside, but the ligustrum and arborvitae and vines—Connie couldn't identify most of them, beyond wisteria and clematis and some others that might have been poison ivy—coiled together so tightly it was impossible to see through. The hedge was bursting in new, waxy green leaves, so freshly green they were nearly yellow, the bright yellow-green of tree frogs. Connie almost imagined she could see them breathe.

Inside the hedge, the happy sound of Arlo barking.

"Ask Arlo to unlock it," Sam said.

"Arlo?" Connie called. "Will you unlock the gate?"

Snuffling and sounds of play, but not of obedience.

"Well?" Sam said. "I guess we could eat in the car."

"Wait." Connie rooted in her jeans pocket and pulled out the antique iron key. She'd found it in this house, after all. But when she tried to fit it to the rusted keyhole in the gate, it wasn't a match. The shape was wrong. The shank too thin. It wouldn't fill the keyhole, much less turn.

"Worth a shot," Connie muttered, stuffing the key back in her pocket. She gazed up. The Milk Street house had a hidden roof, with a secret peak. Vines draped from the hedge with the heavy, billowing luster of a circus tent, arcing low and then rising up to riot around the rubble of the chimney.

"I wonder if we could climb over," Connie mused.

"Not without my rappelling gear," Sam said.

"Oh!" a voice called from the pathway that wound into the woods at the end of the street.

Connie wasn't quite sure how deep the woods went. In her summer of living at the house she'd wandered the woods on occasion, but she'd never seemed to get in very far. Her feet favored the crushed-oyster-shell trail that wound back to the road. Somewhere deep in those woods a pond shimmered. Connie could faintly smell it when the air was right. But she had never found it.

"Mom?" she called, shading her eyes with one hand. The evening sun lingered behind the treeline, painting the sky rose-pink and white, throwing the woods into shadow. Connie thought she saw movement, the silhouette of a woman moving through the trees. It looked like Grace. But in a long dress. Grace never wore dresses. Caftans, but only on special occasions.

"Mom!" Connie waved. "The gate's locked!" She rose on tiptoe, flapping her hand to catch the figure's attention.

"No, it's not," said Grace, from behind Connie.

Grace, two long gray braids over her shoulders, pale eyes shining, was dressed in a plaid work shirt and old Levi's with mud-stained cuffs. Her arms were full of a lemony-smelling herb.

"Oh! You scared me." Connie's heart was thudding, and she felt silly.

"Sorry," Grace said, smiling, lifting the armload of herbs to Connie's face. Connie breathed in the aroma. "The sun's in Aries, you know. Best time to gather verbena."

"Oh, is it," Connie said.

"Hi, Grace," interjected Sam.

Grace smiled a careful smile at Sam. "Come on in." She pushed open the gate and stepped inside the garden, met immediately by the happy barks of Arlo. "Well, hello there!" she said, stooping to rub his ear.

Connie looked at the gate.

"Guess we didn't push hard enough," Sam said. He gestured with an arm for Connie to precede him.

Under the canopy of vines, the Milk Street house garden was turning in its sleep and stretching, stirring its feet under the coverlet of spring. Here and there daffodil heads poked up through dried webs of last year's plantings. The perennial herbs, the rosemary, sage, and thyme, were flushing green, thinking of blooming, tiny purple flowers hinting around the edges of their oily leaves. The ash and the alder were putting out new shoots, shrugging off their winter sleep. The air under the canopy smelled rich and new, stirring with possibility.

Arlo was nosing around in the corner of the garden given over to tomatoes and nightshades, inspecting a fat, hairy-leaved plant that seemed about a month from blooming. He sniffed, then sampled a leaf with a pink tongue.

"Don't do that, little creature," Grace said, edging him away with a duck boot. He looked up at her and wagged. "That'll give you an awful headache."

"What's that one?" Connie asked, eying it from a safe vantage point on the flagstone pathway. She knew there were mandrakes in the garden. For all its lushness and abundance, the yard was crawling with death.

"Looks like a weed," Sam whispered as Grace opened the front door to the house, pausing long enough to kiss her fingertips and touch them briefly to the horseshoe nailed on the jamb overhead.

"*Jusquiamus*," Grace called over her shoulder as she moved into the dim recesses of the dining room with her armload of verbena. "Henbane. Pigs love it. Makes them drunk as skunks. But it can be toxic to other animals. I'm talking to you," she said to the doglike creature who trotted along at her feet, his fur the dark and mottled color of the floorboards in the dining room.

"What did you say?" In the front hall, Connie caught sight of herself in the small mirror over the end table that held the telephone. Her cheeks were pale. She drew the tail end of her braid up under her nose in a thoughtful mustache.

"Henbane," Grace repeated. "Sam, do you want a beer?"

"Sure." Sam edged past Connie in the narrow front hall. "Is she going to put us in the twin beds again?" he whispered. Connie wished she could have a beer too.

"No, I heard that part. You called it something else," Connie said.

Grace reappeared in the doorway from the darkened dining room to the kitchen, backlit by the lone lightbulb buzzing over the sink.

"Where's the switch in here?" Connie was groping along the dining room wall, surprised that she didn't remember.

"You know what? I don't think there is one," Grace came over with an open bottle of Sam Adams for Sam and relieved him of the sack of groceries. "What have we here?" she said, peering into the sack. "Steak?"

"Steak," Sam confirmed. He held the beer up in a mock toast to the silent portrait of the woman who watched over the dining room. In the half-light of the coming evening, the portrait's eyes looked vacant and dead. Sam took a swig of the beer and followed Grace into the kitchen.

"My goodness," said Grace mildly. "I didn't know we were eating meat now."

"Oh, you'll love it," Sam teased. "Anyway, it's local."

The friendly sounds of kitchen noises, knives found and cutting boards hunted up and vegetables put in the old-fashioned icebox, filled the kitchen with happy bustle that overflowed into the somber dining room, where Connie loitered by the hearth. This room had once been the hall, the living heart of the original part of the house. Like many houses built in the first few decades of New England settlement, the Milk Street house had grown and changed over its long and varied life. Start with two simple rooms—hall and keeping—then add a steep central stair, lift the roof, and make two bedrooms upstairs. Add a lean-to on the back, for storage or later as a kitchen. Come the twentieth century, tack on some plumbing, an unsteady water line and a cramped bathroom with a claw-footed tub up under the eaves. The house breathed and changed, expanding to accommodate ever more people, ever longer passages of time.

Connie retrieved a box of kitchen matches from the fireplace mantel in the dining room, striking one and holding it gently to the wick of a beeswax candle in a single brass candlestick holder, the kind with a loop for carrying around to see at night. A round, warm orange glow spilled over the mantel. The fireplace in the dining room was the largest in the house, five feet wide, bristling with iron hooks and andirons. In its heyday it would have hosted as many as three fires at once, different temperatures, for cooking different things. The beehive oven, built into the brick, was full of forgotten iron cookware that had rusted in place.

Connie turned to the dining table, which was newer—a round Queen Anne with polite slipper feet, its surface dotted with pale water stains. Two iron candelabra stood on the table holding melted red candles, and as Connie touched the match to each candle in turn, the warmth in the room rose, chasing the shadows into corners and under end tables. Connie blew out the blackened nub of match and tossed it into the fireplace.

"Mom?" she called, leaning on the mantel and gazing at the painting. In the candlelight she could see a tiny nameplate in the peeling gilt-edge frame. *Temperance Hobbs*. A wasp-waisted, slope-shouldered girl, brown hair in ringlets over her ears, with a yellowish terrier-like animal tucked under her arm. Her dress had at one time been pale pink, but had yellowed with age and varnish. She wore an unreadable expression. Not quite a smile.

"Hmmm?" Grace reappeared carrying one full glass of wine and one half-full. She handed the half-full one to Connie.

"What was the word you used before?" Connie asked. "For henbane."

"*Jusquiamus*." Grace was rooting through a drawer in the credenza at the opposite end of the room. She pulled out three delicate linen napkins. "The Latin name. The old one."

"Do you know the Latin names of all the plants you use?" Connie asked.

Grace dug up a couple of very old-looking three-tined dinner forks and three horn-handled serrated knives, and turned to set three places at the table. "Doesn't it look nice in here, with the candles lit?" she said. "I usually eat in the den, where the fire's going."

"Do you?" Connie pressed.

"Oh, I guess so," Grace said airily. From the kitchen a sizzling sound was shortly followed by the bubbling smell of browning meat. "Have you decided what you're going to do?" Grace said, so quietly Connie almost couldn't hear it.

Connie glanced nervously at the kitchen. "No," she said. "I mean, yes. But—"

Sam reappeared carrying a wooden bowl full of tossed salad. "Middle?" he asked Grace, who nodded, and he placed the bowl on the dining table between the candelabra and disappeared back into the kitchen.

Grace lifted a finger and pressed it to her lips, her pale eyes flicking to the kitchen door. "Later," she mouthed.

Connie's cheeks flushed.

"Ten minutes!" Sam called from the kitchen.

"I hate to admit it, but it does smell good," Grace said.

"Just for the sake of argument"—Connie pulled the small notebook out of her jeans pocket—"do you think you'd know the English names for all these?"

Grace took the notebook out of Connie's hand and scanned the list. "Oh, sure. Let's see. There's henbane—oh, I see now, yes—henbane and rose, of course. Salvia is sage. Iris is the same in English. Nettle, organy, daffodil, marigold . . ."

"Wait!" Connie said, patting down her pockets for a pencil. "I have to write this all down."

"I'll write it down for you after dinner." Grace handed back the notebook and straightened out one of the place settings on the table. "Where did that list come from, I wonder."

Connie stuffed the notebook back in her pocket. "Oh, you know," she demurred.

From the kitchen came the sounds of the gas stove being switched off, and of plates rattling.

"It's from her book," Sam called. "Pretty cool, huh?"

Grace shook her head, smiling. "My stubborn girl," she said, not without affection. "Always going by the book."

Sam appeared with two plates in his left hand and one in his right, each with a slab of medium-done steak decorated with a sprig of parsley, like a button right in the middle.

"Parsley?" Connie teased.

"Yes. Tonight, we dine," said Sam. He put down the plates and pulled out a chair for Grace with exaggerated formality. He caught Connie's eye, and the brackets around his own eyes deepened. *It'll be okay*, his smile said. *She's just being Grace. Go with it.*

Connie pulled out her own seat and lifted her wineglass and gazed at her boyfriend and mother across the flickering taper candles.

"Happy Ostara, Mom," Connie said.

"Merry meet, and merry part, and merry meet again," Grace agreed. She lifted her own wineglass and added, "May the coming sun warm us all, present and past and those to come." And the flickering candlelight brought the illusion of glimmering life to the eyes of the young woman in the portrait—Temperance, whoever and whenever she might have been.

Connie rolled onto her back and kicked the quilt off her feet. Immediately, the cold chilled her naked toes. She pulled the quilt back over herself with a shiver, rubbing her feet together. In the twin bed an arm's length away from her, Sam's mouth fell open in a snore, his arms sprawled overhead, carefree.

Connie punched her sagging feather pillow into a firmer shape and twisted onto her side. Moonlight, beaming in from the skylight in the sloping eave overhead, lit the room a whitish blue. Bright enough to read by. Connie rooted herself into the horsehair mattress and put her arm over her eyes.

She waited for what felt like a long time.

It was no use.

She was awake.

Connie sat up.

The house breathed with secret nighttime sounds. Little creaks and sighs. Old wood. Old plaster. Generations of mice, moving about unseen. She heard Sam's slow and even breathing. He was right there. Safe. Everything was fine. He was fine.

They were fine.

She thought about reaching over to touch Sam's arm, to reassure herself that he was here. That she had enough time to solve this—*thing* she didn't believe in, but feared. She turned on her side and watched him sleep. In the blue light, she could see every detail of his face. The nubbled texture of his cheek and chin. The furrow between his eyes.

He snuffled and sighed and rolled over on his side, facing away from her.

Connie got up and pulled on her old Mount Holyoke sweatshirt, scratched the sleep out of her hair, and moved quietly toward the narrow stair. She had to duck to get under the door. The floor creaked softly under her bare feet. She groped for the stair in the darkness, pressing her hands on the ceiling for balance, as there was no banister. Her toes hung over the edge of each step. Sometimes Connie wondered how long Grace could live in this house safely. Maybe the challenge of climbing up and down this ladderlike staircase would keep Grace supple and aware. Or maybe Connie didn't want to think about her mother getting older.

Downstairs, in the den, the last of the embers in the fireplace glowed orange in a nest of ashes. Connie settled in the armchair near the fire and stretched her bare feet out to the hearth, warming her toes, stuffing her hands in the kangaroo pocket of her sweatshirt.

"Can't sleep?" Grace said softly.

Connie looked sleepily over at the couch and found her mother curled there under an afghan, holding a mug of tea. Arlo dozed beside her, paws twitching in sleep.

"I didn't see you," Connie said.

"I know." Grace combed a hand through Arlo's fur. "You want some tea?"

"No, thanks," Connie said.

They sat for a while in silence, each thinking her own thoughts. A wisp of smoke sighed up the chimney as the last of the embers slowly winked out.

"There has to be some way around it," Connie said at length.

Grace looked into her mug, swirling the contents. She frowned at whatever she saw there. "You always were stubborn," she remarked. "It's one of my favorite things about you. Made you a real handful, though."

"You mean no one has solved this? They all die? No matter what we do?"

Grace traced the lip of her mug with a thumb and said, "You don't think we tried?" To herself, she added, "I know I did."

"What about Granna's parents? What happened to them?" Granna was Sophia, Grace's mother. She and her husband, Lemuel, had lived in the Milk Street house. Lemuel was crushed by a woodpile. Granna died of old age.

"Oh, let's see," Grace said. "Granna's mother's name was Charity. Charity Crowninshield. Her maiden name was Lawrence, I think. When I was a girl I thought her name was so funny! Oh, but she hated her name. Her friends all called her Char." Grace pronounced it soft, like *Shah*. "Mother and I saw her weekends, when I was growing up. She made the most dreadful codfish balls. And liver!" Grace shuddered at the memory. "I used to beg her to make me Jell-O, but she never would. All the other girls' mothers and grandmothers made the most amazing Jell-O molds. Such bright colors. So cheerful. I used to think Jell-O was so fancy. I positively coveted it."

Connie smiled. It was hard to imagine Grace, unreconstructed hippie that she was, ever coveting something so unnatural as Jell-O.

"What was she like?" Connie asked, folding her feet underneath her in the armchair. "Char."

Grace got up and placed another applewood log on the fire. "She was . . . angry, actually."

This was not what Connie expected Grace to say.

"What makes you say that?"

"Oh, you know." She settled back onto the sofa and rubbed one of Arlo's ears. He didn't wake up.

"I don't," Connie pointed out.

Grace pulled the blanket up to her shoulders. Arlo yawned and rolled onto his back, paws splayed. Sometimes, in low firelight like this, Connie could see the contours of Grace's younger face. It was easy to forget that her mother had once been young too.

Grace said, "I suppose she just—she was never a very warm person, is all. I could see that she and Mother were always uneasy with each other." Grace stretched her feet nearer the low fire. "They were desperately poor, for one thing."

"They were?" Connie looked around the sitting room, with its threadbare carpet and hairy-pawed desk.

"Sure. Char got married when she was, what, twenty? Grandpa was a lobsterman. That's hard work. She kept house, had Mother right away. This was 1910, you know. You wouldn't know it now, but Marblehead was poor then. Not many people in town had electricity, I don't think. Some people had cars, but they were awfully expensive. Mother and Dad got the first one Char ever rode in."

"And Char's husband? Grandpa?"

Grace put her mug on the floor by her feet and took up Arlo's tail, petting it softly. "I never knew him," she said carefully.

A pool of ice opened within Connie. Without thinking, she wrapped her arms around herself.

"Char was awfully young, you know. Mother told me that when she was growing up, they lived on charity from the town. Without the Female Humane Society, they wouldn't have been able to eat. Four dollars a month, they got."

The Female Humane Society began in Marblehead in 1816, to provide relief for widows and children who lost their breadwinners to the Grand Banks, or to impressment in the War of 1812. It still carried on, as far as Connie knew, discreetly, lifting up people in town when they needed help. She wondered if Granna had relied on them too, and never told anyone. Probably.

Connie drew her knees up to her chest and grabbed her toes with her hands. They were cold. Her hands were cold. Her cheeks, her shoulders, even her teeth were cold.

"It's awfully hard, you know." Grace's voice was low.

"What is?" Connie asked.

"Doing it alone," Grace said, looking on Connie with pale gray eyes.

Chapter Eleven

Salem, Massachusetts

Late March

2000

"This is it?" Zazi seemed incredulous.

"What did you expect?" Connie gently pumped the brake pedal as they creaked through the stoplight on Washington Street.

Zazi pressed her nose to the passenger window of Connie's Volvo and peered at the passing storefronts. The day was cold and gray, a typical spring day in New England. Connie enjoyed late-March days—sweater-without-gloves days—but they seemed to be bringing Zazi down. People from sunny climates often got depressed in long New England winters. Maybe the weather was doing it. Zazi certainly seemed down. Almost sullen.

"I don't know," Zazi said. "Old stuff?"

It was true. Much of downtown Salem was modern. "A lot of it went down in a fire," Connie said. "In the nineteenth century."

Zazi muttered something in Spanish, clearly disappointed.

"Here," Connie said, turning left off Derby Street and rolling past the imposing nineteenth-century post-office building. "We'll park in the fancy part."

Connie eased the car across Summer Street and rolled into the narrow, tightly built McIntire district, the sedate center of Salem's fine eighteenth- and early-nineteenth-century houses. While the nineteenth century had sent Marblehead's fortunes skidding, Salem had flourished. Waves of immigration, clippers bound for China and St. Petersburg, cobbled streets awash in money. Any trace of the seventeenth century, with its poverty and superstition and embarrassing witch trials, had been burned down, paved over, rebuilt. Even into the twentieth century, the witch trials weren't discussed in polite company in Salem. Maybe that was why Grace had never entirely warmed to Connie's research.

Maybe she was embarrassed.

"Whoa." Zazi watched the plush houses of ship captains roll by, all bright white trim and polished door knockers and fresh black shutters. "This is more like it."

"I can't believe you've never been to Salem before," Connie said. "What kind of colonial historian are you?"

"One who works on the South and Southwest?" Zazi said. The brick sidewalks of the McIntire gleamed with spring rain, and a stray cat skittered around a chestnut tree and vanished under a hemlock hedge.

"Touché," said Connie.

The Volvo creaked to a halt across from Hamilton Hall, and Connie threw it in Park and put on the emergency brake, just in case the car got any ideas. Zazi was glaring at her cell phone.

"You sure you don't mind helping me out today?" Connie asked.

Zazi stuffed the phone back into her bag and shook her head. "No, I'm psyched. It'll be fun. Along with the fifteen an hour." Zazi held her hand up and rubbed her thumb and fingertips together in the universal sign for cash.

Connie well remembered her own grad school poverty. The day she and Liz had discovered that the Harvard Faculty Club had free hors d'oeuvres had been a fine day indeed. Bite-sized spanakopita could, it turned out, make a pretty decent dinner.

Zazi gazed with satisfaction on the dentil molding, the greening chestnut trees, the Federal and Georgian faces of the grand houses lining Chestnut Street like postcards from the Bicentennial.

"Not bad," she pronounced.

They started along an uneven brick path, wending their way to the probate office. Zazi pulled out her phone again, read a text, frowned, and started texting back without looking up.

"Everything okay?" Connie asked. How could Zazi walk and text at the same time? Without tripping, or falling into a pit?

"Oh, yeah." Zazi sighed in a way that meant things were obviously not okay.

"What's going on?" Connie said.

Zazi's nostrils flared. "I'm just pissed. There's a great job coming up next year and it's too early for me to apply."

"You sure it's too early? ABDs apply all the time."

All But Dissertation students—the unofficial no-woman's-land of life after the qualifying exam and before the doctoral defense—often went on the job market for the experience, if nothing else. Most likely Connie would, if asked, have given Zazi the same advice she gave Thomas, though. *Wait, get your book ready, and then go for it when you're really competitive.* But there was something different about Zazi. Some indefinable spark. Charisma, maybe. It shouldn't matter in the life of the mind, and yet somehow, it always did.

"Not ABDs with none of the dissertation written," Zazi pointed out. "I'd need at least a chapter. Preferably two. Anyway, I'm just pissed. I know some of the people applying, and the job is so awesome, and they are such douchebags, and it pisses me off." Zazi thrust her hands in the pockets of her jeans.

"What's the job?" Connie asked. Zazi was right—it was too early for her. That must be disappointing. There was so little in this process that was under anyone's control. Zazi's need for control mirrored Connie's own. She wondered what in Zazi's past had made it so. Then again, maybe it didn't work that way. Perhaps controlling people were born, not made.

Zazi said, "You haven't heard?"

"No. Heard what?"

"They're doing a search to fill Steve Hapsburg's job."

Connie stopped short, so abruptly that Zazi half bumped into her. "What?" Connie said.

"The colonial history job. At Harvard. Hapsburg's job."

But it wasn't Hapsburg's job. Steven Hapsburg had been brought in to fill the yawning void left by Connie's old advisor. They were looking to replace Manning Chilton.

Connie recovered herself enough to start walking again, thrusting her own hands in her own jeans pockets. "That's quite an opportunity," she said dully. She thought of the dry, patrician smile of the man under whom she had come to Harvard to study. The smell of pipe tobacco. Pipe tobacco used to be a pleasant smell to Connie. It used to represent something permanent and warm.

"What rank?" Connie asked, hoping as she did so that she did it lightly enough.

"Assistant," Zazi said.

"Wow," said Connie. "Everyone must be freaking out."

"You have no idea," Zazi said.

Connie chewed the inside of her cheek. Her boots picked their way along the brick sidewalk. So that was Thomas's scheme. He was gunning for Chilton's job. And he didn't want Connie to know, because assistant professors at other institutions could, in theory, also apply. Assistant professors like Constance Goodwin, colonial historian at Northeastern University. With a tenure packet almost submitted, and a book under contract.

What would it feel like, to profess at Harvard? Sometimes there was a special brutality to working at the institution where one had also studied. Colleagues remembered you before your ideas were cooked through. The wormy underbelly of institutional politics, kept so carefully hidden from students and alumni, was an unavoidable part of a job in the professoriate. Nothing would burn away Connie's nostalgia faster than her first faculty meeting. And then there was the fact that no one, but no one, ever got tenure at Harvard unless they came in with it. And sometimes not even then. Connie could apply, but if she actually got Chilton's job it might, paradoxically, ruin her career. For a grad student like Zazi or a postdoc like Thomas, though, even failing to get tenure at Harvard would be all right. If Harvard is your first job, you can go anywhere.

"Come on," Connie said, plucking Zazi's sleeve. "The probate office is only open for four more hours."

Zazi perched at a computer terminal on the far side of the probate office, a pair of cool-girl spectacles on her nose as her fingers flew over the keyboard. Connie had given Zazi what she thought would be the easy job— Goodwin women (men, really—she needed to know about the men) from Charity Crowninshield, working backward. Charity Crowninshield, née Char Lawrence, had been born in Marblehead in 1889, and died in Marblehead—perhaps she had never even left Essex County— in 1963. No burial site. She had been cremated, Grace said, and thrown into the sea, off the lighthouse point on Marblehead Neck. Connie knew Char had outlived her husband by decades. Who was Char's mother? She didn't know. What about Char's father? Neither she nor Grace had any idea. So Zazi was starting with the more recent probates, for the more recent Goodwin women. Late nineteenth century, working backward.

Connie, on the other hand, was starting at the opposite end. She knew Deliverance Dane's story, down to the tiniest detail—such detail as was knowable. Born in a region of England called East Anglia—probably. She embarked from there when she emigrated, anyway. A little late for the Great Migration, but Deliverance Haseltine (also spelled Hazeldine, and Hasseltine, and probably half a dozen other ways) had left Ipswich, England, with her parents in the late winter of 1661 and immigrated to Salem Town. No mention of Deliverance's father, Robert, after the passenger list. Connie couldn't say for certain what had become of him, but his wife, Anna, and Deliverance had boarded with another family in Salem Town—probably helping with household labor to partly offset their rent—before moving into a small cottage in Salem Village, inland, where there was more space to be cheaply had. Deliverance had married Nathaniel Dane—Connie didn't know when. And Nathaniel was alive during Deliverance's slander trial in the 1680s. But by her trial for witchcraft in 1692 he had disappeared from the record.

Deliverance had gone to the gallows in 1692. Leaving a lone daughter, and a small cottage in Marblehead, on what would later be known as Milk Street.

Deliverance's daughter, Mercy, had the married name Lamson by 1714, when her own daughter, Prudence, appeared in the births, marriages, and deaths index for Marblehead. Mercy had fled Salem to the neighboring town to escape her mother's fate, or perhaps to escape her mother's reputation. Mercy sued Salem Town to clear Deliverance's name in around 1710, but her suit failed.

Connie didn't know why it had failed. Many similar suits were successful. But Connie did know that Mercy had lived out her life in something close to abject poverty and died a decade before the Revolution under the care of her daughter, Prudence Lamson, married name Bartlett, installed by then in the Milk Street house with a family of her own. Prudence had kept a methodical and taciturn accounting of her work as a midwife, which Connie had read while working on her dissertation. Prudence was driven by something—poverty? desperation? shame?—to sell Deliverance Dane's physick book to a social-climbing book collector for not much more than the price of a good milk cow. Not that milk cows weren't expensive. And important. But even so.

"Better than magic beans, I guess," Connie thought as she paged through eighteenth-century records grimy with disuse.

So. What had happened to Prudence's husband? And who came next?

Connie pulled the end of her braid under nose in her mustache of thought. Did Zazi know Thomas was applying for Chilton's job? She must. That could account for the chilly reception Zazi had given him at Charlie's Kitchen the other night. Thomas was a couple of years ahead of her, with more writing and teaching to his credit. Zazi would have an uphill battle against him for the department's support. That would explain her feelings for him, but not vice versa.

Douchebags, Zazi had said. Connie wasn't used to hearing Zazi be so harsh. Was she talking about Thomas? Connie had known Thomas since he was in college. A kid, basically. Earnest, a dyed-in-the-wool history nerd.

"Hey!" Zazi cried. She scribbled something in her notebook and then skipped over to Connie's table. "Check it out. I found Char's mom."

"Already?" Connie said, leaning over Zazi's book.

"Wasn't hard. Here she is. Chastity Lawrence, born Marblehead, Mass 1867, died—oh, man. 1889."

"Whoa," Connie said. "1889? That's the same year Char was born."

"I know."

"Did she die in childbirth?" Connie's clinical question masked a wave of insensible sadness. Chastity had been twenty-two. Younger than Zazi. A kid. Terrified, and in pain. Connie hoped she hadn't been alone.

Zazi peered at her notes. "Doesn't say."

"Who was her husband?" Connie asked.

"Also doesn't say." Zazi looked up. "Guess her name was kind of ironic, huh?"

"I guess." Connie walked her pencil over her knuckles. "I mean, he could have been a fisherman. By the late nineteenth century Marblehead had a substantial shoe-manufacturing industry—"

"Professor G," Zazi said.

"—but they still had an active fishing fleet. He could have been lost on the Grand Banks, or—"

"Professor G." Across the room the copier whirred to life.

"—or any number of other things. Lobstering, for instance, or he could have been a craftsman—"

"Connie!" Zazi put her hand on Connie's forearm. "Chastity was a prostitute."

Zazi pointed to her notes from Chastity's probate record, which showed her only belongings of value being some paste jewelry and an antique silk mantua, reworked. The belongings were left to her mother. Whose last name was also Lawrence.

"Oh," Connie said.

"I mean, of course she was. Right?" Zazi pointed out.

"No. You're right. It makes total sense." Connie sat back.

Well, sure. What choice would she have had? It was a hardscrabble life, in small fishing towns. No money. No way to make money. Piece-work for the shoe factories would only go so far. And there would have been no shortage of young men, frightened, lonely, with money in their pockets, about to ship out for months at a time, in brutal work conditions that were often fatal. Connie imagined a pretty girl with pale, calculating eyes, cheeks rouged, hair crimped into ringlets with a hot iron. She would have studied the plates in *Godey's Lady's Book* and remade her hand-me-down gowns into modern silhouettes, with tight waists and high bustles contrived from old rags sewn together. Bodice cut low to show her young throat and chest. Laughing into taverns with young men she'd known her whole life, and some newcomers, strangers come out from the countryside, or from distant shores. Connie pictured Chastity leaning close, her lips almost brushing the ear of whoever she was talking to. Holding out her hand.

"Wives are nothing but scab workers for whores," Zazi said.

"Whoa. Quotable," Connie said. The copier across the room spat out its last sheet of paper and settled back into a hum.

"It *is* a quote. Emma Goldman," Zazi said. "At least Chastity was the one in control, right? Making her own money. Pretty badass, if you ask me."

"Maybe," Connie said. But she wasn't so sure.

She bent back to her list of eighteenth-century probates. Flip a page, run her finger down the column of names, scanning for Prudence Bartlett, Marblehead, second half of the eighteenth century. The names in the ledger were for all of Essex County, not just the town. All in order of their death, with no cross-referencing or alphabetization. 1780—nope. Nothing.

Connie flipped another page, ran her finger down a fresh list. Name after name after name after name. Town after town after town. Topsfield. Newbury. Newburyport. Essex. Lawrence. Danvers. 1781. Nope.

She flipped the page again. 1782. Nope.

"I've got it!" Zazi hollered.

"Already?" Connie was stunned. Computers, man. They made history research so fast Connie almost couldn't believe it.

"Already," Zazi confirmed, making notes from the entry on her computer screen. Then she loped over to Connie with the notebook. "Chastity's mother was named Verity Lawrence."

"Verity!" Connie exclaimed. "Is that not the most nineteenth-century name you've ever heard?"

"I can think of others," Zazi said. "Anyway. Her maiden name was Bishop."

"Like Bridget?" Connie asked. Bridget Bishop had been the first woman hanged at Salem for witchcraft, during the 1692 panic. Amazing, how none of these families moved away. Everyone just stayed put, working, fishing, gossiping, intermarrying, scratching out a life on the edge of the ocean.

"I guess so," said Zazi.

"What were her dates?" Connie asked, excited.

"Born in Marblehead, 1841. Lived in Marblehead. Probated in . . . wow. 1924." Zazi looked up. "That's pretty old."

"Yeah," Connie said. "What about her husband?"

Zazi peered at her notes. "She left the house to her granddaughter."

"Char," Connie said.

"Right," Zazi confirmed. "And all its contents, which wasn't much. Some furniture. No money."

"None?" Connie asked.

"None. Actually, her estate was in debt. Like two hundred dollars. Sucks for Char, huh."

"Yeah." Connie slid a fingernail between her teeth before she caught herself and stopped. "What did she do to make money?"

"Looks like she ran a school for a time," Zazi said. "But it got shut down."

"What kind of school?"

"Navigation?" Zazi said.

"That can't be right." Connie pulled the notebook nearer so she could read the notes.

"Why not?"

Sure enough, Zazi had written "navigation academy," with a reference to an advertisement in the classifieds from the *Salem Gazette* in 1870. That hardly made sense. Plenty of North Shore towns had navigation academies—Salem, Beverly, Manchester. It stood to reason Marblehead would have had one too. In the eighteenth and nineteenth centuries, after boys learned reading and writing and basic math, they would enroll in navigation schools before shipping out on the merchant ships. But the age of the clippers was ending by the 1860s. With the advent of steam travel and the opening of the Suez Canal, there was no need for trade to be done by small, fast clippers. The demand for navigation schools would have tanked. Also, the academies were usually taught by men—ship captains or mates looking to stay closer to home, or too badly maimed to go to sea again. What was Verity doing? How did she learn celestial navigation, anyway?

"It's just . . . it all just seems really unlikely, that's all," Connie said, perplexed. "What happened to Verity's husband?"

"Yellow fever," Zazi said. "When she was thirty."

"And she never remarried?" Connie said.

"Nope," said Zazi.

The contours of Verity's life resolved slowly, strangely into the form of a smart woman—maybe even a brilliant woman, given the math involved—standing in a plain high-collared dress, with a blackboard behind her covered in equations, and braids looped over her ears. Verity had brushed her fingertips over the lip of a cup full of more economic security than her family had enjoyed in generations—perhaps ever. And then something happened. Her fortunes were dashed so thoroughly that by the time Verity was forty-eight years old, her only daughter was selling herself in the street.

"Well," said Connie, turning back to her ledger. "You're totally schooling me on this today."

"Magic fingers," Zazi said, wiggling them like a pianist warming up before a concert. She smiled with self-satisfaction and adjourned back to her computer terminal.

Connie sighed and turned another page. She was up to 1789.

Scanning, scanning, scanning. Flip. Scanning scanning scanning. Flip.

Connie yawned.

"Thirty minutes!" announced the archivist behind the front desk. All the researchers looked up at once, like startled prairie dogs, then hunched their shoulders and bent to their ledgers with renewed vigor.

1792. Scanning scanning scanning. Flip. 1793.

Connie glanced over at Zazi, to see if she'd managed to go any earlier than Verity in record time. Zazi was wrinkling her nose and squinting at the computer screen through her spectacles. It didn't look promising.

1794. Scanning scanning scanning. Flip. 1795.

Connie unconsciously fingered the rattling charm tied around her left wrist. Whenever the twine got wet, which it did every day when Connie showered, the twine seemed to thicken and tighten. She'd never get it off now. A halfhearted attempt to snip it off with scissors the previous week had come to naught. Grace's command of twine was superhuman, it seemed.

Flip. Flip. Flip. Ugh, where was Prudence? What was she doing? How the heck was she living this long? She must have been nearly ninety.

"Ten minutes," the archivist announced. "If everyone would please begin packing up now. Thank you."

"Dammit," Connie whispered under her breath. 1797. Flip flip flip flip flip.

One at a time, lights started snapping off. Zazi booted down the terminal where she was working, stretched her arms over her head with a yawn, and started stuffing her notebooks and pencils back in her shoulder bag.

Connie flipped faster. Scanning name after name after name after name after name until then, her eye tripped.

She squinted.

Prewdense Bartlet, it said. *Midwife.* Born 1714, Marblehead, Massachusetts. Died same, 1798. Only two years shy of the nineteenth century. Leaving a probated estate consisting of a small house in Marblehead, a cow, two pigs, linens, sundry cookware, a Bible, and seven chickens. Worth about thirty-nine dollars in total after outstanding debts. Left to only issue:

Patience.

Interlude

——————

Marblehead, Massachusetts

May

1778

Patty Jacobs bent over and opened her mouth and screamed, one hand on her swollen belly, the other twisting the counterpane, her hair hanging in her face, her cheeks reddened and dripping sweat. Prudence Bartlett took up a cool rag from the washstand and daubed it across Patty's forehead, wiping the strands of plastered hair out of her eyes. Patty's eyes, blue-gray like the sea, darkened in pain.

"Mama," she panted, her teeth gritted. "Mama!"

"Stop it," Prudence said. "Ain't nothing I haven't seen a thousand times. Now buck up."

Patty threw her head back and keened, on her hands and knees on the bedstead, her back arched like a frightened cat's. Sweat soaked through her shift, in a vee of damp down her back. Prudence placed a hand between Patty's shoulder blades, getting a feel for how much distress her daughter was feeling. All women screamed in travail. There was no way round it. The trick was telling when they were screaming just to scream, and when they were screaming because things were about to go sideways.

"Maybe you want to check on things, Prue," worried Martha

Morrison, her neighbor from up Gingerbread Hill. Martha was about Prue's age, sixty-some-odd, a free black spinster keeping house for her elderly brother. She sat straight as a busk in the corner of the keeping room, mobcap low over her ears, fichu wrapped over her chest, a hand-kerchief twisting in her hands. She was making herself utterly useless. Patty would probably have an easier time if she weren't even here.

"I'll do that," Prudence snapped. "Look, Martha, go and boil more water for us, would you?"

"All right." Martha got quickly to her feet and hurried out of the room. Her place in the armchair near the hearth was immediately taken by a vaguely sized doggish creature, who rested his chin on the armrest and stared at his mistresses with worried eyes.

Patty's mouth fell open and she stretched back on her haunches and bellowed like a cow.

Prue pushed her sleeves up above her elbows.

"On your back now," she barked. "Let's have a look."

Whimpering, shivering, Patty crawled until her head was back by the bolster near the headboard and flopped onto her back. She curled up like a baby, arms around her knees, and tears squeezed out of the corners of her eyes.

"Well, I can't get a look if you don't open 'em up," Prudence pointed out as she poured water over her hands at the washstand and wiped them dry. She came over and tapped Patty on the knees. "Come along, there's a good girl."

Patty gulped down a sob and opened her knees, her eyes staring vacantly at the beams in the ceiling.

Prudence settled at the foot of the bed and reached in.

"Hmm," she was careful to say only to herself. Head was engaging all right, but Patty wasn't opening up. Prudence saw the waves of tension running over her daughter's body, clenching her jaw shut, prying her eyes open. That would never do. You have to help them along as best you can. Make it easy on them.

"Patty," Prudence said.

Her daughter didn't respond. She'd taken herself away, somehow. Her body was on the bed, but her mind was floating off, waiting for the pain to be over. Patty couldn't just betake herself away like that. Death comes even to those whose eyes are closed.

"Patty." This time Prudence tried to make her voice go softer. She jostled her daughter's knee gently. Patty blinked once, twice, the light coming back into her eyes. When Patty's eye fell on her mother's face, Prudence did her best to smile broadly and mean it.

"I know just what we need," Prudence said. She went to her tool kit, where she kept rolls of linen bandage, chasteberry tincture, matches, needle and thread, and other odds and ends of her trade. She pulled out a small pair of sewing shears.

"No!" Patty screamed.

"Pffft." Prudence came over to her daughter's bedside. "We're not there yet." She leaned over and took Patty's trembling left hand in hers.

Around Patty's wrist was wrapped a woven leather thong, dangling a single heavy charm. The charm seemed to be a pebble set in a silver frame, and it rattled whenever Patty's arm moved. Prudence leaned across her daughter's considerable girth and fitted the scissors around the leather thong.

"You ready?" Prudence said. "Soon's this comes off, you'll get a surge like you never saw."

Mutely Patty nodded, eyes wide.

Prudence snipped the leather. The charm came off in her hand.

Silence settled on the room, broken only by Patty's shallow gasps.

Then, as Prudence watched, another surge rolled up and over Patty, like an ocean wave licking over the beach. Patty's eyes rolled back in their sockets and her mouth opened, but no sound came out.

"Here, sit up," Prudence said, wrestling Patty up with her hands around her knees.

The wave kept coming, rolling and rolling and gradually a groan began deep in Patty's chest. It built and built, surging up her throat and around her head and then out of her mouth. An unreal, unholy animal groan. Prudence wavered. She'd never heard a sound come out of a woman like that.

"Is she poorly?" asked Martha from the doorway of the keeping room, a steaming kettle hanging from her hand.

"She'll be fine," Prudence said.

"I brought the water," Martha said, looking down. Trying not to look at Patty's nakedness, the spread knees, her moist shift clinging to her swollen breasts.

"Very good, Martha, thank you."

Martha poured some of the boiling water into the basin on the wash-stand and set the kettle on the hearth.

"Shall I fetch someone?" Martha asked, handkerchief back in her anxious hands. "Her husband, maybe?"

"Not unless you know where Washington's camped in New Jersey," Prudence muttered. "Absconding bastard. Rather stare down lobsterbacks with nothing but a rake in his hand. Anyhow, won't be long now." Prudence hoped she was telling the truth. "Come, you take hold of her other hand."

Martha sat on the other side of Patty, unsure at first, but then Patty's weight sagged against her and Martha stiffened with new resolve, one arm behind Patty's back and the other hand taking hold of her knee.

"I'm not going to lie," Martha said over Patty's head. "I'm just as glad I never had to do this."

Prudence laughed. "You forget it right off," she assured her neighbor. "It's like magic, the way God wipes the memories of pain from your head."

Martha rubbed her hand over Patty's knee. "If you say so," she said.

Patty panted, "I'm thirsty."

Prudence got up and went to fetch her a taste of small beer from the hall. "You keep an eye on her. I'll just be a moment," she said to Martha.

In the other room in the house, afternoon sun slanted in through the narrow glass windows, falling across the weathered wide pine floor. The fire was going well, and it made the hall close and warm, even with the windows open. Some potatoes and carrots and celeriac waited on the trestle table to be made into stew. Overhead, varied kinds of herbs, thymes and sages and parsleys hung in drying bunches from the rafters. Prudence set about pouring beer for Patty, and as she did it she pulled down a few bunches of different herbs, muttering quietly over each bunch, and wrapped them into a poultice.

All at once a scream rang out, and the doggish creature appeared at the doorway to the hall, barking, followed by Martha hollering, "Prue!"

Prudence hurried back to the keeping room. Patty was sitting straight up, her face drained of color. Below her, a dark red stain was seeping into the bedclothes and all under the underside of her legs.

"Oh, my God," Prudence whispered.

"What do we do?" Martha cried. There was blood on her apron and mantua and petticoats and both her hands up to her elbows. Fear crazed her eyes.

"Let's turn her over," Prudence said.

Together they turned the silent, trembling Patty onto her side. Prudence slipped the poultice up between her daughter's thighs to help stanch the bleeding, and put her hands on Patty's belly to feel for clues.

Patty's womb was hard as a boulder. Had Prudence cut the aetite off too soon? No. There must have been a tearing in the afterbirth. They'd have to get this done quickly.

"Shall we bleed her?" Martha asked.

"Crooked doctor's nonsense," Prudence said. "No. The opposite."

What she needed, Prudence realized with sickening horror, was her recipe book. The one she'd sold, the year they desperately needed the coin. What was strong enough, among the recipes she knew? Nothing. For two decades now she'd made do with basic charms and poultices, simple things she knew by rote. But rote wouldn't cut it today.

She needed the weather work. But she didn't have it. She only recalled bits and pieces, here and there. Snippets, half-remembered phrases. And she was missing half the ingredients.

The poultice physick she'd made was strong, but it wouldn't be strong enough alone. She must help it along. And trust Patty's body to listen. The book was gone. Sold. She could still feel the weight of the fat little leather bag that the man had put in her palm after she slid it across the tavern table to him. All she could do was all she could do, right here. Right now.

"Martha," Prudence said, trying to project an air of calmness and control. "In the writing desk over there, under that window. There's a rattle. Would you get it for me?"

Martha set to hunting through the papers and letters and inky quill nubs on the desk where Prudence kept her accounting books. Prudence took Patty's cheeks in her hands and looked into her daughter's terrified eyes.

"I want you to listen to me very carefully," Prudence said quietly.

Patty nodded.

"We're going to do a little work together," Prudence said. "You won't have seen it before. But never mind. It'll help. And then you'll be delivered. All right?"

Patty swallowed and whispered, "All right."

"This it?" Martha said, holding up a fine small silver rattle, with bells on one end and a teething coral on the other.

"That's it," Prudence said. She took the toy from her friend. With the rattle cradled in her hands, she pressed her hands to her heart and closed her eyes, sending a silent prayer up, in case anyone was listening to the likes of her. Then she opened her eyes and pressed the coral tip to Patty's forehead. She traced it in a slow, cool, deliberate line down Patty's nose, over her panting lips, down her chin, her throat, between her breasts, all along the globe of her belly. When she reached the belly, Prudence began to trace slow, careful circles, from the outermost edge, in a spiral working in towards Patty's distended navel. As she traced, she recited a long list of half-remembered Latin.

"What are you doing?" Martha said.

Prudence didn't answer. Another surge began trembling and washing through Patty's body, but she didn't cry out. Instead she breathed long and deep, through her mouth, letting the wave come and take her. The bloodstain stopped growing as the poultice did its work.

Outside the narrow windows of the keeping room, in the garden, the May sunshine wavered, as though an invisible hand were drawing a gauze curtain over the sky. Far away, a breath of thunder rumbled.

Prudence continued tracing slow and even circles around Patty's taut belly, whispering her Latin words. Martha began murmuring the Twenty-third Psalm. "Yea, though I walk through the valley of the shadow of death"—Martha's hand held tightly to Patty's—"I shall fear no evil, for thou art with me."

Patty stared, unblinking, unattending, her cheeks flushing slowly with new life.

When Prudence finally reached Patty's navel with the coral, she closed her eyes, placed her hand on Patty's forehead, and searched deep into her mind for the charm Mercy had taught her when she was a gangling girl, fifty-odd years ago, and only once, and told her never to use except in the most desperate extremity. Where was it? She'd locked it away, inside a drawer in her mind, and hidden the key.

The truth was, Prudence was afraid of the weather work.

"As it grows, supplant beneath the sea," Prudence chanted. Within the palms of her hands a deep and throbbing pain stirred and began to awaken. It felt pulpy and hot, the pain, as though her palms were sponging up the sensations gripping Patty's body and soaking them into her own.

Outside the cottage, a wind kicked up, lifting the alder leaves to show their undersides.

"So harden it to rock upon the air," Prudence continued.

She felt Martha's eyes on her, watching. Martha reached the end of her whispered psalm, smoothed the hair away from Patty's forehead, then started the psalm over again. Prudence heard a whimper, as from a dog hiding under the bedstead. And thunder rumbling nearer.

"Thus upon aliveness so decree." Prudence put more strength into her words to distract her from the pain coiling and twisting up her arms. "From where we be, transport us safe to there."

As she finished, she ran both hands over Patty's stomach and down over the poultice between her legs. Then back over the stomach, then back between her legs. Keeping her hands in constant motion, over the belly, between the legs, over the belly, between the legs. Under the pressure of her fingertips, Patty's belly almost seemed to glow with a faint and snapping bluish light. But the light in the whole room had gone blue and clouded. A chill squall of rain rolled down the hill at the center of the peninsula and settled over Milk Street, tapping light fingers on the roof.

Under her hands, within and beneath the pain, Prudence felt a flutter. A lightening movement. A liveliness, and a twisting, as of shoulders finding a way. She sent her quick hands down between Patty's thighs, and felt it there.

"Now, girl," she cried. "Now!"

Thunder rolled as the room went white with lightning. Patty screamed, and then Prudence's palm felt something wet and round, a squirming thing moving into her hands. She sent her other hand down and felt for the shoulders, twisting about and through, and the little curve of back and buttocks and then at last a pair of perfect, grayish feet.

She took the new creature into her aproned lap, being careful of its neck. It was limp, with a milky caul sealed over its face. Prue ripped the caul open with her thumbnail and wiped it away. She leaned down and sucked the infant's nose and turned and spat. Then she held it up, still tethered to its mother by a long ribbon pulsing with shared life, and she smacked it on its bottom.

It coughed.

And paused.

Drawing a first uncertain breath. Tiny pig-nose wrinkling in effort.

And then it squalled, mouth opening as the skies outside opened with sheets of rain. Battering on the windowpanes, hammering on the wooden shingles of the roof.

As the worried, squalling face pinkened with health, Prudence let out a long, slow breath she didn't know she'd been holding. And then, she started to laugh.

"I'll be goddamned," Martha breathed from her place by Patty's knee. "I knew you were cunning, Prudence Bartlett, so I did. Look at that perfect wee thing!"

Patty gasped, returning to herself. She lifted her head weakly to look.

"Is she all right?" Patty asked through lips cracked with exhaustion.

The tiny anemone girl clawed the air with her sea-creature fingers and kicked her little feet, wailing and wailing and wailing.

"She's right as rain," Prudence said, beaming with relief, petting the infant's face and cheeks and gathering the wet caul up and slipping it into her pocket. "Just as right as rain."

Chapter Twelve

~⌒

Marblehead, Massachusetts

Early April

2000

Connie dropped the sack full of final undergrad research papers to grade on the paw-footed desk in the sitting room of the house on Milk Street. Arlo wandered in behind her, leapt casually up onto the sofa, turned around twice, and settled down.

"So where is Grace, again?" Sam stumped into the front hall behind Connie with two suitcases bumping his shins.

"A two-week silent yoga retreat," said Connie.

"Well, of course she is," Sam said. "Can we at least stay in the master bedroom? Those twin beds kill me."

"Sure." Connie was flipping idly through a pile of mail on the desk. Omega Institute newsletter. *Modern Herbalist* magazine. *Yoga Journal*. And, at the very bottom of the pile, under the grocery store circular and the Marblehead *Reporter*, a copy of *Organic Pregnancy*, addressed to Constance Goodwin.

"Terrific," said Connie.

Overhead, creaking footsteps marked Sam's progress with the suitcases into her mother's bedroom, the one with the four-poster double bed. Held together with ropes. And a feather mattress.

"Spring break!" Connie cried to Arlo, aping an MTV party animal, her arms held cheering overhead. But when she turned to him for appreciation of how clever and funny she was, he had disappeared.

She pulled out the desk chair and settled into the same spot where she had begun her dissertation research. The desk faced a window of wavering glass panes held together with lead. Outside, shards of sunlight glittered in the garden, somehow piercing through the protecting drapery of vines. Connie wondered if it was too soon to put the tomatoes in. Probably.

"So," Sam said, coming back downstairs and placing his hands on her shoulders. "What shall we do tonight?"

She smiled a twisty smile up at him. "I'm just excited not to wake up to the sounds of the auto repair shop guys about to beat someone to death with a wrench."

Sam settled on the couch where Arlo had lately been. "I personally am excited that I can sleep an hour later than usual since I don't have to drive up here from Cambridge to scrape and paint the cupola of Old North in Marblehead, Massachusetts."

"No commute!" Connie agreed. She opened her shoulder bag and slid out the thick stack of research papers.

Sam yawned and stretched his arms over his head and propped his feet on the coffee table.

Connie felt his gaze settle on her back. She uncapped her pen and flipped back the first cover page of the first paper. RUFUS KING AND QUEERING THE AMERICAN PRESIDENCY. Hmm. Promising.

"You know," Sam ventured. "When you think about it. There's nothing really keeping us in Cambridge."

Connie lifted her eyes from the paper and stared out the window. Arlo had found a patch of speckled tulips, their colors jumbled together after ages of cross-pollinating, and was lying on his back among them, hind legs splayed in a small patch of sun.

"I need the library," she said, but as she said it she knew it wasn't true. Northeastern had its own library. She could get anything they didn't have on interlibrary loan. But Cambridge had Liz, and Abner's, and the Common, and . . .

"Most of my work is on the North Shore," Sam remarked.

Connie folded an arm over the back of her chair, wrist geode rattling, and looked at him. His fingers were knitted behind his head, and he was leaning back on the sofa, feet up, gazing with lidded eyes on the beamed ceiling.

"Northeastern's an hour from here," Connie said.

"It's an hour from our apartment too," Sam countered.

"Not if I take the car," Connie pointed out.

"Since when do you take the car?" said Sam.

"I take the car."

"That car is held together with masking tape."

Connie turned back to her work, picking up her green grading pen and underlining a few instances of passive voice.

"We might need to be in Cambridge," she said, not looking around.

"What are you talking about?" Sam said.

Connie's fist tightened around the green pen.

"Well. I'm considering applying to the Harvard job," she said. "Chilton's old one. They're doing a search. Assistant."

"Assistant," Sam said. "But you already have a job."

"I know." Connie didn't look around.

"You're a lock for tenure at Northeastern," Sam said.

Connie said, "Maybe."

"And you know they won't give it to you, at Harvard. That job would last five years, max, and then we'd have to move somewhere else."

Connie said, "There's a first time for everything."

She heard the soft rustlings and creakings of Sam getting up out of the sofa and moving behind her to the doorway to the front hall. Then the sound of him lacing up his work boots and pulling on a sweatshirt. His silence sounded exasperated.

"I'm going to go cut us some firewood," he said tightly.

Then the creak of the front door opening, but not followed by the sound of him stepping outside. He was waiting. Trying to goad her into saying something.

"When were you going to discuss this with me?" he said at length.

When Sam got angry, which was rarely, his words got shorter. And his voice got very quiet.

"I am discussing it," she said, eyes on the surface of the desk. "This is the discussion."

"Harvard? Are you freaking kidding me with this?" His voice rose. "After all these years of hard work, we've finally got everything set up. You wanted a job in Boston, and you got one. Your tenure packet is going in. We know what our life is, now. And it's the one that we both want!"

Connie looked up, staring out the window. A gentle breeze ruffled the tulip patch, but Arlo had disappeared. Sam was right. She'd done a focused search. Those never work. Against all odds, Northeastern had come through for her. She could have ended up anywhere. Someplace where she knew no one. Where Sam might not have gone with her. Instead, she'd gotten what she wanted. Why did she want this next shining thing? This thing she didn't need, which might actually be a bad choice?

Sam rested an arm on the doorjamb and a hand on his hip, frowning at his boots.

"It's just—" She addressed herself to the paper on the desk between her elbows. "It's so hard for me to turn it off."

"I guess I don't understand," he said.

"Understand what?" she asked, with some trepidation.

"Why you're always going on to the next thing. Why what we have"— Sam shook his head—"all that you've accomplished. Why that isn't enough for you."

The paint on the windowsill was peeling. Pale green. Boat-bottom paint.

"It's enough for me," Sam said simply. Then he pulled on his coat and stepped out into the crisp spring afternoon.

The front door slammed behind him.

Evening sneaked into the sitting room where Connie sat at work, creeping out from under the desk and gathering in the corners and along the windowsills. She chewed the end of her pen. This paper was terrible. A dull retread of points she'd made in class. Woodenly written, ineptly footnoted. It was so bad it was starting to make Connie angry. There often came a moment in grading when Connie struggled with anger at her students. That was usually when it was time to stop for the night.

Irritated, she shuffled the offending paper out of the way and instead pulled out the list of English names that Grace had given her, translations of the Latin list she'd copied from Deliverance's physick book. She leaned on her elbow and stared at it.

Most were plants. Henbane, iris, rose, sage. Some were animals. Eel. Kite. Goat buck—her favorite. Some repeated over and over. What for? Not a recipe, surely. You couldn't combine a goat buck with anything. You could feed it almost everything else on the list. Even eels. But a kite? That didn't make any sense.

Connie sat back in her chair and rubbed her hands over her face. She'd had to leave the top button of her jeans undone. She was wearing one of Sam's Marblehead Anti-Fouling Green Bottom Paint T-shirts, and its looseness masked her secret from anyone but the keenest spy. Even then she could probably explain it away as too many nachos. But not for much longer.

Sam did have a point. If she tried to make the jump to Harvard she'd be taking a huge gamble. One that was almost certain not to pan out. Even staying at Northeastern meant a crazy year next year. She would have to tell her department. She'd have to figure out what to do in the fall. She would have to solve the intractable problem, and she'd have to do it without tipping her hand to Sam about what was up. She would have to get a bigger apartment, and a car seat, and clothes, and who knew what else, and if she was considering applying to the Harvard job she'd have to put together a job talk and a research proposal and a teaching philosophy all at the same time.

It was, she saw suddenly, completely insane.

Enough. What does "enough" feel like? When happiness and contentment happen, how do you know?

Connie stretched her arms over her head and groaned aloud. A furred chin appeared on her knee. She leaned down to rub Arlo's ear.

"Don't worry," she said to the animal. "We'll be okay."

Through the window, she spied a shadowy figure trudging up the flag-stone path, bent under a leather wood carrier. Warmth tingled along her scalp, spreading down her neck and shoulders, and she knew what she had to do.

"Come on," she said to Arlo. "Let's get the door for him."

She moved into the front hall, now deep in shadow from the gloaming, and pushed open the front door. Sam dropped the firewood on the stoop and leaned up with his hands on his lower back, breathing hard. He smelled pleasantly of sweat and applewood chips and smoke.

"Well," he said. He seemed less angry after all the chopping. There was tremendous moral clarity to be found in chopping wood. "That ought to hold us. For a day or two, at least."

Connie twined her arms around his neck and pressed her lips to his throat. "I'm sorry," she breathed into his neck. "I'm so sorry. You're right."

Surprised, he moved his hands to her waist. His mouth found hers, they stepped backward through the front door, under the horseshoe charm, into the darkness, Sam's hands pulling up the tail of her T-shirt and her own hands groping for the buttons on his flannel. She moved her lips to his neck, tasting the salt of him, smiling, tasting again, and then pulling the skin into her mouth with gentle suction.

"Hey!" he cried, laughing. "I have to look professional tomorrow!"

Connie laughed and nipped him with her teeth.

Sam hoisted her up, draping her over his shoulder as she wiggled in mock protest, squealing with laughter, and started for the narrow winding stair. She pretended to hit him, pretended to kick, and felt his laughter through his shoulders and chest.

"This is never going to work, you have to walk up," he said when her rear end contacted the beam over the staircase.

"All right," said Connie.

Later, after the dishes were put away and the fire banked down to smolder, Connie lay awake in her mother's bed, listening to Sam breathe. It might freeze that night, the news had said. A late-season freeze. Those used to be more common, in the old days. Even when Connie was a girl in Concord, they'd get freezes in April and nobody would think much about it. Now an April hard freeze made the news. Every year, it seemed, was warmer than the last.

She turned on her side, trying to get comfortable in the give and sway of the ropes. Listening to Sam softly snoring, listening for Arlo's paws on the stairs. Listening to the silence as frost crept stealthily through the garden, icing over new green leaves, stilling the tulip cups. Webbing itself across the panes of glass in the windows.

Sam was right—there was no real reason for them to be in Cambridge anymore. Not if she got tenure. Maybe it was time. Time to accept that her twenties were really over. Time to face the fact that everything changes.

Time to grow up.

But knowing and changing weren't the same.

Would she get tenure? Janine Silva thought yes. It would be better if her book were out already, though. Not just forthcoming. Ugh. Her book. She was still behind. Grading always took longer than she thought it would. And then getting the last of the tenure packet together . . . Of course her book was late. That's just how it goes. She'd better crank on it this summer, though. Or sooner. Maybe if she pushed really hard on the grading she could finish tomorrow, and then take the rest of spring break in Grace's house to work on the book. That would be ideal. She always got a lot done at Milk Street. No distractions. Comfortable fireplaces. The garden. That woman's supervisory portrait, like a Foucaultian panopticon, staring at her whenever she passed through the dining room.

Connie's own eyes opened. Up in the darkness collected by the ceiling, a couple of metal spikes were driven into the oak frame. What had those been for? A canopy? A lantern?

Connie pushed herself upright.

How much time did she have before Sam was in real danger? She didn't know. She had no way to guess. Would something happen to him right after the baby? Would it be months? Would it be days?

Hours?

Connie climbed into her Mount Holyoke sweatshirt and pulled on some woolen socks and got up on silent feet, trying not to creak the floor-boards while Sam slept. She crept out of the bedroom and down the stairs, arms folded over her chest against the cold.

In the front hall she groped for matches and the brass candleholder, touching the match flame to the candle nub and shaking it out. She picked up the candle and made her way into the dining room.

"What are you looking at?" Connie whispered at the portrait of Temperance Hobbs as she ghosted through the dining room.

In the kitchen Connie considered snapping on the lone overhead lightbulb, and decided against it. She set the candle on the counter and opened the icebox, its chilly breath washing over her knuckles as she reached inside. She pulled out a half pound of Gouda and put it on a cutting board and started looking for a knife.

A small doglike creature appeared in the narrow space between the icebox and the wall.

"Oh sure, you show up now that there's cheese," she said, carving off a few slices and popping one in her mouth.

The animal licked its lips.

Maybe Sam was right. Maybe it did make sense for them to move to the North Shore. Maybe even to Marblehead. Not here, obviously. With Grace? Connie shuddered at the idea. But maybe close by. One of the new houses on West Shore Drive, with cable television and internet access and functional doorknobs and plumbing that worked nearly all the time.

She took her sliced cheese and her candle and shuffled on stocking feet back to the sitting room, where she settled on the couch near the last embers of their evening fire. At least Grace wouldn't sneak up on her this time. Connie could ruminate in peace. She slipped more cheese in her mouth and chewed. An ember popped, sending a thin ribbon of smoke up that was pushed back out of the chimney by the downdraft of cold and curled instead over the mantel before dissipating by the ceiling.

Smoke gets rid of vermin, Grace had taught her. Connie got up and took the candle over to Granna's desk. There was the grading to do. Outside, a faint gloss of moonlight shone over the freezing garden. The tulips tinkling together like glass.

Her eyes refocused, and instead of seeing the garden she saw her own face, faintly reflected in the window, lit by feeble candlelight. Her face looked drawn and worried. Almost unrecognizable.

Connie drew her knees up to her chest and pulled the sweatshirt down over her knees so she sat completely inside it, turtling. She reached for the list that Grace had written down for her.

Maybe the list didn't mean anything. Maybe it was just some weird notation, or something some long-vanished Dane woman had scribbled, like a doodle. Maybe she was just obsessing over it because she hoped it might have an answer, at a moment in her life when answers were hard to find.

She drew her legs back out of her sweatshirt and leafed to the original cipher, the Latin version. Something about that repetition. It had to mean something.

Connie pulled out a fresh sheet of notebook paper and picked up a pencil. She wrote down the English words in the same order as the original Latin, repetitions and all, and stared at that.

Turtledove henbane eel wild teasel eel alder turtledove henbane eel rose wild teasel organy rose kite iris sage turtledove organy organy sage turtledove rose organy nettle goat buck iris alder marigold henbane iris daffodil iris nettle goat buck turtledove henbane eel wild teasel eel alder turtledove henbane eel rose wild teasel organy rose kite

Behind her, Arlo appeared, paws on either side of the cheese plate on the coffee table, mustache clearly hiding something in his mouth.

"Thief," she said.

He wagged.

Connie turned back to her list and tried reading it aloud. "Organy organy," she whispered to herself when she was done. Why those two together?

"Organy organy organy organy."

She stuck the end of her pencil in her mouth.

Then she took up another fresh sheet of notebook paper. This time she copied down the jumble of words in order, vertically, like a shopping list. Or like a list of ingredients in a recipe.

Turtledove
Henbane
Eel
Wild teasel
Eel
Alder
Turtledove
Henbane
Eel
Rose
Wild teasel
Organy
Rose
Kite
Iris
Sage
Turtledove
Organy
Organy
Sage
Turtledove
Rose
Organy
Nettle
Goat Buck
Iris
Alder
Marigold
Henbane
Iris
Daffodil
Iris

Nettle
Goat Buck
Turtledove
Henbane
Eel
Wild Teasel
Eel
Alder
Turtledove
Henbane
Eel
Rose
Wild Teasel
Organy
Rose
Kite

She sat back and stared again. Outside, the moonlight slowly paled. A breeze ruffled the alder leaves, the soft dry sound of frozen leaves brushing together.

"It's the same," she said aloud.

Arlo stretched out by the hearth and yawned.

"No, I mean it," she said to him. "Look. The first fourteen things on the list. And the last fourteen things on the list. They're identical."

Arlo kneaded his front paws on the hearth bricks.

Why would the list repeat like that? Connie's hand crept up and fingered the long bark-colored braid snaking over her shoulder. Taking up her pencil, she drew a box around the first fourteen objects. Then she moved to draw a box around the last fourteen. Carefully, the pencil lead scraped along the paper, drawing a line down the left margin, alongside the first letters on the list. As she drew, veins of ice bloomed across the glass panes of the window facing the garden. They shot out florets of ice crystal, spreading until the panes were encased in frost.

Connie stopped. Pencil hovering over the paper.

"Oh, my God," she whispered.

Slowly, hand shaking, she lowered the pencil lead back to the paper and drew a trembling line down the left margin, and back up, circling only the first letters of the list of mysterious words. She put the pencil down.

The . . . Weather . . . Work . . . Is . . . Too . . . Strong . . . I . . . Am . . . Hiding . . . The . . . Weather . . . Work.

She looked up at the abruptly frosted glass, so clouded that her reflection had completely disappeared.

Chapter Thirteen

"You're never up this early." Sam leaned against the kitchen sink in the half-light of dawn, a coffee mug in his hand. It was around six, six thirty, and Connie, who hadn't been back to bed, was bustling around him in the kitchen, reaching behind him for coffee, then across him to get to the icebox for milk.

"Just, you know. Couldn't sleep," Connie said, not meeting his eyes.

"Have you asked your doctor about this?" Sam asked. "You need sleep. I mean, you always need sleep, but. You know."

"Bah," said Connie, dumping milk into her coffee and, though it was now her one allowable caffeinated cup of the day, tossing it back in a long swallow. She wiped her mouth on her sleeve and said, "It's fine. I'm fine. I've just—I've got to go."

She hurried out of the kitchen, heading for the desk with her notebooks and pens, and started shoving them into her shoulder bag. She hadn't washed her hair. Her braid was wound up on top of her head in a greasy knot. She didn't even know what shirt she had on. Maybe the one she had been sleeping in. Which may have been the one she was wearing yesterday.

"Go where?" Sam followed her into the sitting room.

"Probate office," she said. "Salem."

"You think a government office is going to be open for business at six thirty in the morning?"

"Sam!" Connie exclaimed, exasperated. "I don't know! I've just got to go."

She shuffled around the papers on Granna's desk, stuffing the pages with the broken code into the inner pocket of her bag where they would be safe.

"What're you doing at the probate office anyway?" Sam pressed. "I thought this whole point of this week was so you could get your grading done."

"Sam!" She widened her pale eyes at him in an *I don't have time for this* expression that she hoped would work.

"Jeez." He held up a hand to fend off the look.

"Sorry." Connie edged past him and into the front hallway, where she started hunting up a jacket and boots. She found an old Army surplus thing of Grace's and threw it on over her sweatshirt. "It's book stuff. I've just . . . I had an idea, and I've got to figure it out."

"Far be it from me to stand in your way," said Sam. "Good luck."

She paused with her hand on the doorknob and turned back to Sam. Maybe she should tell him. It's not that she was acting like a lunatic for no reason. She had to figure it out before anything happened.

He saw her looking and cocked his head at her with a smile.

How could he understand? It was insane. She barely believed it herself. No. She had to solve it on her own. Connie stepped up and quickly placed a peck on his cheek.

"I love you," she said. "I promise I won't always act like this."

The smile lines around Sam's eyes deepened. "Sure, you won't."

She smiled with relief. "Be careful on that cupola."

"Always," said Sam.

Sam's strange illness that long-ago summer had first seized him when he was working on a scaffolding, high by the ceiling of a church with extensive water damage. He'd plunged to the floor, falling two stories at least. He'd shattered his leg. It was bad, but it could have been worse.

Much worse. If he had hit a pew on the way down. If he'd landed on his head. She had made him swear to wear his harness any time his boots left the floor. Which was every day. Every time the boots left the floor was another opportunity for disaster.

Connie hurried down the flagstone path, shoulders hunched against the unseasonable cold, passed through the closely twined gate, and got into her Volvo. The door creaked when she slammed it closed.

Just beyond the steering wheel, the mist from her breath fogged up the view to the woods at the end of Milk Street. "Please," she whispered to the universe at large. "Let me find her today. If she exists. And please let her exist."

Connie shifted the car into Drive and pulled away.

Outside the courthouse, Connie sat in her car, heater on, chewing a Boston cream doughnut and slurping lukewarm decaf coffee from Honey Dew Donuts. Preferring Honey Dew to Dunkin was something of a sacrilege, in greater Boston, but Connie didn't mind being an iconoclast. At least she followed the Red Sox. Some fidelities were nonnegotiable.

She checked her watch. Seven forty-five. The courthouse would open at eight.

Slowly downtown Salem shook itself awake. The sun crept off the horizon and the first commuter trains pulled away for Boston. The shops wouldn't open for another hour or two, and the restaurants later than that, but civic Salem was beginning to stir. Men walking to the train station with briefcases and trench coats. Women in slacks and sunglasses and silk scarves against the chill. Then, along Federal Street, Connie spotted a familiar figure approaching, a tired-looking woman in sensible shoes and skirt suit. The courthouse registrar, Luisa Pereira.

Connie stuffed the last of her doughnut in her mouth, wiped chocolate frosting off her chin, crumpled the wax paper wrapper, tossed the remnants of her breakfast down into the passenger footwell of her car, and got out.

"Morning," she said to Luisa, who was fumbling out a set of keys.

"Oh," Luisa said, taking in Connie's dirty hair and beat-up Army jacket. She adjusted her glasses on her nose. "Constance. I didn't recognize you."

"Oh," Connie said, not realizing that Luisa knew her name. "Yeah." She looked down at herself and realized she was only a step or two from looking like a vagrant. Or maybe she finally looked professorial? Liz used to joke that when she was an undergrad at Cornell, she and the girls in her sorority would play "Homeless? Or tenured professor?" while driving around the streets of Ithaca. It was a hard game.

"Sorry. I got dressed in a hurry."

"Uh-huh," said Luisa. "Come on in."

The two women stepped into the courthouse and down a shadowy hallway lined with frosted glass doors, their footsteps echoing in syncopation. It was 7:51.

They passed through the doors marked "Will and Probate" and Connie settled at her usual table. Luisa Pereira disappeared into the back. One by one, fluorescent lights snapped on overhead. Connie squinted against the glare. She was getting too old to stay up all night. Today was going to be a hard day.

She pulled out her notebooks and pencils and tried to figure out where she and Zazi had left off. There it was: Verity Lawrence. Née Bishop, mother of Chastity, she of the sadly ironic name. Verity died in 1924, outliving both her husband and her unfortunate daughter, leaving the Milk Street house and all its furnishings, such as they were, to her granddaughter, Charity.

All right, Connie thought. *So who was your mother, Verity Bishop Lawrence?*

Alternatively, Connie could start from the other end, seeing what had happened to Patience Bartlett. God, these names. She paused to be thankful that her own cardinal virtue was easily abbreviated to something less precious.

"Here you go," said a voice at her elbow, and Connie was surprised to find Luisa dropping off the indexes for wills probated between 1860 and 1890.

"Wow, thanks," said Connie. "How did you know?"

"We here in Wills and Probate are knowers of the unknowable. The only ones more powerful are those in the Registry of Deeds." Luisa waved her fingers in a mock-mysterious way and went back behind the desk.

Connie stretched her hands in front of her, cracking her knuckles, and opened the ledger.

What she wanted didn't take long to find. Verity had been born in Marblehead—presumably in the Milk Street house—in 1841, to Faith and Knott Bishop.

"Knott?" Connie knew old-time Marbleheaders often had distinct nicknames. A few minutes' researching revealed that sure enough, Knott Bishop was a cordwainer, who'd sewn shoes in a ten-footer, a local term for a home workshop, owned by one of his neighbors around the corner from the Milk Street house. But if Connie had any hopes that it was Faith who had cracked the code of the doomed Dane men, they were soon dashed. Knott's probate appeared in 1863, along with a petition by Faith for a pension as a Union widow. By that time Faith was in her fifties, with a newly married twenty-three-year-old daughter and a son-in-law under her roof, along with an elderly boarder named Obadiah.

A boarder. That was a hallmark of a woman in poverty.

I should have seen that coming, Connie thought.

She tried to picture what the Milk Street house might have looked like in the 1860s. Her mind drifted through the gate—not as rusted as it was today, but well used. The garden perhaps in better shape, with chickens here and there, though it was beginning to be cheaper to buy chicken at the market than raise them oneself. Her mind floated along the flagstone path and up to the door, with a new-looking horseshoe nailed to the threshold overhead.

Inside, the house seemed much the same to Connie's imagination. A couple of older sofas perhaps, stuffed with horsehair, and too hard-used to survive into the twentieth century. Many more books, which were becoming more affordable. Somewhere along the line the attic roof had been raised, making space for proper bedrooms (such as they were) under the rafters. In the sitting room the paw-footed desk sat in the same attitude toward the window, only covered with papers with mathematical calculations on them, and a few mysterious-looking instruments. A sextant?

"Weird," Connie whispered to herself, squinting through closed eyes.

A young woman—Verity, she guessed, plaits over her ears, in a neat gray dress with ballooning sleeves, round skirts, and a high-buttoned bodice—leaned over to tend the fire in the sitting room. She wiped her imaginary hands on her apron and looked around for her sewing before settling in the armchair near the fire. Her face was intelligent and pointed, with gray eyes and freckled cheeks.

In the front hall, Connie passed a hat rack bristling with worn bowlers and scarves and mittens attached to each other with yarn before her imagination carried her into the dining room. Same dining table, same dishes, same overlarge hearth, same watching portrait. A low fire was going in the hearth, still used for cooking. The tiny rear kitchen would have been a twentieth-century addition. A washstand stood in the corner, and a fiftyish woman in faded black taffeta sat at the head of the dining table, shuffling a deck of cards in her hands and then turning them over on the table, one at a time. This would be Faith. She looked fragile and tired, older than Connie would have guessed. Careworn. Her hair was thinning along the tight part at her scalp. Her fingers gnarled. Her dress was of good quality, but plain, resewn a few times into different shapes. Connie could see the discoloration around the ends of Faith's sleeves where they had been taken in, then let out again.

Faith studied the cards on the table and laid a finger alongside her temple. She shook her head, picked up the cards, shuffled, and dealt again.

"Oh," Connie whispered. "I get it now."

Faith was a fortune-teller. Nothing so remarkable in that, though there couldn't have been much money in it. The papers and calculations on the desk in the sitting room could as easily be used for astrology as they were for celestial navigation. In a seafaring town there was more than one way to scratch out a living by computing the position of the stars.

An elderly man moved haltingly into the room. A few long threads of white hair clung to his spotted scalp, and he was bent nearly in half, a knotty fist leaning on a cane. He moved with care, mindful of tables and chairs and the nearness of the wall. The woman at the table looked up, nodded hello to the man, and looked back at her cards.

"Huh," said Connie. She opened her eyes and stared straight ahead across the reference-room table.

She got up and went over to the computer terminal that Zazi had used on their last trip here. She booted up the computer and her fingers flew over the keyboard, hunting up digitized copies of the United States census records. She'd heard that a bunch of census records had been scanned, but she hadn't had a chance to use the digital version yet. She suspected the Harvard university library would have bought access if such a thing were available. Her grad student library ID number still worked.

There it was. No eighteenth-century records yet, but! The nineteenth century!

First stop, 1870. Massachusetts. Essex County. Marblehead. Street names scrolled past Connie's eyes, one after the other after the other. Then—there.

The Milk Street house in 1870 contained Verity Lawrence, age twenty-nine, head of household. Daughter, Chastity Lawrence, age three. Mother, Faith Bishop, age sixty. No husband for Verity. No servants.

And there he was, like an afterthought. Obadiah. Just Obadiah. Age ninety-six.

Obadiah was old. Very, very old. Not impossible. But unusual. She squinted closer. Maybe the first figure wasn't a 9. The handwriting was spiky and inkblotty, that nineteenth-century hand that sometimes made numbers resemble each other. Yes, now she could see. It must have been a 7. Yes. That made more sense—76.

Next stop, 1880. Connie typed, pointed, clicked, clicked again, and there it was. Massachusetts. County of Essex. Town of Marblehead. Then the list of streets. This census was more detailed, signifying the changing priorities of the federal government, but the census taker for that year had much fainter handwriting. What Connie would have given to go back in time and give all census takers permanent markers. The Milk Street house residents for 1880 included Verity Lawrence, age thirty-nine. Birthplace, Marblehead, Mass. Head of household. Occupation, teacher. (Connie guessed they didn't distinguish between navigation schools and grammar schools on the census.) Literate. Native language, English. Next resident: Faith Bishop, age seventy. Also born in Marblehead. Also literate. Occupation, keeping house. No need to advertise fortune-telling to the census taker, apparently, or else Faith had given it up. Native language, English. Next resident: Chastity Lawrence, age thirteen. Birthplace, Marblehead. Occupation, none. Literate. Native language, English.

The next few entries were blurry. Connie leaned nearer the computer screen, squinting.

Yes, there he was. Obadiah. Under "Last name," which had been left vacant in 1870, she made out something that might have been "Hobbled." Birthplace, Beverly, Mass. Occupation, mariner. Literate. Native language, English. Age . . .

Connie squinted harder, so hard her upper lip curled up and revealed her teeth.

"No way," she said aloud.

"What's up?" Luisa peered over the counter.

"The census says this guy is a hundred and six," Connie exclaimed.

"No way," the registrar agreed.

"Right? That's not possible."

"I mean"—Luisa stuck a pencil in the sharpener on her desk, whirring it to a fine point, and continued—"it's *possible*. It's just not very likely."

Connie looked again, thinking the last digit was a misplaced inkblot. It certainly looked like a 6.

"Say," Connie called across the otherwise empty reference room. "Could I see the ledger for wills probated in the 1850s?"

"Sure. Give me a couple minutes." Luisa disappeared into the back, and Connie hurried back to her desk, where she thumbed idly through the 1860–1880 ledgers while she waited. She didn't learn much. Only that most people in Essex County, when they died, seemed to have more money than Faith, Verity, and their family. These latter-day Deliverance Dane descendants were consistently in the bottom quadrant of wealth. Only the house and furnishings kept them from destitution.

"Here you go," Luisa said, depositing a large leather-bound book that hadn't been dusted in some time on the table at Connie's elbow.

"Oh, goody," Connie said, eying the grimy volume, then pulling it over and creaking it open.

She scanned all of 1850 in about fifteen, twenty minutes—nothing.

Connie flipped to 1851. More scanning. More scanning. Her eyes started to ache with the gentle reminder that humans weren't necessarily meant to spend this much time hunched over books.

She flipped to 1852 and settled in for the long haul.

An hour or so later, after half a dozen visitors had passed her table—sweatered genealogists with ballpoint pens for the old records, suited attorneys with attaché cases for the new ones—Connie had made it to the middle of 1859, and was beginning to lose heart.

"Anything?" Luisa asked after situating two professional genealogists at a conference table with the probate records from Beverly in the 1780s.

"Nah," said Connie.

Flip. Flip. Flip. She leaned her cheek on her hand, leaving a smear of archive dust on her cheek.

Flip. Flip.

Flip. Flip.

She stretched her arms over her head and felt her spine pop in relief. Almost done.

November, 1859.

One small cottage, Milk Street, Marblehead, Massachusetts, and all contents (the probate didn't go into any detail about the contents), left to one Faith Bishop, age forty-nine.

Well. There it was.

Connie ran her finger down the grubby page, one letter at a time. She didn't want to miss it. She couldn't.

Underneath that entry, a codicil.

The same will left a meager competence to Obadiah Hobbs (not "Hobbled" but "Hobbs"), age eighty-five. The codicil included the right to remain, for the term of his natural life, in the home owned by his late wife:

Temperance Hobbs.

The woman in the portrait in the dining room, with the doglike creature under her arm. And the secretive smile.

"You," Connie said. "I should've known it was you. Sneaky witch."

Interlude

Temperance Jacobs scrambled down the oyster-shell lane that wound away from town and into the woods behind her house, shells sharp under her naked, dirty feet, tears stinging her eyes. She hated Mehitable Palfrey. Hated her! Hated her hated her hated her hated her!

Her big toe snagged one of the holes in the hem of her dress and Temperance whumped to the ground, face first. Stars burst behind her eyes. She swallowed her tears and got a mouthful of dust and half sobbed, half coughed. Startled, shaking, she took stock of herself, facedown against the gravel.

"Ow," she said into the ground, because there was no point in crying. Nobody would hear her. Nothing was broken, anyway. Slowly, shaken, she got to her hands and knees and then sat up on her haunches. Her fingers hunted around for injuries. Her big toe was wrenched, and the hole in the skirt torn open. She'd have to mend it before her mother saw. Her elbows were scraped pink and raw. Knees too. Oyster-shell dust all over her throat and chest and face, and when she stretched her jaw, it popped painfully. Gingerly she moved her fingertips to her chin, testing, and they came away red.

"Ho there," a young male voice called.

Temperance glanced up with alarm, half expecting to find the leering face of one of her tormentors. Mehitable had all kinds of lackeys, everywhere in town. Oh, but she hated Mehitable Palfrey.

The voice belonged to a boy a little older than herself. He was tall and skinny—too tall, by a long shot. Nobody needed a boy that tall. And his breeches didn't fit. They were baggy at the knees, as if they'd been stretched out by his big brother. His coat too. Probably his father's. It hung from his shoulders so he had to shrug to keep it on. He came loping toward her from outside her mother's gate.

"That was some fall," the boy said when he was near enough.

Temperance dabbed at her bleeding chin with the hem of her apron.

"Are you all right?" the boy pressed.

Temperance sniffed. "I guess."

"You sure? I saw. It looked bad." He indicated her red and chafed palms and her scabbing chin.

"Who're you?" she said, glowering.

"Me?" he blinked. "Obadiah Hobbs. Of the Beverly Hobbses."

Temperance was unimpressed. Who knew who that was, anyway?

"Who're you?" He knelt in the roadway next to her.

"Tempe. What're you doing at my house?"

"Tempe? Like Temperance?" The boy's eyes widened. They were nice enough eyes, she guessed. Kind of stupid, but. "Are you *that* Temperance?"

She stuck out her tongue at him.

"You're famous," he teased.

"I am not."

She wanted this boy to go away. Or maybe she didn't. She didn't know. What did he want to be asking her so many questions for? What if Mehitable and them saw? She'd never hear the end of it. Temperance glanced over her shoulder to see if her pursuers had followed as far as the turn down Milk Street. They usually didn't. They said children should never go down there, or they'd get boiled and eaten for supper by Temperance's mother. They said she used the woods for sacrifices. They said the woods were haunted, and Temperance's mother could command the spirits to rip out people's tongues and throw them down to wag in the dirt. Sometimes, they would dare each other to walk past the cottage. Temperance would hear them on the other side of the hedge while she worked in the garden—whispering, tiptoeing, and then a rock might come sailing through the hedge leaves, followed by whoops and screams and the sound of running feet. The turnspit dog would chase them, barking and snarling until they went away.

"What you running from?" the boy asked.

A pig with black-and-white patches on its ears snuffled by, shat in the gutter, wagged its curly tail, and kept going. No other signs of life marked the lane. A few early yellow dandelions poked through the oyster shells, giving the lane a weedy look. The day was unseasonably warm. It made folks dozy.

Her cheeks flushed in shame. "Nobody."

"Nobody must run pretty fast."

Her mouth twisted in a smile against her will. "No," she said, because she felt like being disagreeable.

"If nobody runs fast," the boy reasoned, "then I guess it's safe for us to walk."

He offered her a hand, but she didn't take it. She got up on her own, lifting her bloody chin. He took her elbow on the way up anyway. His fingers were gentle.

"I guess," she allowed.

They fell in step together, Temperance shaking the dust out of her skirts. One hand crept up to toy with a hank of her hair, which fell loose and wavy to her waist. She liked it loose. It was so long she could wrap it around her neck like a scarf if she wanted. She wound a hank into a knot around her finger and unwound it.

"You don't crimp it?" the boy said, groping for conversation. "My sister crimps hers."

"Well," said Temperance. "Huzzah for her."

The boy—Obadiah—clasped his hands behind his back. The coat slipped a little, and he shrugged it back in place. The lane wound lazily down the hill, past the cottage, and petered out into the woods. Temperance looked down at her bare feet. Her toenails were dirty.

"I'm going to sea soon." He kicked a dandelion and it exploded in a puff of seeds. "As a cabin boy, for Captain Gage. On the *Defiance*."

"To sea?" This boy was too young to do a man's job. And far too skinny. He'd slip through the gaps in the deck. Nobody would even see him go.

"You're too young to go to sea," she informed him.

They reached the edge of the wood. Scraps of sunlight danced through the trees.

"I'm fourteen!" he said, kind of insulted.

"Just so," said Temperance. She slowly plaited her hair into a ragged braid and let it hang over her shoulder. "You ought to stay home and help your mother." She hoped her chin had stopped bleeding.

"Well, she would agree with you." He cast a glance over to the chimney of the Milk Street house, barely visible over a thickly tangled canopy of vines. A thin stream of smoke drifted skyward, speaking of mysteries within.

"She calling on Mama?" Temperance said.

The boy nodded.

"When she due?" Temperance knew her mother, Patty, was as famous among women as she was infamous among children. In Salem. Lawrence. Newburyport, even.

"My sister says June. But she doesn't know anything." The boy and Temperance stepped together over a fallen log, rippled with turkey-tail mushrooms and soft with moss. Through the stand of trees they could see shards of sunlight glinting across the pond. Temperance thought of it as her pond, though she supposed it didn't really belong to anyone. It was cooler by the pond, and quieter. Except when the frogs were out.

"Say," said the boy, as if it had just occurred to him, though he obviously had been looking for a way to bring it up from the beginning. "Is it true?"

"Is what true?" Temperance wasn't going to make it easy for him. Wasn't any of his business anyhow.

A soft brown something flickered in the shadow of the log, and quick as a wink Temperance was on her knees with her hands around it. Warm life fluttered in her palms, and she cracked open a narrow space between her thumbs to peek inside. Two nonplussed toad's eyes blinked back at her. She got to her feet and held out her hands to show the boy her prize. But when she opened her palms again the toad saw his chance, worming through her fingers and springing free back to the forest floor. Temperance laughed as the boy said, "Oh!"

She was still giggling when he recovered himself and said, "You know. About the caul."

"So what if it is?" Temperance yanked up a yellow dandelion and wound its stem between her fingers. Thin white milk squeezed out of the stem.

"Have you still got it?" he asked.

She dropped the crushed dandelion. "Why?"

The bank sloped gently to the lip of the pond, where a boulder warmed in the sun. Temperance clambered on top of it and sat down, extending her naked feet into the water. It was cold. It felt good on her throbbing toe.

"They're good luck," he said, climbing uneasily up to sit next to her. He kept his skinny knees up, buckled shoes clear of the water. His stockings sagged too. "Especially for sailors," he added, as if this were an afterthought, and not the whole point of the conversation.

Temperance flicked the water with her toes, watching the ripples move outward in circles. "You could get a lot of money for it," he pointed out.

She wondered idly how far such circles might go in the open ocean. They might go on for a very long time indeed.

"I'll trade you for it." He touched the back of her hand.

She made a *pfffft* sound between her lips. "You haven't got anything."

"I have so," he said.

"What?" she asked, suspicious.

He stuck out a leg and rummaged in the pocket of his coat. The shoes didn't much fit him, either. It was a wonder he could keep them on.

"This," he said, pulling a small something out and holding in his cupped hand for her to see.

It was a doll. Small, and perfect. Made of knotted cornhusk, with yellow hair of feather-soft corn silk. She wore a dimity dress and apron, trimmed and tucked with tiny rolls of lace, with a lace mobcap sewn on, and a cheery bow about her neck made of marigold-colored yarn. She had painted eyes and a broad painted smile, and tiny hands and feet of knotted husk. She was perfect. Temperance had never seen a doll so fine.

"Oh," she gasped.

He passed it to her.

Temperance brushed her fingers lovingly over the hair and down the skirts. The doll even had two tiny mother-of-pearl pins for earrings. Temperance lifted the doll's skirt and found her dressed in minute lace pantaloons.

"I made her. A present for my sister," Obadiah said.

A craving for this precious toy bloomed in Temperance's chest. What a lucky girl his sister was. Temperance bet she had plenty of nice dolls like this. She probably wouldn't even appreciate it. Temperance supposed his sister was like Mehitable Palfrey, with lots of dolls, and fine clothes, and tasty things to eat.

"What's her name?" Temperance smoothed the doll's skirt back down and fingered her tiny hands. The doll's smile was warm. Temperance loved her blindly.

"Hasn't got one," he said. "You decide."

"Oh!" Temperance couldn't hide her pleasure. "I shall call her Hannah. Hannah's a good name, don't you think?"

"Perfect." Obadiah stroked the doll's corn-silk hair with a fingertip. "It's a palindrome."

"I knoooow," Temperance said, cradling the doll in her lap. She wanted to hug it, but feared crushing its dried husk body.

But then she remembered what she must trade.

With a leaden heart, she loosened her grip on the doll and held it back out to Obadiah, turning her face away.

"Don't you like it?" he said, sounding disappointed.

"I can't," Temperance said. And for an instant she was afraid she might cry.

"My sister won't miss it. I can make her another."

Temperance struggled against the sob rising in her throat. "It's—I can't trade the caul. Mama won't have it."

"Oh." He was disappointed.

"She says I must keep it. In case."

He nodded. He picked up a pebble and threw it into the pond.

"I understand," he said. Temperance thought he had a sob caught in his throat. Boys young enough to sob ought not go away to sea.

"I'm sorry," she exclaimed.

"It's all right," he said, wiping under his eyes with a fist.

She tried to put the doll back in his hands, but he wouldn't take it.

"You keep it," he said.

"I can't." Her cheeks flushed with shame.

"Really," he said. His eyes were dark, fringed with luscious eyelashes, long as a girl's. His nose and cheeks were sunburned. He had no whiskers, but he would soon. Not a boy after all. But not yet a man. "I want you to keep it."

She clutched the doll to her chest, "All right." She closed her eyes, dizzy with love and good fortune.

He wiped at his eyes again with his fingertips. "Will you think of me, though?" he asked without looking at her.

"Why?" she whispered into the doll's hair.

"I'm afraid to go," he said.

Temperance reached over and took his hand in hers. She turned it palm upward and, using her fingertip, she softly traced a pattern on the inside of his palm. Back and forth, across, and away, drawing a star shape. She glanced up at him, to see if he would squeal if she did the next part. He was watching, lips parted. She decided the next step would be worth the risk. She drew back and spat into the center of his palm. Then dipped her finger in the spit and drew the star shape again, whispering a short string of Latin words. A warm small crackling coalesced in the palm of her hand, vibrating quietly down her finger, zapping a mild static shock into the center of his palm. He gasped, but he didn't say anything.

And he didn't look afraid. She kissed the center of his palm to make the hurt go away.

"You'll come back," she said.

Chapter Fourteen

Marblehead, Massachusetts

Early April

2000

"Shut *up*," Connie shouted behind the wheel of the Volvo. She beat her palms on the steering wheel. She bounced inside her seat belt, bursting with the need to tell someone what she'd found. Temperance! It had been Temperance all this time. Just sitting there, in the dining room, with that enigmatic little smile on her face, that smug nineteenth-century minx. Connie wished she could punch Temperance on the shoulder, like she did Liz when she hadn't seen her in months, and say, *Shut up! It was you this whole time?*

Without warning, a Saab peeled out of a side street in front of her and she leaned on the horn, shouting, "Get out of the way! Jesus!"

The Saab flipped her off and turned, and Connie stomped on the accelerator, hunching over the steering wheel as if she could bodily urge the tired car to go faster.

"Shut up shut up shut up! I can't believe it!" she continued, sailing through a yellow light and leaving a trail of honks behind her. "Who the hell was Temperance? What the heck was she up to? What does 'weather work' even mean?"

Behind her, in the backseat of the Volvo, Arlo's paws shifted around for purchase on the seat. He lifted his nose to the cracked window, nostrils trembling.

"Oh, my God," Connie continued. "What do I do now? What do I do?"

Without warning, she peeled over to the curb and stopped, Arlo scrabbling off the seat and into the footwell in back with a thump. Connie leapt out of the car, leaving it running, dashed into the phone booth she'd spotted outside some nondescript pizza place, shut the glass door behind her, and busted out her day planner. She riffled through pages, found the number she wanted, jammed the receiver under her ear, and fed quarters into the phone.

"Pick up pick up pick up pick up," she chanted as the line rang once, twice, three times.

"Hi!" chirped a voice on the other end of the line.

"Hey, Zazi? It's Profess—"

"This is Zazi," the voicemail continued brightly. "You know what to do." Then a beep.

"Dammit," muttered Connie. "Hey, Zazi? This is Prof— This is Connie. Listen. I've got to talk to you. I've found some pretty . . . It's about that project I hired you to help me with. For the book. The code? I could use another pair of eyes, basically. I just need to talk to you. If you could give me a call back, that would be great. I'm staying at my mother's house. I think you've got the number. Okay. Thanks." She hesitated.

"This is Connie," she said again, just in case.

She hung up. She had to tell someone. Sam was up scraping the paint off a church steeple in Marblehead, and nowhere near a phone. She flipped through her address book, looking up Liz's work number.

As she flipped, the pay phone rang.

Connie stared at the receiver. It rang again. Connie hovered her hand over the receiver, puzzled, and then picked it up.

"Hello?"

"Hey, who is this?" said the phone receiver.

"Who did you call?" Connie said, suspicious.

Two kids in Red Sox hats came out of the nondescript pizza place, and one of them dropped his slice of pepperoni. The other one pointed and laughed. "Connie? Is that you?"

"Zazi?" Connie said.

"What time is it?" Zazi sounded sleepy. Connie heard rummaging, as of a hand searching for an alarm clock.

"It's late." Connie checked her watch. "Almost eleven."

"Oh, man." Zazi yawned.

"I just called you." Connie pressed a hand to the glass wall of the phone booth and looked back at her car. A pair of animal eyes watched her from the backseat.

"I know. What number is this?"

"I'm in a pay phone."

"A *pay phone*?" The kid with the dropped pepperoni shoved the other kid, who shoved him back. A guy in a white apron came outside and shouted at both of them.

"Well. Yeah," Connie said. "I didn't think you were there. Why didn't you pick up?"

"Connie," Zazi said patiently. "Nobody picks up unknown numbers."

"Right." Connie was pinching the skin at the bridge of her nose. "So, listen."

"If you had a cell phone," Zazi continued, "I'd know to pick up, because you'd be in my contacts list. The number would come up as you."

"Okay, okay, I get it. Listen. I broke the code."

"What?" Sounds of rustling, as Zazi sat up in bed.

"And that's not all." Connie watched as one of the Red-Sox-hat-wearing kids shouted back at the guy in the apron and started pimp-rolling away. "There's more. But I don't know where to look for it."

"First things first. There was a message embedded in that list? What was the message?"

"It says 'The weather work is too strong I am hiding the weather work.'"

Outside, in the backseat of the Volvo, Arlo barked, the sound muffled by the running engine. Connie's breath was beginning to fog the glass of the phone booth.

"The weather work?" Zazi said. "What does that mean?"

"It means . . ." Connie leaned her forehead against the phone booth glass, abruptly aware of her missed night of sleep. "Actually, I have no idea what it means. That's what I'm calling about."

"Huh," said Zazi around a thumbnail in her mouth. "Weather work," she tested out the phase.

"That's what it said."

"That's a new one. Okay. So what's next?"

Connie thought. "Have you got a car?"

"I've got Zipcar. Where we going?"

"Zipcar?" Connie repeated.

"It's a car-sharing—never mind. I've got a car, basically. Where'm I going?"

"Have you got a pen handy?" Connie said. "It's a little hard to find."

The Volvo rolled to a stop outside the hedge that hid the Milk Street house and Arlo and Connie tumbled out in a tangle of legs and feet and tail and bookbag and dashed for the gate. Connie didn't stop to observe the state of the garden as it moved and parted to make way for her, pulling its springtime shoots out of the way of her running feet. She sprinted unseeing down the flagstone path to the front door, grabbed the handle, and pushed.

Locked. Connie swore under her breath and started digging through her bag for her keychain. She hoped Zazi could find the house. It had taken Connie and Liz forever to find it the first time. And it wasn't as if Grace had trimmed the hedges since then.

"Gah," she said, finally finding the keys. She fit the key in the lock and turned it and leaned her shoulder into the door to open it.

It was stuck.

"Oh, come on!" Connie wailed at the overcast April sky.

When she did so, she noticed the rusted horseshoe nailed over the door. She remembered Grace kissing her fingers and touching them to the horseshoe. Connie looked left, and looked right, knowing there was no one nearby to observe her, but feeling self-conscious anyway. She kissed the tips of the fingers on her right hand and touched them softly to the horseshoe.

When her fingertips made contact, a warm living spark traveled between her body and the metal, like a shock of static electricity. Connie said, "Ow," and pulled her fingers away, kissing them again to soothe away the hurt. A fleet blue sheen traveled over the horseshoe while her attention was on her fingertips.

When she closed her hand over the door handle and pushed, the door opened without protest.

Inside, Connie tossed off her boots and headed straight for the dining room. She planted her hands on her hips and stared at the portrait of Temperance Hobbs.

The portrait smiled placidly back at her.

Connie rummaged on the mantel for the kitchen matches, flaming up two at a time and touching them to the half-melted red candles on the dining room table, gradually lightening the room until Temperance stood illuminated by a warm orange glow.

"All right, you," Connie said. "Tell me where you put it."

Temperance looked as though she had been painted in what the English would call the Regency period, though of course in North America there was no regent anymore, and so the period was usually called Jacksonian. Connie took one of the brass candleholders and held the flame up to the painting to get a better look.

The varnish had yellowed in two hundred years, making the background of the painting dim and hard to make out. Underneath the thick residue of time and smoke stains, Connie saw that Temperance was seated at a trestle-style dining table. At one time the tabletop in the painting must have looked soft and gleaming, as tactile in its polished shine as a John Singleton Copley portrait, the one of the boy with the folded ear and the delicate flying squirrel on a thin golden chain. Temperance's skin was soft and translucent, unnaturally pale, and probably, Connie reflected, idealized by the painter. Nobody had skin that good. Especially not before the smallpox vaccine.

Temperance sat in three-quarter view, with her right elbow leaning on the table and her left hand in her lap. There were some papers under her elbow, with the shadowy hint of writing on them, but when Connie brought the candle in closer she saw that the writing was abstracted scribbles rather than actual letters. Nothing to decode there.

The woman in the painting was young, but not a girl—in her twenties, Connie guessed, with glossy bark-brown hair parted in the middle and plaited tightly back to the nape of her neck. Her dress had probably been pale pink at one time, but now it had faded to a suggestion of rose-gray, like roses left out to dry. Her forehead was high and smooth, her eyebrows dark and arched in an inquiring way. Her eyes were an unsettling shade of pale oyster-shell gray. Her nose was rather long, and her smile seemed knowing. Or was Connie projecting? Had Temperance's smile always looked so smug?

The woman in the portrait wore no jewelry, though under the plait over her right ear, faintly drawn in with watery paint, hung the faded suggestion of an earring. It didn't look like much of an earring. It wasn't gold, for one thing, and platinum didn't come into wide use for jewelry until later. If anything, Connie would have guessed that Temperance was wearing a delicate fishhook through her ear. But that couldn't be right. Maybe it was just a smudge on the surface of the paint, or a scratch.

Under Temperance's arm, in the crook of her elbow, lurked the shadowy outline of a smallish doglike creature, shaggy enough that its own eyes weren't visible. Indeed, it appeared in a strange attitude relative to the sitter—as if there wasn't enough space under her arm for the animal to be there, yet there it was. A paradox, or a mistake of badly executed perspective and shading, done by some self-trained itinerant portraitist.

In the background of the painting Connie observed a window rather like the window in the dining room: the same sash, the same shutters, pinned back, the same tendrils of ivy coiling over the sill and digging into the wood with tenacious roots. Yet the window in the painting didn't look out over the garden, as the real window did. Connie held the candle up, shading it with her palm.

The window in the portrait looked out over Marblehead harbor. Connie recognized the dim outlines of the jutting rock park with the lighthouse on the Neck, though the lighthouse in the painting was smaller, squat, most likely made of wood. The harbor was dotted with boats, their sails put away, reduced to smudges of paint and scumbling to show froth upon the surface of the water.

"Hello?" a young woman called from somewhere outside.

"In here!" Connie put the candle on the dining table and hurried to the front door, stepping into her discarded boots as she did so, but leaving the laces loose since she'd only have to run out into the street for a minute. But when she opened the front door, she found Zazi standing there, fist raised as though about to knock.

"You found it!" Connie exclaimed.

"Well, yeah." Zazi held up a couple of sheets of paper. "Mapquest."

"Great!" Connie was stunned that Zazi had gotten there so quickly. "Great great great. I'm so glad you could make it." She gestured for Zazi to come in.

Zazi looked Connie up and down. "Are you okay?" she asked as she stepped inside and knelt to take off her shoes.

"What?" Connie looked down at herself. She really ought to have showered. And changed her shirt. And probably eaten something that wasn't a doughnut. "Oh, yeah. Sure. Just preoccupied."

"Whatever it is, must be good," Zazi remarked. "When I was finishing my thesis I didn't wash my hair for like a week. Two? I don't remember."

"It's good." Connie closed the front door and cleared a peg in the entryway for Zazi's scarf. "Come on in."

Zazi's socks didn't match. One was bright yellow-and-red stripes, and the other patterned in stars. "Wow." She looked into the study, examining the oak beams overhead. "This your house?"

"Well. Sort of." Connie nudged a curious Arlo out of Zazi's way with her toe. "My mother lives here."

"Ah," said Zazi. "This town is really nice. Kind of reminds me of like an Anglo San Miguel."

"Oh yeah? I've never been." Connie ushered Zazi into the dining room.

"It's like this," Zazi said. "Only, you know. Spanish. And bigger." Her eye took in the Queen Anne dining table, the brass candlesticks, the iron candle chandelier, the open fireplace bristling with hooks and chains and cooking implements. She moved over to the built-in hutch next to the fireplace and ran a gentle finger along the edge of a China-export bowl. She held the finger up and examined the thin sugaring of dust. "My nana lives there."

"Your nana?"

"You know. My *abuela*." She looked at Connie. "In San Miguel de Allende."

"Oh. Right," said Connie. "So. Can I get you anything? You want some coffee?"

"No thanks." Zazi minutely adjusted the bowl on its shelf to perfect its spacing. "I just want to see what you found."

They sat together at the dining table and Connie spread her notes and printouts of the probate lists across its surface, weighing them down against passing drafts with the candlesticks. Zazi puzzled over the list Connie had made of the words in English, with the message circled down the side as in a word-finder puzzle.

"'The weather work is too strong,'" Zazi read aloud. "'I am hiding the weather work.'" She placed her chin on her fist and frowned down at the paper. "And you figured out who hid this message in the book?"

"I have a theory," Connie said. She pointed at the portrait.

Zazi looked up at Temperance, who smiled down at them.

"Her?" Zazi said. "Why do you think it was her?"

They both stared at the painting while Connie tried to come up with a way to explain it to Zazi that wouldn't sound insane. She had to make it about the book. Just keep it about the book.

"Well," Connie hesitated.

"She looks like you," interrupted Zazi.

"What?"

"She does. Look. The nose. The eyes. Same hair." Zazi looked at Connie. "This isn't just about your book, is it?"

Connie took the eagle stone between her fingers and thumb and twisted it. It rattled.

"Not exactly," she said.

Zazi leaned forward. "Spill," she said.

Connie got to her feet and paced back and forth. "It's hard to know where to start."

"A lot of times, it runs in families." Zazi picked a bit of fluff off her sweater. "You see that all over the South. This folklorist, Henry Hyatt? He went around interviewing people in the 1930s. White, black, didn't matter. Whole families. Half of them will do conjure work, and the other half won't consider making a move without it. Even now."

Connie stopped with a hand on the back of one of the shield-backed dining chairs. "How did you know?"

Zazi drew up a knee and rested it against the table, looking critically at Connie. "Lucky guess?" she said.

Connie pressed her fists to her eyes. "Here's the thing." She sat down again. "I've got to find where she hid it."

"The weather work?"

"The recipe for it," Connie said. "I need to find it. I need to find it, like, yesterday." Arlo wormed his way under her arm and looked up at her.

"And you think she left that message in the physick book as a hint," Zazi said.

Connie nodded.

"But I thought you said the physick book got sold to some nouveau riche book collector. Before the Revolution. That's what your dissertation said," Zazi pointed out. "She obviously came later. What were her dates?"

Connie considered Temperance. "Born in Marblehead, 1778," she said. "Died same, 1859."

"That's a generation after the Revolution. How'd she get access to the book, to add anything?" Zazi said.

"It was in a library by then," Connie said. "The Salem Athenaeum. The library was formed in 1810. She lived right here, only one town over. I assume she would've been able to go and see it whenever she wanted."

Zazi looked up at the woman in the painting. Temperance was probably about Zazi's age when it was painted. Maybe a little older.

"So she went to the trouble to go to the library, take out her grandmama's book, put in a secret code, but not put in the recipe itself," Zazi reasoned.

"That's my theory," said Connie.

"And you don't know where she would have put it."

"No idea."

"And you don't know what the weather work does," said Zazi.

"You come across weather charms, sometimes, in coastal towns," said Connie. "And at one point, working on the diss, I found mention of people who specialized in it. But other than that, no. I don't know what it does."

Zazi chewed her lip and stared at the painting.

"Most conjure doesn't really deal with the weather," she reflected. "It's about the house, or the body. Luck, and love. Money, obviously. And fixing enemies. It's about power for the self, and influence over others. Charms get delivered by washes for the floor, or bath salts for the body. Candle work. Bible work. It's small and personal. The weather's big. Impersonal. Although"—she drew up her other knee against the edge of the table and clasped her hands around them—"I did come across one instance of priests in Mexico trying to repel hurricanes. Using the consecrated host. That was in the 1500s."

"Did it work?" Connie paced to the other side of the fireplace.

"What do you think?" Zazi dropped her knees and leaned with her elbows on the dining table.

"Figured," said Connie. She pulled out a chair and sat at the table, opposite the portrait.

Zazi cocked her head. "Oh, wait," she said softly. Her dark eyes widened. "You know what Temperance lived through?"

"The War of 1812?" Connie said.

Zazi leaned across the table and put her hand on Connie's arm. "The year without a summer," she said.

"Oh, my God," Connie said.

"1816, right? The year without a summer!" Zazi's voice rose.

She was right. That year, for whatever reason, summer had never come. Frost killed off crops all over the Eastern Seaboard, as late as May. The effects were global, and devastating. In Europe, in the East Indies, everywhere. Starvation. Freezing. And nowhere had it worse than New England. The year without a summer was so devastating that it permanently changed patterns of settlement in the United States. Farmers gave up and moved west, pushing deeper into western New York State, into Ohio, looking for something new. Escaping desperation and loss.

The year without a summer came close to destroying civilization as it stood in 1816. And even in 2000, no one knew for sure what had caused it.

"'The weather work,'" breathed Connie, "'is too strong.' It's too strong!"

"So," said Zazi. "Where would she have hidden something that powerful? Something important to her, that she wanted someone in her family to be able to find, but maybe nobody else?"

"You were talking about conjure work," Connie said. "That it dealt with bodies, and houses, and candles."

"Yeah. And Bibles," said Zazi.

"And Bibles," Connie said, getting to her feet.

Chapter Fifteen

On the floor of the study Connie and Zazi sat, legs splayed, the two large family Bibles from the bottom shelf of Granna's books open between them. Connie had pulled down the Psalter too, for good measure. They'd riffled quickly through all the pages, looking for marginalia, or scraps of paper, or circled letters, or underlined passages—anything, really, out of the ordinary.

"It has to be here," Connie muttered, paging through the older of the two Bibles slowly, onionskin paper crinkling as she turned the leaves.

"What makes you so sure?" Zazi running her finger down a page of the Psalter.

"You said Bible work is a big part of conjure," said Connie. "It's part of early modern English folk magic too. I got started on my dissertation because of this Bible." She got to her feet and ran her hands along the fireplace mantel, groping through knickknacks for the fragile item she was looking for. She found it leaning forgotten against a blown-glass terrarium full of moss and fogged with moisture. "See?" she said, holding out the tiny object.

Zazi took the item into her hands gently. Connie watched her examine the cornhusk doll, with its yarn bow and faded dimity apron and crayon smile.

"Creepy," said Zazi.

"I found that in the bookshelf," Connie told her. "Hidden behind the Bible."

"No kidding." Zazi turned the doll over in her hands. "There's no pins in this, are there?"

"I don't think so," Connie said, taking it back and inspecting it. "Oh. Wait." She pressed her thumbnail against the doll's tiny earring. It was a fragment of pearl shell, affixed on a sewing stickpin. "That's one."

"Maybe you should put it down," Zazi said. "Just in case."

Connie laughed, placing the doll with care back in its resting place, its arm around the base of the glass terrarium. "My point is," Connie said, "if Temperance were going to hide something in the house, I'd think it would be in the Bible. Or at least, in the bookshelf."

Both women stared back at the shelves upon shelves upon shelves of books. *The Decline and Fall of the Roman Empire. The Yachtsman's Omnibus. Uncle Tom's Cabin.*

"These are all later," said Zazi.

"Yeah," Connie said, reaching for a pen to walk over her knuckles.

"Have you got a copy of *The Pilgrim's Progress*? That's the kind of book a Jacksonian-era white girl would have," Zazi said.

Connie ran her fingertips along the spines of the books, one after the other. She came upon a small, brown leather-bound volume that crumbled slightly to the touch. When she pulled it off the shelf a rain of page fragments followed, and the dust tickled her nose into a sneeze.

"Bless you," said Zazi as Connie wiped her nose on the shoulder of her flannel shirt. She should really change clothes, like, immediately.

Connie eased the cover open with a thumbnail and softly paged through the front matter until she found the title page. Sure enough, it was *The Pilgrim's Progress*. A later edition, probably from the 1750s. Printed in Boston.

"You called it." Connie knelt next to Zazi before the fireplace, holding the volume out for both of them to see. Delicately, softly, Connie turned the pages.

But when they got to the end of the book, they had found nothing. The Pilgrim progressed, but without the help of any hidden notes.

"Drat," said Connie. Zazi was lost in her own thoughts, staring into the middle distance.

"Everything okay?" Connie asked.

Zazi shook herself and came back. "Yeah. I'm just still annoyed about something from yesterday."

"What's up?" Connie slid the small leather-bound book back into place on the shelf.

"Oh, you know"—Zazi waved her hand—"I talked to Professor Beaumont. About the colonial history job. I wanted to feel him out about a rec letter."

"What did he say?" Connie said, trying and failing to keep her voice from sounding cold at the mention of Harold Beaumont.

"He said"—Zazi put on a broad, patently fake Foghorn Leghorn southern accent and waved her fingers in scare quotes—"'Well, you can apply all you want to, but I don't know as it's such a good idea.'"

"That's pretty annoying," Connie said.

"It's ridiculous," Zazi said. "I'm just as qualified as anybody for that job. But I already know who's got his support. And it pisses me off."

Thomas.

"It wouldn't bother me if I thought the guy was a decent scholar," Zazi continued, and Connie noticed she wasn't naming names. "But he's—" She caught herself, suddenly aware of Connie watching her. "Anyway. I'm just disappointed."

"So. What are you going to do?" Connie settled back on the floor next to Zazi. A half-burned pine-cone skeleton sat in the ashes of the fireplace. The scent of burnt pine sap lingered by the hearth.

Zazi fiddled with a corner of the Bible on the floor between her knees. "I don't know. Talk to Janine, I guess."

"Janine will tell you to go for it," said Connie. Zazi thought Thomas was a bad scholar. That was odd. Connie had always known him to be serious. Attentive. Meticulous. Maybe not inspiring. Of course, his paper at the grad student conference hadn't been ready. He should probably have waited to present it. But who hasn't given a paper too early in a career?

"I guess. I don't know," Zazi said.

Connie took up a poker and nudged the pine-cone skeleton. It crumbled apart into ash, going from form to formlessness. To everything, its season. The pine cone grew into being, burned bright, and now it had disappeared. That was natural.

Connie knew what she had to do.

"I'll write you a rec letter," Connie said.

The silence in the sitting room was the silence of hope.

"You will?" Zazi had clasped her hands under her chin. Her eyes were wet. "That would be. I mean. Really?"

Connie laughed. "It's my job."

Zazi sniffed her eyes dry. "That would be awesome. Thank you."

"You're welcome," Connie said.

Zazi got to her feet and began inspecting another shelf of books. "Where else should we look?" she said. Connie could see she was embarrassed, getting emotional about work.

Connie leaned back on her elbows and gazed up at the rows upon rows of books. She knew from previous experience that Temperance's recipe wouldn't be in the kitchen. She'd cleaned out the entire kitchen herself, years ago. All those glass jars, full of strange rotting things. Ugh. The smell had been terrific. And she'd read every single one of Granna's recipe index cards. Though some of them had been, one might say, unconventional, none of them were the weather work.

"I guess we could try the bedrooms," Connie said. "But there's not much up there. The trunks are all just storage for quilts."

"And moths," Zazi added.

"And mice," Connie said, wrinkling her nose.

"Ew." Zazi rose on tiptoe and reached for a slim volume on a top shelf. It was newer, maybe mid-nineteenth century. Zazi touched the faded lettering on the spine. "You ever read this?" she asked Connie, holding out the book.

It was a first edition of *The House of the Seven Gables* by Nathaniel Hawthorne. Published by Ticknor and Fields, Boston. 1851.

"Um." Connie thought. "Maybe? I can't tell if it's one of those books I've actually read, or just one of those that I think I've read."

"Do you remember the plot?" Zazi pressed.

"Uhh . . ." Connie closed her eyes and riffled through the drawers full of note cards in her mind, looking to see if she could find the plot to this book. Something about Salem. Right? But Hawthorne wrote about Salem all the time. And a house. Obviously. The house itself was still in Salem, serving as a historical museum.

Zazi knelt on the floor next to Connie. "A family gets cursed from the gallows during the Salem witch trials because they steal the deed to a guy's land, and then accuse him of witchcraft to get him out of the way," she prodded. "You know. 'I am no more a witch than you are a wizard, and if you take away my life, God will give you blood to drink'?"

"Sarah Good actually said that," said Connie. "From the gallows. I *wish* I were that badass."

"Yeah, well, nobody in the nineteenth century thought women ever said anything important, so Hawthorne gave that line to a guy," said Zazi. "Matthew Maule. And then the guy he cursed—the judge, I mean, Judge Pyncheon—chokes to death on his own blood. Just like Nicholas Noyes in real life."

"Okay," said Connie, a memory of the story stirring in the recesses of her mind. Rosebushes and insanity and a cent shop and a spinster. Now she remembered. "So what's your point?"

"Hawthorne grew up around here, didn't he?"

"In Salem," Connie said.

Zazi put her hand on Connie's shoulder. "Maybe that's not the only plot point Hawthorne stole from some local woman he heard about growing up." Zazi's eyes were the fathomless dark of the ocean in a storm. "Do you remember where they find the deed to the guy's land, in the book?"

"Sure," Connie said uncertainly. "It was . . ."

"Behind the patriarch's portrait," finished Zazi.

"The patriarch's portrait?" Connie echoed.

Zazi nodded.

They leapt to their feet and dashed out of the sitting room, skidding in their socks over the polished pine floorboards and sliding to a stop before Temperance's portrait.

The creature under Temperance's arm watched them with a glittering eye. Sounds of snuffling came from under the dining table.

"I am hiding the weather work. *I* am hiding it," Connie said. She approached the painting and ran soft, delicate fingers along the edges of the frame. "Do you think that's what she meant?"

The frame was gilt, wooden, and hadn't been dusted, perhaps ever. It felt grimy to Connie's touch. She pressed her cheek to the plaster wall, but couldn't see anything behind the picture.

"I mean. Maybe?" said Zazi.

"Will you bring over that candle?" Connie asked. Zazi picked up the brass candlestick and passed it to her. The house had darkened with the afternoon. Shadows had begun to collect in the corners of the dining room, and to deepen under the tables and chairs. Connie didn't know what time it was. But it was getting late.

The raking candlelight cast itself up under Temperance's chin, and her eyes seemed to trace to the right, following Connie's questioning fingers.

Connie moved to the left side of the painting, running her fingernails between the frame and the plaster wall. She couldn't feel anything amiss, but then again, she also couldn't lift the painting away from the wall. It wasn't just hanging on a wire. Of course, in museums paintings were often bolted to the wall, to guard against theft. But who would do that in a private house? A painting with no value except to the people living there?

Connie peered along the underside of the frame.

She ran her fingertips underneath the lower edge. It was so quiet in the dining room that Connie could hear herself and Zazi breathing, and the soft, gentle scrape of her fingertips along the painted wood.

Her finger tripped over something.

She traced backward, groping for the something. One millimeter at

a time, Connie pressed her fingertip against the underside of the painting frame.

There it was. A nub.

She glanced back at Zazi, who was watching from behind the candle, lips parted.

"I think," said Connie, "this might be a button."

"Well, push it!" cried Zazi.

Connie did so. It didn't budge.

"It's stuck," she said.

"Do you have any WD-40?" Zazi asked.

"There's olive oil in the kitchen," Connie said.

"I don't know," Zazi demurred. "Oil could take off the gilding."

Connie brought her fingertip to the little brass nub and rested it there.
Open, she thought. She pictured the brass button, small, corroded from
generations unobserved in salty air. Untouched. Forgotten. She pictured
the corrosion flaking away and falling, harmless, to the floor. Pictured the
mechanism of the button loosening. She invited it to go back to how it
used to be. To feel like a button, instead of like a shadow of one.

Open for me.

A warm tingling sensation flickered to life in Connie's palm. It was a
sensation she remembered, and she knew that in a moment the flickering and snapping would resolve into pain. But for now, it felt soft, crackly,
like the static around a balloon, softly drawing up the hairs along an arm.

The tingling circled the inside of Connie's palm, sending itself around
her index finger like a ring, before vibrating along her nerves to the fingertip. The vibrating grew to just this side of pain. Like grasping a frayed
lamp cord. Connie caught her breath.

The button depressed. As it did so, a puff of dust released into the air,
shimmering in the thin afternoon light of the dining room, and the right
edge of the portrait popped away from the wall.

"Holy crap," whispered Zazi.

The tingling dissipated from Connie's hand, and she flexed it by her
side to get rid of the crawling feeling.

"Okay," she said softly. "Here we go."

She reached for the loosened edge of the painting and gently, slowly, eased it away from the wall.

The hinges creaked from decades, maybe even two centuries, of disuse.

"Here," said Zazi, passing Connie the candle.

The painting was mounted to a kind of cabinet door. The cabinet wasn't large, maybe two feet by one foot, and Connie couldn't tell how deep it was from the shadows. It couldn't be that deep, as it was set into the plaster and lath of the outside wall of the Milk Street house.

Connie held the candle up to shine its orange glow into the depths of the cabinet. Sitting inside was a plain wooden box, thickly coated in dust.

Connie was reaching for the box when the front door swung open and Sam called, "Hello? Anybody home?"

"Oh, my God!" shrieked Zazi.

"Sam!" Connie cried, struggling not to drop the candle.

Sam stood framed in the doorway between the dining room and the front hall, holding a brown paper bag. Arlo appeared from under the dining table and put his paws on Sam's boot, tail a blur of welcome.

"Jesus," Connie said, pressing a hand to her chest. "You scared the pants off me."

"So I see," said Sam, stepping into the room. "Hey. I'm Sam," he said to Zazi, shifting the bag to his other arm and sticking out a hand.

"Zazi." She shook his hand. "God, I just about had a heart attack."

"Everything okay?" Sam asked, sounding uncertain. "I checked in the study first. It looks like it's been ransacked."

"I'm one of Professor Goodwin's students," Zazi said, groping for an explanation. "I was helping her look in the bookcases."

"Sam," Connie said, not bothering to address the disarray they'd left in the other room. "Look."

He peered into the open cabinet set into the wall.

"That's been back there this whole time?" he said. He set the paper bag on the dining table and edged nearer the secret compartment.

"I think," Connie said, "I'm the first person to open it since it was put in."

Sam reached into the darkened hollow of the wall to touch the small wooden box. "Incredible," he said, tracing a fingertip over one of the ellipses in the carving. "Are you going to take it out?"

"We were just about to," said Connie. "Here."

She handed him the candle to hold and reached inside. Her hands met a thick carapace of dust, gritty and cold to the touch.

The box was clotted with grime, locked into its place in the cabinet by centuries of neglect. Connie blew along the lid of the box, stirring up a cloud that burned in her nose and rasped down the back of her throat, making her cough into her sleeve. She ran her fingers along the base of the box, clearing away the crust of dirt. Gently, she wrapped her hands around its rearmost edges, broke the box free, pressed it to her chest, and drew it out of the cabinet.

She turned and set the box carefully down on the dining room table. The three of them bent in close to look.

The box was made of wood, though Connie couldn't tell what kind— oak probably. It was intricately carved with interlocking circles, making flowerlike optical patterns across the surface, but done by a hand that was clearly self-taught. The lid of the box bore the initials *T J H*.

"Temperance Jacobs Hobbs." Connie traced the initials with her fingers.

The box was held closed by an iron lock, hand forged, its strike plate marked by a dark and irregular keyhole. Connie tried pressing here, and pressing there, but it was no use—the box was locked.

"We could force it," said Sam hesitantly. "But we'd probably break it."

"How old, do you think?" Zazi ran her fingertips over the box's lid and scraped a fingernail along the edge of the keyhole.

"Maybe late eighteenth century?" Connie guessed. "Or early nineteenth. It could be a sea chest for papers. Or maybe a lap desk. You see those sometimes from that period."

"So how do we get it open?" asked Zazi.

"I don't know," Connie said. All at once she felt very, very tired. Exhausted. Barely able to stand. She needed a bath. She needed sleep. She needed to understand, and she didn't.

"I do," said Sam. He moved closer to Connie, standing right behind her. He planted a kiss on the crown of her head and reached into her jeans pocket.

His fingers wormed around inside the pocket and reemerged holding the small iron key. With a long, thin, hollow shank. The key that Connie had found hidden in the Bible, all those years ago, during the summer when everything changed.

"Oh, my God," Connie said.

Sam put the key in her hand.

Connie bent to fit the key into the lock on the sea chest. Her hand was shaking. She clenched her fists, closed her eyes, thought, *Get it together, Goodwin,* and opened her eyes again.

She slid the key slowly into the lock.

It clicked into place. A perfect fit.

PART II

CORALLUS

But as they sailed he fell asleep: and there came down a storm
of wind on the lake; and they were filled with water, and were
in jeopardy. And they came to him, and awoke him, saying,
Master, master, we perish. Then he arose, and rebuked the
wind and the raging of the water: and they ceased, and there
was a calm. And he said unto them, Where is your faith? And
they being afraid wondered, saying one to another, What
manner of man is this! for he commandeth even the winds and
water, and they obey him.

Luke 8:23–25
King James Bible

Then said they unto him, What shall we do unto thee, that the
sea may be calm unto us? for the sea wrought, and was tempes-
tuous. And he said unto them, Take me up, and cast me forth
into the sea; so shall the sea be calm unto you: for I know that
for my sake this great tempest is upon you.

Jonah 1:11–12
King James Bible

Chapter Sixteen

Marblehead, Massachusetts

Hoke Day

mid-April

2000

The key turned with a soft click, the gentle pressure of the levers moving against each other inside the lock, and the lid of the box popped open with a creak.

"Oh, wow," Zazi said softly at Connie's elbow.

Connie felt Sam's hand find her lower back. Did he know the real reason this was so important? Should she tell him?

Later, she would tell him. Not now, with Zazi here. She would tell him when they were alone.

Connie evaluated the best way to open the lid of the box. She mustn't force it. The wood would be long dried out, swelled with moisture and then wrung out with freezing, expanding and contracting in a ceaseless cycle for nearly two hundred years. It would be fragile and prone to splintering. Carefully, she placed her hands on the upper corners of the box lid. When her skin met the wood a faint bluish sheen might have washed over the lid of the box. Connie had been awake for nearly thirty-six hours straight. When she was this tired, everything had a muffled feeling of unreality.

Slowly, she eased the lid of the box up. The hinges groaned, surprised at being asked to open. Sam and Zazi both leaned in, peering over Connie's shoulders to see inside. Zazi lifted the candle nearer, and its soft orange glow fell inside the box, long asleep and forgotten inside the wall of the Milk Street house. Under the candlelight the box almost seemed to stir and waken.

The first item Connie spied inside was a small orange pebble, oblong and irregular. Polished smooth. She reached into the box, eagle stone knocking against the wooden side, and closed the pebble between her finger and thumb. It was cool to the touch. She held it up for the others to see and examined it in the candlelight.

"What is it?" Sam asked.

"I don't know," Connie said.

"Agate?" Zazi guessed.

"Agate is usually translucent, isn't it?" Connie said. This pebble was opaque. Connie set the pebble on the dining room table and looked inside the box again.

Next she found a few posies of herbs, tied together with string, which looked so desiccated that she was loath to touch them for fear they would crumble to dust. She looked more closely, but they were so curled that she couldn't tell what they were. As she stared, she felt Sam's warm breath caress the skin behind her ear and along her cheek as he leaned in for a better look, and before her eyes the dried herbs dissolved as if they had been made of sand.

Zazi and Sam both stepped back, and Sam said, "Oh, man. Did I do that?"

"It's okay," Connie said. "It was bound to happen."

She blew a soft stream of air between her pursed lips, clearing the herb dust from whatever lay underneath. The dust drifted up into the air of the dining room and dissipated, settling in a fine film on the table and floor and tumbling on drafts into corners of the room. The candles flickered.

Under the posies Connie discovered a small packet of papers, tied with a string browned by time, and sealed closed with wax. Next to the papers lay what looked like a coil of twine.

She lifted out the twine, laying it softly in her left palm and examining it in the candlelight.

The twine was made of cotton or possibly hemp, rough to the touch, dried out. She took one end between finger and thumb to test and see if it could be safely uncoiled. The twine felt dry and refused to give. There would be no untangling it. In any case, it didn't seem all that remarkable— she couldn't tell how long it was. All she could say for certain was that it had three knots tied in it.

"String?" asked Zazi.

"I guess." Connie tipped her palm and slid the coil of twine gently onto the dining table.

"What's that for?" Sam asked.

"Dunno," said Connie.

She next turned her attention to the packet of papers, peeling it up with two fingers and lifting it out to place it on the tabletop next to the orange pebble and the string.

"Letters?" said Zazi.

"Could be," said Connie.

"Love letters," Sam said.

Connie laughed. "Maybe so. Maybe so."

She tilted her head to the side, looking for a way to open the papers without disturbing the seal. She couldn't see one. She'd either have to break the seal or cut the twine. Or both. Probably both. She hated to disturb an artifact like this, to destroy it in the name of learning about it. But she would have to. This had to be the recipe she was looking for. This had to be what Temperance had gone to so much trouble to hide.

How could she open the packet while minimizing the damage? Connie didn't know. She needed help. Help from someone with experience working with very old, very rare, very fragile documents. Someone with tools and skill and proper lighting.

Dr. Elizabeth Dowers of the Harvard University Art Museums, for example.

"Liz will know what to do with these," Connie said. "I can take them into Cambridge tomorrow."

"There's something else." Zazi lifted the candle higher.

Sure enough, under the tied packet of papers lay an envelope. Using two fingernails, Connie lifted it out. There was no writing on it. It was yellowed, as though stained by water, and crisp from drying. It was still sealed. And there was something odd about the shape. Most envelopes from this period weren't envelopes per se—they were just folded sheets of paper, also sealed with wax. There was no standard shape, though they generally wound up rectangular, as modern envelopes were, because of the shapes of the leaves of paper.

This one was a triangle.

"Has it been cut?" Connie asked.

"Yeah." Zazi reached forward and ran a fingertip along the edge. "It's been sliced in half. On the diagonal."

Connie held the envelope aloft. There was a sheet of thick paper inside, and something else.

"Phaugh," said Sam, lifting his knuckle to his nose.

He was right. The envelope had a strange smell. Not bad, exactly. At least, Connie didn't think it was so bad. Sort of sickly sweet and dry. Like rose petals, long dead. Or stagnant water.

"How odd." Connie turned the half envelope in the candlelight. "I wonder what's inside?"

"Is it heavy?" Zazi asked.

"Sort of," said Connie. "Heavier than if it were just paper."

"Heavier than parchment?"

"I don't know. Maybe. I'll take it to Liz too, and see what she thinks."

"Who's Liz?" asked Zazi.

"My friend from grad school." Connie peered into the box to see if anything else was inside. "She's a medievalist. Works on rare books and manuscripts."

"Cool," said Zazi.

"Well," said Connie. "That's everything."

"There's nothing else?" said Sam. He sounded disappointed.

"Nope," said Connie. She ran a hand lovingly along the open lid, with its rough carved interlocking circles and *T J H* monogram, thinking she might clean it with some lemon oil and get it polished and gleaming and happy-looking.

"Wait," said Zazi.

She stuck a finger into the box and brought it back up, rubbing finger and thumb together critically. When she opened her finger and thumb they were dirty.

"That's not everything," Zazi said.

"What else is there?" asked Connie.

"Dirt," said Zazi, holding out the finger and thumb as evidence.

"Well, sure," said Connie. "It's been stuck in a wall for God knows how long. I'd be surprised if it wasn't dirty."

"No," said Zazi, shaking her head. "It's not dirty. It *contains dirt*."

Connie reached into the box. Her fingertips sank into a long-dried layer of what could only be called dirt. It was about an inch deep. Clotted and crumbly.

"Weird," Connie said. She pressed here and there, groping to see if there was anything hidden in the layer of dirt. It occurred to her that witch bottles often had pins and nails in them, and if there were rusted pins and nails hidden in there she could get tetanus, and that would suck. She pulled her hand out quickly, wiping the residue on her jeans.

"You mean, someone put dirt in there on purpose?" said Sam.

Zazi's brows were furrowed, her dark eyes staring at an idea that neither of the others could see.

"What is it?" Connie prodded her with an elbow.

Zazi blinked. "I don't know. It's just, I didn't think they did that up here."

"Did what?" said Connie, and Sam said, "Yeah, what?"

Zazi pulled on a spiral curl and let it spring back into place.

"Nothing. Just, I wonder if it could be goopher dust."

Connie said, "No way. You think?"

She tipped the box nearer the candle, spilling light into all four corners. The dirt just looked like dirt. The same nondescript blackish-gray dirt that lay under the tangled knots of the garden outside. The same dirt that was clinging to the soles of her boots in the front hall. The same that tinted Arlo's paws a steady shade of gray.

"What's goopher dust?" asked Sam.

"It's kind of dark," said Zazi, eyeing him as though to gauge his appetite for darkness.

"It's graveyard dirt," explained Connie.

"It's *what*?" Sam took an involuntary step backward, startling Arlo, who was standing at perfect trip height behind their clustered legs.

"Told you." Zazi smiled. "Dark, right?"

"I haven't ever heard of that in the Northeast," said Connie. "It's African in origin, right?"

"Well, yeah," said Zazi. "But it's not like there weren't any African people around here then."

"True," said Connie.

"You said yourself, this stuff moves around. The sieve and scissors? You found it in early modern New England. And I found it in the twentieth-century South," Zazi pointed out. "Syncretism," she said to Sam. "That's why I love it. Folk magic makes for strange bedfellows."

"Not half as strange as the fact that you just said 'bedfellows,'" remarked Connie.

Zazi took up a pinch of the dirt and crumbled it into her palm.

"So how do we tell if that's what it is?" Sam cast a wary eye at the otherwise unremarkable dirt inside the box.

"My guess is, we don't. Unless there're shards of bone in there." As soon as Connie said it, she wished she hadn't. Odd herbs and stones she could deal with. Reliquaries, not so much. There was something too intimate, too uncanny, about earth imbued with the deconstructed remnants of long dead people. Which was ridiculous. That's all dirt was, after all. Deconstructed remnants. The residue of life.

Ashes to ashes.

"Gross," said Sam.

All at once a wave of fatigue rose, crested, and broke over Connie. She felt like a wind-up toy twisted past the last forgiving curve of its internal spring.

She looked around, in the serene unreal cloud of crushing fatigue, the early evening sun slanting through the dining room windows, and seized upon the film of posy residue that she had scattered across the floor, illuminated by the raking light.

"I'll get a broom," she said, voice sounding hollow and far away in her ears. To Zazi, she said, "You want to stay for dinner?"

Zazi glanced between Connie and Sam. "I ought to be getting back."

"You sure?" said Sam, pressing the way people press because they feel that they should.

Zazi said, "Yeah. Thanks, though." To Connie, she added, "I've got a cover letter to work on."

Connie smiled weakly at this encyclopedia of southern folk magic masquerading as a curly-headed grad student in beat-up jeans and mismatched socks. Graveyard dust. Connie had just learned about graveyard dust within the past year.

Zazi bent and scratched Arlo behind his ears. His tail helicoptered; then he vanished, only to reappear at the front door, waiting to wag her goodbye.

"So listen," Zazi said as she laced up her boots, "if you're in the Square tomorrow, let me know what you find out, okay?"

"Okay," promised Connie. "And we need to make a time to talk about your letter." She was so tired she couldn't feel her feet. Dr. Belanger had told her that the fatigue might be substantial. Connie hadn't believed her. Or at least, Connie thought grad school had given her a unique insight into what fatigue could be. But she'd never felt anything like this. Fatigue that was crushing. Fatigue that rose up before her eyes and clouded them and made her brain feel detached from her body.

"Thanks, Professor G," Zazi said, adding, "It was nice to meet you, Sam."

"Yeah, you too," Sam said.

Zazi closed the front door behind her, and in a moment, they heard her Zipcar start up and pull away.

Connie sank into one of the dining room chairs and said, "I think I'm going to pass out."

Sam went into the kitchen and emerged holding the vintage broom Granna had stashed there sometime in the 1960s. It was homemade, a slender knotty branch with rushes or some other kind of dried marsh grass knotted at the end.

"You think so? Just take a minute. Breathe." He crouched next to her, his fingers moving into the hair at the nape of her neck.

Connie folded her arms on the dining table and rested her forehead on them. The waistband of her jeans dug into her belly, and she undid the top button with a sigh.

"Maybe you should lie down," he said.

Connie let Sam ease her up out of the chair and wind her arm around his shoulders.

"Yes, please," she muttered into his neck. He smelled good. Furniture polish and turpentine.

"Come on," he said, tightening his grip around her waist.

"Wait." She eased the portrait door closed, hiding Temperance's secret. It felt wrong, leaving the cabinet open. As if she were leaving Temperance naked and exposed. The cabinet clicked back into place.

"Okay." Connie leaned on Sam. "Let's go. I'm wiped."

They made it to the hall and started up the winding stair, one step at a time, with Connie's only thoughts being of the claw-footed bathtub in Granna's old powder room, and pajama pants, and falling asleep with her head on Sam's stomach, listing to the reassuring rhythms of aliveness pulsing under his skin. The lug of his heartbeat and the soft gurgling of life.

Chapter Seventeen

∽

Cambridge, Massachusetts

Late April

2000

"*Inside* the wall?" Liz exclaimed. "You're kidding me, right?"

"I wish," said Connie. She had slept for more than eleven hours in her mother's double bed, sprawled like a skydiver with an arm draped over Sam's chest; still, fatigue stalked behind her and dragged on her like weights around her ankles. She propped her chin in her hand, eagle stone knocking against her wrist.

"So," said Liz, applying a pair of magnifying eyeglasses to her nose. "Let's see what we've got here."

Liz had met Connie in the atrium of the Fogg Museum at Harvard and signed her in to the manuscripts and works on paper department with a nametag and Connie's old grad school ID. Now they clustered around a clean, brightly lit worktable in the center of a preservation studio, lit by tall north-facing windows and recessed fluorescent lights. The walls were a museumy dove-gray, with white pine floors. Liz's desk stood off in a corner, with a wide flat computer monitor and several mesh canisters bristling with brushes and arcane tools. Four worktables stood evenly spaced within the room, each with lights on flexible metal arms, and a large adjustable magnifying glass on a stand, like something out of a horror film set in a dentist's office.

Liz spread out a roll of very fine pale suede, which she fastened down to the worktable at the corners, creating a soft, nonslippery surface.

"Ready," she said.

Connie put her shoulder bag in her lap, opened it, and pulled out a manila file folder. Inside was the sealed packet of letters and the triangular envelope from Temperance's monogrammed box.

"Manila? Connie, come on," chided Liz.

"I didn't have anything nonacidic," Connie apologized.

Liz turned her eyes heavenward and mouthed something that looked like *You see what I have to put up with?*

"At least it's not being stored under a bunch of rotting herbs and on top of dirt anymore!" Connie protested.

"I'm just teasing," said Liz. She snapped on a pair of latex gloves and laid the manila folder on the table in front of her. She opened the folder and clicked on the light under the movable magnifying glass. Gently, carefully, Liz settled first the packet of letters, then the envelope on the roll of suede and maneuvered the light and magnifying glass into position to take a look.

"How old did you say they were supposed to be?"

"Jacksonian," said Connie.

"Looks like it," Liz said. "See the pattern of the fibers in the paper? It's cotton."

Connie looked through the glass and said, "Um. Sure?"

"Goof," said Liz. "Also you can kind of tell by the color of the ink. Now. Let's see how we can get these suckers open."

Liz took up a slender metal probe and prodded the wax seal gently. She tested the tension of the string. And she lifted the cut edge of the envelope, seeing if it had any give.

"Usually," she said, "I'd use steam. But I think . . ."

She put down the metal instrument and picked up another one. This one looked like a thin, flexible, doll-sized spatula.

Liz hunched over the magnifying glass, Connie peering over her shoulder.

"Hey, Dr. Dowers? You going to lunch?" a young woman asked from the doorway of Liz's office, bag over her shoulder and museum ID tag on a lanyard around her neck. She looked about twenty-five—old enough for eyeglasses, young enough that her blouse gapped a little around the buttons.

"Nah," called Liz. "I'll get something later."

"Okay," the girl—her assistant?—said and shut the door behind her.

"*Doctor* Dowers," teased Connie.

"Listen," said Liz, "after all the crap I had to take in grad school, you bet everyone's calling me Doctor. I'll get my cabdriver to do it if I can. I'll make my *mother* do it."

"And the guys you date?"

"Definitely," Liz said. "They love it. Guys *love* women who are educated and successful and self-sufficient. Don't they?"

Their eyes met over the adjustable magnifying glass, and they started giggling. Liz had to put the spatula down.

"Speaking of," said Liz, bringing the light on its flexible arm down lower over the suede, brightening the circle of light around the envelope, "Samuel going to make an honest woman of you? If you're doing it in June, you better hurry. Places get booked up."

Connie's shirt was bloused out around the top of her jeans. Underneath, the jeans button was undone and the zipper half down. The truth was, Connie and Sam had stopped talking about it. They carried on in their lives together, alluding to marriage in coded terms. Making vague plans. It was as though Sam could see into her own denial, could see past it, and respond to the hidden part of her, the part that she seemed to be working so hard to hide from herself.

Connie didn't answer. She traced the webbing of her tote bag's shoulder strap with one thumb.

"Okay, okay," said Liz, turning her attention back to the document. "Motion tabled until the next session."

Connie released the shoulder strap and hooked her thumb under the woven twine bracelet around her wrist. She worried it, but it didn't loosen.

Liz resumed her gentle probing of the sealed papers as if nothing had been said.

"So what's the verdict?" asked Connie after a time.

"The thing about sealing wax," Liz said through her nose as she worked, "is that it can get hard and brittle with age. But that works to our advantage. Steaming would soften it. And that's not what we want."

She slid the spatula against the edge of the wax seal and worked it gently, but insistently, where the wax clung to the paper.

"Come on," she whispered.

Then Connie heard a soft crack.

"Gotcha," said Liz.

She had managed to work the tiny spatula under the seal and lift it completely free of the paper. In one piece. Without tearing the paper underneath.

"Very impressive, Dr. Dowers," said Connie.

"Thank you, thank you," said Liz. She put the spatula aside and took up two long, finely pointed sets of tweezers. "Now for my next trick."

Through the magnifying glass Connie watched Liz affix one tweezer to a coil of the knot in the twine and grasp hold of the other part of the knot with the other tweezer. Liz applied mild pressure, seeing if she could work the threads apart.

They didn't budge.

"Bah," said Liz under her breath. She adjusted the grip of the tweezers on the knot and tried again.

Still, nothing.

"Cut it," said Connie.

"Are you sure?" asked Liz, eyebrows rising.

"It's just string."

"But it's—" Liz looked up from the magnifying glass.

"Cut it," said Connie.

"If you say so."

Liz laid her tweezers aside and took up a razor blade in her gloved fingers.

"Here goes nothing," she said.

Under the magnifying glass, the razor blade loomed into view, bit into the resisting string, and sliced through. The string sprang away from itself.

Connie's breath caught in her throat.

"You realize," said Liz, "that that actually caused me physical pain. As a museum person."

"I know. You're very brave," said Connie.

Liz used the tweezers to inch the string away from the packet of papers, drawing it and the clotted wax seal away completely and laying it aside.

"Now," said Liz. "The fun part."

She laid aside the instruments and, using her gloved fingers, softly, carefully unfolded the sheaf of papers. They crinkled in protest, fibers long locked in place unbending, thinking about breaking but not doing it.

"Hand me that weight?" Liz said.

Connie dragged over a snakelike object that proved to be a suede sock full of sand. Heavy enough to hold curling pages down.

After a minute of gentle rearrangement, the paper opened itself to them like a flower, weighted down at the top and bottom. What had looked like a sheaf of papers was actually one single large sheet, folded many times over until thick.

On the paper was written a long list of numbers and words, under a strange heading.

"What's weather work?" asked Liz.

"We're about to find out," said Connie, leaning in, hungry to see. The handwriting was pretty good, all things considered. Temperance must have had some schooling. Or else a very attentive mother and a house full of books.

Here is what the list said:

E L u I
The Surest Form of the Weather Work
To be used only in the purest extremity
With great care
Or not at all
1 Corallus

3 Knots
5 tincture of Smallage
7 Wolf-Bane
9 Cinque-Foil
1 Hen-bane
3 Hemlock
5 Mandrake, Moon-shade, or other Night-shade
7 Tobacco
9 Opium
1 Saffron
3 Poplar-leaves
5 Pileus naturalis
7 Fat of Children digged out their Graves
9 Dust of ought the strongest sort
First to hold, and next untie, then to boil, then to die.
As it grows, supplant beneath the sea,
So harden it to rocket 'pon the air
Thus upon aliveness so decree,
From here, blest be, transport us safe to there.

At the bottom of the page a faint, watery line of text also appeared, but Connie couldn't read what it said.

"What the everlasting hell is this?" said Liz.

Words failed Connie. It was horrifying. Utterly, completely horrifying.

"You're going to put this in your book?" Liz had lifted her hands clear of the paper and pressed her gloved fingertips together.

"Yes?" said Connie.

"Are you sure about this?" Liz dropped her voice. "Honestly. Connie. The book's fine the way it is. It's late anyway. You don't need to put this in."

"Does that say 'Fat of Children digged out their Graves'?" Connie put a hand to her forehead. She felt hot. Almost sweaty. It was the glaring lights of the conservation table. Or the coming summer sun streaming in through the windows.

"Yeah," said Liz, snapping off her latex gloves and chucking them into a garbage can under her desk. "It does."

Connie got to her feet, but immediately her head swam in protest and she sat back down on the stool next to the worktable. "I—" She faltered. "I don't—"

"Listen," said Liz, pulling the weights off the paper and folding it back up with her naked hands, for once unconcerned about damaging the fragile paper. "If I were you, I'd put this right back where you found it and pretend this never happened."

Connie blinked, trying to clear her head. "It's a primary source," she said.

"So what if it's a primary source. This is crazy," said Liz.

Connie straightened. She wanted to object. It wasn't like Liz to suggest overlooking something on purpose, much less hiding it or destroying it. But she couldn't argue with the revulsion that she, too, felt. A wide sickening pool in her stomach, a rancid smell hovering just outside the realm of perceptibility. As if under the bright clean lights of this bright, clean museum, all the wood was rotting.

"Look." Liz put a hand on Connie's arm. "Didn't you tell me that women who were accused as witches were usually on the outskirts of society?"

"Yeah," said Connie. "They were poor, or they didn't have enough children, or . . ."

"Or they were dangerous," finished Liz.

Connie looked into her friend's serious face. The half-dimple was nowhere to be seen.

"Occam's razor," said Liz. "Come on. What makes the most sense? Do you think a sane person wrote this list?"

"But we can't really—" Connie protested.

"Yeah, yeah, we can't legitimately apply current psychoanalytic categories to people living in the past, because they had a different self-concept, blah blah blah." Liz waved her hand in dismissal. "Real talk now. Was this list written by a sane person?"

Connie chewed the inside of her cheek. "I don't know," she said.

"Okay." Liz got up and went over to her desk. "Have it your way."

"What are you doing?" asked Connie.

Liz leaned over her desk, her back to Connie, and jiggled the mouse to wake up her desktop. "Look," she said without looking around. "You know I love you."

Connie got unsteadily to her feet. "I sense a 'but' coming," she said.

"I have kind of a lot of stuff to get done after lunch, so," said Liz.

"You're not going to open the envelope for me?" asked Connie.

"Honestly?" Liz looked back to Connie by the conservation table. "This is really creeping me out."

Connie retrieved the leaf of paper with its hideous list, folded it carefully back into its tight squares, and slid it, together with the waxed string and the unopened envelope, back into the manila folder.

"I'm sorry," Liz said. "It's just too weird. It makes me really uncomfortable."

Connie hesitated, trying to think of something she could say that would persuade Liz to keep helping her. That would tell Liz how important this was to her. Not to her work, but to her actual life. To her life with Sam. To her life with the mysterious being who was dwelling somewhere inside her. Something that wouldn't make Liz more afraid, as afraid as Connie feared the truth would make her.

She couldn't think of anything.

Liz watched, waiting, Connie guessed, for her to leave. When she didn't, Liz got to her feet and pulled a box down from the shelf over her desk.

"At the very least," said Liz, "you can't keep carrying those things around in a manila folder. Gives me a heart attack just thinking about it."

She rummaged in the box and pulled out a small, clean, acid-free archival envelope, the perfect size for carrying Temperance's two bizarre documents in archive-approved safety.

Connie took the envelope and opened it on the conservation table. When she pulled the folded leaf with the recipe on it out of its manila folder to transfer it to its new container, she saw that the ghostly unreadable handwriting at the bottom of the list had actually been writing on the back of the paper, bleeding through the wove.

It read, in the same spidery handwriting as the list:

Cannot work alone.

Chapter Eighteen

Connie hurried from Liz's office, head down, bag with its secret contents knocking against her flanks, across the quad to Widener Library. The cherry tree—she thought it was a cherry tree—by Houghton was heavy with pink blossoms, and the afternoon air had a springlike softness, the midday sunlight through the trees tinted yellow-orange by pollen and the languor that takes hold of college campuses at the end of the semester. She checked her watch—the library would be open for another three hours. That ought to be enough time to get a start on figuring out what all that stuff on Temperance's list was. She recognized a lot of it—at least most of the list was in English. Henbane, always henbane. Saffron. Poplar leaves. Cinquefoil. Many of those things grew in the garden of the Milk Street house.

But a lot of it was incomprehensible. Smallage? Was that a hint about the amounts that should be used? Maybe Temperance was using a kind of homeopathic approach, and "smallage" meant she should use the least amount of each ingredient possible. Maybe. But that was only one of several mysteries on that list.

Opium, for instance. Not a mystery, exactly. But it was pretty hard to get hold of opium these days.

What did the numbers on the left margin mean? And how should she translate the few Latin items on the list? Liz hadn't known what they meant, suggesting they weren't words common enough for a medievalist to know off the top of her head. And the Latin wasn't even the worst part.

Fat of Children digged out their Graves. A chill worked its way up the back of Connie's neck, until her skin felt as though spiders had been set loose along the length of her arms.

That couldn't possibly mean what it said. Temperance had to be talking about something else. An herb. A plant. Maybe a mandrake? Mandrakes looked like little men, so much so that in the Middle Ages it was widely believed they would scream when pulled out of the earth. Maybe that was it—"Children digged out their Graves" could mean mandrakes pulled out of the garden before maturity.

Except that mandrake showed up elsewhere on the list. There was no good reason for it to appear twice.

"Connie!" someone called out from behind her.

Connie hunched her shoulders, not looking around, hoping whoever it was, was talking to someone else.

"Hey! Connie Goodwin!"

Dammit. She turned and was met with the pale, drawn face of Thomas.

"Oh," said Connie. "Hi." Without thinking she drew her shoulder bag in front of her and folded her arms across it.

"Hey! Hi. You haven't answered my email." He pushed his glasses up the bridge of his nose.

"Oh. Yeah. Sorry," said Connie.

"Well?" said Thomas expectantly.

"Well what?" said Connie. Thomas fell into step alongside her, his hands thrust in the pockets of his khakis. She observed that his left ear was scarlet. Only the left one.

"Will you?" said Thomas.

"Will I what?" said Connie, confused, and fighting through a swell of annoyance.

She'd been inundated with emails from her undergrads after she returned their papers, as her students ran the math and figured out what grade they would need to get on the final exam to come out with an A in her course. Would there be review sessions? Would she provide a study guide? Was there an opportunity for extra credit? Could the grade on the paper be discussed? Could it be regraded? In desperation Connie had put on an autoreply and not checked email for a few days. This happened at the end of every semester. No matter how many times she reassured her students that a B would not stand in the way of their going on to live happy, well-adjusted lives, complete with jobs and houses and dogs and loving partners, and that in the long run this one particular grade on this one particular assignment would fail to rate in the catalogue of horrors bested in the course of their young lives, the despair of her students' emails at the end of the semester never failed to overwhelm.

Thomas stopped. "You haven't even read it?"

A chill late-spring breeze stirred the leaves on the Quad, lifting a layer of pink petals from the cherry tree and drifting them over the brick path where Thomas and Connie stood, soft and light as snow.

"I don't have to tell you how swamped I am right now, do I?" Connie said, exasperated. "You've been teaching long enough to understand what it's like. I just got the tenure packet in. I did your conference panel as a favor to Janine. And frankly, that's just the stuff I've told you about."

Connie tightened her grip on her tote bag against the chill. Behind Thomas, a bright yellow Frisbee sailed by and landed, unattended, on the grass.

His crimson ear flush deepened. "Well. It's important."

"What?" said Connie, unable to hide her exasperation. "What's so important that it can't wait until May?"

"I need to know you'll write me a recommendation letter for the Harvard job," said Thomas.

"Thomas—" she began.

"I really need this commitment from you," he said over her coming objection. "I'm the best candidate. I'm the one with most seniority coming out of the program. I mean, you're not applying, are you? You already have a job. A really good one."

That was true. Northeastern was a great job. For all her grousing, Connie loved her students. She loved the campus. She loved the library. She loved that the Museum of Fine Arts was up the road, with its Cecilia Beaux paintings of nineteenth-century Boston clotted with snow. She loved the Green Line trolleys dinging along the avenue, heavy with commuters. She loved her cinderblock office with her floral armchair from grad school and her walls of books. And, if she was honest, she loved that she had a good shot at tenure. With tenure came stability. Academic freedom. Authority. Harvard would offer none of those things. Well, it would offer authority. For the short four or five years anyone in that job would be likely to last.

"I already have the department's support," Thomas continued. "Professor Beaumont is writing for me. And after the grad conference I met with Professor Hayden. He wants some changes to my project, but once I've done them, he says he'll write for me too. I just need one more."

"I think it's premature to be locking down your letters," she said tightly. She tried to walk around him, but he put himself in her way. The ear darkened until it became almost purple.

"Who else has asked you?" Thomas said.

"Look," Connie said. "I've got to get to the library. It's going to close."

"Was it Zazi?" Thomas put a hand on Connie's arm and squeezed. She looked at his hand on her arm, surprised. Behind him, a shaggy-haired boy with bare feet jogged through the petal-dusted grass and retrieved the Frisbee. The boy was laughing, and threw it back wherever it came from with a leap that sent the Frisbee under his leg. Thomas didn't look around. His face was drawn and pale, with no smile lines around his mouth or his eyes. As if he hadn't been able to smile for a very long time.

Connie put her hand over his and gently pried it free from her arm.

"Can we talk about this later? I've got a lot to accomplish today," she said.

"I'm the better candidate," said Thomas, with an edge to his voice.

"You're further along," Connie conceded. But the truth was, she didn't know that he was the better scholar. His dissertation had been dull, and so far, Zazi's work—what Connie had seen of it—was fresh. Innovative.

"I'm the better candidate," he repeated. "I deserve it. I've got more teaching experience than her, and I've presented more papers. She doesn't even have a chapter. Look, it's not like she's not a great scholar. I respect Zazi. But she'll have plenty of other chances. This one is mine."

Thomas's eyes were sharp, almost feverish in their intensity. Connie stared at her old advisee, probing his face, and for the first time she saw that underneath the armor of his arrogance, that fragile carapace of his seeming disregard, Thomas was afraid. He was a postdoc now. Every year he spent on the job market was a year his degree grew more stale. And every year he'd be competing against a whole new crop of freshly minted PhDs. His shelf life was already half gone. His young hazel eyes were ringed underneath, the skin of his cheeks slack with fatigue. He even had a thread or two of gray in his sandy hair. Stress was gnawing him up from the inside.

She thought then of her old advisor, Manning Chilton. The man she had trusted above everyone with the questions and contents of her mind. Trusted, the way Thomas trusted her. Chilton had betrayed her. Tried to take her work for himself. Panicking, in her own fever of desperation, Connie had destroyed a primary source rather than let him have it. She'd thrown it into a fire. The flames consuming the book they both had been hunting for burned like tiny pinpricks in the center of each of Chilton's irises, melting the last few shards of sanity in his mind. There's a perverse intimacy between the mentor and the mentored. Both pretend that the power dynamic is static, both ignore that power waxes and wanes like spring rain.

Connie relented. "I'm not saying no. I'm saying we need to talk about this later. All right?"

Thomas pushed up the eyeglasses again, reflexively, as they hadn't slipped.

"All right," he said. "When?"

"Soon, I promise." Connie shuffled her feet in her desperation to escape. "Okay?" She tightened her grip on the bag.

Thomas's eyes tracked from Connie's face to the bag clutched against her chest. Connie's shoulders drew up as if she could protect the contents of the bag with her body.

"You found something," Thomas said. He was stating it as a fact. "From that code Zazi talked about. At Charlie's. What did you find?"

"Look. I've just got work to do." Connie moved the bag from her chest back down to her side and started walking, Thomas trotting alongside when it was clear she wasn't going to stop.

"Please?" he said, and in his voice Connie heard a glimmer of the curiosity of his undergraduate self. "Can I see?"

"Let's talk later," she said.

"This week," he insisted to her retreating back.

"This week," she agreed.

She felt his eyes on her as she hurried away, another chill breeze kicking up and peeling away the cherry blossom petals, drifting them in eddies along the path around her feet.

The last light in the reading room snapped off, and Connie stretched her arms overhead and bent back over the library chair, feeling her spine pop in two different places. Time to go. She started packing up her notebooks and pencils, carefully refolding the leaf of paper with Temperance's list. She'd made some progress.

Smallage, for instance. Rather than being a unit of measurement, it turned out that "smallage" was a word for wild celery. "Tincture of smallage" meant, essentially, celery broth.

A few puzzles remained, however. The numbers on the left side of the page? Right now her best guess was that the numbers represented both an order of operations and, possibly, a proportion. So one *corallus*—whatever that was—plus three knots—whatever that meant—plus five measures of tincture of smallage, and so on.

Even if that supposition was right, plenty of mysteries didn't seem to have any obvious solutions. *Corallus*, for instance, wasn't an herb. At least, it didn't appear in any of the herbals she had checked.

Same with *pileus naturalis*.

Dust of ought the strongest sort, despite being in English, was as vague as anything she'd seen in Deliverance Dane's physick book. How could dust be strong? What made some dust stronger than other dust?

And she was no closer to understanding the most gruesome-seeming ingredient. She couldn't bear to think about it. In all her reading about the Dane women, she had never seen a hint that they might have actually committed the horrors they were so often accused of.

Connie hung her bag over her shoulder and shuffled out of the reading room. She checked her watch. It was just before six. Sam was still working on the Old North steeple project up in Marblehead, so he wouldn't make it back to Cambridge until late. She could go back to the Green Monster and start on dinner. Or she could swing by the Hong Kong and pick up some Chinese. Mapo tofu and spicy string beans and scallion pancakes. At this thought her stomach gurgled in appreciation. The craving was there, and it wouldn't go away, and Connie decided to give in.

As she moved down Widener's silent marble hallways, Connie passed an old bank of pay phones, all polished wood and brass handles, darkened and forgotten. She cupped her hands around her eyes to peer inside one of the glass doors, and saw that sure enough, the booths still contained telephones. She slipped inside, closed the glass door, fed a quarter into the slot, and dialed the number of the Milk Street house.

"Hello, darling!" Grace answered after half a ring.

"Hi, Mom. How was Kripalu?" Connie pressed her hand to the glass of the booth. It felt cold.

"It hasn't changed a bit," Grace said airily. "Even the food was the same."

"That's good," said Connie. Carob and oat bran and sprouts. And codfish balls. Connie's childhood on the commune had been flavored with equal parts New England and New Age. Silence descended between them as Connie considered Grace's cooking, such as it was, and that she could actually go for a codfish ball, now that she thought about it.

"Did you and Sam have a nice week up here? Thanks for taking in the mail," Grace tried.

"Oh, yes," said Connie. "Thanks."

She wrapped the telephone cord around her thumb. The eagle stone rattled. A weird artifact of the past, aiming at the future. An intrusive, constrictive contradiction. Not unlike Grace herself.

"I like that I can tell when you've been in the house," Grace said. "Everything on the desk in tidy piles."

"Mom?" Connie paused. "Can I ask you something?"

"Shoot," said Grace. In the background on her end of the line, the front door creaked open. She liked to lean in the doorway and survey the springtime evening sky between the greening vines over the garden. Connie could picture it as clearly as if she were standing in the sitting room, watching Grace gaze out the front door.

"You seem really up on your Linnaean terminology," Connie began.

"Mm-hmm," said Grace, and from the tone of her voice Connie knew her eyes were closed, so she could breathe in the loamy smell of the garden wakening in spring. Grace used to say that you could smell spring before you could see it.

"Do you know what *pileus naturalis* means?" Connie asked.

Down the hall, Connie heard heavy doors opening and the commanding voice of a security guard calling, "Library's closed!" Another door slammed. Echoes of tired students' shuffling feet.

"Why are you asking?" Grace said, her voice light.

"Do you know?"

"Yes," said Grace, with a tightness in her voice. Grace was rarely tight. When she dropped out of Radcliffe to marry Leonard, she had left all tightness behind. Tight collars, tight knee socks, the tightness of a narrow Massachusetts life. But she couldn't deny who she was, any more than Connie could. The tightness lay inside Grace, waiting.

Connie heard down the telephone line a robin's chirp, stretching his voice for the first time that season. Followed by the sound of leaves lifting on an evening breeze.

"Can you tell me?" Connie asked.

"I suppose," said Grace, still with that strange uncanny distance in her voice. "If you really want to know."

"Please. Yes," Connie said. "I want to know."

Grace said, "It's a caul."

Connie wasn't sure she'd heard correctly. A call?

"No, a *caul*," said Grace, as if Connie had voiced her confusion out loud. "Now. Suppose you tell me why you're asking?"

"Why would anybody want that?" Connie said.

Grace laughed gently. "You know, for a historian, there's an awful lot you don't know."

"Mom." Connie's fist closed around the telephone cord.

"In my day, some of us thought it was important to bury the afterbirth," Grace said. Connie could tell that she had stepped out through the front door into the garden, the phone cord unspooling behind her. Faint grating of herb shrubs against Grace's jeans cuffs. "I planted yours under the rosebush. I can see it from where I'm standing."

Connie knew which rosebush she meant. She'd clipped blossoms from it and arranged them in a coffee can in the sitting room, leaning her nose close enough to breathe in the delicate aroma, soft as a baby's skin.

"Cauls are important, my dear," Grace continued. "Anyone born with one intact is bound to be a powerful person. Oftentimes they have second sight. Or they're able to do things with technique the likes of which haven't been seen before. Back in the old days, cauls were considered very powerful good luck charms. Midwives would save them."

"Ew!" Connie exclaimed.

Grace laughed gently. "They were very valuable. For sailors especially."

"Why sailors?" Connie's mind's eye turned to the boats moored in Marblehead harbor, a few minutes' walk from Milk Street. The harbor was full, boats tied up so close together you could almost cross to the Neck by hopping from bow to stern. They were mostly yachts now, though a small lobster fleet pressed on, undaunted by the coming twenty-first century. But in the old days—in Temperance's day—the harbor would have held a fishing fleet. Bringing cod, from the Grand Banks, or lobsters. Salem and Beverly had the China clippers, their holds full of cow skins and guano and rum. But Marblehead had fish.

"Perhaps because they came out over the baby's nose," Grace said. "Or held in the birth waters. Hard to say. For whatever reason, cauls were prized by sailors. To guard against drowning."

Connie hunted in her shoulder bag for the archival folder Liz had given her. She wedged the phone receiver under her chin and cracked the folder open. With finger and thumb, she pulled out the dried and discolored envelope she'd found in Temperance's hidden weather work box.

The unlabeled one that had been sliced in half. As if whatever was inside had been half-used.

The one with a strange and unplaceable smell.

Pileus naturalis, the recipe said.

"Constance," Grace broke in. "Is there something you want to tell me?"

Connie inhaled sharply.

"On second thought, don't tell me," Grace said.

"What?" Connie was confused.

"You're obviously not ready to talk about it," Grace said. "I can tell by your color. It's all right. It can wait."

Connie pinched the skin at the bridge of her nose. Grace was talking about her aura—that was what she meant when she said color. Not the flush of her cheeks or the sheen on her pale eye. The invisible cloud of whatever it was Grace thought she was able to see around people. Well, Grace wasn't right all the time.

"I found Temperance's recipe for the weather work," Connie said quietly. "It was in a secret compartment behind her portrait in the dining room. The recipe is pretty long and obscure, but I think—I think Temperance solved the problem. Temperance Hobbs had both. Her husband outlived her." Connie swallowed. "He outlived her to an almost impossible degree. He didn't die 'til he was a hundred and ten. A hundred and ten!"

An exhaled breath sighed its way down the telephone lines.

"Constance," Grace said carefully. "Are you sure you know what you're doing?"

"What do you mean, am I sure?"

The air in the phone booth was close and warm; Connie stood there in her coat, her bag dragging on her shoulder until the muscle under her scapula twinged in protest. She shifted her weight from one foot to the other and flexed her toes inside her boots. Her toes were swollen.

"All right," Grace said slowly. "But I want you to consider."

"There's nothing to consider," Connie said.

"Consider what it must have cost," Grace insisted. "Not just her. Recipes this powerful . . . sometimes, they have ripple effects. Things one doesn't anticipate. Things one can't control."

Was Grace talking about the pain? Connie had felt the pain before.

"It's okay," Connie said with resolve. "I'm ready. I'm not afraid."

"Not yet," Grace said.

A fist banged on the glass door of the phone booth, and Connie nodded at the security guard outside the door, who shouted, "Come on, miss, library's closed!" She raised a finger to show she would be off in one minute, but the guard said, "Now!" and stalked off.

"The library's closing. Love you, Mom," Connie said, eyeing the darkening hallway outside the phone booth.

"But soon," said Grace.

Chapter Nineteen

Cambridge, Massachusetts

Late April

2000

The next morning in the kitchen of their apartment, a mug of cold coffee in her hand, Connie stood staring into the middle distance at nothing.

"Are you okay?" Sam whisked a couple of eggs together with a fork and dumped them into a frying pan on the stove. They sizzled. "Don't take this the wrong way, but you look terrible."

Connie rubbed under her eye with her fingertips and felt the texture of her skin there, slack with fatigue. Her sleep had gotten worse. After Sam's reading light went out each night, Connie would lie on her back and stare at the egg-and-dart molding, listening to the creakings and rustlings of the Green Monster around her. Muffled voices through the plaster walls. Footsteps on the stairs. Sara crashing home to the apartment abutting their kitchen wall, screaming at someone on the phone. Rap music three floors up, beats palpable through the floor. Undergrads outside on Massachusetts Avenue, shouting. Normally these murmurings, these thrums of life that swelled within and without the apartment building, innervating it, receded to become the background noise of everyday life. But for some reason now the sounds stalked into Connie's attention.

"Thanks." She slurped from her mug of lukewarm decaf coffee. "Just tired, I guess. God, I miss real coffee."

Sam shoved a spatula under the cooking omelet, ripping it as he flipped it over. A thread of half-cooked egg spattered the counter. "How many more days of class?" he asked. He held out his hand, and when Connie didn't move from her spot by the sink, he snapped the dishrag off the refrigerator handle and wiped up the egg.

"Um," Connie hunted around in the mental version of her datebook. "May Day," she said when she found it. "That's the final. I have one lecture left."

"Mayday," said Sam. "That's funny." He spatulaed half the omelet onto one plate and half onto another, which he set with some force onto the counter at Connie's elbow. He took his own plate up and ate, leaning over the sink. Late.

Connie laughed weakly.

"You're pushing yourself too hard," Sam insisted through a mouthful of egg. "And there's no good reason for it."

She looked into her coffee mug.

"What if you didn't go in today?" Sam set his empty plate on the floor, where Arlo appeared to inspect for leftovers.

"I have office hours," Connie objected.

"Have the kids email you," he said, picking up the other plate and trying to put it into her hands.

The grounds at the bottom of Connie's mug had collected in the whorl of a tiny galaxy. Was it possible to read the future in coffee grounds, as in tea leaves?

The truth was, she didn't have office hours.

"I have to be there," she said.

Sam picked up a hank of her bark-colored hair, hanging loose and sleep-rumpled over her shoulders, and coiled it around his finger. When he let go, it uncoiled itself.

"All right. But take it easy," he said. His hands rested on top of her shoulders, his fingers in her hair.

"I'll try," she said.

He planted a kiss on top of her head and said, "See you tonight."

The weather was gray and dismal, a day of wet flower petals collecting in the gutters of Cambridge and sodden boots. Connie squinted through the windshield of the Volvo, through the rivulets streaming down the glass and the thudding of the windshield wipers, trying to read unfamiliar street names. A Mapquest printout sat in a wrinkled heap on the passenger seat next to her, and she plucked it up and held it against the steering wheel, upside down, then right side up.

Also on the seat next to her sat a small bouquet of tulips, hothouse yellow and white.

She was lost. She knew the place she was looking for was in Belmont, a sedate professorial suburb next to Cambridge, where houses with peaked roofs and blank windows watched on guard for unfamiliar cars, holding themselves in dystopian aloofness from the blur of Harvard Square. Somewhere within this sylvan enclave of secret wealth, with its pebbled driveways and gardens of larkspur and lilac and perfect putting-green grass, at the end of a long winding drive, atop a grassy green dotted with chestnut trees that flamed red in autumn, stood a complex of sprawling yellow-and-white wedding-cake houses that housed Ivy League–caliber minds gone mad.

McLean Hospital was famous, sort of. It had a legacy of glamour, of two hundred years of pacing poets and cracked intellectuals, people whose brilliance had burned a hole in their minds. When the greatest thinkers of New England went awry, McLean was where they went.

If Sam or Liz figured out what she was up to with this Temperance recipe stuff, Connie wouldn't be too surprised to find herself there one day.

She put on her blinker, passing a stacked stone wall, into what looked like a well-mown private park. The grassy slopes were perfect, and deserted. Even the birds roosted more quietly at McLean.

As the Volvo rolled over gentle swells, Connie mulled over what she hoped to learn from this probably misguided expedition. While plenty of the things on Temperance's list still needed explanation, only one item still required definition—*corallus*.

Grace had claimed to not know what it was.

Connie could usually tell by subtle shifts in tone when Grace was lying. In this case, she hadn't detected that telltale tonal rise. Connie felt certain if it had been an herb, Grace would have known what it was. And even if Grace didn't want to tell her, Connie should have been able to find it in one of the herbals. But it was nowhere.

That left the possibility that *corallus* was an element. Or perhaps a kind of rock. The kind of substance called for in alchemical work, rather than in the techniques that the untutored commonly referred to as witchcraft.

Connie knew of only one person who had absolute command over alchemical knowledge. That person was her former advisor, Manning Chilton.

Chilton's nominal specialty had been, like Connie's, the history of the colonial period in English North America. She had gone to Harvard specifically to work with him, and he had taken her under his—not wing, exactly, unless wings were made of tweed. Tutelage. Shepherding her through an oral exam that still made her shudder to recall it. He urged her to challenge herself in her dissertation research. He broadened her mind. And then . . .

Near the end of Connie's long sojourn in graduate school, his true scholarly passion had been revealed: early modern alchemy, the theory that held that substances could be perfected through chemical manipulation, and that so could the human soul. One awful night, the summer she started her dissertation research, Chilton had appeared at the Milk Street house, unhinged, threatening, wanting to take Connie's research for himself, his mind warped by years of exposure to mercury, or so they said afterward. When the Harvard history department discovered he had expanded his inquiries from the theoretical to the physical, poisoning both his body and his mind in the process, he'd been quietly removed from the faculty. It was common knowledge that Chilton—whatever might be left of the eminent Brahmin scholar he had once been—was living out his remaining days, such as they were, in McLean.

In the years since their rift, Connie had grown into a scholar and mentor in her own right. Now on the other side of the conference table, Connie saw the unease and confusion with which young scholars approached their apprenticeships. Her students often didn't know what a mentor was supposed to be. A friend? A parent? Neither of those things, of course. But in moments of uncharacteristic self-analysis, Connie could admit Chilton's sway over her had been tangled up with a relational void in her life. Even today, the smell of pipe tobacco made Connie burn with fear of disappointing him.

It was the primary reason she had never gone to visit him.

Unless the real reason was that she was afraid.

Would Chilton see her? Connie didn't know.

If nothing else, she thought with grim certainty, there was no way he would have forgotten her.

Ahead Connie spotted the tidy white-and-yellow house that served as the main administration building of the hospital complex. She rolled to a stop, creaked up the parking brake, and leaned her head back in the seat with her eyes closed.

What if he wouldn't see her?

Connie stared grimly out at the sodden lawn rolling away from the parking lot. A wet willow sagged under the springtime rain, its tendrils stirring softly.

There was no choice.

He would have to tell her.

Connie got out of the car, tucking the tulips under her arm, pale eyes darkening as if they'd taken up shreds of rain cloud from outside, and tiny storms were brewing inside each iris.

"Are you family?" asked the woman at the reception desk.

"Am I? No," said Connie, writing her name in the visitor log. She accepted a visitor pass and read something odd in the woman's expression.

"You haven't been to see Professor Chilton before?" the woman said.

Connie wasn't sure whether she was an administrator or a nurse. She could have been either. Professional and brusque. Protective.

"No, I haven't," Connie said, pinning the pass to the lapel of her blazer.

The woman didn't elaborate. She was bent over the check-in desk, writing directions down on a small slip of paper. She ripped the directions from the pad and held the sheet out for Connie to take. But when Connie grasped the paper, the woman didn't release it immediately.

"Try not to register any surprise," she said. "When you see him."

"Surprise," Connie echoed.

"He finds it very upsetting," the woman added.

Connie hesitated.

"Of course," Connie said.

The woman released the paper.

"Visiting hours are over at four," she said.

Connie's footsteps echoed on a plain institutional hallway that smelled clean and freshly bleached. The directions the woman had written down directed Connie to a private room, in a building apparently given over to long-term residents. Most of the doors she passed were open. People idling on beds, reading books. Some in hospital-issued gowns, some in pajamas. A girl with a shaved head playing solitaire. A boy with tattoos on his neck doing pushups between two twin beds. Several doors away, a muffled scream.

It was the last room at the end of the hall, a corner room, its door partway open. The room next door seemed to be empty. This end of the hallway was quiet.

Connie crushed the tulip bouquet to her chest, lifted her hand, and rapped softly on the door.

"Come in," said a familiar voice, grown graveled with age.

Connie pushed the door open.

The room was neat and unassuming. A hospital bed, made up tightly. A nightstand with a brass reading lamp, some old leather-bound books, and a carafe of water. On the wall, in an elaborate gilt frame, a seascape of Boston harbor crowded with ships at dusk, painted sometime in the nineteenth century. The painting was all soft pinks and oranges, with clumps of pure white pigment for sea foam and smudges of blue and black in place of faces on the ships.

"Well, well," said a stooping figure sitting backlit by the window. "Now this is a surprise."

Connie stepped inside.

"Professor Chilton," she said, her voice sounding stronger than it felt.

The figure was shrunken, bent almost double, knobbed knees together, elbows on the armrests of a wheelchair. Her old advisor wore pressed pin-stripe pajamas and a velvet dressing gown with a crest embroidered over the breast pocket. Soft leather slippers. He reached down and adjusted the wheels of the chair, creaking himself away from the window and into the light.

Connie hoped her horror didn't show on her face.

His weathered mouth pulled down at the corners. His eyes narrowed.

He saw her horror.

And he hated her for it.

Professor Manning Chilton looked as if he had aged thirty years, instead of nine. His body had withered in on itself. His cheeks were sunken, his eyes were ringed with darkness, the skin pouched and sallow, as though he hadn't slept in years. He was barely in his seventies. But he looked like living death. Connie didn't want to step closer. Her inner animal cringed away from him, from this space, from the unseen horrors lurking in this room.

Perhaps that was why the room next to his was empty. Perhaps other human animals could smell the contagion that haunted him.

She forced herself to take another step inside and held out the tulips in front of her like a talisman.

He wheeled nearer. Staring at her.

"I brought these for you," she said.

Chilton grunted and wheeled himself the few inches back to look out the window.

"How kind," he said darkly.

Connie set the flowers on the nightstand, not seeing an obvious vase or container to put them into.

"So, my girl." Chilton laid a bony finger alongside his temple, stroking the withered skin. "You're looking well."

Inside his tone lurked something—Connie couldn't tell if it was judgment or envy. Perhaps both.

"Thank you," she said. There was a red damask armchair situated near the painting, with a matching tasseled footstool. Should she sit? Should she wait for him to invite her to sit?

"To what do I owe this unexpected honor?" he said. His voice sounded ragged. Almost torn from fatigue. He coughed, a deep pipe smoker's hack, and recovered himself. "This visit from the celebrated professor Constance Goodwin?"

Connie hadn't realized that Chilton was following her career.

"Northeastern's a fine school," Chilton continued. "And you're up for tenure, no less." He leaned his head back to gaze down his long patrician nose out the window at a rosebush dotted with tight green knots of buds. "But no book yet. One wonders what you're waiting for."

Connie decided to sit. She perched on the edge of the damask armchair, hands clasped over her knees. It smelled distinguished and old, like dust and lemon oil soap. She imagined it had been taken out of his Back Bay townhouse. Together with the painting, and his books. A meager corner of the life to which Chilton had been born, and which he believed to be his by right.

"Best make it quick," he continued, tracing the armrest of his chair with a fingertip. "We don't have much time."

Connie said, "How much?"

He toyed with a loose thread of his dressing gown and said, "Don't you know?"

The fingers of Connie's right hand were twisting and untwisting the eagle stone around her wrist, digging the knotted twine into her skin. Knots. Knotted twine.

"I wanted to ask you a question," she began.

"Ah," said Chilton. "Very well. I thought you might. It should be Thomas."

"Thomas?" Connie said. The knots tightened in her grip, purpling her wrist.

"To support for my former chair," Chilton said, ripping off the errant thread, examining it in the thin afternoon light, and releasing it to drift to the floor. "It's obvious it should be Thomas."

"That wasn't my question," she said.

"Well," he said. "It certainly can't be you. Not without your book done."

Connie released the knotted twine and flexed her fingers as blood rushed into her hand. The skin grew hot. "I considered it," she said.

"You'd have wasted your time." He resumed petting the armrest of the wheelchair. *As you wasted mine*, he didn't say. "But no matter. We can't all profess at Harvard, now, can we? Sometimes the best we can hope for is proximity to stardom. Thomas, for instance. That is a special young man."

He creaked his chair a quarter turn, to gaze up at the painting.

"Do you like it?" he asked.

She followed his gaze. Nests of masts crowded together in Boston harbor at the gloaming, when the water assumes the white-gray sheen of an opal or moonstone. In the foreground a small gig with two blurry figures rode over a cresting wave. The light was well handled, the work a Luminist precursor of Impressionism. But the proportions were off. The stern transom of the gig skewed at the wrong angle to the hull. Its sails filled with wind coming from the wrong direction, according to the waves. The artist understood texture and light without understanding space and depth.

"It's fine, I suppose," she said.

"You are correct. It *is* fine. It is very fine indeed." Chilton wheeled nearer, the afternoon light moving over his cheek. "Look at the delicacy of the light. That sheen in the air. That, my girl, is a fineness that only a true Americanist can appreciate. Its fineness is invisible to those who don't truly love it. To those not in a position to appreciate all that is truly fine, in American history. Those without a deep connection to the soil."

Perhaps this was a symptom of Chilton's poisoned mind, this rambling. This inattention. By her count she had already been there for four minutes, give or take. How many did that leave? Not quite ten?

"Professor Chilton," she said, "I'm in final revisions on my book. The one based on my dissertation. And I want to include a recipe I just found. But I need to know what one of the ingredients is. It's not an herb. I think it's a kind of stone. Like what would have been used in alchemy. I need your help."

Chilton's hand fell on one of the leather volumes on the sideboard under the painting. The title had been worn away long ago.

"Thomas," he continued as if she hadn't spoken, "is a real American-ist. Has he told you about his current project? On altered states in the early modern? I should think you'd want to share some of your resources with him. His project sounds very promising indeed."

"He doesn't need my help." Connie didn't think Thomas's project sounded promising. In fact, she didn't think it had an original argument at all. He must have many changes planned, if Marcus Hayden was going to write a letter for him. Unless Marcus wasn't going to write for him. Unless he'd lied to her.

"Ah." Chilton dissolved into another hacking cough. "But imagine how good his work will be, when you do."

So. Chilton knew the answer to her question. And he would give it to her, but only if she gave him what he wanted. Her fingers had knot-ted together. Her eyes had grown very, very pale.

"Professor Thomas Rutherford," Chilton mused. "It has a nice ring to it, doesn't it? A certain . . . rightness. A professorial name for a profes-sorial man. The kind of man who can appreciate where the discipline has been. The heritage of our work. Don't we owe it to ourselves—to the future of our work—to maintain what is right?"

Before Connie could object, could point out all the new directions that history had taken in the years that Chilton had been shuttered away, he continued.

"And just think—he'll be your protégé. With a great debt of grati-tude to you. Your name, and his. Linked." For the first time since she entered the room, Chilton's eyes came to rest on her face.

"If I promise to review his book proposal when it's done," Connie said, "will you tell me what I need to know?"

"And?" he said. "What might that be, I wonder?"

"I need to know what *corallus* means," she said.

Chilton's withered mouth twisted as though he was amused at a private joke.

"You have a little mystery for your little book project," he said. "For which you need to ask my help. And yet, in return, you are willing to review his book proposal? Do I have that correctly? But that's not what I asked you for."

Connie's hands tightened in her lap. How much time did they have now? Seven minutes?

"I wonder if you know what's at stake," Chilton said, "in what I'm asking of you."

Connie yearned to leave. So much so that at some point in the course of their interview her car keys had appeared in her hand without her knowing it.

"Safeguarding the practice of history for those who are truly suited for it," he continued.

Connie's eyes found her wristwatch, and she saw that she had misjudged the time. They had three minutes.

"By those with a personal stake in our nation's past," Chilton said, voice dropping. "Not these newcomers, who will never be in a position to understand."

Connie's cheek twitched, and without thinking she got to her feet.

"Sadly, I refer also," Chilton continued, watching her mildly, "to your own interests. You will write Thomas Rutherford a recommendation letter, a glowing one, to complement my own, and that of Harold Beaumont. It should present no difficulty for you, given how well you know his work—and shall come to know it. And how perfectly suited he is to follow me."

A curtain of red misted across Connie's vision, and she took an unconscious step toward him, her hands flexing as if she could wring the answer she needed out of him. "Personal stake?" she started to say, rage pushing the words sourly out of her mouth, but before she could finish her outburst, Chilton's head lolled to the side.

A faint, bluish spark kindled to life, two tiny flaming pinpoints in the very centers of his irises. Small enough that the casual observer would never notice them. But Connie had seen that sizzling hot blue before.

His head lolled further, and the blue flamed larger, thickening, until his eyes looked as though they had been occluded by a billow of smoke.

His mouth fell open, releasing a shuddering groan, loud enough to fill Connie's ears, loud enough to fill the room, loud enough to cause Connie to clap her hands over her ears and fall to her knees, loud enough to fill her head with the sound of a soul on fire.

Then the convulsions started.

His body seemed to pull itself apart from the inside, to disassemble from a coherent whole, falling into discrete parts. A trembling started from somewhere deep inside his body, vibrating through layers of bone and sinew and wasted muscle, all the way to the surface of his skin. Chilton shuddered so hard that he seemed to be shaken in the mouth of an invisible animal. Connie cowered in the shadow of the damask armchair, watching with horror the full fury of the curse that had gripped Chilton for the past nine years. The curse that ripped through him, regular as the tide. The curse that consumed him every fifteen minutes, day or night, waking or sleeping, fair or flood, and that would devour him one shred at a time until the tearing proved too much for a fragile human animal to withstand, that would rip through his body and soul until he dropped dead.

Interlude

———

"How much?" the young man from Beverly asked. His hands worried his hat, bending its long brim in half. He bowed his head low, as if he were in church and not in her kitchen. His hands were older than his face. Roughened by work. The webbing between his forefinger and thumb bore a small tattooed anchor, blurred at the edges.

"Lemme look at you," Temperance said.

She took the tattooed hand in hers and turned it palm up. The lines were deep, burned in by hard work and salt water. She traced along one of them with her fingertip, but the calluses were so thick he probably couldn't feel it. She glanced up at him, sharpish, and read his eyes. They were gray and flecked, bloodshot from being warmed by rum when out to sea.

"Press gang?" she asked.

"Once," he said.

"Mr. Madison's War," Temperance said with disdain, letting go of the hand. It was hard to tell, with palms that rough. Even so, it didn't look good. "When you shipping out, then?"

"Next week," the young man said. He stared at the fishhook hanging from her earlobe, which gave Temperance the odd sensation that some-one was standing just behind her.

The latch gave and the door to the kitchen creaked open, revealing an old woman in an even older dress, much hemmed and taken in and out, a knitted woolen scarf tucked over her tired bosom. Her hands trembled. A small creature, the household ratter, wound through her skirts and around her ankles as a cat might, yawned, and padded into the room, disappearing under the worktable heaped with dandelion greens. A hard crust of cornbread sat forgotten at Temperance's elbow. A weevil squirmed in its crumbs.

"Faith's done her dinner," said the woman—Patty, Temperance's mother. Her voice shook too, and her chin.

"I'm working," Temperance said.

Patty took in the young man from Beverly with a watery blue eye, then went back out of the room.

"All right," Temperance said to the young man, who had turned his attention to the herbs hung to dry from the rafters.

"She brought me out," the young man said softly.

"What?"

"Your mama. She brought me out," he said. "Brought out all my sis-tren too."

"Did she now," said Temperance, bored by the secret revelation that so many of her clients felt compelled to share, once they laid eyes on her long-storied mother.

"Yes, ma'am," he continued. "Mother wouldn't trust nobody else."

"You haven't any brothers?"

"No, ma'am," he said.

Temperance felt a twist of guilt at what she'd seen in the young man's hand. "You got a wife?" she said.

"Yes, ma'am," he said. Eyes back on the fishhook.

"What's she do, then?" Temperance made as if she were going to scratch behind her ear, but brought a hank of hair over her shoulder instead. No one ever wanted to look her in the face. But she wasn't above tricking people into it.

"She sells fish," the young man said.

"All right." Temperance got to her feet and went over to the sewing table under the window.

"That you?" She knew he meant the painted likeness hanging on the wall, staring them down while she worked.

"Yep." She hated having herself on the wall like that. Should've insisted on coin.

"It's a fair likeness." He sounded sort of surprised. "Your hair and that."

"It was payment," Temperance said, impatient with his fumbled compliments.

"Oh." He looked down at his feet. "I ain't got so much."

Well, that makes two of us, Temperance thought. Every time, it was the same. They'd come. She knew what they wanted. They'd be nervous and ashamed of their fear. She'd try to put them at ease, and she would fail. If they caught sight of Patty, they'd confess their previous connection to Temperance's family. Dropping the curtain to reveal the shadow of their childlike selves. Then, ashamed of the shadow, of their infantile weakness, they'd plead poverty.

Temperance pulled out the drawer of the sewing table and reached inside the hanging bag. She grabbed one of the precut coils of twine in the belly of the bag, one of the ones with three knots along it. Not much different from the knotted cordage used on shipboard for taking the measure of the wind.

"Half a dollar," she said.

His eyes widened, and the hat brim suffered for it.

"But—" The young man tried to find a way to object.

Temperance held the knotted cord up between finger and thumb for him to see, dangling like a dead garden snake.

"It's worth it," she said. "See? You untie the first one, and that gives you a fine calm. You unknot the second, and that brings on winds just right to make sail. Unknot the third, and it blows a gale."

"It work?" he asked. Thumbs digging into the felt of his suffering hat.

"Guaranteed." Temperance gave him a knowing smile.

She heard the telltale creak of a floorboard overhead. At least one member of the household was listening at the knothole in the ceiling.

The young man from Beverly thrust his hand into his duck trouser pocket and fished around inside.

"I've got a nickel," he said, holding the coin out in the palm of his weathered hand.

"That all?" Temperance said. But the eyes of the young man from Beverly were fixed on the knotted length of twine with a hunger that could only be genuine.

Poor bastard, Temperance thought.

She sighed heavily, and a gleam of hope alit in the young man's eyes as he saw that she was going to cave in.

"All right," she said, peeling the coin out of his hand and sliding it into her own pocket. She pressed the knotted twine between her hands and whispered a quick incantation, just enough to feel the warm crackling in her palms that let her know it was working. The pain was acute enough that she took notice of it. But Temperance was good at removing herself from the pain. She could step aside from it, and observe it from a distance. From outside herself, she saw that the pain was nothing. Especially if followed by a nickel.

She dropped the twine into his waiting hand. A puff of invisible blue smoke coiled up as it left her fingers.

The young man cupped the twine in his palms as if it were a precious jewel.

Just then the kitchen door burst open and a child of six or seven whirled in. Brown curls flying, shirttail aflap. The child was in bare feet and boy's breeches. She came skidding around the trestle worktable and collided with Temperance's legs, the ratter bursting from under the table with barks and leaps and merry paws all over everything.

Temperance put her hand on the child's head. "Go back to Grandmother. Mama's working." But in truth she was pleased by the interruption.

The sailor's fingertips smeared away the moisture from his eyes and nose, and he slid the knotted length of twine into his pocket.

"No!" the child objected. "You said times tables after dinner." She gathered the ratter up into her arms, the animal wiggling and kicking its hind feet, and rested her face in the creature's fur.

Temperance widened her eyes to show she meant business, and pointed at the kitchen door. Her daughter slunk away, the vaguely colored animal struggling in her considerable grip. The door closed behind her.

The young man didn't make a move to go.

"All right, then?" Temperance said.

His feet shuffled in the sand on the floor, boots grating on the wood.

"What," Temperance said.

"It's just." The sailor's gaze met hers for the first time since he'd stepped through the door. She knew exactly what he wanted. That same thing everyone wanted.

"It's not for sale." She brushed a hand over her busk, unawares, as if to reassure herself that she still stood there.

"But if you only knew what it might mean for me." The young man thrust the knotted string into his empty pocket. His fist bunched inside.

"Not for a nickel," Temperance said, growing irritated. "Best be off with you." She held out her hand to shake.

The young man stuck his crumpled hat back on his hanging head. He pressed his lips together, his face paling under its suntan. Then he squeezed her hand once and let it go. The kitchen door clicked shut behind him.

Through the plaster, Temperance heard the young man bid Patty good evening in the sitting room across from the front hall. She sank into a ladderback chair at the trestle worktable and massaged a temple with her fingertips.

Footsteps on the boards overhead, a fine rain of sand falling between the gaps, and then the same footsteps whumped down the stair and into the kitchen.

"Don't start," Temperance said without looking up.

"A nickel?" cried Obadiah.

She dug the coin out of her pocket, set it on her closed fist, and used her thumb to fling it singing across the room. Obie snatched the singing coin out of the air, gave it a tentative bite, and stuck it in his pocket.

"All he had," Temperance said.

"Rot," said Obie, coming over to her. "He had more."

Temperance looked helplessly up at her husband. His face was weathered by sun and salt wind. Graying temples. His hair in a long pigtail, tied with ribbon, old fashioned, because she liked it.

"He didn't," she said.

Obie put his hand on her neck and scratched in her hair with a stout thumb. The aching muscles there felt crisp and raw.

"Perhaps your mother?" he said, gently as he could.

"You know she can't," Temperance snapped. Tendrils of pain wound about her nerves, slow to dissipate.

Patty's hands shook around the same time every afternoon, until her first nip of rum, and afterward they only shook now and again. Her eyes were clouded from rum, or age, or both. Her days delivering babies were done.

Obie pulled out a chair and sat down next to his wife.

"You have to charge more," he said.

"They won't pay."

"They will."

"They haven't got it!" she shouted, and the kitchen door opened to the pressure of the ratter's nose as he snuffled into the kitchen and disappeared back under the worktable.

"Mama?" called Faith from the other room.

Temperance curled her hands into fists, then shook them out. She wanted to kick over the soup and rip the herbs from the rafters.

"Coming," she called to her daughter, her voice thin.

But Obie grabbed her hand and held it, hard. "Did you eat today?" he said.

"I boiled up some dandelion greens," she said.

"Look," Obie said, getting to his feet. "The Orne brothers. They've offered me a berth, to the Grand Banks."

Temperance's thumbnail scraped against the wood grain of the trestle table.

"No," she said.

"The weather's fine this time of year. They're good sailors. And I can ask for some pay in advance."

"Absolutely not." Temperance kept her tone reasonable.

"Two months, they said. Not a day longer."

Temperance put her hands over her eyes and laughed, at the edge of hysteria.

"You can fix it aright," he said in an urgent whisper. "What else is it for? Good God! All this work for others, but let your family starve?"

In the other room, Faith's voice rose shrilly: "Mama?" Patty murmured to shush her, but a hiccupping sound meant that Faith had started to cry, as she often did when they argued. Patty tried to keep them from hearing her sobs by holding the child's face to her grandmotherly shoulder.

Obie's eyes were warm and brown. Whenever Temperance looked into them, she felt safe, and she didn't mind drinking dandelion broth made of weeds she'd gleaned in the woods behind the cottage.

Faith. Her dandelion soup had had an egg in it. Tempe had sneaked an egg into Patty's too. Her mother was growing reedy with age, the weight falling from her in slow, steady measure. But they were nearly out of eggs. The Beverly man's nickel would buy food, but for how long? A month? By then the fleet would be gone, and no scared young men would scratch at her door again until the dog days of summer.

Springtime. The starving time.

Obadiah cupped her cheek in his weathered hand.

She sank two anxious fingers between the swell of her breasts, rooting in the warmth between her flesh and the ruffles sewn inside. Her fingernail caught the corner of a sheet of paper, folded small and square, and sealed closed. She always carried it. Her mother had said it would be safe in the house. But Temperance knew better. Everyone knew how to find their house. Everyone knew there was nothing of value in the house, save this one rare thing. A thing of special value for anyone living off the sea.

Temperance slowly withdrew the paper from its hiding place and held it up between two fingers. Her eyes met Obadiah's. And misted over until they were almost solid white.

Chapter Twenty

Belmont, Massachusetts
Late April
2000

The Volvo's engine rumbled through the chassis and the steering wheel and into Connie's fists, and she forced herself to pay attention. The needle on the speedometer hovered past fifty miles per hour. The engine was only rated up to eighty-five.

"Stop it." She forced her foot to ease off the gas pedal, and the engine's shuddering receded, the car's speed dropping back to something manageable—and legal. The sun slipped lower behind the Charles River, staining the ribbon of water winding between Boston and Cambridge the orangey-purple of a cabochon opal. Connie slowed further as the Volvo descended into the snaking red taillights of rush hour traffic. A single scull pulled along the river, oars dipping and rising.

Sam would be getting home now. Connie felt a driving need to lay eyes upon him, to touch him, to sniff his skin and reassure herself that he was all right.

She nosed the car out of the traffic on the drive along the riverbank, turning down a lane that wound into a neighborhood shaded by trees, peeling around a corner and back onto the familiar stretch of

Massachusetts Avenue. The sky behind her apartment building paled with the coming evening. Streetlights winked on one after the other.

Connie squealed the car to a halt with one wheel over the curb, leapt out, and dashed up the steps, her keys in her hand. She flung open the front door of the building and vaulted over a passing cat who'd escaped from Sara's apartment in back, scraped her key into the door of their apartment, and burst inside, calling, "Sam!"

He appeared from the galley kitchen, carrying a small tumbler of bourbon over ice.

"Oh, hey. You're home," he said, surprised.

Connie threw herself onto him, her arms around his neck, her cheek pressed to his. It was stubbly and warm. She closed her eyes and squeezed and breathed in his smell. Turpentine and flannel.

"Oh, hey now," he said. "Whoa. Hi."

"Hi," she said. She squeezed harder. She became aware of a cold clammy patch between her shoulder blades—he'd accidentally dumped bourbon down her back. Sam set the empty tumbler on the mail table and put his arms around her waist. One of his hands found the back of her head and combed his fingers through her hair.

"That must have been some office hours," he said lightly.

"I didn't go to office hours," she confessed into his shoulder. "I went to go see Chilton."

He said, "You what?"

"He said I'd better support Thomas over Zazi for the Harvard job. He did everything he could to force me to agree."

"Why'd you even go see him?" Sam released her and gripped the back of the futon with both hands. "What the hell is going on?"

Connie's throat began to close tight against all she was trying not to say.

"I had a question," she said, her voice going small.

"What question could he possibly answer that you can't answer for yourself?" Sam said. His grip on the futon cushion tightened.

"I wanted to know what *corallus* meant," Connie said.

Sam was on the point of saying something, but the phone rang.

It rang again.

"You going to get it?" Sam asked.

Connie picked up the receiver and said, "Hello?"

"Hey, are you okay?" the woman on the other side of the receiver said.

"Liz?"

"Yeah. I wasn't sure I'd get you. You sound terrible." Liz sounded concerned. A dullness behind her on the line suggested she was still in her office at the Fogg, and everyone else had already gone home.

"It's—I'm—" Connie pinched the bridge of her nose. "Just tired. I'm fine."

Outside, a siren wailed past the apartment. "Is Sam there?" Liz asked.

Sam was looking into his empty bourbon tumbler.

"Yes," said Connie.

"I'll make it quick then," Liz said. "I had an idea. About your problem."

"Which one?" Connie wished she could have a tumbler of bourbon too.

Liz laughed through her nose and said, "Right. I was referring to the impossible ingredient. The really disgusting one. Since I know you well enough to know that my disapproving of what you want to do isn't about to keep you from doing it."

Fat of Children digged out of their Graves. It was horrid, like something out of a dark fairy tale. The kind told in the old days, before 1950s American popular culture cleaned them up and made witches into harmless old women, toothless and unthreatening in their silly hats. No. That ingredient dated from an earlier imagination of witches. When they were tools of fear. When they receded from the visible world and became hideous, appetitive phantoms. Hansel and Gretel, starving and lost and alone, seduced by a house built of sticky candy walls, imprisoned in cages of woven reeds and fatted slowly for the oven.

Connie held the receiver closer to her mouth and said, "I'm listening."

Rustling down the telephone line as Liz leaned nearer. "When you came to see me the other day," she said, dropping her voice, "did you happen to spend any time in the galleries?"

"I didn't," Connie said, feeling sheepish.

"So you didn't see the photography show that's up right now," Liz continued.

"No," Connie said.

"It's about Victorian death culture," said Liz.

Across the living room, one of the thin cotton curtains hanging by the window to the auto repair shop had worn away to a ragged hole.

"Death culture," Connie echoed. "Like mourning jewelry. And hair jewelry. Stuff like that."

"Yes," said Liz. "And?"

Sam had disappeared into the kitchen to refill his glass when she first answered the phone and by now had come back into the living room. He mouthed, *Hair jewelry?* "They took photos. When people died. Death portraits."

"And what do we know about mortality rates in the nineteenth century?" Liz continued, excited.

"Really high." Connie sat down hard on the futon. "Especially for children."

"Correctamundo," said Liz. "Now here's the important part. What are photos made of? Not daguerreotypes, mind you. Photographs. Old ones, printed on paper."

"Egg albumen," Connie said. Her right foot started to jiggle with nervous energy.

"I mean," Liz said, talking around a pen cap between her teeth. "Egg albumen is a kind of fat. Right?"

Folk magic used images to stand in for the real thing all the time. Connie considered the cornhusk doll she had found hidden in the bookshelf of the Milk Street house, bristling with pins. Even the witch bottles used in the old days, holding nails sealed inside a bottle of urine—that was a common example of the part standing in for the whole. Urine from the bewitched person, standing in for the person's body. Sympathy, and synecdoche.

"Yeah," Connie said at length. "Yeah, it is."

Sam sat on the futon next to her. "What's going on? Is that Liz?"

"See?" Liz said.

"But," Connie objected, "where do I get one of those? If they're so rare that they're in an exhibition at the Fogg?"

"That, I can't help you with," Liz said. "But I will say, they're not as rare as you think. Plenty of examples out there aren't museum quality."

"I can't believe you're telling me to do what I think you're telling me to do," Connie said. She glanced at Sam.

I have to tell you something, he mouthed. *It's important.*

Connie nodded.

"Well," said Liz. "What can I say? The world is full of mysteries I cannot explain."

"Truer words were rarely spoke," Connie said. "Thanks."

"Okay. Let me know how it goes."

"What was that all about?" Sam asked when Connie had hung up the phone.

"Is there an antiques store in Harvard Square?" Connie asked.

"A couple," said Sam. "You want to see if they have any figurines made of coral?"

"Any what?" Connie said.

"Coral," Sam repeated with a crooked smile. He propped a bare foot on the coffee table and took a sip of his fresh bourbon. His naked toes flexed, the knuckles cracking.

"Coral?" Connie repeated. She took her bangs in her fists and tightened her grip. "Oh, my God. *Corallus!*"

"Yep." Sam took another sip of bourbon and followed it up with, "I don't know why you didn't ask me sooner."

Connie started to laugh. The laughter rose until it was too high, and too loud, and not funny anymore, and Connie was afraid she was going to cry. Sam put his arms around her and brought her head into his shoulder. The flannel of his shirt tickled her nose, and her laughter became gasps, and his hand went to the back of her neck and the warmth of his touch felt like it was untying a knot at the base of her skull that she hadn't known was there.

"It's okay," Sam murmured as her near-hysterical gasps dissolved into a sob. "No one is supposed to do all this stuff alone, Cornell." His lips brushed the skin behind her ear. "Not even you."

Chapter Twenty-one

Cambridge, Massachusetts

Late April

2000

Connie had thirty minutes before she was due to meet Zazi at Dado Tea in Harvard Square to give notes on Zazi's cover letter for the Harvard history job. Thirty minutes was enough time, wasn't it? If she promised herself not to linger. Connie put on her turn signal and rolled into an unassuming gravel parking lot with a commanding view of the silver ribbon of the Charles River winding between Cambridge and Boston.

Mahoney's Garden Shop, the knotty sylvan wilderness hidden behind this gravel parking lot, camped along the Charles, surrounded on all sides by newish Brutalist apartment buildings all owned and administered by Harvard University. The garden shop clung to the riverbank, tenacious, with fingernails made of shrubbery, and today Mahoney's appeared as an azalea fairyland, flowers studding its wall of greenery like hot pink nests.

On the front seat next to her sagged a grubby tote bag, into which Connie had already stashed some of the ingredients that Temperance's recipe for weather work required. Connie guessed that much of what was missing could be had at Mahoney's.

She reviewed Temperance's list in her head. Coral—that one might prove challenging. If she lived in a beach town, there might be shops with coral paperweights and doodads. But Boston and the North Shore weren't coral doodad beach towns. Beach glass, lobster buoys, and anchor-patterned throw pillows were more like it. She'd have to look someplace else for coral. A rock shop? Did they have those? Another alternative—sometimes coral was used for decorative figurines and jewelry in the nineteenth century. Where might she find something like that? Hard to tell.

Knots—she had the small knotted length of twine from Temperance's hidden box, safely ensconced in Liz's acid-free archival envelope in the tote bag next to her. And if Temperance's original twine proved too fragile to handle, or tie, or untie, or whatever she was supposed to do with it, she supposed that any length of twine might do.

Next, tincture of smallage—a head of freezer-burned celery, forgotten in the salad crisper in her refrigerator, sat in the tote bag ready to be boiled for broth.

Wolfsbane, cinquefoil, henbane, hemlock, and moonshade—those would all be at Mahoney's. And if not there, she could probably find them up in Marblehead, at the house, if it came to that.

Tobacco? The tote bag contained a cellophane-wrapped pack of Camels Connie had picked up at the newsstand in Harvard Square, for the exorbitant-seeming price of seven dollars. She'd held it under her nose after she bought it, cellophane crinkling. It smelled sweet, toasty, and addictive.

Opium—Connie felt pretty smug about how she'd solved this one. Opium was hard to find, and even harder to prepare. But she had discovered, in the medicine cabinet of their apartment in the Green Monster, behind rattling bottles of Tylenol and blister foils of decongestant and a half-empty bottle of mouthwash with a sticky ring around the bottom, an old expired prescription written to Samuel Hartley for Tylenol with codeine, left over from when he'd had his wisdom teeth out. When she'd pried open the pill bottle she discovered three tablets inside, powdery with age. Now they, too, were in the tote bag.

Saffron she found hidden among the cooking herbs in their apartment, in a forgotten glass jar with the label peeling off. Into the tote bag.

Poplar leaves? Maybe those would be at Mahoney's too.

Then, *pileus naturalis.* The caul, still sealed in its antique envelope, squirreled away in the tote bag.

All that would remain, after all these disparate items were assembled, were the two most opaque entries on Temperance's list. *Fat of Children digged out of their Graves*—for that she would need somehow to lay her hands on an original nineteenth-century photograph of a dead child. Assuming Liz's idea would work.

And lastly, *dust of ought the strongest sort.*

She didn't know what that meant. Like, at all.

Connie shifted the car into park. Her temples were beginning to ache. She took up the tote bag and stepped out of the car.

Inside Mahoney's, Connie roamed shaded racks of springtime greenery, long tables covered in new baby plants waiting to be taken away in flats and urged to bloom. In a stand of narrow adolescent trees Connie combed her fingers through a poplar's leaves, her thumbnail breaking three of them off at the stem and slipping them into her tote bag.

How had Temperance come up with this madness? It was hard enough keeping straight all the steps and ingredients, remembering the order of things, the words. That's why these women had written them down. The audacity, the gall it must have taken for Temperance to throw deadly ingredients together in a pot and boil until reduced to a potion so dangerous that she would hide it away from everyone, even her own daughter, despite the fact that it worked.

Or seemed to work.

Connie passed a small hemlock shrub gasping for water, rootbound in a pot in the far corner of the garden lot, and brushed a palm over its prickly branches. She tried to sever three fingers of hemlock with her thumbnail, but the dried bark resisted. Connie scanned to make sure no one was paying attention to her, then withdrew a slim pocket knife from her tote bag and started sawing at an unobtrusive branch.

"The hell do you think you're doing?"

Connie gasped, looking up into the scowling, bearded face of a deeply tanned white guy who could have been anywhere between twenty-five and fifty. The faded brown of his T-shirt suggested that he belonged there in the garden shop, spiritually if not professionally.

Connie said. "I was just—"

"You gonna buy that?" The bearded man pointed at the pitiful hemlock. It would be lucky to last a week.

"I wasn't," Connie said. She tightened her grip on the tote bag with its contraband contents and smiled in what she hoped was an apologetic way.

The man bent over, picked up the gasping hemlock, and thrust the pot into her arms.

"Here," he said.

Connie glared at the man. As her hands met the terra-cotta, a faint buzzing of static electricity bloomed to life in the palms of her hands. A momentary glimmer of green flushed along the tips of the hemlock needles nearest her face.

The man's glare became uncertain.

"Over there." He pointed to a cash register under a knotted bower of honeysuckle.

"But I'm not done," Connie objected.

"You're done." The man backed away. He held his hands palms-out in front of him, the unconscious gesture of a warded-off attack.

Connie scuttled with the hemlock shrub to the register. What was she still missing? Wolfsbane. Cinquefoil. Mandrake. They wouldn't have that anyway. Nightshades, always nightshades.

"That'll be thirty-one fifty," the woman at the register said. Like the man who had rebuked her, the woman at the register was browned and ageless from the sun, with permanently blackened fingernails.

"For this?" Connie exclaimed. "You're kidding." It was, truly, a pitiful plant.

"They're getting harder and harder to keep going, around here." The woman rubbed a needled stalk thoughtfully. "Used to be native, hemlocks. Not anymore."

Connie fished in her jeans pocket for the money to pay for her unwanted prize. "Why's that?" she asked, finding two crumpled twenty-dollar bills and putting them in the woman's outstretched hand. The register rang and spat open the change drawer.

"Wooly adelgids," the woman said. "Parasites." She counted dollar bills out to Connie. "The climate is changing. The freezes aren't hard enough anymore to kill them, and the hemlocks can't fight 'em off. It's a shame. You mess too much with the weather, and you never can predict what will happen." She dropped some coins on top of the ones and added, "Soon we won't have any hemlocks in New England at all."

Connie tightened her grip around the pot. "I didn't know that."

The woman said, "Take good care of it."

Connie looked into the dried and wasted shrub and said, "All right."

The Volvo crept along a side street off Harvard Square, and Connie pushed a needled hemlock branch away from her cheek as she squinted through the windshield, hunting for a parking space. Something prickled on her lip, and Connie spat, plucking a hemlock needle from inside her mouth. Temperance had just had all these ingredients lying around. Of course, Granna's garden and her panoply of kitchen jars full of rotting things had probably contained its own hideous secrets. Garden herbs and cookbooks, feigning innocence, papering over horrors.

Connie flexed her left hand around the steering wheel, trying to wring out the squirming, uncomfortable prickle she had felt when her arms had closed around the hemlock. That bluish snapping pain.

She didn't like to think about the pain.

Connie spied a parking spot that could easily have been legal, though she wouldn't have sworn to it, and gently backed the Volvo in, rolling a rear tire up onto the brick sidewalk. She wouldn't be that long. Connie considered leaving a note on the dashboard that said, I KNOW JUST FIVE MINUTES, but decided against it.

She was late. Of course. She shouldn't have stopped. Zazi was waiting for her, leaning with crossed arms against the picture window by the door of Dado Tea. The skin under her student's dark eyes was purpled, her eyelids puffy and pinkish. Her freckled nose was chapped and pink too.

"Hey. Hi. I'm here. Sorry." Connie arrived out of breath at Zazi's side.

Zazi seemed to shake off some thought, and did her best to smile. "It's fine. I just got here." She had clearly been crying. Hard.

"Are you okay?" Connie asked. She started to reach for Zazi's shoulder, but stopped herself.

"Eh." Zazi wiped under her eye with her fingertips. "Yeah. Sure."

A tour group of bright-eyed high school students gawped by, trailed by exhausted-looking parents. Zazi glanced at Connie under her eyelashes and then said, "No."

"What's going on?" Connie asked.

"Oh, you know." Zazi kicked the wall of the building with her bootheel. "Just grad school. Everyone told me it was going to suck, and they were right."

Connie said, "You know. We don't have to do this now."

Zazi chewed the inside of her cheek. "Really? You don't mind if we push it?"

Connie smiled. "Nah. Everyone needs a break sometimes." She looked through the picture window into the café, crowded with worried students bent over laptops and bowls of bibimbap. "You still want to get tea?"

"To be totally honest? I hate tea," said Zazi. Connie laughed as Zazi continued, "Now, shopping, on the other hand . . ."

"Know what?" said Connie. "I have something I need to find anyway. I was going to hit this antique store that's supposed to be around here."

"There's a place on this block I like," Zazi said, and they moved together down the brick sidewalk. "Always a bitch to find, though."

On the corner of a nameless block in Harvard Square, near a poetry bookstore that was often shuttered and around the corner from a used-record store, Connie and Zazi stood, their hands in their respective jeans pockets. It was an unseasonably warm spring evening, the air carrying the heavy pollen smell of coming summer. Connie looked up into the late-afternoon sky. Overcast. Pregnant with rain.

"What store were you going to hit?" Zazi asked.

"Rafferty and Sons," Connie said, squinting at door fronts for a sign. A window crowded with old desks and barbershop poles. She'd lived in

Harvard Square for long enough that she thought she knew every lunch counter and joke shop and magazine store. But she'd never, somehow, been on this block before. "Block" was too generous a word—it was more of an alley. An alley with, Sam had promised before leaving for work that morning, an antiques store run by the same family of Irish New Englanders for going on four generations.

"Will they have old cartes de visite?" Connie had asked him over her morning decaf (she still couldn't believe she'd had to switch to decaf).

"All I know is," Sam had said, "when I've needed brass candle sconces for restoration jobs, and no place else has had them for less than three hundred dollars a pop, Rafferty's somehow always had some."

"For less than three hundred dollars?" Connie had paled a little around the edges. Until her tenure vote came through, she and Sam were bringing in ramen-noodle wages. Cambridge was expensive.

"You'll see," Sam had said, tugging on the end of her braid.

Now, as she and Zazi stood under a sky growing leaden with springtime rain, she didn't see anything that looked as if it might be Rafferty and Sons.

"Oh yeah. I love that place," Zazi said. "I never remember where it is."

"Let's try this way," Connie said.

The two women fell into step together, both with their eyes on their feet. The muffled donging of the clock tower in the Yard told them that the day was drawing to a close.

"That douchebag," Zazi muttered presently.

Connie watched Zazi out of the corner of her eye. Zazi's tears had dried, and her eyes were darkening. Angry.

"What douchebag?" Connie asked, keeping her voice mild.

"Nothing." Zazi stopped outside a carved wooden door that seemed to belong to an early-twentieth-century apartment building. "Now here we go," she said. "I thought it was on this block."

"This is it?" Connie asked.

"You've never been?" Zazi leaned on the doorbell, and a buzzing emanated from somewhere deep within the brick walls.

"I guess not," Connie marveled. The front door creaked open a hairsbreadth.

Zazi pushed.

The door wouldn't open all the way. They had to edge inside, and Connie's throat closed against the smell of mildew and dust. She stifled a cough.

"Isn't it great?" Zazi exclaimed.

They were crammed into a narrow entry hallway with Victorian hall-stands stacked three deep, heaped with top hats, scarves, lace; there was a whole umbrella stand bristling with walking sticks. A riot of different Turkey-work carpets competed for attention on what little floor space was visible between paw feet and iron cookware and rusted weathervanes.

"I can't believe this is real," Connie said, holding her tote bag to her chest.

"This is just the hall," Zazi said.

She took Connie's hand and led her through a beaded curtain into what must have at one time been a parlor. There were no other people in the store. In fact, it didn't even feel much like a store. It felt like a trap-door to another Cambridge, at another time. If it hadn't been for the distant wail of a siren wending down Massachusetts Avenue, she could almost believe that present-day Cambridge had fallen away.

A walnut dining room credenza filled the front window of the par-lor, its entire surface covered in crystal balls of varying size. Some stood on little brass stands; some rolled loose in nests of velvet. Handwritten price tags were affixed here and there with cellophane tape. One bore a calligraphed label that read "owned by the celebrated Mrs. Dee."

"I like to come here when I'm depressed," Zazi said. "It's like a *botánica*, only better." She drew a circle through the dust on one of the larger crys-tal balls with a finger.

"Not Newbury Street?" Connie said drily. Newbury Street was the fancy shopping district in downtown Boston. Connie couldn't afford to shop there. Neither could Zazi.

"Har har," said Zazi as she disappeared down a narrow aisle crowded with Chinese export porcelain and heavy cut-crystal ashtrays.

Connie moved down another aisle, this one with racks of Currier and Ives prints in discolored matting, castoff haberdasher's signs, and beer steins in the shape of bearded fishermen in sou'wester hats

A thick mahogany bookshelf offered faded hardbacks arranged roughly by size. She trailed her fingertips along the spines of the books. A pictorial guide to Boston in 1876. A gilt-embossed edition of Boswell's *Life of Johnson*. A book of fashion plates, also from the 1870s. Her finger alit on a spine with an etched image under a faded, illegible title. The gilded outline of a primitive-style woman. Naked, grinning, her knees spread, her teeth bared like a skeleton's, with the letters *E L U I* over her head.

Connie drew the book down from the shelf, blowing off dust. The title page read *Sheela-na-Gigs: The Goddess Revealed*. She opened the book to the frontispiece to find a black-and-white photograph, paled in the manner of tipped-in photos in books from the 1960s. The photograph was of a stone carving, like the abstraction on the spine—a hideous grinning woman, spreading herself, her head covered in a kind of coif.

"Weird," Connie said to herself, brushing a fingertip over the photograph. Her fingertip tingled.

"What's weird?" Zazi said. Connie couldn't see her through all the bric-a-brac.

"Nothing," Connie said, sliding the book back into place and wiping her fingers on the seat of her jeans. "Just, this whole place. It's crazy."

"Word," said Zazi.

Connie continued down the aisle, the jumble of junk crowding in around her tightly enough that she had to turn sideways to peel herself around a large antique globe with curling seams, and expanses of ocean marked with snarling beasts and the inscription HERE THERE BE MONSTERS. On the other side of the globe, tucked into the letter-sorting cubbies of a water-stained Victorian desk, Connie discovered a set of stereoscope cards. She pulled them out. Here, a double image of a man on a tightrope with a stove on his back, suspended over Niagara Falls. There, a double image of a masked woman in Halloween costume, with a pointed hat on her head and a broomstick in her hand.

Another siren wailed by outside.

Connie heard the gentle sound of rummaging, presumably Zazi one aisle over, sifting jade beads in a bowl. Then an irritated sigh.

"That douchebag," Zazi said again under her breath.

In another cubbyhole, Connie found secreted a collection of cartes de visite, one of the most common formats of early photography. Small enough to fit in the palm of a hand, or in a pocket, printed on cardboard. Made of egg albumen. She took the pile of cards in her hands. Grime came off onto her fingers.

"You know," she said, loudly enough for Zazi to hear, "you can tell me. If something's bothering you."

Jade beads continued stirring in a glass bowl in the next aisle over. Connie shuffled through the photograph cards she had discovered. They were silvery with age. The first one was of a middle-aged white man with long sideburns, dressed in a suit with a watch chain across his belly. He sat, one leg crossed over the other, in profile. He dated from the 1880s, to judge by his dress and hairstyle. His eyes were opaque, staring into himself.

Invisible behind a stack of 78 rpm records, Zazi said in a low voice, "It's okay. I have to fight my own battles."

The next photo was of a chubby-cheeked, lace-bonneted white baby, its tiny hands balled into fists, staring at the camera. Someone had written "Claudette" in spidery pencil underneath the image. Connie smiled down at the chubster. Those cheeks! Claudette's dress was long, with eyelets and needlepoint hemming. That must have been some time to be a baby. By her teens there would be cars. Telephones. A whole other world. Connie brought the photograph closer to her eyes, eagle stone rattling at her wrist. What was the baby sitting on? It looked like a sheeted, oddly-shaped chair.

No, the baby wasn't sitting up on her own—instead she was being propped up by a dark hand peeking out from the sheeting. The oddly shaped chair wasn't a chair at all. It was a woman, the baby's nurse, sheeted to be kept hidden, literally out of the picture. Connie returned the photograph to its cubbyhole.

"What's this battle about? That you are completely capable of fighting by yourself," Connie said.

She turned her attention to the next photograph. This was another baby—or maybe the same baby?—sitting up in an elaborate wicker carriage with narrow wheels. Yes, it must be the same baby. The backdrop looked the same, as though all three pictures had been taken at the same studio. Even the rug was the same. It could even have been taken on the same day. No name this time. Connie considered keeping this one, but put it back in the cubbyhole.

"Graduate History Association," Zazi said, voice low with irritation. "We were taking a vote. It got kind of contentious."

"On what?" Connie asked.

The next photo was the same baby, now grown marginally bigger. It was unusual for a nineteenth-century family to have so many pictures taken of themselves. Photography was expensive. And time-consuming. In this shot, the baby was on the floor, on all fours, a new crawler, nose to nose with a spaniel. Connie smiled.

"Unionizing," Zazi said. "If we want to back the union drive by the GSA. Doesn't matter."

"Unionization?" Connie looked up from her photographs.

"Yeah. Whatever, doesn't matter," Zazi said. Shuffling sounds of her fingers walking through Victrola records.

"So what was so contentious?"

Zazi moved deeper into her own aisle. Connie heard her pick up a small ceramic bowl and put it down again on a wooden surface. "Nothing. I just got into it with some guy. Some guy who thinks he's a better scholar than me, even though he isn't. Doesn't matter."

The next photo was of the first man in the pile, now a shade older, with threads of silvery white in his whiskers, sitting knee to knee with an unsmiling white woman. Her hair was parted in the middle and pulled back from her forehead, and her eyes looked tired. The couple weren't touching each other. She was in a dove-gray dress, with a laurel-leaf cameo at her throat. Connie looked at the back of the card, but didn't find any identifying information. Back into the cubbyhole.

"Huh," Connie said. An ambulance screamed several blocks away, followed by the elephant-honk of a fire truck.

"It just got weirdly personal, is all," Zazi continued, irritation plain in her voice. "Things were said. It sucked." In a lower voice, she grumbled "'Go back to Mexico.' Hah. I'm Texan. I'm not even *from* Mexico."

Connie stiffened. In her hands, the next picture was of the same baby—Claudette. About a year old, now. In a version of the same starched white eyelet smock and bonnet. She was laid out, head cradled by a satin pillow. Her eyes were closed.

"I'm really sorry to hear that," Connie said. Her fingertip brushed over the image of the baby's face. She looked as if she were asleep.

"He totally flipped out. Threw some stuff and left. Said people like me were ruining history. You believe that? *People like me.*"

Connie said, "That's appalling."

Flowers heaped around the baby bonnet—lilies, the kind with a heavy, sickly-sweet fragrance. Tiny hands down at her sides. Linens and satin tucked around the smock, clearly the lining of a coffin.

Connie had to look away.

"What people? I said. People smarter than you? Is that it?" Zazi's voice rose.

"Good," said Connie. "Sounds like he deserved it."

There was an ashtray. Locke-Ober's. Stolen. Next to it, another ashtray, also stolen, this one from the Parker House hotel.

"'Don't be ugly,'" Zazi said, calmer now. "That's what my mother always says. 'Esperanza, don't you be ugly, now.' But I'll tell you. It's hard."

Connie looked back at the carte de visite cradled in the palm of her hand. She knew she should be excited. She had found what she was looking for.

But it was horrible.

Horrible, and only five dollars.

"Come on," Connie said, her voice going cold. "Let's get out of here."

"You find something?" Zazi reappeared through a narrow gap between two dressing-room mirrors, startling Connie with the illusion that she had materialized out of nowhere.

"Yeah," Connie said, though her voice was dark. "Where do I get rung up?"

Zazi smiled strangely and said, "Over this way."

She led Connie deeper into the store, away from the light filtering through the front parlor window, until they came upon a glass counter vitrine in the rear, its shelves heavy with paste brooches, cameos, bracelets made of woven hair, and earrings of polished black onyx. Behind the vitrine, long velvet scarves edged with fringe, and—disconcertingly—a 1930s vintage mannequin, with rosebud lips and flat blue eyes, wearing an oversized straw picture hat and an ermine coat.

No live person stood behind the vitrine.

"Hello?" Connie called.

Zazi pointed to a hand-calligraphed card next to the mannequin. It stood in a shallow porcelain glove tray, which contained a few stray dollar bills, a pressed crisp two-dollar bill, and several disparate vintages of change.

The sign read *Honor System*, with a tiny asterisk.

At the bottom, next to the asterisk, in smaller font, small enough that Connie almost couldn't read it, the sign added, *You're being watched.*

Then a smiley face.

"Um." Connie eyed the mannequin. The mannequin's dead eyes stared back.

Another fire truck honked past outside, nearer, followed by yet another siren.

"It's okay," Zazi assured her. "They always do this."

"They do?" Connie fished in her pocket, wondering if she had a five-dollar bill.

"Oh, yeah," Zazi said. "In fact, I don't think I've ever seen anybody working here. Fun, right?"

Connie glanced at the image of the dead baby in her hand, made of chemicals and egg fat. *Fat of a child dug out of her grave.* The store itself was a kind of grave. A mausoleum of memories pried free of the people who might otherwise care for them.

She found five crumpled one-dollar bills in her pocket and left them on the glove tray.

"Fun," she agreed, though her tone didn't match the word. She gave a last look at the dead-eyed mannequin, slid the carte de visite into her tote bag, and looped the bag's straps over her arm and head, so she could wear it crosswise across her body. A nervous laugh bubbled up in her throat. "You wanna leave? Let's leave, okay?"

Zazi laughed. "Yeah, all right. Let's go."

They moved together down winding aisles of Yankee detritus, back into the cluttered front hall. Without their having to ask or press a button, the front door buzzed itself open. Connie and Zazi exchanged a look and giggled. Then they edged one at a time back out the door.

Outside, the early evening was weirdly lit. Like sunset, only not. The air smelled of roasting wood. Connie looked up at the narrow strip of sky visible between the buildings in the alley.

The sky flushed an angry orange, the sickly wrongness of polluted air. The street echoed with a riot of sirens. Another ambulance screamed by, flashing past the opening of the alley.

"What's going on?" Zazi asked.

As she spoke, a soft gray flake drifted from the reddening sky and settled on Connie's cheek.

Ash.

Connie strained to hear direction out of the echoing, overlapping sirens. It seemed to be coming from the east. Toward Central Square.

"Come on," Connie cried, hauling Zazi up the street to the corner where she'd left the Volvo. They tumbled into the car before Connie could consciously decide what she thought was happening. She gunned the engine, rammed into the back bumper of the Ford parked in front of her, backed up onto the sidewalk with a bounce, spun the steering wheel, and peeled out of the alley onto Massachusetts Avenue. They were only a few blocks away. The sky filling with red, a spreading bloodstain, tinted black at the edges with smoke, like the blackening crust of a scab. Spinning red and white lights splashing up the faces of buildings, pedestrians stopping on the sidewalk, shading their eyes, staring down the street, asking each other could they see? What building was it? What was going on? What was on fire?

Connie stamped on the gas pedal, engine grinding as she rushed back to the burning Green Monster.

Back to Sam.

Back home.

Interlude

───────

Salem, Massachusetts

April 23

1816

"All right there, Tempe?" the woman asked from atop a step stool. She had a few books in her hands and was peering at the spines, comparing whatever she saw there with what she found on the shelf.

"Hi, Charlotte," Temperance said, looking around. She hadn't yet been to see the new Athenaeum building. Goodness, but it was fancy. Polished wood floors. Greek columns. A few plaster busts, newly painted to look like marble.

Charlotte Coffin, the librarian, slid the last of her volumes onto the shelf and came over. "Looks nice, doesn't it?" she said, surveying the reading room with satisfaction. Afternoon spring sun glinted through tall windows. Long library tables of polished wood.

"I'll say," Temperance said, feeling shabby.

"You see the garden?" Charlotte waved a hand at the back doors. They were crisp with new white paint, open to the soft springtime afternoon. It was going to be a hot summer.

"Not yet." Temperance looked at the doors, at the ceiling, at Charlotte's tidy desk, at the library table with its new wooden chairs and oil lamps, at the bolts of sunshine streaking through the big new windows.

So unlike the cramped and dark inside of her house on Milk Street, where she was always ducking her head under eaves and lighting another candle to see.

"Haven't seen you around much lately," Charlotte said. She and Temperance had been at grammar school together. Charlotte lived with another woman—her particular friend—in rented rooms on Chestnut Street. They were the sort of women who attended lectures and advocated dress reform and abolition. Serious women, but merry too: punners and poem-quoters. Charlotte had always been like that. When they were girls together she had vowed to Tempe that she would never marry— she had no use for men, their drink and their bluster, and she could make her own money.

Temperance said, "I've been working."

Something glimmered behind Charlotte's eyes. She reached over and gently dandled the fishhook that hung from Temperance's earlobe.

"Shall I show you to the stacks, then?" Charlotte asked.

Temperance nodded, her eyes on her feet.

"This way." Charlotte plucked at her sleeve.

Charlotte fitted a pretty brass key to the new keyhole in a door on the side of the room, edged it open, looked left and right—the Athenaeum was empty of patrons, save for a white-whiskered sea captain dozing in a winged chair in the afternoon sunshine, and a fat tabby lolling on its back under the reading table—and ushered her into the stacks.

Temperance took an almost physical pleasure in proximity to so many books. Tracts and novels—novels!—and bound newspapers and magazines and commonplace books and who knew what-all else. A bloom of envy alit in her breast as she glanced at the braided nape of Charlotte's neck, that Charlotte got to spend her days lost among stories, not spinning ones for hungry sailors who never wanted to pay.

"I haven't kept up my fees," Temperance confessed.

"I know," Charlotte said. "No matter. It's yours anyway." She glanced over her shoulder and added, "You ask me, your grandmama never should've sold it."

Temperance knew she should thank Charlotte for this gesture of solidarity, but she was too ashamed. Poverty was common enough on the rocky spit of Marblehead, but Salem's streets rolled with money. Pin-tucked dresses, literary societies, musical clubs with dances at the holidays and spiced cider and beer. Schools for girls to learn sewing and French. Faith would never be able to go to such a school.

Faith would probably wind up selling fish.

"Here we are." Charlotte led Temperance around a corner and into a narrow aisle lined on both sides with thick, leather-bound volumes crumbling with age. Charlotte got to her knees, took hold of one of the thickest and oldest on the bottom shelf, and eased it out of its resting place.

A hot, prickling feeling crawled across Temperance's palms, and she flexed her fingers to shake the unpleasant sensation off. Charlotte, meantime, had gotten to her feet, the heavy book clutched to her chest, and was leading Temperance to a small desk and chair tucked at the end of the aisle. A lone oil lamp burned on the desk, smoking heavily. It needed trimming.

Charlotte laid the book on the desk and gestured for Temperance to take the chair. Then, with a reassuring squeeze of Temperance's shoulder, she withdrew.

"I'll put it back," she said. "Just leave it there when you're done."

Temperance said, "All right."

When Charlotte was gone, she laid her hands softly on the cover of the nameless book. She closed her eyes. A silent wish formed itself, deep inside her mind, in the quiet room where she went when she needed to be alone.

She opened the volume and got to work.

That night, the kitchen warm from cooking, the windows propped open to the still spring air, Temperance and Obie leaned together over her notes. He was in his shirtsleeves, rolled up on strong tanned forearms, and she'd unknotted her hair, brushing out the curls over her ears and pinning them off her forehead so she could see. Obie kept glancing at her when he thought she wasn't looking. Once she caught him doing it and arched her eyebrow in inquisition. Instead of answering he touched her cheek.

"Smallage still going?" she asked him.

Obie went over to the hearth and peered into the iron cauldron hanging on a hook over the fire.

"Boiling," he confirmed.

"Edge it off," she said. "Don't want it rolling."

Obie used a tong to rotate the hook holding the cauldron over the hottest of the fires, edging the pot off the heat. A thin, celery-scented steam drifted up the chimney. Temperance's stomach growled. Smallage for supper. Again.

She stared down at the list she'd jotted, culling ideas from several different entries of several different vintages in Deliverance Dane's physick book. Temperance never minded improvisation. In fact, she preferred to set about the recipes by smell and feel. And in this instance, she had no choice.

In truth, she doubted it could be done at all.

Temperance scratched her fingers over her scalp.

The door to the hall bounced open and Faith strode in, loose pantaloons rolled over her knees, ratter trotting at her bare heels. Faith was chewing something with her mouth open. She wandered over and put her elbows on the trestle table and took up a lock of Temperance's long hair and pulled on it.

"Mama?" she said through the something she was chewing. Temperance leaned over and sniffed her daughter's breath. Pine sap.

"Yes," Temperance said. She disengaged her daughter's hand from her hair. It left a piney residue. She kissed the hand and put it down on the table. To Obie, she said, "Would you take the creature and get him to dig up a mandrake for me?"

Obie said, "All right," and lifted his chin to summon the ratter. It trotted over, tail merry, and together they ventured out the back door.

"Whatcha doing?" Faith asked, peering at the list.

"Working," Temperance answered.

"Can I help?" Faith asked.

"Where's Grandmother?" Temperance asked.

"She's resting," said Faith, the corners of her mouth pulling down. They both knew what that meant.

"You can watch," Temperance said.

Faith sat down at the worktable, feet swinging.

Temperance stood, fingers knitted atop her head like a hat, elbows splayed, and stared at the dried herbs hanging from the ceiling, considering. She reached up and pulled down a packet of wolfsbane, seven stalks' worth. Cinquefoil next. How much? Nine leaves? Why not. The dried leaves rustled in her hands, and smelled desiccated and sharp. She went over to the hearth, crumbled the leaves in her fists, and rained them into the pot.

The broth, bubbling, swallowed the plant matter in a gulp and belched up a small cloud of blue smoke. Temperance sniffed the smoke and frowned into the cauldron.

"Faith," she said.

Her daughter scrambled to her feet. "Yes?"

"How about you run out to the garden and bring me some poplar leaves."

"How many?" the little girl asked. She was always very mathy. Faith liked percentages. She liked measurements to be precise.

Temperance thought. "Three," she said at length, for reasons that escaped her, but that nevertheless felt right.

"Which poplar?" Faith said. "North or south?"

Temperance put her hands on her hips. "You pick."

"What's it for?" Faith asked.

Temperance hesitated. "Papa has to go to sea," she said.

"Why don't you send him with a knotted string, like you do the others?" Faith asked.

Temperance laid a hand on top of Faith's head. Flosses of curls escaped her sloppy braid, like resting a hand on a bird's nest of woven grass.

"I will," she said. "But that's just for fair winds. Papa needs . . ." Temperance tried to come up with a way to explain. That would tell her daughter the truth, but that wouldn't crush her hope. In Faith's pale, careful eyes Temperance saw a glimmer of comprehension.

"North," the girl said, and scampered out the kitchen door.

A moment later the door creaked open on Obie's elbow, and he came back into the kitchen, clay pipe in his mouth, his hands full of three hemlock branches and some odd pods on long green stems. At his heels trotted the ratter, smug, a rooty protuberance in its mouth.

"Look what we found," Obie said, grinning around his pipe. He held up the pods.

"What's that?" Temperance bent and, shielding her hand with a dish-rag, gently disengaged the root from the animal's mouth. She scratched him behind a rosebud ear, and his hind end blurred with pleasure.

"Poppies," Obie said. "Gone to seed." He went to the hearth and held them over the bubbling cauldron, then glanced back at her with a cocked eyebrow, waiting for permission.

Temperance laughed. "Go ahead," she said. "They'll make you sleepy, if nothing else."

The stew swallowed them with a hiss. A coil of white smoke snaked over the lip of the hearth, thickening near the ceiling.

Temperance used the dishrag to rub the dirt off the root the creature had dug up. A fat conical bulb with four chubby cilia, like arms and legs, coiling into gnarls clotted with mud. A mandrake if ever there was one. Small, about the size of her palm and five fingers together. Once it was clean enough she dropped it into the pot. The white smoke thickened, becoming an almost chemical column.

Temperance reviewed her notes, Obie looking over her shoulder. The kitchen door squeaked open to reveal Faith, poplar leaves bunched in her first. She smiled sagely at her parents and, without asking, went over and dropped them into the cauldron. Deep inside the column of white smoke, a ribbon of an indescribable color twisted to life.

"Well?" Obie said.

Temperance put her fingertip into the column of smoke, ripping a small hole in the dense billow, drawing a circle inside. She withdrew the fingertip and waved it under her nose. The aroma was close—it carried the same burning tension as the calm before a gale, when the electricity in the air enlivens, drawing the hairs up, disrupting the skin.

"I think we're ready," Temperance said.

She steered Obie to sit on the bench alongside the trestle table. In a rush of inspiration, she plucked the clay pipe out of his mouth and dumped its smoldering tobacco into the cauldron. A fizzing crackle rippled across the surface of the boiling liquid. Temperance thrust her finger back into the column of smoke, stirred it in a spiral, and held the finger under her nose again. Now the smell of a tree trunk split by lightning drifted into her nostrils, and Temperance smiled.

"All right," she said.

She laid a length of thrice-knotted twine in Obie's waiting hands. To Faith, she said, "Get the rattle."

Faith disappeared up the narrow stairs to the attic overhead, where Obie had raised the roof and turned it sideways, making two bedchambers from what had been storerooms when Temperance was small. Temperance and Obie traced the pounding of her small feet overhead, bits of sand sifting between the floorboards and ticking onto the trestle table. Temperance brushed them away with the side of her hand.

"It'll work, won't it?" Obie asked quietly.

Temperance put a hand under his bearded chin. His warm brown eyes bathed her in their confidence. Temperance often wished to be the woman her husband believed her to be.

"Yes," she said.

Faith stumped down the attic stairs and reappeared in the kitchen to a bark from the ratter, holding a small silver rattle with a pink coral teething nub on one end over her head in triumph.

"Good girl," said Temperance. To Obie, she said, "Now. When I sign to you, you're to untie each knot. But not a moment before. All right?"

He nodded. His nervous fingers worked the knots in the length of twine, worrying them like a rosary.

Temperance turned to the hearth. With tongs she edged the cauldron back over the hotter part of the fire. The boiling grew angry, the smell of lightning thickening in the room. The billow of white smoke glimmered on the inside, shot through here and there with shards and ellipses of color, like the colors striping the surface of the ocean when the sun drops in the evening.

First to hold. And next untie. Then to boil. And then to die.

She lifted her hands, readying herself against the coming pain that she knew would rip through her nerves with such hideous intensity that she would have difficulty not falling to the floor. Pain unlike any other pain. Pain which, unlike the transient pain of childbirth, which though it seems so all-encompassing when in the grip of it, when abandoning one's body to it, instead disappears from memory. This pain, Temperance knew, would never disappear.

"As it gr—" Temperance started to incant.

Before the words could leave her lips, the door to the kitchen flew open and her mother's voice shouted, "Stop! You don't know what you're doing! *Stop!*"

Chapter Twenty-two

Cambridge, Massachusetts

Late April

2000

Connie couldn't get through. Police barricades blocked Massachusetts Avenue, horns blaring, policemen and Staties with orange flashlights waving off traffic, trying vainly to get cars to turn down side streets and away. Spinning lights, red and white and red and white running through her eyes until Connie could see nothing but the lights, the lights and her own panic were the same, because behind the lights all she saw was smoke.

"Turn right!" Zazi shouted, and Connie obeyed without thinking or signaling, the Volvo jouncing up over a median to the furious blare of horns and sirens, and peeled down a side street.

"Remington," Connie cried, and Zazi said, "Yeah, they won't have that closed off. Left! Left!"

Connie spun the wheel, the hemlock pot falling over and dumping earth across the back seat, Zazi bracing herself with a hand on the car ceiling.

Please let him be okay, please let him be okay, please let him be okay. She'd taken too long. She hadn't fixed it. She was lazy, and slow, and she had no business being a history professor, or a person, and certainly not someone's mother. She was a sham, and now everyone would know it, and even worse than everyone knowing was the dawning certainty that Sam was hurt, or dead, and it was all her fault. Sam loved her, and was paying for it with his life.

"Here it is, here it is!" Zazi shouted, pointing, and Connie spun the wheel, the Volvo lifting off two of its tires, coming down with a slam that scraped the undercarriage on a curb. Remington Street was a short neighborhood alley, only a block long, a tunnel of trees with winking yellow streetlights. Now the tunnel burst into red and white and red and white with the spinning of firetruck lights, and the smoke lay so thick under the canopy that Connie could smell the stench in the car with the windows closed.

Connie gunned the engine with what little power it had left and the car rocketed forward, bouncing over a curb and squealing to a stop in the auto repair shop parking lot next door to the Green Monster.

Connie stared up through the windshield at the face of her apartment building. Two ineffectual streams of water spewed pitifully from fire trucks parked on Massachusetts Avenue into the second-floor windows and onto the gaping, smoking hole where the roof had been. The green paint on the clapboards was bubbling and peeling, and the white trim around the windows had blackened. Smoke belched out of windows in oily columns, oozing among the treetops, weaving orange rings around the streetlights.

In front of her car, at the parlor level of the house, the windows of their bedroom—where she lay early in the morning hazy with sleep, listening to the musical cursing of the mechanics, where the pleasant roasting smell of coffee tickled her awake, where she had come home and opened the door to the welcome blur of Arlo and a room so full of daffodils she could barely see the walls of books—danced with hot orange flames.

"No," Connie whispered. She shrank into herself. Her reason rebelled against what she was seeing. It was impossible. It wasn't happening. It wasn't.

"Connie!" a muffled voice cried, slowed down, thick, as if under water. "We've got to get out! Come on!"

Time wound down through the layers of her shock. Connie's eye landed on the rearview mirror, which revealed two uniformed policemen, mouths open. Were they running to her car? They were. Her eyes tracked back to the windshield. Inside the roiling mouth of the fire she saw a shadow tip and fall—the bookcase by their bed. Sparks curled up in a gorgeous shower, dancing upward on the blast of heat, and Connie had time to reflect that cinders looked a lot like fireworks.

"Connie!" the slowed-down voice came again, only this time Zazi got hold of her shoulder and shook her, hard.

Connie's hand found the door handle and she tumbled out of the car, falling on her hands and knees on the pavement of the parking lot. A hot blast seared her face. Now she understood what all those policemen were shouting. An official hand took hold of her upper arm and she stumbled away from the Volvo, its doors standing open like bat wings, silhouetted against the raging inferno that used to be her home.

"Where is he?" Connie shouted into the ear of the police officer who had hold of her arm. "Sam Hartley! Where is he?"

The police officer didn't respond. He was talking into some kind of receiver on his shoulder. Then Zazi was there, her arm around Connie's waist, and the officer heaped Connie into Zazi's arms, shouted, "Stay back!" and vanished into a knot of other police officers, their shouts inaudible over the cracking and roaring of the flames and scream of sirens. Another stream spat out of a hose held by several Cambridge firefighters, shoulders up, helmets down, and disappeared into the devouring maw of the fire in the Green Monster.

"This is awesome," someone said.

Connie looked up from Zazi's shoulder and saw that the speaker was Sara, her punk-rock first-floor neighbor. She was in ripped fishnets and heavy eyeliner, her arms full of a placid black cat, its tail flicking left and right.

"Sara!" Connie cried, pulling herself from Zazi's grip. "Did they get everyone out?"

Sara stared at Connie as if she couldn't quite place her—Sara's standard mode of address—and said, "I guess so?"

They both stared back at the apartment house as another section of roof sighed into the top floor and released a plume of sparks into the sky.

"Where's Sam? Did you see him?"

"Sam?" Sara repeated.

"My boyfriend. Sam Hartley. Who lives with me. Next door to you! Where'd they take everyone, when they got them out?" Connie's voice was rising.

Sara said, "Wait. Sam was home?"

A pit of ice opened inside Connie and spread like a sinkhole, devouring all the warmth she had ever felt in her life, leaving her fingers and toes numb. Sara's face twisted in dawning horror and she cried, "You mean Sam was in there?"

Connie couldn't answer. She didn't know what to do. She didn't know where to look.

"Come sit down," Zazi commanded. She led Connie away between police cars, over to where an ambulance sat waiting, back doors open, its inside harshly lit. Connie allowed herself to be led. She wrapped her arms around her softly swollen middle, eagle stone twine digging into her wrist. Something was rough around her middle. Connie looked down. Oh. The tote bag. She was still wearing her tote bag.

"I—" Connie faltered.

"Don't," said Zazi. "You need to sit down."

Connie looked around at the gawking faces in the crowd, clustered together like worshippers at a pagan bonfire. What was it about fire that was so compelling to people? They were drawn to it. Like moths. Like flies.

In the crowd of strangers Connie recognized the MIT grad students from upstairs. They were speaking Mandarin, and one of them was crying, and one of them had his shirt on backward, and they all had soot on their faces. But they were all there. Not far from them stood the alcoholic dad from the apartment above theirs. His feet were bare, his cheeks and nose red with burst capillaries. His son was riding on his shoulders, clutching a small stuffed dog.

Connie strained her eyes in the dark, looking at all the faces, hunting for Sam. He must have gotten out. Everyone else got out. They were always setting the smoke alarm off in the kitchen. It was deafening. No way he didn't get out.

"Excuse me." Zazi poked the shoulder of an EMT outside the ambulance, who looked around, concerned.

"Yes?" said the EMT.

"My friend's in shock."

Connie heard Zazi say this, and had time to marvel at it. In shock? Her? No, she was fine. She just had to find Sam.

A bright light flared into her eyes, and she squinted against it, blinded, as a voice said "Miss? Can you tell me your name? Miss?"

Connie held up her hands to fend off the light. "Where's Sam?" she said.

"Sam? Is that your name?" The light blared brighter. "Sam, I need you to sit down, okay?"

"No! Jesus!" Connie shouted. "My boyfriend. Sam Hartley. He was inside. I have to find him! Have you seen him?"

The light disappeared and a crinkly silver Mylar blanket was folded around her shoulders. In the sudden absence of light Connie could see nothing but afterglare.

"What was the name again?" the EMT asked.

"Sam!" she shouted into the black void that was closing in around her. "Sam!" She could hear nothing but the sound of her own panic, not even the roar of the fire and the groan as a beam holding up the second-floor staircase thinned and collapsed, bringing half the upper wall down with it.

"Sam! Where are you? Sam!" Connie's scream pierced the night and she clutched the Mylar blanket to her chest and knew, in her bones, that if she had lost Sam her heart would freeze and shatter and never be whole again.

"Cornell!"

Was that him? Or was it her panic? How would she know the difference?

Then he was there. She still couldn't see. She felt him, she smelled him—wood polish and turpentine and then flannel against her cheek, and his arms were around her waist, and his stubbled chin grazed the top of her head. Her eyes squinted closed, burning with tears, and she buried her nose in his shirt and breathed him in.

"I'm so sorry," she sobbed. "Sam! I'm so so sorry!"

"It's okay. I'm here. I'm fine." His body took her weight as she leaned on him. She wanted to climb inside his shirt, to climb into his skin. His shirt reeked of wood smoke.

She babbled, "It's all my fault. I'm sorry. I didn't fix it yet. I thought I had more time! Oh my God! I'm so very sorry!"

"What are you talking about?" Sam smoothed her hair off her forehead. "It was a prank, they said."

"It was a what?" Connie wiped her face and nose with a palm, smearing hot tears across her face.

"You know. A prank. A flaming bag of dog poop on the stoop, you ring the bell, someone comes out and steps on it, gets poop on their shoe. Only this time, no one answered the bell. Me, I didn't even hear it. And the rose bush out front was dead. It caught fire."

The green-white afterglare was fading from Connie's eyes, and Sam stood limned before her, his cheeks smudged with soot, wrapped in his own silver Mylar blanket. His hazel eyes were veiled and uncertain.

"No," she said, sickened with herself. "Maybe that's what they're saying caused it, but they're wrong."

He wasn't going to believe her. And if he did, he would hate her. She would lose him. But it didn't matter anymore. Connie had to tell him that every minute he spent loving her was a minute that brought him closer to death.

She took a deep breath, closed her eyes, and said, "It's me. I caused it. It was my fault."

"I don't think it was you who put a flaming bag on our stoop by the dead rosebush, do you?" His fingers combed her hair away from her forehead. She would miss his hands in her hair.

"No." Connie pressed a palm to one of her eyes and rubbed. "No, I didn't. But come on. Who ever heard of that prank burning down a whole apartment building? No. It's my fault."

Sam glanced over Connie's shoulder, and a shadow passed through his eyes. Connie turned to look, and saw their upstairs neighbor with his son on his shoulders. The boy, Caleb was his name, had started to cry, crushing his stuffed dog to his face.

"Sam," Connie said. Her voice felt brittle. "Where's Arlo?"

Sam tightened his grip on her waist. Heat and salt flushed through her cheeks and nose, and a hard knot tied in her throat.

"Where is he?" she said, but when she saw Sam go stricken, she knew. Red and white emergency lights striped his face.

"He woke me up. Barking," Sam said, haltingly. He wiped his nose with a fist. "I was asleep, on the couch. I'd been in Beverly all day, I was wiped."

"And then?" Arlo. Her Arlo. A dog, but not exactly. Arlos arrive when you are ready for them. Their names aren't always Arlo. They are called lots of things. And Arlos don't die. Not exactly. They just change. Connie knew this.

"And then I—" Sam wiped his eye, hard. He gulped for air, tried again. "I was in the entryway." His voice caught. "It was full of smoke. Caleb was on the stairs, and he tripped. I—That is, I had to—" Sam looked into the reddened sky and cried, "I got Caleb out, but they wouldn't let me go back inside. They wouldn't let me go back inside!"

Connie's face splintered. The ice chasm inside her widened, eating her stomach and her lungs and her soul and her heart. Her mouth pulled apart at the seams. Sam's hands cradled her shoulders. Arlo trotting out from under a hedge in grad school and following her home. Showing up, and vanishing at will. Her familiar. Her Arlo. Connie opened her mouth into the flannel of Sam's shirt and keened.

"Watch out!" someone screamed, and a *whoomp* and a blast of heat hit Connie like a wall. Stars burst across her vision with a shattering of pain.

"Goddammit! I told you not to park your car there!" someone else shouted.

Connie's eyes opened. She and Sam had been knocked sideways, smack into the side of the ambulance. The top story of the Green Monster was completely eaten now, save for its charred brick chimney reaching naked into the sky. In the parking lot of the auto repair shop stood the shell of her exploded Volvo, its winglike doors still splayed, hood peeled back like a sardine can. A smaller, secondary ball of flame ripped though the back seat—the hemlock, engulfed and curling. One of the tires burst and the car's shell settled in to burn.

Connie brought a hand up to her cheek. Her fingers came away wet. "Oh, my God," she said. Her home. Her car. All her books. Her computer. Her familiar. All of them, gone.

"There you are," said Zazi, appearing next to them by the ambulance. "Sam! You're okay! Oh, thank God."

Sam was crying, his mouth drawn down into a grimace. But he nodded and clutched Connie to him. The three of them huddled together, a still point within the maelstrom of firefighters and police officers and gawkers and sirens. Across the street, a firefighter took an ax to the driver's-side window of a sedan that was illegally parked by a hydrant. The hose was fed through the sedan's broken windows, unrolled across Massachusetts Avenue, lined with men holding it in place, and the water was turned on. A third stream aimed into the bay window that used to look out from Connie and Sam's living room over the rosebush. A billow of black smoke belched through the shattered glass.

Zazi said, "Well. Guess we shouldn't have parked there, huh."

Connie looked at Zazi. She had soot flecks on her cheeks, and her face was tight. Then, because she saw that Zazi needed her to do it, Connie laughed. Weakly. But it was a laugh.

"It was on its last legs anyway," Connie said, looking at the flaming shell of the Volvo.

Sam wiped his eyes and his nose, coming back to himself. "Oh, my God. All our books. All our books!" he cried.

"They're just books," Connie said. Books could be replaced, even if they were very fine and rare and dangerous and hard to use. She'd learned that lesson well enough.

But you only get one familiar, in a given life. Only one.

"It's a wonder everyone got out okay," Zazi said.

The three of them watched in silence as the last clapboards from the third floor, silhouetted against the night sky like ribs, crumbled into ash.

"What did you mean? When you said it was your fault," Sam asked, voice quiet.

Connie put her fists to her temples.

"The Lord giveth," she said. "And the Lord taketh away."

"What does that mean?" Sam asked.

Connie spoke softly. "That's how Grace explained it to me. That we get to have this thing. This particular ability. But that it comes with a cost. The cost is pain. Physical, and emotional too. The worst pain you could possibly imagine."

"What are you talking about?" Sam said at the same time that Zazi said, "Oh."

"Deliverance Dane," Connie continued after a breath, "was my great-many-times-removed grandmother. Her physick book really works. That's why Chilton wanted to take it from me all those years ago. That's why I had to destroy it."

"Are you serious?" Sam said. The stench of burning wood hung thick in the air, and the smoke was making Connie's eyes and nose raw.

"I am serious. And that's not the worst part." She took hold of Sam's upper arm. "Anyone who marries into my family dies a horrible early death."

"That doesn't make any sense," Sam said. "Are you in shock?"

"No, Sam," Connie said. Zazi was cupping her elbows with her opposite hands to stop herself from shivering. "That's what gave you those seizures, when we met. It wasn't Chilton. It was because you had the terrible misfortune to love me."

The heat of the burning apartment building pressed against Connie's back, through the Mylar. Heat, and pressure.

"So it's fine," he said, one eye squinting in thought. "I got better. It's fine."

"No," Connie said. "I was right about the pattern, but I was wrong about the cause. It happens when"—and here she found herself strangely unwilling to name the truth, but she knew she must—"when the next generation is set."

"You're—!" Zazi exclaimed, but stopped herself from saying anything else.

"And how fast it happens seems somehow connected to the weather," Connie said, growing exhausted. "I don't understand how. I think I've maybe found a way to stop it, and that's what I've been researching the last couple of months, and I'm so scared I won't get it right and something will happen to you that I've stopped sleeping. When I saw the Green Monster was on fire I was afraid I'd failed, and I'd lost you. And I should've told you sooner, and I'm sorry I didn't, but I was afraid you'd think I was crazy. I won't blame you if you do."

It was out. Dizziness buzzed inside her head, like bees stirred up in a hive. Her eyes were closed so she didn't have to see Sam's face. She could feel Zazi's nervous energy next to her. One by one the police sirens turned off, leaving only the sound of the crackling fire and the chatter of bystanders. A creak and a sigh as another section of wall collapsed into ash.

"Wow," said Sam.

Zazi said, "That's. That's really." But she didn't finish.

Connie screwed up the courage to open her eyes and look to see the effect of what she'd had to say, on the man in whom her whole world was contained.

Sam's mouth settled into a firm line. "You're in shock," he announced. "You don't know what you're saying." He turned to Zazi. "Are you hearing this?"

"I'm hearing it," said Zazi.

He put his hands on Connie's shoulders and shook her, gently. "Come on. Snap out of it," he said.

"I'm not in shock," Connie told him.

"I should get that EMT to come over here and check you out," Sam insisted.

"He did," said Connie. "I'm fine. I'm telling you the truth."

Connie cupped Sam's cheeks in her hands and steered him to look her full in the face. His hazel eyes were red-rimmed from smoke. Through her palms she could feel how tired he was. How afraid he had been. How afraid he still was, after what she had told him.

"Watch," she whispered.

She focused on the minute gray flecks in his irises. She loved those flecks. They looked like tiny constellations. As if his eyes contained an entire universe that she alone could see.

As she gazed on him, her hands pressed to his cheeks, a warm tingling began to spread from the centers of her palms. Sharp stinging flickered along the nerves in her fingers. She knew he could feel it. Warmth, in her hands. Vibrating. Sam's lips parted in bafflement. Connie smiled, slowly.

Now, he would know.

Sam's eyes widened as he watched the pale mist created by her mind collect in her irises, filling in, thickening, whitening her eyes until they were completely blank, like a marble statue. Sam whispered, "No way," in the manner of someone realizing something he already knew. As she held his face, she told his pain and fear to go away. She felt it, seeping from inside his head, into her hands, spreading a dull throbbing pain up as far as her elbows. His forehead softened.

She gently released his cheeks, leaving behind faint glowing blue fingerprints on his skin. He touched his cheek with disbelief.

Her eyes cleared, leaving a residual ache in her temples. She said, "Do you see?"

"It's really true?" Sam brushed a fingertip along Connie's eyebrow.

Connie nodded.

"You're really—"

"Yes," Connie said. Even within the haze of pain she found that she felt lighter. Her shoulders lowered. Relief. She had told him, and he hadn't run away. A line drifted into her mind, dredged up from the depths of her memory:

And ye shall know the truth, and the truth shall make you free.

Connie turned to Zazi. "Well?" Connie said to her.

Zazi twisted a curl around her finger. "I mean," she said presently, "my mom's friend Nancy thinks she saw the Virgin Mary in her French toast. So."

Another *whoomp* and burst of breaking glass, and the Volvo's alarm ground to life for three sorry wails before a stream of water hissed the fire into submission, leaving only its charred skeleton in a circle of ash in the auto repair shop parking lot.

Zazi said, "Suppose what you're saying is true. About Sam. Seems like maybe we should stop wasting time. Right?"

Connie clutched her tote bag to her chest. "Tonight," she said. "I think we have to do it tonight."

"So what do we do?" Sam asked.

"We've got to get to Grace's house," Connie said. "In Marblehead."

"I'll get us a Zipcar," Zazi said.

Interlude

————

Marblehead, Massachusetts

Evening, April 23

1816

Temperance held her hands basketed before her, the electrical pulses zinging between her fingertips.

"Stop!" came the command again, filling the kitchen with unaccustomed force.

In the doorway from the hall that led to the sitting room stood Patty Jacobs—Patience being her full Christian name. Temperance's mother.

Patty leaned on the doorframe, her body swaying with constant subtle motion not unlike the wave-sickness of sailors who set foot back on land after many months at sea. Patty had never been in a boat in her life. In her free hand she held a heavy glass bottle, empty—her daily ration of rum. Patty's eyes, once cool and gray like Temperance's own, had grown clouded in the past few years. Her sunken cheeks were marked by starbursts of pink capillaries; her nose was reddened and swollen. The rum got into her body, soaked through her skin, and breathed out of her pores till she smelled of stale Christmas cake.

"I can't stop!" Temperance cried. A blue vein of electricity snapped from her index finger into her own palm, ripping along the nerves all the way down the side of her body and into her foot.

"You must!" Patty's rum bottle exploded across the floor, shards of blue glass skittering into the fire. Faith screamed, Obie pushed his chair back from the trestle table, and Temperance covered her face against the shards of glass, breaking the electric tension between her hands. Patty eased into the room, managing to walk to the hearth with a hand on the sideboard, then a chair back, then Temperance's shoulder. She leaned in close, close enough that Tempe could smell her sour breath.

"Why you be doing this, now?" Patty said.

Temperance drew away, nearer to Obie. She took hold of his inner elbow.

"I can't lose him," she said. "I refuse."

Patty peered over Tempe's shoulder at the notes scattered across the trestle table. "You refuse?" she said.

"I refuse," Temperance repeated as Obie put his hand over hers.

"I see." Patty inched nearer, sniffing over Temperance's other shoulder, where steam rose from the cauldron. It smelled pale and savory, like celery, with an undercurrent of spice and flowers. The poppyseed pods had opened in the broth.

Faith muffled her sobs in the fur of the ratter, who had materialized in her arms. The animal's vaguely colored eyes watched them.

"Clean that up, girl," Patty barked, waving a hand at the shards of glass glinting in the hearthlight.

Wiping her nose on her sleeve, Faith set the animal down and took up the broom in the corner. No sound in the kitchen of the Milk Street house but the popping of the fire and the scrape, scrape, scrape of dried rushes failing to sweep up broken glass.

"This won't do it," Patty said, flicking her fingers at the notes on the trestle table. "Something missing."

"I know," Temperance said. She withdrew the envelope that lived concealed in her busk, held it up between finger and thumb, and tapped its corner against her temple.

Patty said, "Not that."

Her bleary eye settled on Faith, still gamely trying to sweep up the glass, but so far managing only to heap it into an untidy pile. She'd caught a cinder in the rushes and stomped on it to put it out.

"Girl!" Patty shouted, and Faith looked up like a startled cat. She favored Obie, in her face and tangles of russet hair, but there was no mistaking whose eyes those were. Paler, even, than her mother's.

"I can't get them all," she objected. "The shards're too fine."

"Leave it," Patty said. She crooked a finger to summon the child. Patty rested a gnarled hand atop her granddaughter's head and looked down into her face. "Good girl. Now then. What were we learning about, the other day?"

Faith stiffened, and tried to look back to Temperance for reassurance, but her grandmother's hand on her hair kept her head from moving.

"How to multiply two three-digit numbers together," Faith answered, but there was a question in her voice.

"Not Wednesday," Patty said. "What we were studying the other day?"

Faith shrank into herself. Temperance moved instinctively to take a step toward them, but Obie held her back.

"Plants," Faith said, voice shriveled down to a croak. "And animals."

"That's right." Patty's thin lips drew back in a smile, revealing preternaturally white and even teeth. To Temperance, she added, "How plants and animals work. And can be made to work, together."

Temperance knew her mother had been schooling the girl in basic physick. She also knew Faith didn't much care for it. Her fascinations lay in manipulating numbers, measuring things, adding things together, taking them back apart. It might be just as well. No money in babies or charms anymore. Maybe Faith wouldn't sell fish. Maybe she'd cut shoe patterns.

"Do you recall," Patty said to her granddaughter, "what we learned was of special strength, in matters occult, such as these?"

Faith attempted to squirm out of her grandmother's grip, but the older woman held her fast, keeping one hand on top of her head and bringing the other up under the girl's chin, squeezing her cheeks until her lips pillowed out like a fish's.

"Mother!" Temperance exclaimed, breaking free of Obie and pulling her daughter away. Faith's eyes welled with tears, but she swallowed them.

"Those cheeks!" Patty exclaimed. "Such fat in them. So hale and hearty! I remember when yours looked just the same," she said to Temperance. "As round and fat as ripe peaches."

A black cloud stirred to life in Tempe's chest, split through with cracks of lightning. She grabbed hold of Faith's upper arm and held her close.

"No," she said.

"Ah, now she remembers," Patty cackled. She bent over, hands on her knees to look into Faith's face.

"Kid fat," Patty said to Faith. "Dug fresh from the grave."

The color drained out of Faith's young face, and Obie cried, "The hell are you talking about!"

"Stop it, Mother," Temperance snapped. Faith was trembling, her pale eyes leaping between her mother and grandmother. Whimpering emanated from under the trestle table.

"What's she talking about, Tempe?" Obie said.

"Nothing," Temperance said, glaring at her mother to dare her to disagree with her. "A fairy story."

"Oh, it's no fairy story." Patty's laughter dissolved into a cough. "It's older than fairies. You look at them old carvings they used to have, in the churches." Patty gazed into the middle distance, her blood-rimmed eyes turning inward. "The Sheelas. Life and death. Always bound up together." On unsteady legs she lowered herself into one of the chairs.

"What's she on about?" Obie said in a low voice to Temperance.

In truth, Tempe had no idea. Sometimes Patty babbled when the evening came on. It usually meant it was time to make up her trundle in the sitting room, time for the rest of them to withdraw into the attic bedrooms, under quilts and quiet.

Patty raised her voice. "I'm sitting right here, and I'm making perfect sense. Life and death. You can't have one without the other."

Temperance stared at Obie, who was glaring at her mother, and rested a gentle hand on top of Faith's head. The girl's hair needed washing.

"But—" Obie started to object.

"No buts about it." Patty leaned her head against the splat of the chair and closed her eyes.

"Obie," Temperance said.

"Well," Obie said, "I'm still shipping out."

Patty abruptly pushed her chair away from the table and rose, sway-ing, to her feet. "All right," she said to the room at large. To Temper-ance, she said, "You ready to go?"

"Go?" Temperance said.

"Them two can stay here. Make sure it doesn't all boil off. You and me, we've got to go. Ready?"

"You said there's no point," Temperance objected.

Patty was groping in her pockets for something. On a shelf nearby she found a small, stoppered bottle, smiled lovingly at it, and slipped it into her skirt pocket. "Didn't," she said. "Said nothing of the sort. Look you, getting so married to how you think things ought to be. Come along." She pointed at the ceiling, its rafters crowded with dried herbs, and recited from Revelations. "Blessed is he that readeth, and they that hear the words of this prophecy, and keep those things which are writ-ten therein: for the time is at hand."

Temperance, with a last puzzled glance exchanged with Obie, helped her mother to the door. They stepped together out into the close and humid springtime night.

Chapter Twenty-three

Marblehead, Massachusetts

Last night of April

2000

"What happened?" The night was dark, moonless, and Connie couldn't see anything other than the black mass of the hedge that hid the Milk Street house. But she heard her mother's voice. As her eyes accustomed themselves to the darkness, Connie saw her.

Grace Goodwin stood, bareheaded and barefoot, a fringed shawl tucked around her shoulders, at the gate in the hedge. Connie, Sam, and Zazi climbed out of the Zipcar—a Kia, lime green—and trudged together to the gate. Oyster shells crunched under their feet. The night felt close and hot, more like summer than spring. Toads croaked unseen in the woods at the end of the lane.

"Oh, my God. You all look terrible." Grace squinted at them in the dark. Milk Street had streetlights, had had them since the fifties, but they didn't reach all the way to the end of the lane. The woods had a way of swallowing artificial light. "What is that, soot?"

"Hi, Grace," Sam said. His voice was weary.

"Hello, Mrs. Goodwin," Zazi said. "Is it okay if I park there?"

"Mom, there was a. There was—" The words stuck in Connie's mouth, bitter as ashes.

Grace put a hand on Connie's shoulder. "Tell me what happened," she said.

Connie started to cry.

"We're all right," Sam hurried to say. "It's just been a long night."

"Come inside," Grace said. "I'll put the kettle on."

She wrapped an arm around Connie's waist, and Connie leaned into her mother, breathing in her familiar scent of lavender and patchouli. Grace's hair, long like hers, had gone wiry as it went gray. The skin of Grace's cheek was soft as paper. Maybe it was going to be all right.

"Is Arlo with you?" Grace asked.

Connie put her hands over her face and sobbed.

"Oh," said Grace. A trembling passed through her body which Connie felt through her mother's arm.

Sam and Zazi followed behind them along the flagstone path, through the droning of toads under leaves in the garden. Here and there, toad eyes glimmered.

Inside, the house was uncomfortably warm. Windows were propped open for any passing breeze, but none was passing. Grace disappeared into the rear kitchen as Connie, Sam, and Zazi collapsed into shield-back chairs around the dining table. Two red candelabras cast a warm flickering glow over the room. On the wall opposite the hearth, between the windows open to the garden, the portrait of Temperance Hobbs stared down at them, the firelight giving her painted eyes the illusion of life. A fire was going in the big hearth. A little one, in one corner. Grace was baking something in the beehive oven.

Connie breathed deep.

Sourdough.

The terrierlike creature under Temperance's arm in the painting had glittering eyes too. Connie stared at her lap. She toyed with the tote bag so she wouldn't have to look at the painting.

"What's in there?" Sam pointed to the bag.

When Connie didn't answer, Zazi said, "We were at Rafferty's. When we saw the fire."

"You went to Rafferty's?" Sam said. "Did you find any corals?"

"What do you need coral for?" Grace asked from the kitchen door, which she was easing open with a hip. She held a tray with four mismatched mugs and an old copper kettle. Steam breathed from the kettle's lip, scented with jasmine. Grace set the tray at one end of the table and, without asking who wanted what, started apportioning tea, some with lemon, some with milk.

"I need it," Connie said. "For—"

"Wait." Grace went over to the portrait of Temperance, ran her fingers expertly along the underside of the frame, found the catch, and pressed it. The hidden compartment sprang open. Grace took out the secret box and set it on the dining table. She patted Connie's shoulder. "I'm sorry about your apartment building," Grace said as she turned the key they'd left in the keyhole, opening the lid on delicate fingertips and hunting about inside. "All your books. Arlo. It must be terribly upsetting."

"But how did you—" Zazi was interrupted by a burst of electronic disco music from somewhere under the table. It sounded like "More than a Woman." "Oh, my God, I'm sorry." She dug in her shoulder bag and produced her Nokia. Zazi bent over to answer, her hand over her mouth.

"Mami? Hello?" she said. Then she spoke quickly in Spanish, punctuated with a few English phrases. Connie caught "fire engines" and "Zipcar" and "North Shore," but not much else. Zazi paused while the person on the other end of the line spoke—a woman, who sounded annoyed—and then Zazi added a few more phrases, at a higher volume. Zazi rolled her eyes, said, "Okay, love you, bye," with two kisses, and hung up.

"I'm *so* sorry." Zazi stuffed the cell phone back in her bag.

"Did you tell your mother it's totally fine you staying the night with us?" Grace passed Zazi her mug of tea. "She's probably worried sick."

"I . . . Yeah." Zazi looked at Grace strangely as she accepted the cup. "Thanks." She took a sip. To Connie she said in a low voice, "Your mom and my mom should start a club."

Connie smiled weakly.

"Tell her," Sam prodded. "Tell her what you think you have to do."

Connie said, "She knows."

Grace chuckled to herself. "Indeed," she said. "I'd have done it myself. If I knew how." She opened the lid and combed her fingers through the dirt inside. When she found what she was looking for, she held it up.

"Coral," she announced.

It was the small reddish pebble from inside the box. Polished smooth, like the nub of a finger snipped off, or the tip of a tongue. Connie held out her hand, eagle stone knocking at her wrist. Grace dropped the coral pebble into her waiting palm and Connie stared down at it.

"I think"—Connie looked at Sam and Zazi and Grace in turn—"that might be everything."

"This is going to be awesome," Zazi said, her knees bobbing under the table with excess energy.

"Constance," Grace said, a hand on Connie's arm. "Are you sure you've thought this through?"

Connie closed her fist tight around the piece of coral and held it up to her forehead. When she closed her eyes, she saw the Green Monster folding in on itself, swallowed by fire. She opened her eyes so she didn't have to watch it burn.

"Yes," Connie said.

Grace squeezed her arm. A passing breath of air caused the candlelight to flicker, dancing their shadows around the dining room. "Well then," she said. "Let's get started."

A suitably cauldron-like receptacle wasn't forthcoming, but it didn't take long for Grace to dig up an aluminum spaghetti pot that seemed as if it would be big enough.

"I can't find the lid," she said apologetically as she struggled with it from the kitchen sink into the dining room, sloshing water on the floor.

"That's okay," Connie said. She was kneeling at the hearth, feeding sticks of firewood into the fire.

"God." Sam fanned himself at the dining table. "It's like a sauna in here."

"Sorry," Connie said, her attention close on the fire. "I don't know how else to do it."

Zazi sat with her heels on the seat of the dining chair, arms around her knees, dark eyes shining as she watched Connie's preparations.

"Have you got everything with you?" Zazi asked, reaching for the tote bag on the dining table and peering inside.

"Almost. But whatever we still need, we can probably find in the garden," said Connie, sitting back on her heels. She looked up at Grace. "How do we put the pot in the fire? We can't just sit it on top. It'll fall over."

Grace lifted the wire handle of the spaghetti pot and hung it from her hand. "Behold," she said. Using a pair of fireplace tongs, she maneuvered an iron hook from the back of the hearth. The hook squealed into place over the fire, raining flecks of rust. Grace hung the pot on it, waiting with her hands nearby to make sure the iron didn't snap from the weight, and when it didn't, she used the tongs to ease the spaghetti pot over the hottest part of the fire. Tiny air bubbles began to form around the rim of the water's surface.

"Now then," said Grace, dusting her hands on her jeans. "Where's this weather work recipe I've been hearing so much about?"

Back at the dining table, Connie reached into her tote bag and pulled out the notebook in which she'd been puzzling out Temperance's recipe. She opened it and flipped through the pages.

"All right." Connie's index finger marked the place to begin. "So. First, we've got to make the ointment. And then, there's a sort of incantation I have to do." Connie watched Sam as she spoke, waiting for him to realize what she was really saying, and change his mind. He sat at the head of the dining table, arms folded over his chest. But he didn't look worried. In fact, he wore the same open, guileless expression that he'd had the first night they'd gone out together, to a bar in the old sail loft downtown. Over beers, Sam had tried to convince her that people's belief in magic should matter.

"Come on," she'd said, slurping beer foam from the top of her glass.

"But if people organize their lives assuming that something is true," Sam pointed out, "shouldn't we pay attention?"

To prove his point that night, he'd led her by the hand through darkened yards and alleyways, trespassing across wet lawns, hiding in shadows. Finally, they found what he wanted her to see: a long-forgotten boundary marker, carved with a grinning stick figure, its arms and legs splayed. Like the Sheelas in that book she and Zazi had found at Rafferty's. A protector. She hadn't believed it at first.

"There was something here to be afraid of," he'd said.

Now, safe in the firelight around her grandmother's Queen Anne dining table, Sam smiled at her. His look said, *Remember? I'm the one who first showed you that magic could be real. The trick is, you have to believe.*

Grace held out a hand to stop her. "Wait," she said.

She disappeared into the kitchen. One of the candles in the center of the dining table started to smoke. Then Grace reappeared, her fists full of dried sage.

"*Mom*," Connie started to object.

"Excuse me. Whose house is this?" Grace said, more sharply than was usual for her. All of Grace's years in the New Age, all her self-actualization and meditation, hadn't been able entirely to purge her of the New England trait of expressing worry in the form of anger. In the sharpness, Connie heard that Grace was afraid.

"I'm sorry." Connie loathed reverting to her teenage self, a self embarrassed by her hippie mother in front of her preppy Concord friends. Penny loafers and knee socks and shame.

Grace thrust the sage into the hearth fire.

"This'll only take a second," Grace said tightly.

The sage bloomed to life, catching fire, filling the room with a sweet-savory cloud. Grace shook out the flaming ends in the hearth in a shower of sparks, reducing the flames to a blue-gray smolder. Grace turned to Connie, cupping her hand around the smoking ends of the smudge to keep embers from falling on the pine floor. She held the smoking sage aloft over Connie's head.

Grace's eyes slowly paled, as though occluded with whitening smoke.

"I, Grace Goodwin, a servant of God, call upon, desire, and conjure thee, Abael, Banech, by the most holy words Agios, Tetragrammaton, Eschiros, Adonai, Alpha et Omega, Raphael, Michael, Uriel, Schmaradiel, Zaday, and by all the known names of Almighty God, by whatsoever thou, Abael, canst be compelled, that thou appear before me, in a human form, and fulfill what I desire, to keep my daughter Constance safe, and reveal to us who put her partner Sam in danger for his life. Fiat, fiat, fiat."

With each "fiat," Grace waved the sage smudge from the top of Connie's head, to her right shoulder, to her left shoulder, and then to her nose. Then Grace shook the sage up by the rafters, then down by the floor, raining ash in a semicircle around Connie's sneakered feet, and then with a few last words muttered under her breath, she tossed the sage smudge into the fire. It vanished with a poof of gray-blue smoke.

"That was awesome." Zazi was grinning.

Grace said, "Water's boiling, my dear."

"What's that supposed to do?" Connie asked. She had never heard that charm before. It seemed too old-school for Grace, who preferred physick of the Reiki-and-crystals variety.

Grace busied her hands with the fire. "Maybe nothing. Maybe it will help to keep you safe, while you do the work. Maybe, if there's a will behind the danger to Sam, it will help us to know whose it is. *Il est bon à savoir*, after all."

"How would it do that?" Zazi asked from behind her knees.

Grace leaned the fireplace poker against the wall. "You're a historian," she said. "You tell me."

Zazi dropped first one leg, then the other. "Well," she said, "I know during the Salem thing, some of the villagers testified that they'd seen the shapes of other people in town come in through the window."

"That was a huge theological debate at the time," Connie said. "Whether or not the devil could assume the shape of an innocent person."

"Can he?" Grace asked without looking round.

"Cotton Mather thought no," Connie said. "But Increase Mather thought yes."

Grace shook out the hand that had held the sage, massaging the palm with the thumb of her other hand. As if it were sore.

"Whether any of us is ever really innocent," Grace said, "is perhaps another question."

Another of the candle flames lengthened, sending a plume of black smoke coiling up to the rafters.

"I guess we should get started," Connie said. She fanned the contents of the tote bag across the surface of the dining table. A shadow of pain tingled along the nerves in her hands, and she flexed them to discharge it. She handed Zazi the recipe sheet. "You tell me how much of everything we need."

"It doesn't say," said Zazi, examining the paper.

"The numbers," Connie said. "Just tell me what they are. Okay?"

"Okay."

Connie took up the freezer-burned celery. It was limp, a head made up of five wilting stalks, browning at the tips. To Sam, she said, "Step one. Make smallage."

"Mmmmm," said Sam. "Smallage."

Connie dropped the celery into the simmering spaghetti pot with a plop. The room began to smell faintly, lightly, of boiling vegetables.

"Step two," Connie continued to Grace. "Add a piece of coral."

She held the polished red pebble from Temperance's box up in the candlelight. It shone. Connie rubbed it with a thumb, enjoying its smoothness, before tossing it into the spaghetti pot. It landed in the water, spitting up a fat droplet from the bubbling center.

"In alchemical tradition, it's both a plant and a stone," Grace remarked to Zazi. "Very powerful, in the right circumstances. As are all things that move in liminal spaces."

The smallage was beginning to steam. Moisture beaded on Connie's cheeks.

"What's next on the list?" she asked.

"Seven wolfsbane," said Zazi.

"We'll have to get that from the garden. What else?"

Zazi scanned down the list. "There's like five things here you're missing. Next one on the list that you've got is seven tobacco."

"Aha," said Connie. She picked up the pack of Camels, held it up for everyone to see like an illusionist about to do a magic trick, unwrapped the cellophane, and pulled out seven cigarettes, holding them in a fan shape between her fingers.

"I'm so glad you never smoked," Grace remarked to herself.

Connie laughed.

"You didn't, did you?" Grace exclaimed.

"Who can remember?" countered Connie. She slit each cigarette lengthwise with a thumbnail, and rained the contents one at a time into the spaghetti pot. Faint bubbling and hissing marked the flecks of tobacco falling into the smallage, and an addictive, toasted aroma filled the kitchen. To Zazi, Connie said, "Next?"

"Nine opium?" Zazi looked up. "How the heck are you going to get opium? Nobody has opium. I wouldn't even know where to look for opium."

"I'm cheating a little," said Connie. She took up the expired pill bottle with Sam's old prescription for Tylenol with codeine. She twisted off the cap and shook the three remaining pills into her palm. They were powdery with age.

"Mom?" said Connie.

Grace got up and went into the kitchen. She reappeared a moment later with a wooden cutting board and a small paring knife.

Connie placed each pill on the cutting board and said, "Behold. The power of math."

She sliced each pill into thirds. Then Connie carried the cutting board with its nine crumbling measures of modern opium over to the spaghetti pot, tipped the board sideways, and used the knife to scrape the pills into the brew. When the pills landed, the boiling liquid spat and sizzled; a hot fleck of water hit Connie's cheek. She squinted against it, but some of the fluid had gotten into her eye. She saw white and felt stinging, like nettles under her eyelid. She pressed a palm to her eye. "Ow."

"One saffron," continued Zazi, picking up the glass vial of kitchen herb (1973 vintage, judging from the peeling yellow label) and holding it up for Connie to take.

Still squinting, an irritated tear welling in her lower lid, Connie accepted the jar and withdrew the small envelope of saffron from within, dropping it whole into the spaghetti pot. The aroma emanating from the hearth went mallowy. Sort of sickening. Like rotting leaves, or logs blistered with mushrooms. A soft throb rose in Connie's temples.

"Three poplar leaves. Is that what these are?" Zazi indicated the three heart-shaped, pointed leaves Connie had stolen from Mahoney's, browning around the edges. The throb in her temples pulsed. Connie nodded. Zazi handed the leaves to her, and Connie dropped them whole into the pot. The bubbles gurgled and swallowed the leaves into a thin black liquid. An oily scum began to collect on the surface.

The steam thickened, and thickened some more, until it formed a column of dense white smoke. The smell was overpowering. Of rotting, and worms, and larvae. The secret rustlings of cockroaches and ants and beetles, if insect rustling could have a smell. Bile rose in the back of Connie's throat. She leaned on the dining table, breathing through her mouth.

"Let's step outside for a minute," Grace suggested. "Give it a bit to simmer. And we can collect whatever else we need."

Connie swallowed the sour bubble in her throat and chest, and the four of them filed through the hall, out the front door into the humid spring night.

The tide must have been coming in, because as soon as she stepped outside Connie smelled the ocean. Even though the Milk Street house stood on a narrow alley in the woods in the center of the peninsula, not within sight of the water, she could sense where the ocean was. East. Always east. Connie sucked the briny air deep into her lungs. The throb in her temples receded. Night was blacker under the canopy of vines over the garden, and the toads quieted their calling when they saw four people emerge from inside the house. The kitchen windows, propped open, cast warm semicircles of firelight into the garden.

"Wolfsbane, you say?" Grace's feet and head were bare, and she stepped through the overgrown garden lightly, the soles of her feet dark with dirt. Somewhere along the line she had pulled on a pair of old gardening gloves, and she rubbed her palms on her jeans as she approached a tall flowering shrub, with weedy leaves and nodding spire-shaped flowers, colored a rich enough violet that they were almost invisible in the dark.

"Seven," confirmed Zazi, holding the list up to the light. She stood directly under the rusted horseshoe that had always been over the front door.

Grace clipped off seven wolfsbane flowers with pruning shears, cupping them in one of her gloved hands.

Not far away, car tires crunched softly over the oyster shells of the alleyway. They all paused, listening. Milk Street was a dead end. Cars didn't often come down the lane unexpectedly.

Even the toads were quiet. The tires rolled to a stop a ways away, and a lone toad droned. Grace turned her attention to twisting the corners of her shawl into a makeshift bag for the dark violet flower heads. Connie waded into the greenery of the garden, sharp herbal leaves brushing against her shins. She trod lightly. At one point her toe nudged toad flesh, and a rippling of leaves marked the animal's flight.

"What next?" Grace asked.

"Cinquefoil?" guessed Connie.

"That's right," Zazi agreed.

"Over here," said Grace, beckoning to Sam. "It grows near the roses. They all like to stick together, you know." Sam followed her, picking through the overgrowth. A toad leapt away from his right boot, ribbiting into the dark.

"Technically cinquefoil's sort of a weed," Grace continued. She knelt by a plot of tangled rosebushes, their buds closed knots of green, their gnarled roots obscured by a riot of woody five-leafed vines. "But I'm rather partial to it."

Sam joined Grace on his knees and ran his hands over the small yellow flowers shimmering under the rosebushes.

"It's odd," Grace said quietly. "They bloom so early now."

Connie bent and rubbed a papery sage leaf between her finger and thumb, and brought her hand up to her nose to smell. Well down the lane, a car door slammed, muffled by the dense leaves of the hedge. The slam echoed inside Connie's skull. She breathed in the smell of the sage oil and it wafted into her skull too, mixing with the smoke and the echo.

"How many?" Sam called to Zazi.

Zazi's eyes were in shadow from the light in the hall behind her, which shone through her curls like a halo. Connie squinted at her. The shadows made Zazi look strange. Almost skeletal. "Nine," Zazi said, answering Sam. The word echoed in Connie's head.

"Huh," Connie said aloud, and the word had an almost physical presence inside her mouth. A roundness and a squirming on her tongue. She leaned over with her hands on her knees. The squirming in her mouth worsened, and she heaved and coughed to get rid of the feeling, but when she tried to spit out another word she instead spied a tiny toad flickering away under a leaf at her feet.

"Don't worry," Grace reassured Sam. "You don't need gloves for these ones."

Sam reached into the snarls of vines under the rose bush and snapped off a yellow five-petaled flower. He yelped in pain, bringing his thumb to his mouth.

"Except for the thorns," said Grace.

Sam finished picking the cinquefoil while Zazi laughed. Their laughter sounded slowed down. Unwound like a loosened wire.

"Now, henbane," said Zazi. "Just one."

"Hmmmm," said Grace, sitting on her heels. "Probably over with the nightshades. Don't you think so, my darling?"

Connie, hands still on her knees, eyed the desiccated tomato plants at the far corner of the house, crisp and rustling from the previous year. They would reseed themselves soon, the new children of rotting fruit fallen at the end of summer. The tomatoes dominated that side of the house, a webbing of sour-smelling flowers and leaves cycling in and out of death. The nightshade corner.

"Yes," she said thickly. Her mouth tasted of toad.

The henbane grew near the rear of the house, away from the light of the open kitchen windows. The vines and spires in the nightshade corner shimmered in the dark. Connie moved deeper into the nightshades, leaves rustling around her ankles, dried vines clawing at her hair.

At last, blooming under the midnight shadow of the alder tree, loomed a tall set of stalks, studded with sharp-sided leaves as wide as cabbages, and topped by flowers with pale petals and oxblood-red cups. The dark voids in the center of white petals in the night gave the henbane the eerie look of a medusa, with dozens of eyes mounted on leafy stalks. Watching her.

A breeze tripped through the garden, bringing with it the cool breath of the ocean, raising the hairs along Connie's arms.

"You get it yet?" called Sam.

Connie took one of the eye-flowers in her hand and pulled.

It wouldn't come off.

She got her thumbnail into the stalk and worried the flower back and forth until it came away with a snap. When the stalk broke, a spray of fluid flecked Connie's lips and eyes. Startled, she stepped backward, and the arch of her foot met soft toad flesh. It stirred and croaked out of harm's way, and Connie leapt straight up.

For an instant, she had the illusion of feeling suspended in midair. Connie had time to think *This is weird*, but instantly the sensation was gone and she landed hard on the ground, twisting her ankle. She swore and bent to touch her twisted joint, but the act of bending over made her head blur. Not with nausea. This was more like vertigo. She was unsure of her body's relationship to itself in space.

"Whoa," she said, bent double, one hand on her thigh. The other clutched the henbane stalk. Plant flesh in her hand. Prickly. Hot. Heat in her ankle too, and in her temples, moving to the crown of her head.

"What's taking her so long?" Sam said to someone else.

"Where is she?" That was Zazi. "I can't see her."

"I'm here," Connie said. Her tongue felt furred and alien in her mouth.

"You okay?" Sam called.

Connie shook her head, trying to be rid of the eerie, spinning, weightless feeling. "Yeah," she said to the ground. "I tripped."

"Next we need hemlock," Zazi said. Her voice reached Connie as if from a great distance away. Traveling through ripples of water.

"How much?" asked Grace from the opposite side of the garden. Her mother sounded muffled too. As though she were speaking through snow.

"Three," called Zazi.

Connie lifted her head, looking up at the vine canopy overhead. Little flashes of light bloomed and winked out in her field of vision, like static, or a filmstrip with holes burned through it, pulling apart in the film projector. She thought she heard footsteps. Footsteps on oyster shell. But she couldn't tell how close or far away anything was. Her mother sounded as though she were across a valley, and yet at the same time she was close enough that Connie could hear her gardening shears clipping the branches of a hemlock growing in the corner of the garden devoted to pines and sharp, needly things.

Connie crept back to the front garden, away from the nightshades, back to the safety of the firelight through the kitchen windows. When she rounded the corner of the house she found Sam and Zazi on the stoop by the front door, looking at the list, and Grace approaching from the other side of the house with her gloved hands full of hemlock.

"Oh, my darling, you didn't pick that barehanded, did you?" Grace said when she saw Connie.

Connie looked down at her fist closed around the henbane.

"Last thing," Zazi broke in, her voice rising with excitement. "Mandrake. Then we can go back in and finish!"

"Mandrake. Now that's what I'm talking about. I've always wanted to see one of those," someone said from over by the gate.

Connie squinted into the darkness, but the henbane must have been messing with her perceptions, because the darkness kept swelling and deepening whenever she tried to focus her eyes. But she recognized the voice.

"Who the hell are you?" Sam shouted.

Zazi folded her arms over her chest. "Thomas."

Interlude

Marblehead, Massachusetts

Night, April 23

1816

"Mother!" Temperance hissed. Night had come on thick under the canopy of the Milk Street garden, and Temperance could hardly see her.

"Come along," Patty whispered.

The ratter stuck close to Temperance's heels, worming around her ankles. When they reached the gate through the hedge she tried to edge him away with a toe, but he wasn't going.

"Shhh," Patty said, a bony finger to her lips.

She pushed open the gate with a faint creak, and Temperance was surprised that the air outside the boundary of the garden hedge was sharp again with the tang of winter. Not enough to freeze, but enough to make her shiver and wish she'd thought to wear a cloak.

"Hmm," Patty muttered as she moved deeper into the darkness.

"Mother!" Temperance shout-whispered at the retreating woman's back. "Where are we going?"

"Palfreys' goat shed," her mother whispered back.

"What! Why?" But Patty only plucked at Temperance's sleeve to get her to follow.

They crept down the lane past sleeping clapboard houses, shutters closed and front-door lanterns snuffed for the night. Two speckled pigs dozed in the gutter together, an ear flapping against flies. The moon had yet to rise. The night stars glinted with the eerie crispness that they only get in winter, as though it weren't April at all.

When they arrived at the home of Temperance's childhood nemesis, long since faded into mild and temperate personhood, married with four children and a breast scarred with cancer, they found a lone candle burning in a window overhead.

Patty's hand appeared around Temperance's wrist, and the two women flattened themselves into the shadows by the gate leading into the Palfrey yard. Softly clucking hens. A breeze kicked up and ruffled the nodding squash flowers in the garden. The wind was cold.

Patty fished in her skirt pocket for the stoppered bottle, uncorked it, took a long swallow, and offered it to Temperance.

Craving warmth, Temperance took the bottle out of her mother's hand and poured some of the liquid down her throat. It burned. When it met the black storm cloud in her chest, the rum rumbled like thunder and dissolved into vapor. Temperance coughed.

"Goat shed's in back," Patty whispered.

Silently, her mother eased open the latch to the yard gate and took Temperance by the hand. They crept together along the hoed row of squash. Fuzzy vegetable leaves grated on the hem of Temperance's dress. She glanced up to the candle in the window, steeled for a pale-moon face staring down at them. But she didn't see one.

The goat shed was small and warm, padded with hay and animal breath. Temperance heard the soft rustling of mice in the hay, and the dozing nasal sighs of a nanny curled on her side, bearded chin on her knees. In the darkness the colors in the shed receded to pale silvery grays, and limned in the shelter of the nanny's legs rested two velveteen kids, not more than a few days old. Asleep.

All at once, Temperance understood.

A black form obscured her view. A flurry, and bleating, hay flying, bumping of hooves on wood, and a dull horn grazed Temperance's stomach. She lost her balance, her arms wheeling in space, then fell hard against the wall.

"Hurry," said Patty.

Temperance couldn't see in the dark, but heard a baby goat crying, and the nickering of its mother, and her stamping feet.

Together they slipped out the shed door, Patty bent halfway over, carrying something concealed under her cloak.

"Mother, what—" Temperance started to say.

"Poor devil," Patty said. "Runty little thing. Wouldn't have made it anyway." She got to her hands and knees in the squash patch and commanded, "Help me."

"What are you doing?" Temperance said, blood throbbing in her temples.

"Don't be daft," Patty said. "Dig."

The earth under Temperance's fingernails was cold and hard, colder than it should be for late April. As though the warmth of the past few weeks had been a glamour, cast to disguise the rocky chill of the truth. One of Temperance's nails cracked on a pebble, and she swore, bringing the hurt finger to her lips.

"Good enough," Patty muttered.

She laid a limp, lifeless form, small as a broken doll, in the shallow depression they had made, and started heaping loose dirt on top of it. One tiny hoof gleamed in the starlight.

In the blank second-story window overlooking the side yard, an orange candle flared to life. Temperance and her mother froze, staring up at it.

It flickered.

"Hurry," Patty whispered, her hands scrabbling the dirt away again, digging up what they had laid to temporary rest. Temperance sat frozen, heartbeat in her ears, until Patty cried "Now!" and she set to digging too, gathering the dirt into her lap with the sides of her palms. When the kid was cleared, Patty took it by a floppy hind leg and heaved to her feet.

Temperance had never seen her mother run. As it was, Patty could scarcely walk. But now her mother's cloak billowed out behind her like black owl wings, and Temperance found herself sprinting, gasping for breath as she dashed after the disappearing form of her mother. Her feet pounded the ground, so winter-cold it felt nearly frozen, and behind them Temperance heard a woman's faint voice cry, "Who's there?"

In a trice she was back over the garden gate and into the lane, panting. She withdrew into the shadow of a ten-footer shoe workshop belonging to Mehitable Palfrey's neighbor and flattened herself against its wall.

A hand closed around her wrist and she gasped aloud.

"Shhhh," said Patty, breath hot on her daughter's ear, resting a finger on her lips to keep her from crying out. "We've one more stop to make."

The mud of Milk Street was deeply rutted with wagon tracks and hoofprints, offset by crunched-up oyster shells here and there, but still a treacherous surface for walking at the best of times. Temperance set her foot down and instantly it was enclosed in water up to her ankle. Slushy with cold. In the glinting starlight she could see her breath.

"Mother," she said. She couldn't see Patty.

"This way," Patty answered in a low voice.

They were making their way back down the lane to their house. Stupid thing to do. What if Mehitable saw them? What if she was standing in her nightdress right now, squinting through the dark after them, a shawl over her shoulders and wasted chest? Being charged with theft of livestock would cost them a piece. Court fees. Fines. Hard looks and lost business. Even if it were a sickly little thing they stole.

They drew near to the gate hidden in the hedge, but instead of turning for home, the hunched black form of Temperance's mother continued, crunching along the oyster-shell path.

The lane petered out into a dense thicket, where Temperance used to play as a child. Under the canopy of elms and maples and scrub oaks, toads droned to each other, invisible inside logs and under leaves. When the breeze lifted, branches creaked against each other, a mournful, lonesome sound. Temperance folded her arms against the chill, shivering, and wished she could see the lights in the warm kitchen of their house, the friendly glow of the hearth fire, the smoke drifting lazily up the chimney. Faith stirring the cauldron. Obie picking his molar thoughtfully with a knifepoint.

They moved through the woods, stepping over fallen logs and

shuffling through leaves. After a time, the branches thinned to reveal a small, silty pond, glittering in the starlight, its surface rippled by the breeze. The ripples moved out in concentric circles that met the shore and stopped abruptly—the pond was newly ringed with shards of ice.

Patty's dark shape shifted among the trees, snapping twigs, crunching leaves, and Temperance followed the sound.

"Mother!" she said, her voice a rasp.

"Come along, come along," Patty answered.

Temperance stepped over a fallen log, and her foot met the ground sooner than she expected. The woods had a way of twisting itself around. One afternoon, when she was a girl, not long after she first met Obie, she'd ventured in to hunt for mushrooms and been unable to find her way home 'til the next morning.

She didn't go into the woods as much after that.

She didn't remember this hill, which seemed to be newly rising from within the earth. It steepened so abruptly that soon she had to climb hand over hand, pulling herself up by fistfuls of vine and roots. Now and then a crumble of dirt fell from under her mother's shoe and rained into her face. She spat to get the earth out of her mouth.

"Almost there," Patty urged her on, her voice near its usual volume.

Temperance couldn't believe her mother wasn't winded. Her own arms burned from dragging her weight up this nearly vertical hill, her wet foot nearly frozen with cold, her nose crusted with dirt.

"Where are we going?" she panted, grasping a tree root jutting incongruously out of the side of the hill and hoisting herself up.

A hand closed around her upper arm and lifted her, almost as easily as when she was a child.

"We're there," Patty said.

Temperance brushed the mud and bits of twig off herself and looked around at what she thought was a clearing on the hill above the pond. But they weren't standing in a clearing. Not exactly.

Here and there, slabs of slate leaned this way and that, arched on top and sharp of shoulder. Carved in the arches were faces. Rows and rows of blank-eyed faces, staring at them. On the newer ones, the faces were those of sleeping cherubs, their cheeks fat, lips pursed, eyes closed in repose. But on the older ones, the faces weren't faces at all. They were skulls. Naked teeth, empty eye sockets, noses missing, sitting atop crossed bones, or sometimes flanked by whole skeletons, grinning as they held scythes and hourglasses, dancing their way to the grave.

Temperance and Patty were standing on the crest of the hill that held the old Marblehead burying ground. Away to the east, behind a line of sleeping fishermen's shacks, the gently breathing Atlantic Ocean, black as the night sky, wavetops dusted with starlight. Far away, on the eastern horizon—back where they'd all come from—the barest glimmer of yellow-orange nudged along the horizon line, opening a shimmering path along the surface of the water. Moonrise.

Temperance didn't know how long this hilltop had been used to bury Marblehead's dead. It was said that the first meetinghouse in the settlement had been erected on the rocky ridge where they now stood, but it was long gone. Nothing stood up here now but the headstones. Everyone in her family was buried there. Even the ones who weren't supposed to be.

Temperance stared at her mother, baffled as to how they'd gotten halfway across the peninsula in a matter of moments. Patty's cloak had shifted on her shoulders, and she stood with her nose to the east, her chin lifted, her eyes closed, her lips parted as though she were tasting the breeze. Her withered, drunken mother, here in the moonlight, looked softer. Suppler. More herself.

"What are we doing here, Mama?"

Slowly Patty's eyes opened, and she turned to gaze at her daughter. Graying curls lifted on the ocean breeze. Her mother's eyes had faded until they were completely white.

"You can't do it alone," Patty said.

Temperance said, "What do you mean?"

"Only help of the strongest sort will do what you need done," Patty continued. "Come. She's over here."

A chill started on Temperance's scalp, traveling down her neck and along her limbs until the hairs on her arms stood up, prickled as a cat with a bottle-brush tail. When Patty walked down the hill, picking through the rows of shadowed stones, Temperance followed. She didn't like to think about what lay beneath the stones. What worms and twisted bones, wrapped in roots and roosting beetles.

As the bald dome of the burying ground petered out to scrub and weeds, with the first dry shoots of hollyhocks nosing up for spring, the stones grew sparse. The moon lifted itself another inch or two above the water, its light casting long black shadows between the grave markers. Patty walked bent over, as though sniffing the ground, peering at each stone in turn.

"There," she said, pointing.

Temperance searched into the darkness. She thought she made out a slender, leaning stone, well away from the others, grown over with brambles. Under the brambles a creature seemed to be curled, asleep. A raccoon, or a skunk. It was getting on to be the skunking time of night.

"Go on! Shoo!" Patty said, flapping the hem of her cloak at the animal. It lifted a head incuriously, seemed to yawn. Then a moonlight shimmer, and it disappeared.

Patty knelt by the headstone, gently untangling brambles and brushing away crusts of dirt and moss. The name had been eaten away by time and inattention, but Temperance could make out a few of the letters.

D . . . v . . . n . e.

D . . e.

One of the ones who wasn't supposed to be in hallowed ground.

Temperance got to her knees next to her mother. The ground was hard. The cold made its way from the frozen earth through her layers of skirts, spreading into her knees. They regarded the stone with its paucity of information. No dates. No Bible verse. Only the fading letters and, so shallowly carved as to be nearly invisible after more than a hundred New England winters, an untutored and awkward skeletal figure. Naked skull grinning. But unlike the others, this one's knees were spread, like those of a woman about to give birth. Life, and death. All bound up together. In the corner, under the naked skull's knee, the letters *E L U I.*

"Her?" Temperance asked.

Patty's profile made a black silhouette against the rising moon. "Why?"

"She didn't succeed," Patty said. "But even so."

They both set to digging, pulling the frozen earth apart with their naked hands.

Chapter Twenty-four

Marblehead, Massachusetts

One minute past midnight

Beltane

2000

"Thomas." Connie's body felt unconnected to the ground. As if she were drunk. Or dreaming. The spray of henbane juice sizzled on her cheek.

"Well, now," said Grace softly.

"Who's Thomas?" said Sam.

"A douchebag," Zazi said under her breath.

"My old thesis student," Connie said, marveling.

Thomas stood before them, looking strangely flat in the moonlight. A cardboard cutout of himself. He examined his hands, looking at the palms and then turning them over to peer at the backs. He cast no shadow. Instead of illuminating him, the firelight from the windows seemed to disappear into his skin.

Grace walked over to him, her hands full of hemlock branches and gardening shears. The cardboard-cutout Thomas watched her come, and Connie knew him well enough to see that he was pretending to be confident. But his face warred with itself, a victim of his imperfect control. He was looking down his fine nose, but his chin was stubbled, his polo shirt untucked and spotted with stains. His hair stuck up in a nest of cowlicks. As the older woman drew nearer, Thomas pushed his eyeglasses up the bridge of his nose.

"Hello there," said Grace when she reached him.

"What do you want?" Sam said. "It's the middle of the night."

"I know what he wants," Connie said, though the words felt velvety and thick in her mouth. She moved to stand behind Grace. "He's not going to get it."

Cardboard-cutout Thomas's Adam's apple moved in his throat. "Now, wait a minute," he said, voice rising.

"Hush now." Grace held a hand over Thomas's forehead. Her hand cast no shadow on him. His eyes followed her hand, and as her palm drew nearer, his eyes drew together until they were crossed. She stopped just short of touching him, holding her hand a few millimeters away from his flat, uncanny skin. Grace closed her eyes.

The image of Thomas shimmered, like the picture on an old television with a poor signal, the kind with a round antenna on the back that had to be aimed just right to sift sense out of the invisible chaos of signals zapping through the air. A toad droned near Connie's left foot.

Grace opened her eyes. They were occluded with white.

"You didn't mean to do it, did you?" she said to Thomas.

The image of Thomas stood immobile, hazed with interference, his eyes crossed, staring at Grace's hand hovering near his forehead.

"The fire," said Grace.

"No," Thomas said. His mouth moved unnaturally, like a puppet mouth. Hinged jaw, opening and closing on strings.

"It was an accident, wasn't it?" Grace continued, her voice soft. Almost hypnotic.

"An accident?" Connie said aloud. She was standing close enough to see a faint bluish glow coalescing in Grace's palm. It shone on Thomas's flat and flickering face, bathing him in a cool moonlight blue. The light cast a corona around Thomas, making his image waver, like stretched videotape.

The apparition's eyes welled with tears.

"Yes," he said, his throat catching on a sob.

"You never meant to hurt Sam, did you? You were just angry. Acting out," Grace said kindly.

One tear blurred over Thomas's right eye and snaked down his cheek.

"It's hard," Grace soothed. "Not getting what you want."

The blue-white light around Thomas buzzed and flickered. "I," Thomas tried to say. There was static in his voice.

Connie's eye was stinging from the henbane fluid, and her hand around the stalk was faintly burning.

The weird blue glow intensified in Grace's palm until it focused its crackling heat on the spot exactly in the center of the cardboard-cutout Thomas's forehead. His third eye, the hippie Grace of Connie's childhood would have called it. The doorway of his perception.

"Somewhere along the line, someone told you that the way to get what you want is to undercut other people," Grace said sorrowfully. "That the way to power is to take, and step on, and crush. But that's not the way. Is it."

Chilton. Chilton let Thomas believe the Harvard job was his for the taking. That he didn't have to compete for it. That he deserved it. And when it looked as if he wasn't going to get it, he snapped. Thomas had left the burning bag on their apartment stoop. Thomas had wanted to scare them. Instead Thomas burned the building down, nearly taking Sam and all their neighbors with it. Connie's stomach seized in sickened nausea. Chilton's pride had driven him mad, years ago. Now that sickness had infected Thomas. Had twisted a formerly earnest, nervous boy into this broken young man who was standing before them. Or whose image was conjured before them, hazing and flickering.

The blue-white light outlining Thomas rolled, more signal interference, as he stood immobilized, his eyes crossed, staring hard up at the point on his forehead burning in a bright blue spot.

"Mom," Connie said, reaching out a hand as if to stop Grace.

Grace looked at Connie over her shoulder. Her eyes had gone completely white, with no irises at all. "Yes, my darling," she said, her voice reaching Connie muffled, as though under water. "You're right. We have work to do. And dawn will soon be upon us."

Grace dropped her hand, and the image of Thomas wavered, let out a sickening groan, and sank to his knees, his palms pressed to his forehead.

"I'm sorry," he wailed, shaking inside the static.

They stared at him, Connie and Sam and Grace and Zazi, unmoved.

"We still need a mandrake," Zazi said.

Grace looked down on the sobbing young man. He was going snowy, the hiss of static audible under the droning of the toads. She said, "They're all over. This garden loves mandrakes. And mandrakes love this garden. Love," she emphasized to Thomas. "See what I mean?"

He covered his face with his hands and wept.

"How can we dig one up safely?" Connie said, the henbane burning into the skin of her hand and the reddened rim of her eye. "We don't have Arlo." Connie let some special venom go into that last word.

Grace cocked her head and said, "I bet he would like to help us. Wouldn't you, Thomas?"

The shadow of Connie's former student rubbed his palms miserably over his slacks.

"I always wanted to see a mandrake," the cardboard-cutout Thomas said softly.

"Then dig," said Grace.

The blue-white light around Thomas sharpened, as if a cloud were rolling away from the moon. Obedient, he spread his hands out and began pawing the ground, clearing away earth in a circle around his knees. Where his image-fingertips met the real ground, small bluish sparks flickered to life and burned out, like winking fireflies.

"I wonder," the image of Thomas said in a quiet voice, "if they really scream, when they're dug up."

"Keep digging," said Connie darkly.

Sam and Zazi came down the flagstone path and stood behind Connie and Grace, watching. Zazi shivered, her curls trembling. Sam's breath formed a pale nimbus around his mouth.

"There." Grace pointed. "Now pull that up."

Thomas's hand closed around the base of a leafy weed, like all the weeds carpeting the garden between the clover and dandelions and tufts of crabgrass, dotted at its base with pale violet flowers.

"Connie," Thomas said. "I'm sorry." The electric field around him wavered and snapped.

Then he pulled.

A piercing ring stabbed into Connie's ears, and she clapped her hands over them. It screamed like feedback, dialed up all the way. The sound seemed to be inside her head, created by the resonance of her own skull, and she bent double, her eyes squeezed closed, powerless to block it out. Connie didn't know how long the ringing lasted. Probably no longer than an instant. But it felt eternal. The sound took over her body, filling her head, vibrating her skull. She opened her own mouth to scream.

But as suddenly as the ringing appeared, it was gone. So completely gone it might have never been there.

Zazi and Sam were also bent double with their hands over their ears. Grace stood before them, serene and smiling, a dirty root like a homunculus hanging from her gloved hand.

The image of Thomas had disappeared. As if the television had been snapped off.

"Mom, what—" Connie started to say.

Sam and Zazi were lowering their hands from their ears, yawning like people trying to clear their Eustachian tubes on an airplane.

"Dang," Zazi said, sticking a finger in her ear and rubbing it vigorously. "That was crazy."

"Where did he go?" Connie demanded of Grace.

"Who?" Grace said sweetly. She held up the mandrake by its leaves. Its cilia coiled down like stubby fingers, almost obscene.

"Thomas!" Connie cried shrilly.

Grace started along the flagstone path back to the house. The toads lapsed into silence as she passed.

"You okay, Cornell?" Sam said, bringing the cinquefoil under his nose for a sniff.

Connie had to struggle not to shout. "He was right there! Thomas!"

But in the space where Thomas had knelt and dug was an empty hole. In the shadow of its shallow depth, a toadlike eye glittered.

"Thomas?" Zazi said, following behind Grace with the recipe in her hands.

"What the hell, Mom?" Connie shouted.

Grace stopped at the front door, her hand on the latch. "The Devil goes about like a roaring lion, seeking what he may devour," she said. "And he can take whatever shape he chooses, when we conjure him up."

The henbane had begun to wilt in Connie's hand. Slowly, she walked down the flagstones and approached the door, which Grace held open. Sam and Zazi went in first, and as Connie passed from the garden into the Milk Street house, Grace whispered in her ear, "Never the shape of an innocent, of course."

The spaghetti pot had reached a rolling boil, and much of the afternoon heat had leached away in the creeping frost of midnight. Grace went over and dropped in the mandrake, and the oily smallage belched up a violet cloud as the root was swallowed whole into the brew. Then she fed the three hemlock branches into the pot, slowly, pushing them in as they softened, just as she might with dried spaghetti. As the brew swallowed the branches Connie smelled pine sap and something else—something sharp and intoxicating.

"Here, Sam, put yours in next," Grace urged.

Sam came over and sprinkled the yellow cinquefoil flowers onto the surface of the liquid. They floated for a moment, swirling together, and then sank beneath the surface, a faint yellow cloud lifting like pollen into the hearth chimney.

"Now," Grace said to Zazi. "Why don't you add the wolfsbane, my dear." She indicated the dark purple flower heads held in her shawl.

Zazi said, "Yes, please." She took up the flowers in her two fists and threw them into the pot, laughing. The yellowish mist shaded into purples and golds, ribboning colors through the thickening smoke.

Connie watched all this activity unfold with a growing sense of fascinated unreality. She watched, time seeming to wind down around her, as Grace urged Sam to stand up near the fire, and maneuvered Zazi to stand opposite him. At last Grace rested merry, shining eyes on Connie and said, "We're all set."

Connie moved over to the hearth. She felt as though she were floating. As though her feet weren't contacting the floor.

Inside the spaghetti pot, the concoction of smallage had become thick and oily, the texture of molten tar. The smoke drifting up from it was dense and violet-colored, and when Connie leaned in close, the vapor smelled strangely of ocean air mixed with rotting log split by lightning.

"All right," she said. "Here goes nothing."

Connie held her hand with the wilting henbane flower out over the bubbling pot.

"Here, take my hands," Grace urged, and she and Zazi joined hands around Sam, as children would who were playing ring around the rosy.

Connie opened her hand, and as the henbane flower slowly fell, spinning, drifting on the rising fumes of the smallage, she began to recite the recipe Temperance had hidden in the wall almost two hundred years ago.

"As we grow, like plants beneath the sea . . ."

The words echoed inside Connie's head as she spoke, but she couldn't tell whether that was the psychoactive effect of the nightshades, or whether Grace and Zazi were repeating what she had just said. The henbane disappeared into the pot, belching forth smoke the color of steel. The smoke thickened until there was too much for the chimney to swallow, and wafts of it began to escape toward the dining room ceiling.

"So harden us to rocket on the air," Connie continued.

She reached into the tote bag and withdrew the photograph of the baby—Claudette. Connie peered at it in the dancing firelight. Though she knew the fire was going, knew that the fire was hot and that she should find the kitchen hot too, Connie felt strangely detached from the sensations in the room around her. In fact, she felt cold. Her chill deepened as she stared at the baby's closed eyes. Its tiny, closed fists. Its brief, closed life.

Connie dropped the photograph into the pot so she wouldn't have to look at it anymore. The eagle stone rattled at her wrist.

The photo drifted down to the surface of the brew and came to rest flat atop the membrane of tarry fluid. Its edges started to curl. The emulsion over the baby's face began to bubble and pull away from the cardboard backing, and Connie felt an icy trickle along the back of her neck.

She looked up.

Hanging from one of the rafters was a lone icicle.

Connie swallowed hard, and reached for the triangular shred of caul in its archival envelope. "Thus in our aliveness we decree."

She held the caul suspended between finger and thumb over the boiling potion, now so thickened as to be almost an ointment. She had to drop it in. She had to.

She couldn't. Something was stopping her. Not just the snapping pain sizzling along the nerves in her hands. That, she had expected. That, she was almost used to.

Connie realized she was afraid of what would happen. When Temperance did this, she shattered the weather for an entire year. The year without a summer. Her selfishness had driven farmers off their farms, had spread poverty and hunger all across New England. Had even pushed settlement into the interior, to New York State and as far as Ohio. But it had worked. Temperance had gotten what she wanted. But at a huge cost for her community. For her world. For generations after her.

Was it worth it?

Sam's hands hung loose at his sides, his face warm and trusting. He smiled at Connie, a smile that said, *Nobody would believe this but me, you know.*

The fear dissolved. The pain snapping along her nerves stayed behind, but Connie didn't care.

Connie opened her finger and thumb, and the caul spun slowly into the spaghetti pot.

A gaping maw opened in the oily mass and swallowed it. Instantly the smoke changed color from a rich burnt black to a strangely pulsing opalescence. It was every color, and none. Behind the screen of smoke the bricks of the hearth whitened with frost.

"From fear, blest be, transport us safe and square," Connie finished.

The smoke didn't change. It poured up from the pot as thickly as before, running over the ceiling of the kitchen, thick enough to flow in fluid waves. But its color didn't change. Nothing changed.

Connie tried basketing her fingers before her. Once, years ago, she'd lain on her belly in the grass on Salem Common, her hands basketed just like this, only around a new yellow dandelion. She'd spoken a few words, she didn't remember which ones anymore, and under her eyes the dandelion had bloomed, seeded, and blown away, all in an instant. That was the first time. She concentrated, willing the pale, painful shocks of blue to materialize within the nest of her fingers.

Nothing happened.

Through the haze of nightshade poison that had leached into her skin, through her terror and fatigue, through the surge of unfamiliar hormones coursing through her bloodstream, Connie tried to focus. What was missing?

"The dust!" Zazi cried.

"Oh, my God," Connie said, panic rising in her chest. What was it the list had said? *Dust of ought the strongest sort.*

What did that even mean?

Connie was so tired. And she was so sick of being afraid.

Pain throbbed through her hands, up her arms, wrapping around her shoulders, digging into her brain. She was afraid she would pass out. Her hand found the back of a chair.

She felt someone else watching her. Eyes, resting on her.

Temperance. The portrait behind the dining table. Through Connie's haze of henbane unreality, the eyes glittered in the firelight.

Connie left the bubbling cauldron and went over to where Grace had left Temperance's box open on the dining table. The box that was inexplicably full of dirt. She rested her hand on the lid, with its monogram of *T J H.*

"This box belonged to you," Connie told the painting. "That means this is your dust. And you're the strongest one. You're the only one who's made it work! This is the dust of ought the strongest sort!"

She reached into the box, sank her hand into the crust of dirt, crumbling between her fingers. Then she hurried back to the spaghetti pot and rained the dirt into the potion.

The flecks of dust landed on its boiling surface, hissing like snow on a pond in autumn. A chill breeze kicked up through the kitchen windows, tumbling along the dining table and stirring Grace and Sam and Zazi's hair before it reached Connie, blowing up the back of her neck until her own hair was caught in the updraft. The wind was ice cold. When Connie leaned her head back against the gale, she saw that the smoke flowing across the ceiling had gone as white as snow.

One thing remained.

Connie rooted in the tote bag and withdrew the fragile length of knotted twine. She held it out to Sam.

"When I tell you," she said, "I want you to untie each one. Okay?"

Sam nodded dumbly, taking the twine in his hands. His hands were shaking, from cold or fear.

Connie returned to the spaghetti pot, lifted her hands, and raised her eyes to the ceiling. The smoke was swirling now, moving slowly counterclockwise over the spot in the dining room where Sam and the others were standing.

"First, to hold," she said.

A faint, painful crackling shot across her palms as Sam set to untying the first knot. The twine was old and dried, so fragile it might dissolve in his hands. But Sam was used to old and fragile things. He made his life with them. Using a thumbnail, slowly, carefully, he loosened the first knot. Opening it. Widening it. Then it was free. The twine held stubbornly on to its curves where the knot had been, kinked and twisted.

"And next, untie," Connie continued.

Sam worried at the second knot. This one fought back, perhaps because it was the one in the middle. She watched him work away at it, feeling the electric snap and bite of blue veins of energy sizzle into her fingertips, up her arms, into her shoulder and neck. The temperature in the room slipped another few degrees, and another icicle formed out of nowhere and stretched down from the rafters.

Then Sam had the knot free. A single snowflake drifted down from the kitchen ceiling and landed on her eyelash.

"Then," she went on, "to boil."

Sam set to working on the last of the knots. He frowned. He used a thumbnail.

As he worked, the pain flowed down Connie's sides, wrapping around her hips, sizzling through her thighs. It stirred in her softly swollen belly. Moving around inside. Spreading.

Sam lifted the knot to his teeth and bit the knot free, severing the old twine into two pieces. Shaking, trying to push the pain away and failing, Connie took the pieces of twine from him.

She held them in the column of smoke pouring up from the cauldron, so thick and oily that Connie could feel it press against the back of her hand. Like a thing that could be molded, formed into shapes.

"Last," Connie said through teeth clenched against the pain, "never die."

She let go the twine.

A flash of lightning split through the kitchen. Connie's head threw itself back, her mouth open, her eyes wide, misted with white, and then time seemed to wind down, like a record player grinding to silence. Connie had time to look around herself. She looked first to the cauldron and saw that the twine had disappeared, burned to cinders by the flash of light. Only then, looking down at the hearth, did Connie notice.

Her feet drifted about three feet off the pine boards. Converses waving in space. In this eerie in-between non-time Connie stretched her hands out on either side of herself, marveling. Her braid drifted by, suspended over her shoulder. Around her, all was a haze of cloud and white. Connie swam a hand in front of her face, stirring through the smoke that had borne her aloft. The smoke was cold, made of drifting particles that swirled when she moved through them. Cold, and wet. Almost like . . .

Snow.

Connie started to laugh.

She looked down to where Grace and Zazi stood, frozen in place, hands joined, mouths open as if caught speaking. Between them, standing completely still, his head back, eyes open, face frozen in wonder, staring at Connie, stood Sam.

The snow swirling in eddies up near the dining room ceiling started to fall. It drifted down, somehow falling only on Sam. It collected gently on his shoulders. In his hair. Around his feet. Building up in a pure white drift of ice. The drift reached his knees. Then his hips. His hands, his chest. His skin paled under the pressure of the snow, and the veins in his face and neck went blue, the same blue as the crackles in her palms, the blue of Arctic ice.

"Sam," Connie whispered.

And then, a strange sensation seized her body. Like a fluttering. Butterfly wings. No, a fish. Fish fins swimming. Connie's hands rushed to her midsection. There it was again, a semaphore flag from deep inside her body. From her future.

Connie gasped aloud, and something broke apart. A whoosh of blistering frigid wind, a crash, and everything went dark.

"Is she okay?"

"She'll be fine. Just needs a little air."

"It's so hot in here. She probably fainted."

Connie's eyelids twitched.

"Darling?" A soft hand cupped her cheek. The smell of patchouli told Connie that Grace was leaning over her. "Hmm. Sam, why don't you go get her a glass of water."

"Okay," said Sam. Connie wanted to see him. She had to know if it had worked. She shifted, testing to see if she could sit up.

Her shoulder was pressed against the dining room floor. Her hip too. And her head. Connie assessed her body. Some smarting, there and there, but nothing seemed broken. Her hands. Where were her hands? They

were numb, but somewhere outside the numbness, they were covered in
something sticky.

"Connie?" That was Zazi.

Connie remembered the semaphore flag. She sent her consciousness
deep inside herself, checking to make sure everything in there was all
right. She probed, gently. Here, a foot. There, a hand. Over there, a head,
fast asleep.

Connie sighed with relief and opened her eyes.

Grace and Zazi crowded over her, two worried women's faces, one
young and framed by wild hair, one lined and careworn, staring down
at her.

"There she is." Grace smiled. "Here's Sam with some water."

Sam appeared from the kitchen, a jelly jar of water in his hand.

"Cornell," he said.

Connie blinked. The henbane must have still been working its way
out of her system. When she looked at Sam, she saw odd little flashes
of light. Blue flashes. Here and there. His chin. His ear. His eyebrow. His
tooth.

Then Connie understood.

"You want some water?" Sam said.

Connie nodded and reached for her friends and mother to help
her up.

"Oh," Grace said. "I'll get a towel."

"You knocked the pot over," Sam explained. "When you fainted."

Her hands were coated in a tarry sludge. It was of no particular color.
Or all colors at once. Connie rubbed the substance between her fingers.
It felt soft, like the underbelly of a snail, or like eiderdown, if eiderdown
could be a liquid. It smelled of rotting log and fire and something else.
Something Connie couldn't identify.

"Here we are." Grace reappeared with a damp 1950s dish towel,
monogrammed with Granna's initials. She ran the towel over Connie's
fingers, cleaning her off like when she was a child, and as she did so,
Sam and Zazi took hold of Connie's arms and rolled her up to seated.
Connie accepted the jelly jar of water gratefully from Sam and swallowed
long drafts of it. The water entered her bloodstream, clearing away the

last drops of nightshade poison from her eyes, from her body, from her mind.

Behind them, the portrait of Temperance Hobbs, her ratter under her arm, watched with a glimmer in her eyes that slowly dimmed.

Physick has many names, Connie thought. *And the weather work is only one.*

Interlude

———

Marblehead, Massachusetts

Night, April 23

1816

Temperance and Patty made it back to the kitchen of the Milk Street house in the blink of an eye, faster than Temperance had ever dreamed they could go. The night around them felt unreal, as though the unseasonable cold creeping through the air was slowing time around them, letting them move faster between places. Not five minutes after she looked down on her apron full of dirt from Deliverance Dane's secret resting spot, and without even lifting her head, Temperance found her feet stepping through the gate in the garden hedge, shoe still soaked from the puddle in the lane by Mehitable's house.

"Hurry," Patty urged, a hand on her daughter's upper arm. "We don't want it to boil off."

They burst back into the kitchen and found Faith kneeling by the hearth, feeding logs into the fire. The cold had crept under the garden drapery, into the gaps in the clapboards and under the doors, frosting its way into the kitchen. Obie sometimes tried to insulate the house by stuffing old newspapers into the gaps in the floor, though it helped but little.

When he saw Temperance, Obie leapt to his feet from the bench by the trestle table. She had been gone only a few minutes, maybe an hour, maybe two. But it felt longer. The night felt both eternal and instantaneous.

"No time for that," Patty barked. "Dawn's coming."

Patty pulled the limp form of the kid from somewhere inside her cloak and dropped it into the boiling smallage. The mixture belched, an oily black cloud forming inside the cauldron, and an iridescent scum of fat bubbled up from the depths of the concoction, spiraling its surface with slicks of rainbows. The black smoke thickened, painted inside with ribbons of crimson and navy blue. The smell of thunder deepened.

Temperance walked to the bubbling cauldron, stepping around the rush broom that Faith had left leaning against the hearth. She held her apron corners up together, making a bag, bits of earth spilling out when her knee knocked against it. When she drew close to the fire, her cheeks burned with the heat. The mixture was of no particular color, or all colors together, oozing and changing, like oil or tar. She reached into her apron, took up a fistful of dirt, and held it over the cauldron. Over her shoulder, Temperance saw her mother, bent with age once again, propping herself on the trestle table; Obie, a hand resting over Faith's shoulder. At Faith's feet, the ratter sat at attention.

"Ready?" Temperance asked.

"Yes," said Obie.

"Ready, Mama," Faith said.

"Do it," said Patty.

Temperance steeled herself against the coming pain, and opened her fingers, raining the graveyard dirt into the brew.

"As it grows, sextant across the sea," she said.

The mixture in the cauldron licked up the bits of dirt, and the smoke filled the flue and spilled out of the chimney, overflowing the lip of the hearth and oozing toward the ceiling. The nerves within her palm cracked and snapped. Pain bloomed across her hands, wrapping around her wrists.

"So harden me to rocket 'pon the air."

Temperance took up the delicate silver rattle, one of the few pieces of silver in the house. A treasure, the rattle was, taken generations ago as payment for a charm made for a wealthy boy. She caressed the smooth pink coral tip, almost obscene in its smoothness and pinkness. Temperance was on the point of snapping it off, but she hesitated.

"Will you help me?" She held the rattle out to Faith. She knew it was cruel, asking her daughter to break her toy. But Faith took the rattle and snapped off the coral teether in one try. The child tossed the coral into the cauldron, then took her mother's hand. Her child's cheek flickered when the electric pain snapped from Temperance's palm into Faith's, but Faith didn't let go.

Instead, she held out her other hand to Patty. "You stand there," Patty said to Obie, maneuvering him by his shoulders to stand inside the circle made of the three women—maiden, woman, and crone. Then she took Faith's hand, and Temperance's other hand, closing the circle. When Temperance felt her mother's leathery palm enfold her own, she was surprised to find the snapping electric pain grow duller. Still there. But a little less.

"Thus, 'pon our liveness so decree," Temperance continued.

She withdrew the envelope holding her precious caul from its hiding place in her busk. Taking up a pair of sewing shears from inside the sewing table, she sliced the envelope in half longways, making two equal triangles. One she secreted between her breasts again. The other she held over the cauldron.

She dropped it in.

The envelope vanished into the roiling mass of the brew, as if an aperture had opened in the surface of the water, swallowing the caul in one gulp.

The smoke poured over the ceiling of the kitchen, rippling, thick as wool. The air in the room grew close, the smell of thunderclouds filling Temperance's nostrils, getting into her ears, her eyes, her mouth. The redolence of coming storm was overpowering. She could barely see the faces of Obie and her mother and her daughter through the smoke. Colors swam before her eyes, scraps of color, like silk scarves drifting in a cloud.

Her mother squeezed her hand.

"From here, blest be, transport him safe to there," Tempe said in a low voice.

Obie stood within the circle, his head bowed. A dull crackling sensation moved along Temperance's arms, into her trunk, down her legs, snapping through the soles of her feet. She saw Faith's young face through the thickening haze. Flinching. But the girl didn't let go. Slowly, the smoke hovering along the ceiling began to thicken over the four of them, drawing into itself. Moving, clockwise.

"Now," said Patty. "The string."

Obie groped in his pockets and produced the knotted length of twine. He held it upstretched between his fingers, waiting to be shown what to do.

The pain was making its way into Temperance's face, reaching through her jaw, getting into her teeth, and it was hard to open her mouth. But she had to talk Obie through the untying of the string.

"First, to hold."

Obie, his hands shaking, picked apart the first knot using his thumb and fingernail. It was tight. He had to work to loosen it. As he did so, a faint rumble moved through the smoke overhead, and a chill seeped into Temperance's feet. She looked down, astonished to find the pine board floor frosted in ice.

At last Obie got the knot undone. He swallowed hard, his shining eyes the only warmth in the room other than the fire under the cauldron.

"Next, untie," Temperance said, and Patty and Faith whispered along with her, or at least the words were echoed inside her head.

Obie struggled with the second knot. Overhead, a zigzag of lightning arced through the smoke, cracking against the kitchen ceiling, leaving a burnt scar on the wood. When the knot was loose, he looked at her, his eyes tinted with doubt.

"Then," she said, the pain grinding into her skull like a hand drill, "to boil."

Patty and Faith did their best to repeat the words, but pain must have been grinding into them too. Faith's eyes squeezed closed, and Patty's lips drew back, baring her gums.

The last knot fought back. Obie had to pull at it with his teeth. As he gnawed it loose, the thunder in the kitchen intensified, and the temperature plunged. Icicles formed from nothing on the beams over-head, cracking with cold, reaching transparent fingers down between them. Then Obie got the knot open. He held the twine hanging between finger and thumb.

Temperance reached through the smoke in the room, which curled in on itself, spinning fast, grown thick and shimmering. Her hand left a bluish trail behind it. It took longer than it should have for her fingers to reach the hanging length of twine, and close around it, and take it out of Obie's hand, and for her to turn to face the cauldron bubbling in the hearth behind her.

She held the twine suspended over the cauldron. Temperance could see the fire still burning; but there was no heat, although the viscous fluid was clearly boiling, bubbles rising and bursting, thickly, like boiling tar. The colors on the surface of the fluid blurred, reds and violets and blues and greens braiding together, turning back against themselves, blending into colors that had no name. The bricks on the inside of the hearth were slick with ice.

"And last, not die," Temperance said, her voice sounding far away in her ears. Muffled, as though she had spoken through a cloud.

Temperance opened her hand and watched the twine drift down, slowly, coiling through the smoke, almost borne up on the fumes of the bubbling tincture, twisting on itself, bending and moving as though it were alive. Then an aperture opened in the color-blurred surface of the cauldron, a hole, into which the twine coil disappeared.

Instantly the smoke turned solid white.

Pain seized Temperance's body so total, so intense, that she felt her-self floating apart from it, as if the pain were an object separate from her, an object she could look at and touch. The smoke filled her eyes, took them over. She saw only a solid curtain of whiteness, and underneath the pain she felt the pressure of the smoke, dense as a frozen cloud, wrap-ping itself around her body, around her waist, around her neck, running its fingers through her hair.

Temperance closed her eyes.

When she opened them again, a floss of hair drifted past her face. Her skirts lifted weightless at her ankles. There was Obie, standing between Faith and Patty, his head bowed, his hands folded in a prayerful attitude beneath his chin. Patty had a gnarled hand reaching out for Faith. Faith's hands were pressed to her cheeks, her eyes gazing heavenward, gone blank and white. The rush broom, caught up in the frozen cloud that bore her aloft, drifted near to hand, bumping lazily against the chimney. Only the ratter was animate, looking with bright dark eyes up at Temperance.

He barked.

And then it began to snow.

Snowflakes drifted from the nothingness near the kitchen ceiling where Temperance floated, coalesced into sparkling flecks, and spun glintingly down, collecting on the floor and the trestle table and Patty's shoulders and Faith's open eyes. And they collected most thickly on Obie.

As Temperance watched, dazzled, apart from the pain, apart from her body, a blizzard opened itself inside the kitchen of the Milk Street house. Snowdrifts heaped around Obie's feet, building up to his knees, to his hips, to his elbows, until in a trice Obie was encased in a thick, wavering wall of ice, obscuring his face, swallowing his warmth, blue veins of cold rising under his skin. Locking him in a carapace that nothing could penetrate. Freezing him. Freezing him in place. Freezing him in time.

All at once, Temperance understood.

Through the haze of pain Temperance grew giddy, and she started to laugh. She threw her head back, bumping against the kitchen ceiling, laughing and laughing and laughing and laughing until . . .

A flash, and she heard her mother scream, "Tempe!" and then a million stars burst across her eyes and everything was pain.

Temperance moved one leg.

The splinters of the trestle table rustled in snow beneath her.

She had fallen through the table.

"Mama?"

Temperance gazed up into the concerned face of her daughter. Snow fell from Faith's shoulders, and tiny flecks of snow clung to her eyelashes.

"What happened?" Temperance's voice was hoarse.

The smoke was gone. A charred smell hung in the room, and the corners of the kitchen were deep with drifts of snow. As though a window had been left open in a blizzard.

Next to Faith appeared Patty, her gray curls hanging around her face, her nose red with rum and cold. Patty pressed a weathered hand to Temperance's cheek.

"Anything broken?" Patty asked.

"Where's Obie?" Temperance mentally scanned her body for harm, and discovered twinges in her shoulder, her hip, one rib, and her ankle.

"I'm here," said her husband from over her head. He pressed his lips to her forehead; she smelled wet wool and warmth, and knew he was safe.

"What's burning?" she asked him.

"Shhhh," Patty said. "Let's see if you've got any damage first."

Her knowing midwife's hands prodded the length of Temperance's body. When her fingers felt a fractured spot, Temperance caught her breath at the sharp pain.

"You fainted," Obie told her, his fingers combing through her hair as her mother's inspection continued.

"What's that smell?" Temperance said. She had to get up. Had it really worked?

"One cracked rib and one sprained ankle," Patty pronounced. "Not too bad. Need a new table, but."

"You ready to sit up?" Obie's soft brown eyes gazed into hers and Temperance saw that he didn't know. Whatever had happened—had anything happened?—lay beyond his apprehension. Did Faith know? Her face looked pinched with worry.

"Boiled off," Patty said, as she wormed a wiry arm under Temperance's shoulders and eased her, wincing, up to be seated.

"It boiled off?" Temperance looked around at the wreckage of the kitchen. A casement window waved to and fro on a broken hinge, breathing roils of snowflakes into the kitchen. Obie pulled the window closed against the blizzard outside and latched it tight. Temperance was sitting among the splintered remains of the trestle table. A hundred and fifty years old, now smashed to firewood.

"Yep," Patty said, pulling the pot off the hottest part of the hearth fire. "Scorched. It'll be a beast to scour."

"I can scour it," Faith said. The ratter appeared under her arm, sniffing the sharp burn of the air.

Obie smiled down at Temperance, still combing her hair through his fingers. A glimmer seemed to pass over his face, a soft bluish glint, like the reflection of sunlight on new-fallen snow.

Temperance reached over and took Faith's hand in hers, giving it a warm squeeze.

"No one can do it alone," she said.

Postlude

Connie elbowed her way past a knot of laughing undergrads who were gathered by the door to Abner's Pub, waiting to be summoned to a table with the eager zeal of kids who have finally arrived where they think they belong. It was a madhouse. Even more of a madhouse than usual at the start of a school year. Connie wondered if they'd have room for everyone at the table.

"Hey!" a familiar voice called. Connie rose on tiptoe, scanning the crowd. "Over here!" the voice cried. "In back!"

In the shadow of the snug at the rear of the pub, Connie spied Liz Dowers, looking very museum-y wrapped in a cashmere cowl. Connie waved back and started picking her way through the throng. Someone stumbled into her, sloshing beer down her sleeve, laughing and saying, "Oh, my God, sorry!"

Connie shook the drops off. "Don't worry about it," she said to the culprit, an awkward dark-haired girl who was probably there on a fake ID borrowed from her sister. For the first time, Connie considered that perhaps she was aging out of Abner's. It happened like that. You didn't notice you were getting older, until all of a sudden, there you were.

"There she is!" cried Janine Silva, enfolding Connie in a flowing hug. "We were just talking about the American Historical Association conference." She retrieved her reading glasses from the chain where they hung around her neck, applied them to her nose, and gestured at Zazi, who was tucked into the head of the table at the far end of the snug, somewhat dwarfed by the print of Queen Victoria hanging on the wall behind her head.

"Hey! I heard! Congratulations!" Connie edged behind the chairs and gave Zazi an awkward half hug necessitated by lack of space.

"It's just a first-round interview for the Harvard job," Zazi said, a flush rising in her cheeks. "It's not an on-campus or anything."

She's getting an on-campus, Janine mouthed to Connie.

Zazi's blush deepened. "Come on."

Janine waved her off. "Look, it's a reach for a candidate who hasn't defended yet. This, we know. But for all that, you're in really good shape. Better than that one was, that's for sure."

She arched an eyebrow at Connie, who arched one in return and said, "Gee, thanks."

"Weren't you competing with another kid for the department's support?" Liz said. Connie kicked her under the table, and Liz exclaimed, "What? I thought you told me that!"

"I was, I guess," Zazi said, looking into the depths of her glass. "But last spring, he kind of freaked out. Said he couldn't face another season on the job market. And quit."

Janine shifted her reading glasses to the end of her nose and examined a small leather-bound cocktail menu. "People do it. I wonder if he went to live on a boat too?"

Liz stared moodily into the middle distance and said, "I'd live on a boat. If there were openings for the study of medieval manuscripts. On the boat."

"We need to discuss your job talk," Connie said to Zazi.

"After we talk about your tenure," said Janine.

"And your book, which for some reason isn't dedicated to me," added Liz.

"Congratulations," Janine said quietly. "My letter was easy."

"Thanks," Connie said, a hot flush creeping up her neck. To Liz, she said, "How the heck did you get Abner to open the snug for you? We never get the snug. Nobody gets the snug."

"I may have told him there were special guests coming." She tapped the leading of the small faux-medieval stained-glass window of St. George and the dragon that screened the snug from the rest of the pub.

"You didn't."

"It's possible," Liz continued "that certain people might be paraded about the bar later. That's all I'm saying."

Connie unfolded a cocktail napkin and held it in front of her face, as though hiding.

"Where's Samuel?" Liz was scanning the heads of the crowd.

"He'll be in in a minute," Connie said, taking the drink menu from Janine and looking it over. She didn't know why she bothered—she always got the same thing. "He's dealing with parking."

"How come you call him Samuel?" Zazi asked Liz, bringing her cocktail straw up to her lips and taking a delicate sip.

"Oh," said Connie, "it's just a joke. Not an especially funny one."

Abner swung by the table with pen and pad in his hand and pointed the pen at Connie. "They coming?" he said.

"They'll be here," Connie assured him.

"All right. Old-fashioned?" Abner said.

Connie handed back the menu and said, "Nothing but."

Abner tucked his pen behind his ear and wove through throngs of kids back to the bar.

"So what's the joke?" Zazi said.

Connie and Liz exchanged a smile.

"It's dumb," said Liz. "Just, one night we were all hanging out, and realized all three of us had official nicknames, and real names. And we felt like when people used our real names we were pretending to be someone else. You know, Elizabeth is the one who's a museum curator. I'm just Liz."

"Constance is the history professor," Connie said.

"Tenured history professor," Janine interjected.

"But I'm just Connie."

"The joke is," said Liz, "Sam and Samuel are always the same person. He's like the most on-the-surface guy you'd ever meet. You know exactly what you're getting with him. So I call him Samuel."

"And why does he call you Cornell?" Zazi asked Connie.

Connie raised her eyebrows and looked pointedly at Liz.

"Oh, don't you even!" said Liz, throwing a crumpled cocktail napkin at Connie.

"Long story," said Connie.

Zazi said, "I've got the nickname thing happening too."

"What's Zazi short for?" Liz asked, gesturing for Abner to come back with more ice water.

"Esperanza," Zazi said. She pulled her cocktail straw out of her drink, stuck the wet end in her mouth, and said, "It means hope."

Connie stared at Zazi. "It, does, doesn't it," she said.

Zazi smiled around her cocktail straw.

"To hope," Connie said, offering her old-fashioned glass. Zazi chinked and pulled a curl under nose, releasing it with a *spoing*.

"What's taking him so long?" Janine said, stretching to look toward the door. "I mean, it's all well and good spending time with you girls, but you know who I'm really here to see."

"He's coming," Connie assured her. "It takes longer than you'd think."

Outside, under the awning over the door to Abner's Pub, crowded with undergraduates texting each other, calling each other's names, getting their names on the list, Sam bent over a complicated stroller, muttering to himself.

"Parking brake," he said, reviewing the list that he and Connie both recited whenever making the transition from stroller to everyday life. "Diaper bag. Truthfull in the carrier."

He patted the sleeping head of a three-week-old baby girl, her fists curled under her chin, wearing a Grace-knitted hat patterned like a green cabbage leaf. He had fitted her into a carrier on his chest, snapping the straps into place and adjusting the hip support and getting everything squared away. They always did Truthfull first. Truthfull, they'd learned, could sleep through anything.

"Now then," Sam said, crouching to look into the stroller. "You ready?"

A faint mewling emanated from the second seat of the stroller, where Faithfull, in a Grace-knitted hat shaped like a purple cabbage leaf, waved her arms in protest.

"Well, too bad," Sam said softly, reaching in and fussing with the safety belt.

Faithfull, they'd learned, could sleep through nothing. She came out of the stroller last.

"There's people waiting to meet you," Sam told her.

Faithfull gulped down her sobs and smacked her lips. She blinked up at her father.

"All right, then," murmured Sam as he eased her out of the stroller. "You have your hat on? It's cold out here. So cold, it's like the year without a summer. Which is weird, when you consider this is the hottest year ever recorded. Don't you think that's weird?"

He continued talking as he tucked her into her own sling next to her sleeping sister, adjusting straps, patting down pockets, checking diaper bags, taking one last look at the parking brake. One of the Harvard girls waiting to get into the pub spotted the babies on his chest, squealed, "Ohmigod, they are so cuuuuute!" and clacked over on perilously high heels. Sam turned away from the stroller to fend off the stranger who wanted to plant kisses on his brand-new daughters.

Sam, preoccupied with the twins, didn't notice when two glittering animal eyes opened inside the shrubbery under the window, close to where the stroller was parked out of the way of the front door.

Sam was busy explaining to the door guy that he was there to meet people who were already inside when the creature in the shrubbery materialized out of the sheltering leaves, one molecule at a time, drifting like a waft of pale smoke across the sidewalk, and collecting under the stroller's shadow. Slowly the smoke condensed into the shape of a small puppylike animal, its fur the mottled color of a summer night, sitting at attention, eyes on the door to Abner's pub. Waiting.

And Sam was already inside the bar, joining everyone in the coveted snug to cries of welcome and squeals of joy over the babies, when the creature under the stroller yipped once, and another pair of glittering eyes opened in the shrubbery under the window. The second pair of eyes blinked. None of the students waiting to get into the bar noticed a faint cloud of smoke drift over to the inky shadow under the stroller, where it slowly coalesced into the form of a different sort of animal—almost the size and shape of a kitten. Also sitting at attention. Also staring at the door. Both creatures paling until they were the exact color of a New England autumn night.

Author's Note

Almost immediately after the largest, most deadly, and most widespread witch hunt in North America—Salem—drew to an ignominious close in 1693, the crime of witchcraft ceased to be prosecuted. As the eighteenth century opened in what would become the United States of America, witchcraft stayed on the books as a crime but receded from the courts. Family members of those accused at Salem sued for restitution or to have their good names restored in the first decade of the 1700s. A few witch trials flickered to life in this decade, though their outcomes were wildly different from what had gone before. In Virginia, for instance, in 1706, Grace Sherwood was one of the last women actually convicted of witchcraft in the colonies. She was freed after a relatively short period of incarceration, even going on to reclaim her property from the state, and eventually died of old age in her eighties. A far cry indeed from the spectacle hangings of Salem a mere decade and a half previous. So where did all the witches go?

By 1735 the English anti-witchcraft statute had changed, as Connie notes in the novel, from outlawing witchcraft itself, to outlawing the pretense of witchcraft. Instead of addressing a perceived mortal risk to body or livelihood, the law instead attempted to control the small, persistent cultural practices of conjuring, charming, unbewitching, and finding lost objects that were often done for a fee, and in communities all over the Atlantic world. The stakes were lower for people thought to be witches. But that doesn't mean that belief in witchcraft went away. The phrasing of the 1735 law suggests that the courts felt that people had to be protected, not from felony maleficium wrought on their bodies or crops or farm animals, but from being conned.

The reason for the lowered stakes was that by the 1730s, a consumer revolution was well under way. As common households in Britain and the colonies found it easier to secure food and goods, adjudicating the bewitchment of calves or butter was no longer of the mortal import that it had been in the 1600s. Economics, rather than changed belief, pushed witchcraft off the legal docket. From there, witchcraft moved into the world of folklore, where it has lived comfortably ever since.

The need to exert control over uncontrollable forces didn't go away with the advent of the Scientific Revolution or the spread of relatively greater material prosperity, however. In coastal New England communities that drew their living from farming and the sea, a major area for seeking control lay in the weather. Moll Pitcher, "the sole Pythoness of ancient Lynn," born Mary Diamond in Marblehead to a family with a reputation for weather charming, lived from around 1736—just after the change in the anti-witchcraft statutes—to 1813, and gained particular fame for her purported ability to predict the outcome of voyages. In an earlier generation Moll Pitcher would have been an object of fear and derision, but by the late eighteenth and early nineteenth centuries Pitcher's seeming command of the occult no longer posed a threat to her community. Instead, it could be offered as a benefit. The description of her by the poet John Greenleaf Whittier, however, fixes Pitcher squarely in the mode of a fairy tale witch: "a wasted, gray, and meagre hag, in featured evil as her lot." Whittier even gives her a crooked nose. In real life Pitcher was merely plain-looking, and far from haggish, but her literary ugliness speaks to the disquiet concerning women with a witchy reputation even after they were no longer threatening enough to legislate against.

Moll Pitcher's counsel would have been keenly valued during the real year without a summer, which wreaked havoc around the world, but particularly in New England, beginning in May 1816. The temperature plunge described in Temperance's timeline really occurred, and for the rest of the year, summer never came. Crops failed. The New England economy tanked, and some historians have argued that the hardship brought about by the anomalous weather pattern contributed to migration from the coasts of the former colonies into the interior, to western New York State and to Ohio. Construction on the Erie Canal, which would eventually serve as the primary artery of travel and commerce from the coast to the expanding frontier, began the following July, in 1817. Many factors, of course, contributed to the shifting of population during the Jacksonian period, but the uncertainty of weather was part of that nexus of causality. We are seeing similar unintended consequences play out today, as rising global temperatures force massive changes on coastal areas all over the world. Connie didn't cause that change in weather pattern by herself (fossil fuel dependence did) but she—and all of us—will feel the consequences soon enough.

The specific accounts of witchcraft in this story derive from disparate sources, all with their roots in American folklore. Witches have long been believed to fly, with airborne witches showing up in medieval European woodcuts and in Tituba Indian's confessional testimony at Salem. The flying ointment recipe that Connie finds hidden in the wall of the Milk Street house comes from a rare book of collected European and American folklore and superstitions, first published in the late 1700s and held today at the New York Public Library, which also provided the three-knot sailor charm that Temperance sells. Interestingly, one poisonous ingredient in the flying ointment—henbane—supposedly provides a sensation of flight when consumed. Whether Connie and Temperance really flew, or merely felt themselves to fly, I leave to the reader to decide.

Grace's conjure spell to both protect Connie and also discern the source of her struggles comes from a different real grimoire called the *Sixth and Seventh Book of Moses*, which dates from sometime in the eighteenth or nineteenth century, and which is still available for sale. That text followed a path from Germany (probably) to German immigrants to the Americas, where it grew in popularity among African American hoodoo practitioners in the South. (Notably, it also contains instructions for how to influence the weather.) Zazi's point about folk-magical practices penetrating into different regions and in different cultural contexts derives from my own reading while researching a different project—the sieve-and-scissors divination method described in detail in *The Physick Book of Deliverance Dane* as an artifact of early modern English folk magic, and alluded to here, really does show up almost completely unchanged in an oral history collected by a folklorist working in the American South in the 1920s. (Of course, magical needs sometimes change with current events: that text also contains instructions for a charm to keep a secret liquor still from being raided by the police. Inquiries may be submitted via my website, for a very reasonable fee.)

Lastly, my apologies to the people of Easthorpe, England, for Livvy's dim view of their village, which I assure them I do not share. Their church, however, did contain a real Sheela-na-gig, the primitive carving of a grinning, naked older woman that reminds Livvy that female power takes many guises, not all of them welcome in the halls of patriarchy. Sheelas are not widely understood, but have been documented all over Ireland, in parts of Scotland, and in England as far east as Easthorpe. Their iconography reminded me of the grinning figure on the charmed boundary stone still standing in Byfield, Massachusetts—another concrete example of the never-ending struggle by individuals to assert power, agency, and safety in an uncertain and heavily circumscribed world. May we all of us some day settle in a city named for peace, as Livvy's mother, Anna, sought to do, even if that place lies not on a thickly forested faraway coast, but somewhere inside ourselves.

Acknowledgments

Deep and heartfelt thanks to my fabulous editor, Barbara Jones, and her right hand, Ruby Rose Lee, for doing yeoman's duty shepherding this story into the book that it has become, to Hannah Campbell for the great Thanskgiving ellipsis slaughter of 2018, and to everyone else at Henry Holt for giving this novel such a welcome and happy home. My gratitude also to my agent, Suzanne Gluck, and her own right hand, Andrea Blatt, for career and life guidance on matters both mighty and picayune.

I began percolating this story while a visiting scholar at the Center for Advanced Study in Behavioral Sciences at Stanford, where I enjoyed work space, library services, good fellowship, and lively meals through the generosity of the center's director, Margaret Levi. I conducted the research and writing of this book while in residence at the Wertheim Study at the New York Public Library, a resource of research, space, and time so abundant and luxurious that I dream of never leaving. And I completed revisions and copyedits at my favorite café in Salem, Massachusetts: Front Street Café. Thanks to Chris and all the staff for feeding me, caffeinating me, and giving me the wifi password. Everyone should go eat there immediately. Just don't take my table.

My love and thanks to the CASBS class of 2015–2016, the vinho verde sharers of Tuesday Dinner, the players of the Springfield Street Coffee Table, the castaways of End Times Island, the cast of the Real Housewives of Ithaca, Gen Xer trivia night at the Lobster Shanty, and the crew of the Menage, all of whom keep me sane and writing in their own special ways.

Novelists' families must contend with sharing their home with someone who only has one foot (and sometimes no feet) rooted in reality, and for their patience and forbearance I thank my parents, George and Katherine S. Howe, my brother-in-law, Eli "the Ward" Hyman, my sister-in-law, Rachel Hyman, and Milo, who personally ensures that I leave the house at least once a day. Most of all, thanks to my husband, Louis Hyman, who fires my imagination more than anyone else, who makes sure I never lose the plot, and who keeps me from going so deep into the zone that I can't find my way back.

Finally, I owe this book most of all to the readers of *The Physick Book of Deliverance Dane* who told me—in bookstores, over email, on Twitter, and on the occasional airplane—that they wanted to read it. I never dared to believe I might have a career writing novels, but as it happens, just because you don't believe in something doesn't mean it isn't true. Thank you.

About the Author

KATHERINE HOWE, the author of *New York Times* bestsellers *The Physick Book of Deliverance Dane* and *The House of Velvet and Glass* as well as of the YA novels *Conversion* and *The Appearance of Annie van Sinderen*, is also the editor of *The Penguin Book of Witches* and Anderson Cooper's collaborator on two forthcoming nonfiction books. Descended from three women who were tried for witchcraft in Salem, she lives with her family in New England and New York City.

Reading Group Guide for

The Daughters of Temperance Hobbs

1. Witches have stalked literature in many forms over the years. How does the depiction of magic in this novel contrast with that of witches' magic in other fiction, such as the crones gathered around a cauldron in *Macbeth* or the Quidditch-playing wizards of *Harry Potter*? How are the witches in Physick World different from other literary witches that you have read about?

2. Connie is at a stage in her life where the pull of family responsibility is beginning to conflict with the career path she's built over the past decade. How does she grapple with this tension, and how do her decisions compare to those of her ancestors who faced similar choices? Have you ever had to weigh being pulled in two different directions like Connie?

3. Connie advises a graduate student named Esperanza "Zazi" Molina, whose experiences with class and gender hierarchy in academia are similar to those Connie encountered herself when she was a student. How do Zazi and Connie's points of view align, and how do they differ? How does Zazi's research into different kinds of magic affect her outlook?

4. Connie, Zazi, and Thomas all must confront ambition as a simultaneously motivating and warping force in their lives. While Zazi manages to thrive in academia's competitive environment, Connie's previous thesis student Thomas ultimately does not. What do their different paths illustrate about ambition?

5. How is motherhood represented in Physick World? The novel presents several mother/daughter dyads at various points in history, and in many respects is about Connie's journey to discovering what motherhood means for her. Motherhood can be empowering, can be restrictive, can be defining, can be fraught. Which mother/daughter dyad speaks to you, and why?

6. All uses of magic in *The Daughters of Temperance Hobbs* come at a high price of physical pain, emotional pain, or sometimes both. Would you want to be a witch if any expression of supernatural power involved pain?

7. What exactly is "weather work" in this book? And why does each occasion of the weather work arrive in slightly different wording?

8. One of the novel's key characters is Arlo, who remains by Connie's side for much of the story. Do you believe Arlo is a real dog? What is the evidence that supports your argument? What role does Arlo play in the story, and what role does he play in Connie's life?

9. The novel moves between two distinct timelines, one set in 2000 and one set in 1816. What has changed for the women in these two timelines? What has, perhaps unexpectedly, stayed the same?

10. Connie's story is one in a strand of stories about gifted women in her family, stretching all the way from 1661 to the present day. What story about this female lineage would you write next?